no direction home

no direction home

elizabeth burns

water rabbit

water rabbit
PO Box 247
Ranchos de Taos, NM 87557

For more information or for bulk orders, please contact ecbee63@msn.com

ISBN 978-0-9989011-0-7

for A,
as always

I

My parents really made a striking couple and I gazed upon them with admiration.

Mom was in her mid-fifties. Her fine, straight, polychrome hair—silver, gold and platinum—brushed her shoulders. Her blush was applied a little too thickly, but her lips were the right shade of red, not too pink and girly nor too scarlet and garish. She wore an expensive knee-length dress of deep purple silk with thin black stripes, and on her feet were two-inch heeled black patent leather pumps. She was wearing a pair of earrings I'd never seen before, obviously fake diamonds, which was odd because I knew she had a pair of real ones given to her by my father for her fortieth birthday.

Dad was of the same age. An arched nose and a slightly upturned chin called to mind the puppet Punch, but overall he was handsome rather than comical. His suit was not bespoke, but of a high quality and charcoal grey, a color that favored any man who wore it. A silk tie, striped in forest green and a dark purple that almost matched my mother's dress, a pale blue Oxford cloth shirt and black tasseled loafers completed his ensemble. His wavy hair, dark brown, greying at the temples, was smoothed down with a light coating of pomade.

They could have been on their way to a sumptuous dinner with good friends. Chateaubriand, glasses of expensive Pinot Noir and talk of a recent trip to Paris or London.

Studying my mother more closely, I discerned her make-up disguised an ugly purple contusion on her left cheek. Something about my father's face wasn't right, either. An attempt had been made to repair and conceal a deep gash in his forehead.

The bile rose in my stomach. I threw up into a small waste-basket I found lurking in a corner. Afterward, I dug a tissue out of my bag and wiped my mouth.

In the private viewing room of Hillier & Son Funeral Home, I tried to wake up from the nightmare, the worst nightmare I'd ever had. It had to a nightmare because the reality was impossible to bear. Both my parents were dead and I, the only child of only children, was alone.

2

On the day my parents died I'd been far away, in a tiny apartment in Cusco that had been my home for several months. I'd spent a year teaching English in Chile, until a doomed love affair drove me north to try my luck in Peru. Changing cities, countries, even continents was the way I dealt with any setback. It wasn't working out too well in the ancient Incan capital. I'd quit my job at the university because my students had more important things to do than show up for class at seven-forty-five in the morning. I had private students who paid for their lessons with profuse thank-yous instead of *soles*. I was losing the battle for control of my bedroom to the fleas that lived in the floorboards. My waist was encircled by belt of tiny red bites that drove me into spasms of furious scratching. I was feeling lonely and wanting to hear a familiar voice. It was one PM on a Sunday. My parents might be home.

Successfully eluding Señora Quintanilla, who lived in the apartment below and was forever curious about the comings and goings of the young American, I slipped out the heavy wooden door of the courtyard into the street.

The nearest telephone center was just off the *Plaza de Armas*. I wrote my parents' number on a slip of white paper and handed it to the clerk.

"*Cabina dos,*" he said without taking his eyes off the *fútbol* match he was watching on a small black and white TV.

I sat on the metal stool in the cabina and stared at the telephone on a small shelf. The moment it rang, I grabbed the receiver and placing it to my ear, heard the ringing tone one, two, three, four, five times. After the fifth ring, I knew the answering machine would pick up and my father's voice, expressionless, would inform me that Jack and Margaret Grayson were unable to take the call. If I left my name and number my call would be returned as soon as possible. When the place closed at midnight, they still hadn't answered. It was then I remembered a mentioned weekend trip to the Ericsons' house on Oconomowoc Lake.

The center was dark and locked when I arrived after nine the next morning. Its posted hours were eight till midnight, but being Peru, schedules were often meaningless. I kicked the door in frustration, cursing the lazy clerk. If I didn't call soon my father would leave for the office, if he hadn't already, and my mother may have had an early meeting.

I ambled around the plaza, pointing at my canvas sneakers and giving an apologetic shrug to the urchins, wooden boxes awkwardly clasped under their arms, polish-stained rags in their pockets, who offered to shine my shoes.

At nine-fifteen the center was still closed, as it was at nine-twenty-two, nine-thirty-one and nine-forty-seven. I could have gone to the other call center, but refused on principle and pigheadedness. I wanted to chide the clerk when he eventually showed up, which he did at nine-fifty-six. He handed me the notice he was tearing off the door, a notice I had consistently missed. Phone service had been out in all Cusco because of a downed line. I slunk to the assigned

10

cabina and waited for the call to go through. No answer. No answer in the evening. Was it a three-day weekend and they were coming back from the Ericsons' today? When the machine picked up the following morning I started to freak.

Knowing I wouldn't relax until I had some reassurance, I pulled out the Alice in Wonderland-themed address book Mom (*sometimes she got my taste right*) had given me and thumbed the pages searching for Gale Dickerson's number, which because of my idiosyncratic filing system I found not under G or D but P, for preppy, perky, plump, painful, adjectives that described my mom's best friend since high school. What if Gale was with them I thought as I handed over her number.

Gale answered after the third ring. Her voice was as rough as a gravel road.

"Hi Gale, it's Hunter Grayson," I said, dusting off some seldom-used cheerfulness.

Gale let out a little gasp, followed by a sniffle, but said nothing.

"You all right? You sound like you've got a cold."

"Oh no, I'm okay," Gale replied.

"I know I'm probably being silly. I'm sure they're fine, but I was wondering if you know where my parents are. I've been trying to get a hold of them for a couple of days, but no answer." Almost effortlessly light and casual.

"Oh, Hunter honey," Gale's voice broke and my heart crumbled.

According to the police report, forty-eight hours before my parents, Jack and Margaret Grayson, were heading back from the Ericsons' lake house when their late model BMW hit a patch of black ice causing it to skid off the road and roll down a ravine. If the temperatures hadn't been sub-zero, if they'd been found sooner, the tragedy would have been averted.

❧

The world spun away till I was aware of nothing around me. There was no phone, no cabina, no phone center. I groped my way out to the street. My feet, as though guided by an unseen hand, took me back to my apartment. A small woman in grey skirt and white blouse sent by the American Embassy was talking with Señora Quintanilla, who was shaking her head gravely and clucking her tongue.

Thirty-six hours later I was at Hillier & Son. The woman from the embassy helped arrange a flight and the airline staff were sympathetic and accommodating. They bumped me up to first class from Lima to Miami. My first time in first class and I enjoyed none of the perks. All I wanted was to be unconscious, but I could only stare out the window.

Thinking liquor would help, I asked for a whiskey. I spat it back in the glass. At least first class was nearly empty and I had both seats to myself, no one trying to engage me in mundane conversation. Once on a flight from Tokyo to the U.S. a Christian missionary right out of the corn belt kept trying to talk to me. Even with my nose stuck in a book, the woman had persisted. "So, are you from here?" she asked.

Here? Did she mean Japan? I am about as white as they come with blonde hair and blue eyes.

In Miami, I bought a packet of Unisom and took one as soon as I got on the plane. I had to sleep so I didn't think about why I hadn't cried. A flight attendant woke me in Milwaukee. Groggy and disoriented, my bags made three passes on the carousel before I claimed them.

My plan was to head straight to the funeral home, where Gale had had the bodies transferred. Disorientation made renting a car out of the question. I hailed a cab and gave the driver the address then fell asleep in the back.

The staff at Hillier & Son were as solicitous as the airline's. But that was their job, wasn't it, to ease the grieving process with platitudes on the peacefulness of eternal rest that transitioned to a subtle sales pitch on how the Eternal Slumber cherry wood casket would ensure it.

I was aware of gently rocking side to side. I opened my eyes and saw the pudgy face of Raymond Hillier, Jr.— Raymond Hillier, Sr. had made full use of the mortuary's services several years prior—leaning forward over his desk, his brow knitted with concern. "Can I get you some water, Ms. Grayson?"

My lips wouldn't open. I nodded. He walked over to a crystal pitcher on a credenza and I noticed his strangeness for the first time. A large round head sitting directly on a large, round body, no neck, supported by thin legs, like a snowman on stilts. Was he losing weight or gaining it, I couldn't decide.

Hillier handed me the water, his eyes brimming with compassion. I couldn't believe he really cared if I was okay or not. The man was a professional sympathizer. He dealt with the bereaved every day. Maybe I was being too hard on him. Maybe he did care a little. Maybe it was the company motto: One Light Guides Us. Maybe it was the posters—the marble angel, a tear in her eye; the butterfly; and the daisy dropping its petals, each accompanied by an inspirational quote on grief—decorating the walls that were making me cynical. Leave it to Gale to choose such a cheesy outfit.

God, this couldn't be happening. Hillier again mentioned the Eternal Slumber cherry wood caskets. Why were caskets needed at all? My parents were going to be cremated. Torch thousands of dollars in cherry wood? I'd rather burn the money and save the wood. I opted for the most basic ones, not quite pine boxes, but close.

"Ms. Grayson I'm not trying to sell you anything. It's all paid for. Your parents purchased the plan with us a number of years ago," Hillier said, folding his lumpy hands neatly on his desk.

What? My parents had picked this place, not Gale? Purchased the coffins, paid for cremation when they were in their late forties. I recalled what was happening then and pushed it back into the drawer where I kept events and episodes I preferred not to think about. "Now, about the funeral arrangements," he continued.

A funeral. I'd completely forgotten that there would have to be some kind of service. I couldn't plan a funeral. At that moment, there was a soft tap on the door and Gale Dickerson entered the office. She was a short woman to whom God had endowed a generous pair of hips that made her seem even shorter. Dad had compared her to a garden gnome. With tears staining her face, she lifted me up out of the chair and hugged me tightly. The embrace was unwanted and unpleasant, like a serpent slithering round me, squeezing. My parents were dead and I felt nothing. I couldn't cry, and it repulsed me to be pulled into another person's pain.

"Where are you staying tonight?" she asked.

Oh shit, I had to think fast or I'd be stuck staying at her house, suffocated by her hovering. Do you need anything? Do you want anything? And worse, I might have to talk about my parents and what happened, watching Gale cry and her expecting me to cry, wondering why I didn't.

"At Andy's. You remember Andy Blake, don't you?"

Gale's face puckered liked she'd bitten a sour pickle. She was one of the only people who didn't like Andy. "Well, you call me, honey, if there's anything you need, or if you change your mind."

"I will (*only if every hotel and motel from here to Chicago is booked*), thank you. And Gale," I said, compelling my hand to take hers, "Would you arrange the funeral?"

Her eyes sparkled through her tears, "You are such a dear. It means so much that you'd ask, but it's all taken care of. Your parents gave me detailed instructions, the hymns, the readings, who they wanted to give eulogies, in case they passed suddenly." A stifled moan at her friends' foresight. "They didn't want you (*their useless daughter*) to have to worry about a thing. I've already spoken with Father Stephens. He may want to speak with you, too. He was close to your mother. Can I tell him it's all right to call?"

15

I nodded even though I had every intention of avoiding that conversation. I'd figure out how later.

Gale squeezed out another hug. "You poor child. You poor thing. These next few months are going to be hell for us, but we'll get each other through. I've always thought of you as my daughter, too. I'll call you tomorrow." She reached into her purse and took out a small address book, "What's Andy's number?" It was after Gale left that Hillier asked if I wanted to see my parents. He led me to the small room at the back of the building.

"I'll leave you alone. Press here to call the front desk if you need anything," he said, indicating a button next to the light switch, and closed the door.

Embarrassed about the wastebasket, I left it behind. I found a restroom and furiously rinsed my mouth in the sink. With a fragile calm regained, I returned to Hillier's office and asked to use the telephone.

"Certainly, take as much time as you need," he said and quietly slipped out the door.

I sank into the plush executive chair. On the desk was a photograph of Hillier, his wife and three children. All happy and smiling in their Sunday best, like Dad didn't deal with death every day. Hillier was lumpier in the photo. So he was getting fit. I picked up the phone and called Andy. Please be home, please be home, please be home. When the machine answered, I hung up without leaving a message.

I walked out of the hushed powder blue of the funeral home into a blast of frigid air blowing straight from the

Arctic. The first thud of a headache struck my forehead. Shit, I didn't have a car. I went back inside and called a rental agency. No, no one could pick me up. That wasn't one of their services, said the cool voice on the other end. I wanted to tell the guy to fuck off, my parents were dead, then thought of the awkwardness and pity that would evoke. I cabbed it to their office.

❧

I had no idea where to go so I steered the rented Ford to the freeway and headed south toward downtown. The air was fragrant with the familiar smells of Ambrosia Chocolate and Wonderbread. Every direction into Milwaukee had a smell. From the north, it was the sweet aroma of bread and chocolate. From the west, it was the sour odor of yeast and hops, from the south, the tanneries, and from the east, it was the smell of alewives washed up on the shores of Lake Michigan.

I went east through downtown to Lincoln Memorial Drive that followed Lake Michigan's shore, the lake a slab of grey water under a slab of gray clouds. I went up along Lake Drive lined with the imposing houses that had been the homes of Milwaukee's wealthiest families. I drove past my grade school just as the children were getting out for the day, shouting, running, jumping down the steps as though released from years of captivity. A small few looked shell-shocked. I drove past Milwaukee Academy, my high school, stopping for a time to watch the students, arms laden with books and folders, drift towards the parking lot filled with hand-me-down high-end German makes, the Japanese contingent, and a half dozen clunkers. Clusters of girls in down jackets over blue or green pullovers, corduroy-covered legs sticking out from their Black Watch plaid uniform skirts, responded with disdaining looks to the taunts tossed at them by cocky boys pulling off their required neckties. Nothing had changed in the twelve years since I'd graduated.

I drove past my childhood home where I'd lived until I was fourteen. The street was nearly naked. The beautiful old elm trees that had lined Moreland Court were gone, felled one by one to Dutch Elm disease. Some children were playing in the front yard of our old house. Across the street was the home of Andy's parents. Arthur Blake was sweeping away the last remnants of the recent snow storm from the front walk.

I was shocked by how old he looked. His once full head of black hair was almost completely grey and retreating toward his ears. When he stopped to rest, my hand went to the door handle, on the verge of getting out to say hello. Again, the likely course of the conversation stopped me. "Hello, Mr. Blake." "Oh, hello, Hunter. I'm sorry your parents are dead. A great tragedy. So sad. You must be devastated. You're an orphan now. No family. No one."

I pulled into a gas station with a pay phone, fished out a quarter and dialed Andy's number. A voice, not Andy's, answered.

"Andy's in Chicago. I don't know when he'll be back. Sometime tonight," the voice said.

"Can you tell him Hunter called."

"Will do," the voice responded and rung off.

I collapsed in the driver's seat. My forehead throbbed. My eyes burned with exhaustion. Darkness was swallowing the sky. I couldn't keep driving in circles and I certainly wasn't going to Gale's. I decided to go home.

3

Home. My parents' home. Other than the annual three-week visit (*some years longer if life was really throwing me curve balls*), neither the house nor Milwaukee had been my home since I was nineteen. Ruby slippers wouldn't have sent me to Milwaukee. I loved my parents but I wasn't meant to live in the city. Since graduating from college, I'd been like a pinball, bumping from one country to the next, always hoping I'd find the place where I belonged. I hadn't yet found it.

I parked the car in the driveway of the brick mock-colonial house. Cream City brick they called it, the color of the head of a beer. The house was located in Shorewood, a suburb just outside the city limits. It was the newest house on Stansfield Street. The original house had burned to the ground and the purchasers of the lot had tried to build something in keeping with the character of the neighborhood. To my mind, they hadn't succeeded. It tried so hard to look old that it screamed new. It had a great kitchen and a wonderful garden, Mom said.

The spare key was in its hiding place under a rock in the flowerbed by the front porch. I opened the door and stepped onto the letters and catalogues strewn on the floor. The house smelled as it always had, of pile carpet and roses. I was sixteen years old again, miserable but safe from the slings and arrows of high school. I expected my mother to come out of the kitchen to tell me dinner was almost on the table. Dad to call out from the den, "Hey Susu, what's newnew?" From the moment he first held me I was Susu, even after I'd insisted on going by Hunter, my middle name, in fifth grade.

But Mom didn't come out of the kitchen and Dad never called to me. The house was eerily silent as if it too had died. Coming here was a mistake. I should have gone to a motel. No, I'd have to do this eventually. I ventured further inside. I passed through the dining room where the pink and white tea roses that Mom always had as a centerpiece were dropping their petals.

In the kitchen, I instinctively opened the refrigerator. Eating would give me something to do even though I wasn't hungry. It was nearly empty: half a bottle of wine, some milk, an over-ripe tomato and various bottles and jars of ketchup, mayonnaise and mustard. I closed the door and leaned against it. Scanning the room, my eyes came to rest on a drawing of a horse hanging in the breakfast nook. I'd made it when I was ten, a Christmas present for my parents. I'd worked hard on it, starting over time and again until I was reasonably satisfied with my rendering.

Memories of that Christmas morning came flooding back. My mother's rapturous cries of delight. My father declaring he'd take it to the framers the next day. The shock that had numbed me melted. I sank to the floor.

When the sobbing subsided, I dragged myself and my backpack upstairs. The walls of the stairwell were lined with family photographs, every one familiar to me, but I kept my eyes straight ahead. I wasn't ready to look at them. I went into what had once been my bedroom.

❧

Oblivion. That was what I was seeking when I crawled into bed. A return to the oblivion of my sleep on the airplane, no dreams, no feelings now that I was feeling everything. It mattered little that it was only seven o'clock. I laid back on the pillows and closed my eyes. And that's when it began. Memories pushed and kicked and fought in my head, vying for attention. One minute my parents and I were driving to Florida to visit my grandparents, the next I was trying to have a coherent conversation with my mother after smoking four joints with Andy, and the next Dad and I were in a screaming match about my staying out till four o'clock in the morning with a guy he didn't like.

Then came the terror. When I was a child, outer space petrified me more than anything. I'd make myself cry thinking of being stranded alone in it. That feeling was the only one that came close to describing what the loss of my parents felt like. Life without them would be like the infinite, cold, intangibility of space.

The only thing that didn't come was sleep. I covered my head with the pillow, as if that could block out the din. At ten o'clock I couldn't take it anymore. A search of my bag produced no packet of Unisom. I went to my parents' bathroom and opened the medicine cabinet. There had to be something to knock me out. My mother was, had been, a chronic insomniac. On the second shelf, behind the ibuprofen, I found it: an almost full bottle of Valium.

I took one and headed back to my room, pausing at my parents' bed. I remembered the childhood nights when frightened by a bad dream, I'd sought the security of my parents' company, climbing under the covers between them, the warmth of their bodies lulling me into dreamless sleep. I pulled back the spread and slipped under the flannel sheets and waited for the pill to work its magic.

࿔

The telephone woke me in the morning. I answered it on the fifth ring, the same time as the answering machine. My father's voice was the first voice I heard, the bland recording conveying none of his humor. Tears sprang from my eyes. The machine beeped.

"Hunter, are you there? It's Andy."

"I'm here. Oh fuck. Just a second." I put down the phone, ran into the bathroom, unrolled a wad of toilet paper and blew my nose.

"I'm really sorry about yesterday," Andy said when I picked up again, "The deposition just kept going on and on. I didn't get home until after midnight. How are you doing?"

"Um, I don't know...I..."

"I'll be right over, with ice cream. Mint chocolate chip still your favorite?"

I curled up knees to chest and shoved my head under the pillow. The dread and anxiety of having to make it through the day pushed down on me like a car crusher. When the phone rang again I sprung up to answer it before the machine.

"May I speak with Susan Grayson, please?" asked the meticulous young female voice on the other end.

"Susan?" It took me several seconds to recall that I was Susan Grayson. "Yes, this is Susan."

"Ms. Grayson, this is Deborah Taylor from Martin Taylor's office. Mr. Taylor is your parents' attorney." Her voice rose on the final syllable like she was asking a question. Did she want me to acknowledge I was aware of this? It had never occurred to me that my parents had a lawyer. But of course they would. They had been true adults, at least by the standards I'd been raised to associate with adulthood: stability, responsibility, home ownership, a stock portfolio, insurance, burial plots. I was playing at being adult. I was impressed when I paid a bill without incurring late fees.

"Yes?"

"Firstly, let me say that my fa... Mr. Taylor and I extend you our deepest condolences on your loss. It was a terrible tragedy."

I didn't feel like responding with the expected, "Yes, it was," so I said nothing.

"Ms. Grayson, are you there?"

"Yes."

Deborah cleared her throat and addressed the reason for her call. Mr. Taylor wanted to meet with me to discuss my parents' estate. When could I come to the office?

"I just got into town yesterday. I really haven't had time to...Can it wait till after the funeral?" Please don't make me deal with this now, I wanted to add.

"Oh, I'm so sorry. I didn't realize. The file was on my desk. I thought..." Her voice trailed off into embarrassed silence. I imagined Deborah at her desk, straightening an already perfect stack of files, lips set in distress that her own father would fire her from her first office job for the misstep.

When Deborah spoke again her professionalism was back, "Of course. Please call us at your earliest convenience. We look forward to meeting you." She must have known she'd blundered again because she hurriedly rang off.

Scenes from countless mystery movies were my only reference points for the reading of a will. Women in black dresses with veiled hats and men in dark suits sitting in oak paneled offices, eyeing one another suspiciously, as a crusty, white-haired lawyer read the disposition of the estate of the wealthy and despised deceased.

I doubted the reading of my parents' will was going to be anything like that. I didn't have any brothers or sisters or cousins or aunts and uncles. Maybe a young woman would charge into the office claiming to be the love child of Dad and some woman he'd met on a business trip and demanding a portion of the money. I would gladly give it to her, happy to know I had a sister.

4

Andy Blake, out of shape and with the thick glasses he'd been wearing forever, puffed up the stairs and dropped down on the bed next to me, a pint of ice cream and two spoons in his hands. He was a nerd, he'd always been one, and he probably would have been considered unattractive if it wasn't for his eyes, which were full of life and all its possibilities. He was also super smart—Yale and then Georgetown law school on full scholarships— and despite offers from all the big D.C. firms, he chose to practice environmental law in Milwaukee. We'd been best friends since his family moved into the house across from ours on Moreland Court when we were seven. I went to the public grade school while he went to a Montessori school, but as only children, and about the only children on the block, we'd sought each other out, building elaborate cities out of shoe boxes and Lincoln Logs, having sleepovers, reading stories by flashlight.

I didn't want to be a puddle of misery, but I couldn't help it, seeing that face I knew so well, thick brown hair flopping over his glasses. Andy held me, letting me cry myself dry. When I finally raised my head, he looked at the dark circles under my puffy eyes, my shiny skin and matted hair and wrinkled his nose in disgust. "Hunter, I know you're having a rough time, but that doesn't mean you have to give up completely. When was the last time you bathed?"

"Four days ago."

An onlooker might have been appalled by his apparent disregard for my situation. I knew Andy better. He was the closest thing I had to a brother and I counted on him not to envelop me in a cloak of compassion and commiseration. I was going to get that from enough people. I needed someone who could make me laugh, not treat me as an object of pity.

"No ice cream for you till you've had a shower," Andy declared.

I dangled my hair in his face. "Don't you like the way I look?"

"Not particularly, and I really don't like the way you smell. That better not be patchouli. If you've gone hippy on me I'll have to take away your passport. You can't be trusted traveling on your own."

"It's sandalwood," I replied, heading into the bathroom. "There better be some ice cream left when I come back."

❧

Scrubbed clean and wrapped in a towel, I snatched the ice cream from Andy. The bottom of the container was visible.

"You pig!" I cried.

"There's another one in the freezer so don't get your knockers in a twist."

"It's knickers, you idiot," I laughed and shoved a dripping spoonful into my mouth.

"Since, at this moment, I don't think you're wearing any knickers to get twisted, knockers is more appropriate. Can I bring a date to the funeral?"

"Not a first date, I hope." I said throwing on a black and grey alpaca sweater and a pair of black sweat pants.

"No, a guy I've been seeing for about three months."

"Three months! And you've never said a word," I gasped. Andy'd never had a relationship that lasted more than a month. He was successful at everything except relationships.

"I didn't want to jinx it. His name's Danny. He's a personal trainer."

"Don't tell me you met him at a gym." Andy's idea of exercise was lifting liter bottles of Diet Pepsi.

"No, and I've successfully avoided all his attempts to get me to one. Even the lure of men in unitards has failed to work. We met at a party."

"That's great. I'm really happy for you. Now let's get that other pint."

"Whose hideous Ford is that in the driveway?" Andy asked when he joined me in the kitchen.

"A rental," I replied, then drove the spoon into the rock-hard ice cream. The spoon bent. "I guess I don't need it. I can use my mom's car. Can you follow me to the rental place?"

"No problem." Andy took the ice cream, popped open the microwave and placed the container inside. He set the timer for fifteen seconds. The ice cream came out the perfect consistency and Andy ceremoniously presented it to me and I polished off half of it in a matter of minutes.

"So, are you going to stay with me?" Andy asked.

Andy's place would have been an island where I could wash ashore, but a little voice in my head told me I deserved to get tossed about in a stormy sea. "I think I'm going to stay here. I'll be alright."

"You sure?"

I nodded. If things got too bad there was always the Valium. And if the coming nights were going to be anything like last night, I'd be reaching for those babies a lot.

5

The L-shaped stone hulk of St. Mark's Church sat amidst what in spring and summer was a peaceful garden of roses, hydrangea and lilacs but in winter was a tangle of spindly brown branches. The bronze cherub in the garden fountain shivered in the cold.

Above the heavily carved and iron-worked doors of the church's main entrance, three tall, narrow stained glass windows, the center window taller than the two flanking it, reached upwards toward the gothic cross sitting atop the facade. Smaller arched windows ran down both side walls of the church and dappled the floor of the dim nave with shards of colored light. I stood dumbly by, shifting awkwardly from foot to foot, as Gale and Thomas Caine, the curate, discussed liturgy I didn't believe in, their voices echoing through the quiet space.

Unlike my parents, I wasn't a religious person. That day was the first time I'd been in a church other than as a tourist in years. I couldn't even be dragged to services on major holidays though I knew how happy it would have made my parents. Why did the service have to be in a church? Why couldn't it just be at Gale's house where the reception was going to be? Selfish cow. My parents were dead and here I was thinking about my own comfort. The service was in their memory to be performed by a minister of their faith.

As we were leaving, Gale insisted I come to her house for dinner. "I bet you haven't had a proper meal since you got back," she said.

Did ice cream qualify as a proper meal? I had no appetite for food or Gale's company, but I lacked the strength to refuse.

à♠

Gale's fastidiousness as a home owner was evident from the driveway, which like the path to her shingled house, was shoveled clean of every snowflake. The snow blanketing the small front yard seemed evened to a uniform depth. A wreath of evergreen and holly and a small Welcome sign hung on the front door. My hand hovered over the doorbell. Had Gale heard the car drive up? Was it too late to run away? The curtain of a downstairs window opened slightly then fell closed again. I rang the bell.

"I'm so glad you're here," Gale greeted me, red-nosed, mascara smudged under her eyes.

The house she ushered me into was also immaculate. The hall was decorated with framed, expertly stitched needlepoint samplers. The living room was chintz curtains and over-stuffed chintz furniture. A collection of seashells and porcelain birds lived in a tall, octagonal glass case. On the wall behind a couch strewn with needlepoint pillows, were a series of watercolors of English landscapes. The thick carpet was vacuumed so all the pile was going in one direction. I remembered Dad down on his hands and knees writing, "Hello Gale" in it with his finger. I never liked the cold formalism of our house, which reflected Mom's taste, even the couch in the family room was uncomfortable, but it was better than this homage to Laura Ashley.

Gale guided me into the kitchen and over to the breakfast bar set for two. "Now, you just sit down right here. Dinner'll be ready in two shakes." She returned to the stove and gave the sauce a stir. "I made spaghetti, garlic bread and salad. Nothing fancy. I hope that's okay."

As I watched Gale stirring the contents of a saucepan, I couldn't help making another comparison between my mother and her oldest friend. Gale's preppy style—she was dressed in a ruffled gingham apron over a wool plaid wraparound skirt and red Shetland sweater, the collar of an Izod polo shirt peeking out, her girlish bobbed hair pushed back with a grosgrain headband—was so at odds with Mom's sophisticated Armani suits. Only shared childhood experience could explain the lifelong friendship of such different women.

Gale opened the oven and pulled out a loaf of French bread wrapped in aluminum foil. A basket lined with a chintz napkin was ready to receive it. She flitted around the kitchen, retrieving two plates from the cupboard, draining the noodles and scooping them onto the plates, topping the noodles with sauce, and serving the plates, all the while chirping like a plump canary about Milwaukee Academy, where she was the assistant to the headmaster. It was gossipy and mundane chatter, anything to fill the void that Margaret's death had created. I picked at my food, throwing out the occasional "Hmm" to give the appearance of listening. Not until I heard, "When she survived the big C, I thought she'd be around forever," did it register that Gale was talking of the dark period six years ago when Mom was diagnosed with breast cancer, the event I was pretty sure had brought Hillier & Son into their lives.

I shifted in my seat. The way I'd behaved when Mom was ill was a sore that festered in my heart. I was living in Tokyo when Dad called with the news that Mom had to have a lumpectomy. He tried to sound upbeat, saying the cancer had been caught early, the doctors were optimistic and her chances for a full recovery were good with chemo and radiation. My first thought was why was this happening now, to me? For once I was enjoying life, earning four thousand dollars a month as an English teacher, working only twenty hours a week, going out all night in Roppongi, seeing how many over-paid ex-pat men I could get to buy me drinks. I didn't want to go back to Milwaukee. Then I was plagued with guilt. I was awful. Nothing was happening to me, it was happening to my mother. Cancer. She could die.

I'd never felt so scared in my life. I didn't want to go home and watch Mom waste away. The little I knew of cancer came from the stories Eleanor, a college friend, had told of the year she spent as the live-in caretaker for a cousin who was dying of a rare form of T-cell cancer, bathing her, emptying bedpans, consoling her three-year-old daughter and distraught husband. I wanted to be like Eleanor, but I knew I lacked the selflessness to take care of Mom no matter how much I loved her.

My father hadn't actually asked me to come home. Maybe he and my mother assumed they didn't have to ask, that I would know my presence was desired. Or maybe they didn't expect or want me to. They must have known how useless I'd have been, afraid to look Mom in the face, afraid my slightest touch would hurt her. I convinced myself that it was better for all concerned that I stay in Tokyo, and my parents never said a word. I called every few days and it was easy to convince myself I wasn't needed because Mom didn't sound sick. Dad joked that she'd in fact gained weight, surprising, he added, as she'd lost all her hair, including her eyelashes. But I heard his underlying fear.

Then came the joyous news that Mom was in the clear. The cancer hadn't spread. And with regular check-ups the prognosis was good. I hadn't been needed after all. Going home would've been completely unnecessary. I knew now, though, that I should have because the guilt I had carried around with me took all the fun out of Tokyo life.

Gale wiped her nose and eyes with a monogrammed cotton handkerchief that she always kept in the waistband of her skirt, smearing her mascara even more. I awkwardly tried to comfort her, contemplating the irony of the situation. It came to me what a lonely existence Gale had. Dealing with those rich brats and their parents every day, few friends, divorced with no kids and no real prospects of another man in her life. Her husband, Jerry, had run off with Jonas Gottlieb, the drama teacher at MA, when I was a sophomore. A huge scandal. According to Gale's version, Jerry had been preyed upon, corrupted, and lured away from a happy marriage by a monster, a minion of the devil. To her, all gay men, including Andy, were predators to be assiduously avoided. My mother tried to tell Gale that Jerry had always been gay—they're born not made—but

Gale refused to hear any of it and Mom eventually gave up. "You can lead a horse to water," she sighed. But it was really her friendship with my mom that had always been the primary relationship in Gale's life, and she was fiercely loyal to the woman she idolized and idealized. She'd moved from their hometown of Grand Rapids, Michigan to be close to her. "Your girlfriend's on the phone," Dad would call out to Mom like a teasing brother, knowing how much it would make Gale squirm to be thrown in the same witch's cauldron as Jonas Gottlieb.

Margaret's death must have hit Gale like a left hook. Sympathy made giving comfort a little easier until Gale, with an I-told-you-so shaking of her head, began, "But with the way Jack drove."

She couldn't help herself. Even though my father was dead Gale couldn't resist. She had to take a dig at him. The two had never really gotten along, only tolerated each other for Margaret's sake. On Gale's part, Jack wasn't good enough for my mom (*I doubt she thought any man was*) and on my dad's (*and mine*), Gale was just too Gale, too perky, too fussy, too devoted.

Fortunately for Gale, she didn't pursue her theme because if she had I'd have hit her with a real left hook. It was true that my father only had one speed: fast. And it didn't apply solely to driving. He was always a block ahead of my mother and me walking; he read five-hundred page books in a few days; for him fast food didn't refer to how it was prepared but how it was consumed. The only time I knew him to slow down was when he met my mother in Paris. He slammed the brakes on his twenty-countries-in-six-months tour and never left the City of Light. Of course, Jack being Jack, he'd proposed after one month.

Since their deaths, I'd cursed countless times my father's need for speed and had shuddered when I recalled my mother telling me she knew she'd die in a car crash and was resigned to it. But Gale had absolutely no right to even begin to blame him. Pleading a headache, I fled to Stansfield Street. I popped a Valium, curled up in my parents' bed and waited for oblivion.

6

Clouds trapped the sun which stained them a weak yellow with its light. As befitting the day of a funeral, a sheet of icy rain fell. A stream of dark figures, some under umbrellas or folded newspapers, flowed into the church and filled the pews. White roses, lilies and delphinium were arranged in large vases set on the floor on either side of the altar draped in white. Two acolytes, boys of twelve, ginger haired and freckle faced, twins possibly, dressed in red cassocks and white cottas, lit thin white candles on the altar and fat white candles atop wrought-iron floor-standing holders. On a stone pedestal carved with acanthus leaves and scrolls in the Corinthian style was a single alabaster urn.

All eyes were discreetly on me as I, supported by Andy, walked up the aisle like a tragic bride, to take my seat in the front row. I marveled at the number of attendees. I'd forgotten, or had never known, what a wide social circle my parents had traveled in. Young and old, friend and stranger were there. I stole sidelong glances down the pews, checking out the women's outfits, wondering how many had been purchased for just such occasions, hanging in closets until death called them into service.

I hadn't planned on buying a dress for the funeral, but Leslie, my only girl friend from high school still living in Milwaukee, had come over, scanned my wardrobe and declared there was nothing appropriate. I was the bereaved. Why should I care about what I wear?

"Because in times of trouble and sorrow, shallow concerns are a distraction," Leslie replied sensibly.

"Do you think I can find a dress to match the circles under my eyes," I asked, examining myself in the bathroom mirror. I was amazed how little I looked like the Hunter of only a few weeks ago. My usually creamy skin was sallow and my blonde hair dull. Bright red pimples had popped up around my mouth. I didn't want to leave the house, especially to try on clothes. I was a terrible shopper at the best of times and way worse when I was depressed or lonely and needed the short-lived thrill of something new. It didn't matter if I needed or even liked the dress, or shirt, or skirt, and most of the time I didn't, so when the high wore off, the item joined all the other unworn clothes in my crowded closet.

Leslie took me to Claire de Lune, a boutique popular with the young mothers she socialized with. I counseled myself to take my time, to not buy the first dress I tried on. I took four selections into the dressing room and stripped off my jeans and sweater. Seeing my body in the chartreuse halogen light, throwing into relief dimples of fat on my thighs, my stomach, even my hair had cellulite, my energy flagged. I pulled on a wool dress with three-quarter sleeves and a simple square neck that hit just above the knee. I spun around in front of the mirror checking the fit from all angles. No unsightly bulges, my legs didn't appear stubby.

It was fine. Now I wished I'd walked around in it a bit. The lining made an annoying sound with every move I made. Swish. Swish. Swish.

A black lace doily covering her hair, Gale was down on the kneeler, head bowed in private prayer. Her lips bent into a frown, quickly banished, when Andy placed himself between her and me. The organist, who had been playing softly, confidently struck the opening chords of Hymn 178. *Alleluia, alleluia! Give thanks the Lord has risen.* All attendees rose as the crucifer, followed by Father Stephens proceeded up the aisle.

I mechanically followed the commands to stand, to kneel, and to sit. I opened the prayer book to the designated pages and recited aloud without the faintest clue what I was saying. During the readings, my mind wandered to the summer after college graduation when Mom, Dad and I stayed in a small hotel in Vézelay, France, a stop on a road trip through Burgundy. Crowded into the tiny bathroom, Dad was showing the skeptical hotel manager and his assistant the leaking toilet. The Frenchmen denied the leak's existence, even as water seeped out all over the carpet. We laughed about it for the rest of the trip. We hoped every toilet in every hotel room leaked. It was a happy memory, one that I'd keep close to the surface for easy access.

The eulogies caught and held my attention. Jack's college buddy, Bill Thomas, told of the time he introduced Jack to his parents, a story I never tired of hearing my father tell. As Jack reached out to shake Mr. Thomas's hand, the cork of the champagne bottle he'd hidden under his suit popped out sending a foamy rivulet down his sleeve and onto Mr. Thomas's shoes. In her eulogy for Margaret, Alberta Hart talked of Margaret's inspiring chairmanship of the Art in the Schools Foundation. I was surprised when Bill said Dad had once considered medical school and again when Alberta revealed Mom had placed fourth in a college beauty pageant. I realized there were stories about my parents that I'd never known, stories that now, I'd never know.

After the service, we all gathered at Gale's. The dining table, sideboard and breakfast bar sagged under the weight of smoked salmon, deviled eggs, vegetables and dip, cheese and crackers, stuffed mushrooms, mini quiches, cold ham, fruit, cakes, brownies, cookies, wine, beer, coffee, and tea. Andy surveyed the feast and commented to Leslie and me that it would be a great party if it weren't a funeral. "What is it about death that makes people want to eat?" he asked, piling his plate high with a little bit of everything, "I'm famished."

Hunger was not my problem. I took a plate of grapes to the over-stuffed couch and popped them into my mouth one after the other until they were gone. Leslie got up to refill the plate, returning with eyes wide in disbelief. "Oh my God," she said as she sat down almost spilling the grapes, "Mrs. VanLeiden (*super rich, her family owned a huge engine company*) just dropped a piece of ham on the floor and she kicked it under the counter."

"You expected Trudy VanLeiden to pick up something off the floor?" Andy asked, "She might dirty the cuff of her ultrasuede suit. Hasn't anyone told her the one week that fabric was in fashion ended in 1979?"

"Dirt? In Gale Dickerson's kitchen? Highly unlikely. She washes paper plates before she throws them away," I giggled, a brief moment of levity that abruptly ended when I noticed a woman in a dark suit and upswept hair, vaguely familiar, looking at me from across the room. She said something to Gale. They both looked at me. Then Gale said something to her. Eventually, the woman leaned in close and whispered. Gale nodded. The woman walked over.

"Hello Hunter, I'm Sally Turner. I don't know if you remember me. We met several years ago. You'd just come back from Tokyo, I think."

I rose and shook the hand Sally offered, "I think so."

"I worked for your father at Penner & Grayson. I just wanted to tell you how sorry I am for your loss. Your father, and mother, though I didn't know her as well, were wonderful people and they will be greatly missed."

Sally's coming over broke the spell. Other mourners who'd been reluctant to approach, even those who knew me, as if I were made of the thinnest crystal and the tiniest vibration would shatter me, now came over singly or in pairs to convey their condolences. From acquaintances it was easy because they were awkward, their words short, and once expressed, they beat a hasty retreat. But those from my parents' close friends were torture. They poured out their sadness and shock, hugged me, entreated me to call them if I needed anything, anything they stressed, even if it was just someone to talk to. And when it was all over and I was back at home, I couldn't remember one thing that happened or one person who was there.

Two days later, accompanied by Andy, Leslie and Gale, I interred my parents' ashes at Woodlawn Cemetery.

ॐ

The temperature outside was in the twenties and it felt only a few degrees warmer in the law offices of Martin Taylor. Deborah Taylor, shivering in her Fair Isle sweater and navy corduroy skirt, escorted me to her father's office.

"Come in, Ms. Grayson. Please sit down," Martin Taylor said indicating to a chair at a small conference table, "And bring us some coffee, would you, Debo. You drink coffee, don't you, Ms. Grayson?"

Martin Taylor was a tall, thin man with a thick head of curly auburn hair and tortoise shell glasses. He wore a blue pinstripe shirt and a brown tweed jacket, suede patches on the elbows. He looked more like a college professor than a lawyer. "I only wear a suit when I have to go to court," he said, "which fortunately isn't very often."

Hands wrapped around the steaming mug of coffee hoping to absorb its heat, I listened as Martin explained the trust my parents had set up.

"You are to receive six thousand dollars a month. 'That way you can do whatever makes you happy and not have to worry about money.' Those are your parents' words. The sum is to be increased to eight thousand when you have a child or turn thirty-eight, whichever comes first."

So like my parents. Supportive in every way was what they had always been. "If it makes you happy, then that's what we want too," was their response to my every move, to my every half-baked idea.

Me, age 27: I'm thinking of going back to school to study philosophy (*because of a guy, as usual*).

Mom: A good education is an end in itself and waitressing is an important and undervalued occupation.

Me, age 28: I'm moving to Turkey.

Dad: I've always wanted to visit Istanbul!

I spent three months in Turkey before deciding that I'd be much happier in South America. I never did take a philosophy class.

Six thousand dollars a month was enough for a comfortable life, but not so much that I could be like that cousin of Tom Campbell's, Leslie's husband, who inherited half a million dollars, bought a Porsche 911, two Rolexes, a stereo with tweeters and woofers and sub-woofers and speakers as big as fridges and then blew almost all the rest on trips to Vegas. Not that there was any serious risk I would do something that stupid, materialism was not one of my weaknesses, but I did have rather a casual relationship with money. Never able to balance my checkbook, making just enough to keep afloat, I'd so far avoided serious debt because my needs were minimal and with the exception of London and Tokyo, everywhere I'd lived had been cheap.

In Cusco, I'd washed my dishes and clothes by hand in freezing water. The furnishings in my apartment consisted of a mattress, a table and stool, and a small stove. The water in the shower was heated by an electric shower head flipped on with a breaker stolen from Frankenstein's lab that sent a tingle of current through me every morning. I was literally jolted awake.

My mother winced when she saw the place, my dad applauded. He bragged to his buddies that his daughter's private school education hadn't blinded me to how the world really was. I was out there living it. I never saw it that way. I felt I didn't deserve any better. And despite what Dad said, when I was down to my last few dollars, hunger, eviction, destitution were never truly biting at my ankles. A panicked call. Calm on the other end. Okay, where do we wire the money? I certainly hadn't deserved my parents.

"Hunter," a distant voice said.

"Hunter," this time much louder, startling me out of my daze.

"You didn't hear a word I said, did you?" Martin asked. I shook my head.

"I asked what you wanted to do with the house."

"Sell it." I didn't need any time to think that over.

"That would seem like the best idea. Do you know a realtor?"

I stared at Martin dumbfounded, as if he'd asked me if I knew the pope. I'd lived in Milwaukee for a total of maybe six months in the last ten years. And while I could easily grasp exchange rates, read subway maps, find cheap hotels and restaurants around the world, when it came to the day-to-day, settled life in the United States I was clueless. I didn't understand how my health insurance worked and now I was being asked about a realtor.

Martin assumed my hesitation meant no. "I can recommend someone," he said.

Couldn't someone else handle the whole thing?

He shook his head, "The terms of the trust are explicit. Penner & Grayson, the co-trustee, is to manage the investment portfolio, while all physical property is your responsibility. Only you can decide to sell the house."

7

"Number one in sales! Call me!" the real estate agent, with her toothpaste-ad smile, reminded me every morning from her magnetized business card slapped on the fridge. I ignored her. My parents' clothes were still hung neatly in their closet or folded away in dresser drawers. Their books still lined the walls of the den. China and crystal remained in the dining room breakfront. I'd never liked the house and many of my memories about living there were unhappy ones, but it and everything in it were my only tangible connection to my parents and selling was harder than I ever imagined. After a month, I shoved the card in a drawer.

Sometimes I was swimming in a sea of self-pity. In a corner of their dark closet, wrapped in one of Dad's sweaters, the scent of his cologne clinging to it, or in one of Mom's robes smelling of rose oil, I'd cry myself to sleep, waking hours later, my body cramped and my mind senseless to day and time. Other times I was plagued with guilt about deserting them. If I'd only been in Milwaukee, living close by, I could have saved them somehow. That because of me—one of my periodic life catastrophes for once doing some good— they wouldn't have gone to the Ericsons' that weekend. And way too often, to escape my own head, I'd lose myself in the lives of the scheming, ambitious, cheating, passionate residents of Llanview (*One Life to Life*), Salem (*Days of Our Lives*) and Port Charles (*General Hospital*).

The answering machine was the greatest development in telecommunications since the phone itself. I screened all my calls so I never had to talk to anyone I didn't want to, like Gale, who called frequently in the beginning. She'd leave messages asking me to call her back, please, she needed to talk to me about my parents.

The prospect of consoling a distraught woman I'd never liked sickened me, as did knowing my father's passing would barely be touched upon. I feared that Gale wanted me, despite our difference in age, to take Margaret's place, for us to become best friends bound to one another by death rather than life, and I recoiled at the idea of Gale introducing me as her 'sister in sorrow.' She'd hinted more than once that she wanted to be the one I turned to for consolation. Her primness and exaggerated jollity, however, didn't recommend her as a confidant in general, and her devotion to my mom made her the last person I would ever choose to bare my soul to. In my mind I saw Gale, at first happy to have won my trust, puff up with indignation on Mom's behalf, her pudgy fingers gripping her handkerchief ever more tightly, her mouth hardening into a pinched frown, as I listed my filial sins. The list was a long one.

My performance as a daughter deserved a big fat F. I came into the world in a bad mood that was as much a part of me as my liver and my fingernails. I remembered with great shame all the temper tantrums I'd thrown; all the shouting matches I'd started. The angst and frustrations of my adolescence were vented on my parents because they were there. If I'd screamed and carried on with my friends, I wouldn't have had any friends, and I had too few to risk losing them. A few fights were especially painful, like the time I slapped my mother and stormed out of the house vowing never to return. I couldn't even remember what the fight was about, but the shock and pain on my mother's face were etched in my mind. Or, after vowing that hell would have to freeze over before I'd move back to Milwaukee, I still went ballistic when I found out she'd converted my bedroom into a guest room, removing all the posters of David Bowie, The Clash, and The Rolling Stones from the walls and stowing them away in the attic along with my toys and books. How could she be so cruel, I cried, so insensitive? Didn't she love me at all? Or the time I'd exploded because Dad wanted me to attend a company picnic and I didn't want to go. I cursed and ranted and threw myself on the ground as though possessed by a demon. He had to physically subdue me on the kitchen floor.

And on the day my parents died, I'd been angry with them. They weren't there when I called, when I needed to talk to them, to hear their voices because Oswaldo, my Quechua boyfriend, had just told me he was still in love with a Norwegian girl he'd met the previous year. I knew I was sometimes difficult, needy or bitchy depending on the hour, but to be dumped for a girl who didn't speak Spanish and who'd left Peru eight months earlier was a top-ten low. I wasn't woman enough to make him forget her. But it wasn't just that failed relationship that had me curled up in a tight ball crying that night, but all my failed relationships, over the fear that I never would be woman enough, that I was fated to be unloved, unwanted and unhappy.

Whenever I asked my parents why they'd never had any more children they'd say one was all they ever wanted. But I sensed the truth behind their words. They were terrified they'd produce another me, and one of me was more any parent could be expected to handle. They certainly wouldn't have chosen me from a baby catalog. Girl: 8lb/7oz; blonde hair & blue eyes; pretty; average intelligence; subject to mood swings, rages, sulking.

When I failed to return her calls, Gale's messages got more insistent. She had something to tell me. Something important. Ugh, did she want to acknowledge how awful she'd been to my dad? Playing the role of confessor to her repentant transgressor was even more repugnant than being her shoulder to cry on. Eventually, there was a final message: "I've been too pushy. Margaret used to warn me about that. So I'm going to stop. When you're ready, please call me. Take care until then."

The conversation I imagined Leslie and Tom having prior to her dragging me out one night:

Leslie: "It's so sad. It's been four months and Hunter's still holed up in that big house all alone. She never goes out, Tom. She wears those same awful black sweat pants day in and day out. She's gotten so thin. I'm worried about her."

Tom: "Why don't you two go out Saturday night. I'll watch the girls. You both could use a night on the town."

Leslie: "Really? You'd do that for me? I mean, you're sure you can handle it?"

Tom: "Pshaw, it's a snap. Just one thing, could you feed Schuyler before you go?"

Just before the start of ninth grade, we moved to the house on Stansfield Street, only eight blocks from Moreland Court, but it put me in a different school district. Not that it mattered because I was going to attend MA (*Dad's alma mater, Mom's idea*). Cliquey and hierarchical, it was a tough school to transfer into as a freshman. Most of my classmates had started together in the first grade and they were slow to warm to new-comers, if at all. Marty Simmons, Kitty Caufield, and Polly Vandercamp, neither pretty, smart nor nice, ruled our class with unflinching authority. I, who didn't make friends easily, gave cigarettes to Marty, the meanest and least attractive of the trio, but whose twin brother was the star of the soccer team. I laughed at Polly's nasty jokes about plain, heavy Lauren Feldman. I let Kitty copy my biology homework. It left me feeling ugly and pathetic, like a trained seal whose reward would be acceptance rather than fish. I quit performing and waited— and waited and waited—for the three to notice how clever and fun I was. Leslie, champion of the underdog, guardian angel to down-and-outers, and stray animals, saw my suffering and swooped in to rescue me.

On Saturdays she and I, along with some other girls caught in social limbo, not popular but not total nerds, would descend on Heinemann's for lunch, and while nibbling our BLTs and sipping Tabs, we'd gossip and claw away at Marty, Kitty, and Polly, the very girls we would have stomped all over each other to get in with.

On Saturday nights, we'd pile into Leslie's 1974 Dodge Dart and drive around smoking Merits and singing along to the radio at the tops of our lungs. *"You can ring my be-e-ell. Ring my bell."* And when her parents were out of town, which was frequently, and her wild older sister was babysitting, we'd get drunk on shots from every bottle in their father's liquor cabinet.

After graduation, we'd go months, sometimes a year, without even a postcard, but when we got together it was as if no time had passed.

After pizza at Veneta's I was ready to go home, but Leslie was adamant about keeping the night going. "It's not often I'm let off the leash," she said.

The smoke was thick, the music loud, and the beer cheap at Hanrahan's. All the men turned and stared appreciatively as the door swung shut behind us. Fresh meat. We had first gone there at sixteen, thinking ourselves so sophisticated ordering white wine Spritzers. Now it was tequila shots.

"Do you remember prom sophomore year?" Leslie asked, smacking down her empty shot glass.

It was a night I was unlikely to forget. Six of us were without dates so we threw a non-prom party on the beach below Hannah Nicholson's house. Megan Brenner brought rum in a shampoo bottle that she hadn't rinsed out too well. We got drunk on soapy shots. Prell Punch. Leslie got so drunk she couldn't walk back up the bluff. I had to carry one hundred-twenty pounds of dead weight through the dark and the trees to the house. I'd just gotten her into Hannah's bedroom when she puked all over the floor. I threw her down on the bed and grabbed a towel to clean up the mess, little green flecks and lots of stringy stuff.

"Gross! What did you have for lunch?" I asked.

"A Reuben sandwich," Leslie groaned and threw up into the waste basket.

That drunken story led to another: Me in a Nashville motel room on a school choir trip so drunk I couldn't stand up. I opened the door for Leslie on my hands and knees, barking like a dog, and bit her on the ankle.

Two stools opened up at the bar and we snatched them, ordered another round. For me, alcohol and cigarettes went together like apple pie and ice cream. I rummaged around my purse for the pack of Marlboro Lights I carried for nights like that. I found the crumpled, half-empty pack—it must have been eight months old—extricated a cigarette and stuck it between my lips. Now for the lighter.

A deep, husky voice saying, "Allow me," put an end to my search and had me hoping it had a face to match. His hands, bits of blue paint on the fingernails, flipped open a Zippo lighter and ignited it in one smooth gesture. Our eyes met. In the dim bar he looked a little like Johnny Depp with longish, messy dark hair and deep brown eyes. He wore an old denim shirt fraying at the cuffs. I was staring, but then so was he. I realized I needed to get laid. Flustered, as if he knew what I was thinking, I fumbled out a thank you. I put the cigarette to the flame, inhaled and coughed like a novice on the stale tobacco. Impressive.

My eyes kept wandering up to the bar mirror to check out the guy as Leslie was reminding me of another high school exploit. A couple of times I caught him checking me out.

"Go for it," whispered Leslie, "You know you want him."

"I do not. Wait, is it that obvious?"

"You're only looking in that mirror like every five seconds."

"What do I do?" I asked, stubbing out the cigarette.

"You're asking me? I've been married for six years. You're the one out there having wild sex in foreign countries."

But I was out of practice. For me, going a couple months without sex was a major drought and in my mourning it was the last thing on my mind. Finding myself attracted to a guy came as a surprise.

I let ten minutes pass before I fished out another Marlboro Light, and not bothering to look for my lighter, I asked the guy for a light. After saying thanks, the words dried up. I had no idea how to get a conversation going.

Leslie, sensing my distress, tossed a lifeline, "I'm Leslie and this is Hunter."

"Michael," he said, pushing his hair behind his ear, "I've never seen either of you in here before."

"I think we were in high school the last time I was here. Hunter's just moved back. She's been living in South America."

"Oh yeah? Where?"

"Peru mostly," Leslie said.

"You're shitting me. That's so cool. What were you doing there?"

"Trying to teach English. They all want to learn, but no one has the money to pay for lessons," I said, finding my voice at last.

"So, what do you do, Michael?" Leslie asked.

"I work at a factory to pay the bills, but I'm really an artist." He pointed to a poster on the wall near the door for The Freeloaders, a blues band playing at Hanrahan's the following week. "Go check it out."

It was an Art Nouveau drawing of a woman, hair piled on top of her head with a flower crown, sheets of fabric wrapped around her body creating sensuous curves and folds. He was good.

Before we returned to the bar Leslie said, "Gimme your keys. I'll drop your car off tomorrow. You two are so going home together."

"He's cute, right?"

Leslie's mouth fell open, "Yeah, and girl, you need some fun. Keys, please."

"You know, I think you're right."

"Not bad," I told Michael when we reclaimed our seats.

"I'd like to draw you sometime," he said, his eyes traveling over my body.

"Really? No one's told me that before," I said, leaning in ever so slightly.

"How about tonight?"

I was ready to say let's go right now, my place or yours, instead I laughed, "Maybe one day, but first you can buy me a drink, and my friend."

"No, no more alcohol for me, thanks. I gotta go. You'll make sure Hunter gets home safely, won't you?" Leslie asked Michael. She laid a ten down on the bar, kissed me on the cheek and made for the door.

It would have been nice if she'd stay long enough to know if I actually had a ride.

"Don't worry, I'll get you home."

A bartender, a woman, delivered me a Heineken and cocking her head at Michael said, "It's on him." I recognized her immediately as the woman in the poster and wondered if she and Michael had ever been lovers. I laid a dollar on the bar for a tip and took a swig of beer.

"Hunter's a cool name, different," Michael said.

"It's my middle name. Not because I like dressing up in camo and shooting cute little deer. My name's actually Susan. In grade school I decided I hated the name, mainly because everyone tried to call me Susie."

Michael leaned over and whispered in my ear, "I've noticed something about you."

"Oh yeah, what's that?" I asked dropping my voice a few notches, aroused by his warm breath and his closeness.

"I'm not going to tell you, but it's something good," he replied. "Drink up and let's get out of here."

❧

Approaching his old, dented black Corolla, Michael cried, "Fuck! How long's that been there?"

That was a bumper sticker. YOU BET YOUR DUPA I'M POLISH it declared loud and proud in red letters.

Peeling back the upper left corner while vowing to kill his fucking brother, Michael gave the sticker a swift yank. Only half came off. Now it read UPA I'M POLISH. "Fuck!" he cried again.

"What does *dupa* mean?" I asked.

"You sit on it."

❧

Michael whistled as he sized up my house. "You live here? Alone?"

"Yeah, it's a sad story. I'll tell you one day, but not tonight."

There was no awkward moment of should I or shouldn't I invite him in. We both knew he was staying. He grabbed a sketch book and a pencil case from the pile of clothes and art supplies on the backseat and followed me inside and straight upstairs.

When I was younger, making love with a guy in my parents' bed had been one of my most recurring teenage sexual fantasies, but now that they were dead it seemed like sacrilege, a violation of their space and memory. I led Michael to the bedroom across the hall where the only reminder that it had once been mine was the formerly dilapidated antique dresser that Mom and I had refurbished and painted black.

Michael enveloped me in his arms, "Do you ever know when something is going to happen? Like tonight. As soon as I saw you I knew we'd end up together. I should've written it down on a piece of paper. Then I could have handed it to you and said 'See, I knew it.'"

"If I'm going to bed with or you, I at least need to know your last name. Somehow it makes us seem like we're not total strangers," I said.

"I'll go one better. Michael Casimir Iwinski. Catholic, you know, gotta have a saint's name. Could'a been worse. My parents could'a named me Adalbert or Jozafat. Polish saints have some crazy ass names."

"My great grandmother was Edna Gertrude. She forbid anyone to be named after her."

Michael kissed me, pushing his tongue deep in my mouth.

Now that it was happening, I was nervous, fearing I'd forgotten what to do. Should I get undressed and get into bed, or was that too presumptuous. I felt ridiculous. Being with a man felt like a lifetime ago.

"It's like riding a bike, but if it helps, I'll do all the work to start," Michael said. He kissed me again, unbuttoning my pink cotton blouse. He slipped it off my shoulders and dropped it on the bed, followed by my bra.

He held up my hands and examined them. They were wide, veins and bones prominent. The fingers were slightly crooked with rounded, large-mooned fingernails. A writer's callous had permanently misshapen the nail of the middle finger of my left hand. The palms were crisscrossed by hundreds of lines.

"You have amazing hands. I can't wait to draw them."

He went down on his knees and loosened my belt, surprised when my white linen pants fell to the floor.

"I've lost a little weight recently," I explained.

"That's cool. Makes my job easier," he said and pulled off my panties. He got to his feet and stepped back to look at me as I stood self-consciously naked before him.

"Turn around," he ordered and I obeyed anxious that he was going to give his opinion of my body and if it wasn't up to his standards he was going to leave.

"You're definitely hot. Lie down on the bed with your feet on the floor and your legs spread." Michael returned to his knees and positioned himself between my legs. "I love eating pussy," he announced and buried his face in me. It had been so long since I'd last had sex that I came easily, much to Michael's satisfaction.

He grabbed the sketch pad and pencils off the floor, "This is when I love to draw a woman, when she has that mixture of pleasure and contentment on her face that I gave her. Drawing for me is the ultimate turn on."

I thought of the poster in the bar and knew the answer to my question. Did Michael do this often? Did he go down on a woman every time he wanted to draw? Did he go down on the same woman or did he always want fresh inspiration? Oh shit, what did it matter now.

"How do you want me?" I asked.

He propped the pillows behind my head and tucked the sheet around my body, leaving my breasts exposed.

"Rest your left arm on your head, with your palm facing up and your fingers curled slightly."

"Like this?" I asked, hoping I was following his instructions.

"Perfect. Now, can you hold that for twenty minutes?"

"I think so."

He stared at me for a bit, then began making quick strokes with a pencil, looking up at me frequently.

I didn't know if it was okay to talk, but I was uncomfortable staying silent under such scrutiny. I asked him where he worked.

"Promise not to laugh? A sausage factory."

I couldn't help it, laughter exploded out of me ruining my carefully constructed pose.

"Now look what you've done," Michael said in mock anger, throwing down his sketchbook. "You'll be severely punished for that." He tore off his jeans and was on top of me, his tongue in my mouth and his hard cock pressing against my belly.

❧

Sex was definitely a much better sleep aid than Valium. I awoke in the morning to find Michael getting dressed.

"Sorry, I was trying to be quiet. Gotta go."

Great, he was trying to sneak out, never to be seen again. "But it's Sunday."

"Told my brother I'd help him move some stuff," he said pulling on his boots. "What are you doing tonight? How about going on a real date. I'll buy you dinner and everything."

"That would be nice," I said with relief.

"I'll call you later." He leaned down, gave me a kiss and was gone.

I lay in bed for another hour, going over every detail of the previous night. I felt close to happy for the first time since that dreadful January day. I buried my face in the pillow rich with Michael's scent.

The phone rang. The bedside clock read noon. I must have fallen back asleep.

"Tell me all the dirty details!" Leslie cried when I picked up. "Oh, he's not still there, is he?"

"No, he's gone."

"And...?"

"And what? I don't kiss and tell."

"Since when? So, do you want me to bring your car back or are you going to float over here on a cloud of love?"

8

"Meet me at Tip Top Thai at seven," Michael said when he called, "I can't remember the address, but you can look it up."

I was ready at five o'clock. I tried on several outfits before deciding on jeans, a white tank, a grey cardigan and black sandals. From the neck down I looked pretty good. My hair, on the other hand, looked like chickens had been roosting in it. Down, up, in a ponytail, in pig tails, in braids, nothing worked. Only the fear I'd end up with no hair at all stopped me from taking scissors and hacking off a few inches. Braids hid the fried ends best, though I looked about twelve.

I killed time puttering around the house, picking up clothes, washing dishes that had been piling up in the sink for days and then sat down to read a copy of *The New Yorker* pilfered from my lawyer's office. When I looked at the clock again it was quarter to seven.

It didn't matter that I was late, Michael wasn't at the restaurant. Hovering between fury and humiliation, I was close to walking out when he unapologetically arrived at seven-forty-five.

"You look so hot," he said as he sat down. And so did he in a black tee shirt and faded jeans, a plaid flannel shirt tied around his hips and his hair tied back in a messy ponytail.

"Let's skip the preliminaries and go back to your place and fuck" he suggested, grabbing my knee under the table. My anger evaporated.

"No way! No guy has bought me dinner in months and I'm not giving up a free meal. Sex'll have to wait." But I was flattered that he was so eager to get me back in bed.

As we ate *pad thai* and green curry, Michael told me about growing up on the south side, a traditionally working class area of the city that I'd never been to. I didn't tell him that in high school we'd made fun of "da sout-siders."

His father had been a machinist at Silas-Allen, a manufacturer of farm equipment, until he died of lung cancer when Michael was nineteen. Michael dropped out of Wisconsin State to work full-time to help support his mother, a nurse's assistant at St. Francis Hospital, and his younger brother.

Michael piled his fork with pad thai and before shoving into his mouth, pronounced the meal delicious.

In my opinion it was pretty mediocre. "The food you get in Thailand is so much better." God, I sounded so pretentious.

"You've been to Thailand? That's cool"

"Yeah, I spent nine months in Southeast Asia."

"That's cool."

Michael said, "That's cool" a lot. Whenever I managed to interject something about my life into his monologue, the phrase was included in his response. "You went to school

66

in England? That's cool." "You lived on Tokyo? That's cool." "Your parents just died, that's cool." (*He didn't really say that, but he might have*) And then returned to talking about himself.

That he didn't ask me any questions about myself was a bit of a relief. I didn't want to talk about my parents to some guy I hardly knew, but all the same it irked me that he appeared to have no interest in knowing anything about me. Then again, I'd done and seen so much more than he had, maybe he felt threatened, maybe he was trying to prove he was good enough for me.

Except what he was telling me wasn't all that interesting and he wasn't all that smart. When I talked about traveling in Bolivia, my jaw dropped several inches when he asked where it was. The only books he ever read were comic books. Maybe Michael wasn't right for me. Maybe I needed a guy more worldly, not so south-side. Listen to me, what a hypocrite. Most of the boyfriends I'd had since leaving Milwaukee were blue collar. I hated the rich boys I'd gone to high school with. None of them would even have made good first husbands. I'd turned my back on that conservative-prep-school-country-club-perfect-outside-rotten-inside life as soon as I left Milwaukee. So why was I being a snob about Michael's background? Odd how those early prejudices popped up as unwelcome and unexpected as pimples. At thirty years old I should have outgrown both. Maybe I should just shut up about my life, rein in my need to be fascinating, alluring, and be a good listener for once.

I examined his face across the table. He was gorgeous and he sure wasn't lacking in confidence. But there was something odd about the shape of his nose. The tip was bulbous with a faint ridge dividing it into two parts. It reminded me of the head of a penis.

Back at my house, as soon as we were in the door, Michael was all over me, pulling off my cardigan, pushing me up against the kitchen counter. "You look so hot. I've been waiting all night for this." He ripped off my sandals, jeans and panties, lifted me onto the counter, and put his head between my thighs. Michael was perfect.

∂✿

Four days and another date with Michael later, I was on Downer Avenue on the trendy east side, to meet Andy, who lived nearby. The street was quiet, the usual bustle of shoppers absent. Two women scurried down the sidewalk, heads bent against the rain, purses clutched tightly to their chests, and darted into Salvador Deli. The popular restaurant was my destination too, though I was in no hurry to arrive. Floating on a cloud of love, I was oblivious to the cold and wet, my mind full of Michael, his smell, his taste, the weight of his body on mine.

The deli's decor was an homage to the surrealist painter. Dali's painting "The Persistence of Memory" was reproduced on one wall with melting hamburgers and sandwiches in place of the clocks. On another, Galatea was pieced together with tomatoes rather than spheres. It was crowded and noisy with the din of dozens of conversations. It was the only business thriving on such a miserable day. Andy waved to me from a table by the front window, misty from the heat of so many bodies.

"What's with you? You look almost giddy," Andy asked as I sank down into one of the cafe's custom-made metal chairs.

"I don't know, maybe I'm falling in love," I replied.

"You've been on, what, three dates with the guy. A week ago you were moaning to me about how miserable your life was, no family, no friends, no life and now you're in love. Have you ever called Sonya?" He sounded almost angry.

Sonya was the therapist Andy'd been trying to get me to see for months. She'd helped him come to terms with his sexuality and he thought she could help me 'process my grief.' Processing anything made me think of American cheese. I didn't want to lie on a couch and tell someone I didn't know what a crap daughter I'd been, rehash things I'd said and done that I'd rather forget. I'd blown off Father Stephens so many times he'd stopped calling. And besides, now there was Michael to love.

I pretended not to hear him, wiping a circle in the steamed-up window and gazing out, thinking about the neighbor-hood. Restaurants, boutiques, bookshops, galleries and a cinema filled the blocks of Downer Avenue. On tree-lined side streets were old three-story, brick apartment buildings mixed with single-family homes. There was a lot more going on there than on Stansfield Street.

"Maybe I should move down here," I said, imagining me and Michael getting a place of our own. A two-bedroom apartment with big windows and hardwood floors. We could convert one of the bedrooms into his studio. I would take care of him, cook for him. With my money, he'd be able to quit his job at the factory and be an artist full time, maybe even get a show in New York one day. I would nurture his talent, using my inheritance in a way that would make my parents proud, and I could be his muse. "It's much more convenient. Michael wouldn't have to drive as far."

"What, now you're planning on staying in Milwaukee? Not that I don't like having you around, but I thought you hated it here."

"Well, if things with Michael work out..." I said coyly taking a sip from my mug of Darjeeling.

"What are you going to be? A stay-at-home girlfriend? Now that you've maybe got a boyfriend you don't need to get your shit together?"

God, he was like a Pekinese. Yap. Yap. Yap. Call Sonya. Get help. Talk about your problems. Don't spend so much time in your head, feeling sorry for yourself. Get a job. Do something productive with your time. Get out more. Don't have a boyfriend. What did he know about grief?

"If this relationship, or any relationship is going to work, you've got to get your own life. A boyfriend is not going to solve your problems," he continued.

And when had Andy gotten to be such an expert on relationships? He was supposed to be my friend, the one who made me laugh, not treat me like pitiable orphan. He wasn't supposed to ride my ass about my life.

"You've been with Danny, what, seven months? It's the first relationship you've had that doesn't exist more in your head than in reality and you're giving me relationship advice." It came out nastier than I intended and I apologized. I didn't want to start a fight. "God, Andy, I'm sorry, I didn't mean that."

"As it happens, Danny and I are moving in together. I mean, he's moving into my place."

There weren't many men in the world, let alone Milwaukee, who could keep up with Andy's high energy—caused by the Ritalin he took for narcolepsy—or sleep through the din of his asthmatic snoring. "That's great. I'm happy for you, really," I said, trying to appear happy rather than surprised.

As we said goodbye, Andy gave me a big hug, "Listen, you know I love you, but you gotta get a job or do something other than sit at home and wait for Michael to come over."

Andy was right. I had to be more than just a girlfriend. How many times in my life had I been with a guy just so I wouldn't be alone. I knew I wasn't going to be in Milwaukee forever, but as long as I was there, for as long as I was there, I had to get some kind life of my own. And maybe Michael would want to move with me, whenever I figured out where I wanted to go. He could paint anywhere. The big question was what kind of job should I get. I'd never pursued a career. I didn't even have a résumé. I could look for a job teaching ESL, but that would mean making lesson plans and being happy and genial in class and as happy as I was at that moment, I wasn't sure I could sustain it. Plus, ESL classes were usually at night, which meant I wouldn't be able to see Michael as much. My work experience was slim. I had no references in the US and with the exception of Japan, most of my recent jobs had been under the table. Who would hire me?

A NOW HIRING sign hanging in the window of The Printed Page caught my eye. Working in a bookstore couldn't be that hard. A good time-filler until I figured out what I really wanted to do. I loved books. Instead of walking straight in and applying, I promised to do it tomorrow.

There was a message from Michael when I got home. Something had come up and he had to cancel our date that night. He'd call later.

By ten o'clock, nada. Could it be over already? Had I said or done something that turned him off? Was I bad in bed? Was I ugly? Too fat? Too boring? Too needy? I took a Valium, the first in weeks.

⁂♣

There was no call from Michael the next morning.

Realizing more than ever that I had to get up and get a job, I lay in bed until eleven. Dragging myself to the bathroom, I decided what I really needed was a bath. Soaking in hot water and bubbles would relax my nerves. Any calming effects of the bath were lost when I tackled the issue of what to wear. Outfit after outfit was rejected for making my arms look too big, or my legs too short, or making me look like I had no waist. I was almost in tears before I found something that I didn't feel completely hideous in. The day was ticking by and I hadn't left the house. And no call from Michael.

On Downer Avenue, I wandered around for another hour, passing in front of the bookshop several times before I harnessed the confidence to go in. I asked the girl at the register for an application. She didn't hear me forcing me to ask again in a louder voice. I wanted the fewest number of people to know my purpose, or hear the girl tell me the position was already filled, or I needn't bother applying because I was not at all the type they were looking for. But she handed me an application and pointed to a chair I could sit in to fill it out.

Turning it in, I was informed the owner would like to interview me right away. Not exactly what I had expected or wanted. I hated interviews at the best of times and today I was definitely not at my best. I was led upstairs and into the office of Janine Bosco, the tiny, tightly wound—even her hair was wound into tight curls—proprietor of The Printed Page.

Janine invited me to sit on a cat-hair-covered sofa. The source of the hair was curled up at the far end, a large, lazy calico. Janine perched herself on the edge of her desk like a coiled animal ready to pounce, her head twitching at every chair moving, drawer opening, telephone ringing on the other side of her office door.

The interview went as badly as I expected. My answers were preambled with hems and haws. The only question I answered without hesitation was what were my weaknesses? Interviews, I replied not missing a beat.

"When can you start?" Janine asked.

Wow, she must be really short-staffed. For me, it meant no more job hunting, no more interviews. I could start tomorrow.

To celebrate my joining the gainfully employed, I headed straight to a supermarket for a pint of mint chocolate chip ice cream. Michael was sitting on the front steps, pen and paper in hand when I arrived home.

"Hey, I was just writing you a note. Sorry I never called. My roommate washed my jeans with your number in the pocket."

"Your roommate does your laundry?" I asked not knowing if I should believe him, but so relieved that he was there in front of me I would have accepted any excuse. He'd spit out a wad of gum into it. His dog ate it. A condor swooped down from the sky and plucked it out of his hand.

"A little odd I know. But hey, my clothes are clean."

"I guess I can forgive you this one time. Do you like mint chocolate chip ice cream?"

"My favorite."

9

Janine stood at the front door of the shop, arms folded, foot tapping impatiently, her mouth a thin red line, as I hurried down the sidewalk ten minutes late for my first day of work.

"I hope this is a one-time occurrence, Hunter. UPS always arrives between nine-thirty and ten so you've got to be here by nine-thirty."

"I'm really sorry. It won't happen again," I replied like a chastened school girl. But the cause of my tardiness was making my heart sing. Michael had jumped in the shower with me and, well, one thing led to another, and another, and another and then I was scrambling to get dressed and out the door by nine-fifteen.

"But as it is your first day, I suppose I can let it slide," Janine said with a tense smile.

So keyed up that she was practically hyperventilating, Janine began the tour upstairs where there were three offices. The largest was Janine's. Next to it was Alice's, the bookkeeper, who along with me was one of the four full-time employees. I greeted Alice, who briefly looked up from her adding machine, giving a quick wave. The third office was currently being used by Philip Cox, a freelance computer programmer Janine had hired to develop an inventory software system for the shop and for the book and video catalog devoted to New Age titles she was launching. It's a growing market Janine assured me.

The tour continued downstairs in the shop that was a book lover's paradise. The atmosphere was pleasantly relaxed despite the nervous energy of the owner. The shelves were bulging with popular as well as obscure titles on subjects ranging from psychology to travel, religion to science, fiction to personal development. There was even a large room solely for New Age topics. Several large easy chairs were placed around the shop where customers could spend as much time as they wanted reading with no pressure to buy. The sales staff were almost all part-timers, eleven in all, most of them students at Wisconsin State. They worked four to a shift, three on the floor and one on the register.

Janine then led me down a flight of wooden steps to the basement, where all book orders were received. It was a cool and dreary place, particularly when contrasted with the sunny airiness of the shop and offices. I gulped at the thought of spending my days down there. The concrete walls and floor were dank from fifty years of humid Wisconsin summers. The low ceiling, made even lower by heating ducts, hummed with fluorescent lights. Three long rows of five-tiered metal shelves holding overstock books extended into the gloom of the basement's far corners. A wooden table was set against one wall, a small window above it. On it were a computer, a printer, a metal clamp-on desk lamp and an old coffee can holding pens and a couple of box cutters.

Janine guided me through the shelves pointing out where extra copies of books for the different sections upstairs were stacked. The number of copies stored in the basement would soon rise with the addition of the catalog and so too would the work for the receiver. Instead of four or five copies of a popular book by Marianne Williamson or J.Z. Knight there were now forty. I was shown how a shipment was checked against the purchase order and the invoice and the quantities inputted into the computer. Each book got a label giving the price and the section. Labelled books were put into boxes marked for the different sections then the sales assistants would carry those boxes upstairs and load the books onto carts for shelving. After helping me receive a few small shipments, Janine was confident her new employee understood the process and went back to her office.

The day passed swiftly and I wasn't as lonely as I feared. Stephanie, a twenty-one-year-old English major, caustic as lye, was in the basement often on the pretense of getting books, but really wanting to chat. She had a stud in her nose and her shoulder-length hair was thick, black and straight, cut across her forehead in short, severe bangs. Her thin eyebrows slanted downward from her temples to her nose. She could have been Mr. Spock's daughter.

Stephanie filled me in on the ins and outs of working for the Bat, as Janine was known by the staff. "It's like she has a built-in radar. She always knows where everyone is, if we're talking to a customer or to each other," she said, lifting herself to sit on the table. If someone was about to spill the details of her date the night before, Janine was there wanting to know who the guy was. If an employee paused shelving a cart of books, Janine was by the cart asking why the task hadn't been completed.

"The worst is when you make a mistake. She'll yell at you in front of customers. But you're in the basement so you don't have to worry about that, but you and her have the same schedule so that sucks." She picked up a review copy of *The Shipping News* and idly examined it. "She sells these, you know, even though they're stamped 'Not for Sale.' She cuts out that page. Totally unethical. I don't know how Alice has worked here for ten years."

Greta, a chubby, pockmarked mouse of a girl from a small town in northern Wisconsin, came down and her eyes widened in frightened disbelief when she saw us calmly talking. She grabbed an armful of books and raced back upstairs.

"Poor Greta. She'd quit if she wasn't so afraid Janine would yell at her," Stephanie said as she dropped the book and jumped off the table. She hoisted up a box with books for the travel section, "See ya in a bit."

A little later Jeremy, one of the other full-time employees, came down for boxes. He was in his late thirties, thin, slightly stooped with a weak chin and round wire-rimmed glasses like John Lennon. He'd worked as a researcher in a biology lab, but was going through a transitional phase in his life, he informed me.

"After every shift he sits reading in the kook room," Stephanie said on her next visit.

"What's the kook room?"

"You know, where all the books on Atlantis and channeling are. He asked me once if he could open my chakras.

Sounds kinky, doesn't it? If he wasn't such a weirdo, I might let him. He'll probably ask you too. He asks every female who works here. I think it's his weird way of trying to get a date."

I finished my first day without any major mistakes. I could tell Janine was pleased that I'd caught on so easily. Tomorrow I'd bring a boom box and some tapes to liven up the scene in the basement.

❧

Weeks later I was still looking forward to going to work five days a week. It was pretty mindless, but it got me out of the house and out of my head. I arrived on a Friday morning and was nearly knocked to the ground by a hysterical Greta moving like a runaway train out of the shop. She blubbered an apology and kept on going.

Inside, Janine was cursing loudly, "What the hell am I going to do now? I'm a person short. I guess I'll to have to work the floor." Stephanie, Jeremy, Dora, another part-timer, and Alice stared silently at the floor. Stephanie's hands were clasped behind her back as if that was the only thing stopping her from punching Janine.

"Greta forgot to make the night deposit. Janine went ballistic. She was already in a shitty mood," Stephanie told me when she came downstairs a few minutes later. "God, today's going to suck. It's bad enough when Janine's in her office, but on the floor."

"Why do you work here if you dislike her so much?" I asked.

"Cause I want to nail her somehow. I haven't figured out how yet."

Stephanie's griping was interrupted by someone descending the stairs singing, "Good morning, good morning/Sun beams will soon shine through/Good morning, good morning to you." Philip pointed at me and still singing added, "UPS is here." He turned toward Stephanie, "Hey, hey, hey, Steph, why the long face?"

"The prospect of a whole day on the floor with Janine," she replied.

"Well, I can turn that frown upside down. I just told Janine I'd work the register. Want to see how the new point-of-sale program is working."

In an uncharacteristic display of exuberance, Stephanie threw her arms around Philip and kissed him on the cheek. "You're an absolute angel. Come out with us tonight. We'll all owe you a beer." (Us was Stephanie, Dora, Alice, and until today Greta, who went out for beers every Friday.)

"You're on," he said, "Now I better get back upstairs."

When he was gone, Stephanie swooned, or as close to a swoon as a Vulcan can make, "He's got such kissable lips. I'd have planted that kiss right on them if I could've done it without completely losing control."

All the girls at the shop lusted after Philip. I didn't see what the fuss was about. Ok, so he had kind of a sexy mouth and his eyes were a rare greenish-grey, the color of Spanish moss. And yes, he was always upbeat and so laid back not even the Bat could ruffle him. Not that Janine ever tried. Her infatuation with Philip was an open secret and the source of amusement among the staff. But his ash blond hair was thinning on top, and to me, he was too smooth and open, lacking the rough edges and dark corners I found so compelling in a man. And really, how exciting could a guy be who spent his days hunched over a computer writing code? Phrases Philip used, silly rhymes he made up, singing show tunes, made me speculate he was gay, further evidenced by his having no current girlfriend. I expressed this opinion to Stephanie.

She shot it down immediately. "No, no, he was married. And there was a girl, Jennifer, who worked here a while back who had a fling with him. She was totally NVSP. I thought he'd be deeper than that. Maybe he just had an itch that needed scratching 'cause nothing came of it. But there's no way he's gay."

"NV what?"

"NSVP. No Visible Signs of Personality. You know the type, 'I'm pretty, have big boobs, men love me so I don't need a personality or opinions, or any of that plain girl stuff," Stephanie's voice was an octave higher and her head bobbed from side to side. As she headed for the stairs she suggested I join them after work.

"Can't. Michael's coming over for dinner. It's our month anniversary."

"Wow. A whole month. When's the wedding?"

I brushed off Stephanie's sarcasm. Michael and I had been spending a lot of time together and it was beginning to feel like a relationship. He'd come over in the evenings and we'd have dinner and watch a video, or we'd meet up at a bar or club. Usually he was slipping his hand down my jeans before we were twenty minutes into a movie, or when at a club, he'd grab me from behind and suggest making it an early night. And the sex was three-alarm hot.

He knew a lot about art and was super talented. He'd drawn me dozens of times and I loved being the model and lover of an artist. But God, he was clueless about the world and showed zero interest in learning more. I told him once he was loquacious. He had no clue what it meant, said it sounded like a kind of seafood. He rarely helped prepare the dinners we ate and since our first date his wallet had been locked in his back pocket. But he was really into me and I liked feeling part of something.

At least until recently he'd been really into me. Like some people sensed coming changes in the weather, I sensed the earliest stirrings of doubt in a man, changes so subtle they were undetectable to a less-trained eye. In the last few days I'd been detecting minute changes in Michael. The way he said hello, how he looked just over my shoulder rather than at me when answering my questions about his day, set me worrying that a storm was brewing and kept me from mentioning the anniversary to him. It was my secret.

The evening had to be perfect. The aroma of sautéing cumin and coriander seeds wafted through the kitchen minutes after I returned home. On the cutting board, chopped onions, garlic and broccoli were ready to join the spices in the skillet. A pot of lentils simmered on a back burner. Tandoori chicken was baking in the oven. I'd even risen early that morning to make the *raita* and the chocolate mousse dessert that were chilling in the refrigerator, and to set the table with candles and my mother's china. If Michael questioned the elaborate dinner, I'd laugh it off as a lark, just something I wanted to do. Another motive besides my private celebration, was to remind Michael that cooking was one of my many talents. And the green floral dress I'd wear showed lots of skin and hugged all my curves to remind him how sexy and beautiful I was. I'd purchased the dress with my first pay check, which was so small it barely covered the cost. And after dinner, I'd give him the best blow job of his life.

I was giving the lentils a stir when Michael called.

"I don't think tonight's going to happen" were the first words out of his mouth after "hello." His voice was distant.

"Oh well, Indian food always tastes better the next day," I replied with fake sunniness while tiny fissures formed on my heart.

"Yeah, well, I'm not sure that's going to work either. It's starting to feel too much like a relationship and I really don't want to get tied down right now," Michael continued, "I've got a lot of things I wanna to do, you know, with my art and don't want any distractions."

"Uh huh, I understand," I lied, fighting back tears. The storm had hit before I even had the chance to quell it. Did my sixth sense have to be so infallible? Couldn't it be wrong just once? My heart broke.

"No hard feelings, okay? We can still be friends."

"Yeah, whatever. Hey, I gotta go. Got stuff on the stove," and choking down a sob, I hung up before Michael could say another word. The wooden spoon I was holding flew out of my hand, struck the refrigerator, blotching it with lentils, and clattered to the floor.

IO

"He dumped me," I cried into the phone, "He only wants a relationship with his art."

"Oh honey, I'm sorry," Andy said, "What a prick. Wanna come over? I'm making my infamous tuna casserole with pickle relish and potato chips. I know you love it."

"I'm leaving now."

Fleeing the house like it was on fire, I grabbed the seventy-dollar bottle of wine I'd bought for the dinner and jumped in the car. I pushed in the clutch, shifted into reverse, and hit the accelerator. The car lurched backward and stalled. I slumped against the steering wheel, weeping, my chest shuddering. My vague premonition of Michael's leaving had done nothing to lessen the shock of it. When I calmed down, I dried my cheeks and restarted the engine.

Traffic was unusually heavy. As the traffic light switched from yellow to red, oncoming cars raced through the intersection forcing me to sit through two lights before I could turn onto Downer Avenue. There, cars were bumper to bumper, inching along, stopping and starting. What the hell was going on? Ten minutes only gained me three blocks. My shoulders tensed with irritation, my grip tightened on the steering wheel. I had to get out of there, go another way, but no one would let me change lanes. Each time space opened up, a car shot forward to fill it, cutting me off. Anger boiling just beneath the surface erupted. I slammed my back repeatedly against the seat back. Fuck you, Michael and your penis nose. You fucking loser. Fuck you God, or the Universe, or whoever was responsible for taking my beautiful, generous, loving parents. Fuck you for leaving me all alone.

Five blocks further on the reason for the snarl came into view. A broken-down delivery van had reduced the two lanes to one. A silver Camaro convertible, a fat, balding man in an overstretched tank top at the wheel, his bleach blonde girlfriend in the passenger seat, tried to edge in front of me. In a bit of childish revenge, I sped up and blocked the opening.

The late-June evening was hot and humidity hung in the air like a damp rag. Perspiration was sheening my face and arms by the time I knocked on Andy's door. Downer Avenue was a popular destination on Friday nights and parking spaces were hard to come by. I'd had to park three blocks away, fueling my anger even more. When Andy answered, I thrust the bottle of wine into his hands demanding it be opened. I needed a drink. Andy's whistled when he read the vintage.

I flung myself down on the couch, not even acknowledging Danny, who was in the kitchen pouring me a glass from an already open bottle of Pinot.

"God! Men are such assholes. They're so eager in the beginning, wanting to spend every minute with you and then accuse you of being the one pushing a relationship. I don't get it," I seethed.

"Here you go," Danny said, presenting me the glass.

Without a thank you, I snatched it out of his hands, poured half the contents down my throat and continued my rant, "I am such an idiot. I knew he'd pull some chicken shit move like this. I should have dumped him first. And his art isn't all that great. Who's he kidding? He's never going to be famous."

I finished off the wine and held out the empty glass, a silent demand for more, which Danny fulfilled. I looked up at the striking man with angular features, darks eyes and dark skin. The tee shirt he wore hugged the well-toned body beneath. That he could have had any man but chose Andy endeared him to me. So sweet bringing me the wine and I'd completely ignored him, treated him like a waiter. Why were all the good ones gay?

"Thanks, Danny," I said weakly, my anger spent, my eyes stinging. "What's wrong with me? Will I ever find somebody?"

Andy joined me on the couch and put his arm around me. "Sure you will, but Michael just isn't the one."

"But you told me that night I wasn't woman enough, not sexy enough," I was crying freely now.

"Oh God, how I wish I could take that all back. I was trapped in the closet then. You are beautiful and sexy and smart and any man would be lucky to have you. Michael's an idiot. You told me so yourself, not in those exact words, maybe, but come on, who doesn't know Bolivia's in South America."

That night, the night I'd never forgotten, the night Andy'd been so cruel, was the night of our senior prom.

Andy'd transferred to Milwaukee Academy junior year and was almost immediately popular, a spectacular feat on its own, but even greater given the fact that he was a terrible athlete and had a tendency to fall asleep—later diagnosed as narcolepsy—in the most unexpected places: on the toilet; with a beer to his lips, the bottle splattering across the floor; and once kissing Elizabeth Watts during a drunken game of Spin the Bottle. No one could laugh at Andy because he laughed at himself first. He was completely indifferent to the school's social hierarchy. He befriended anyone and everyone.

We hung out together, as we always had, so everyone assumed we were a couple. Eventually, we did, too. For me, the relationship got me begrudging invitations to the parties of the popular crowd and a date to all the dances.

Andy and I had gone to the prom and then to a party at Kitty Caufield's house. Andy had everyone in stitches with his imitations of some of our more idiosyncratic teachers: Mr. Nyman (*English*) sounding like Elmer Fudd weciting poetwee by the gweat Engwish poets. Mr. Hansen (*geometry*) whose penchant for digression could turn a lesson about solids into a lecture on the price of coffee into a narrative about a summer trip to Spain. And Mrs. Gilman (*French*) whose speech, due to a bottle kept in the lower lefthand drawer of her desk, was slurred by the afternoon.

I was in a glorious mood. Polly Vandercamp had actually been nice to me, even engaged me in a conversation. It didn't matter that she'd had six beers and wasn't sure who she was talking to.

And then there was the big event to look forward to after the party. Andy and I were going to do "it." We said "it" because "making love" was too dopey and "fucking" too ugly.

Andy's parents were gone for the weekend and he'd decided that it was the perfect time to do "it." He'd even bought some condoms. I told my parents I was spending the night at Leslie's.

We transformed Andy's bedroom into a love nest with lots of candles and incense. We drank champagne Andy had purloined from his father's collection as *Dark Side of the Moon* played in the background. It was just the way I'd imagined it would be and I'd been imagining that moment for years. Except that, when it came to the sex part, I had never imagined past the kissing because I had no idea what came next. The few sexual experiences I'd had—the making out and awkward groping under my shirt with Billy Maxwell, a boy I dated for about ten seconds fresh-man year; giving a hand job to Mark Anderson sophomore year only to have him start going out with Danielle Spurling—had not lived up to my romantic notions of what sex was about. They had been crude, almost vulgar, especially the hand job.

Now I was with Andy, my best friend, the boy I thought I was in love with. We hadn't done much experimentation other than long make out sessions. I'd wanted more, but Andy was hesitant and I didn't want to come on too strong, afraid he would think I was a nympho. But tonight we were going to do "it," and it had been Andy's idea. My heart began to tremble. Please let it be perfect. Please let me be good at this, I prayed.

We self-consciously removed our clothes and got under the covers. Andy moved on top of me and began to kiss me mechanically, his body rigid. When I responded passionately, he pulled away falling back onto the bed.

"What's the matter?" I asked uneasily, touching his arm. He twitched like my fingers were covered in needles.

"Nothing. I'm just nervous, I guess. I need to relax."

We lay in silence until Andy again began to kiss me and climbed on top of me only to stop again and complain about nerves. He didn't even have an erection.

"Can I help?" I asked, as I tried to recall a love scene from any movie to help me. I kissed his face and neck trying hard to appear sexy and experienced. I reached down and grabbed his flaccid penis and tugged at it thinking it might help. That's what Leslie had told me to do. She was the resident expert because she'd been going out with Peter Fritz since sophomore year and they'd done "it" over Christmas break. Andy pushed my hand away and rolled over on his side giving his back to me.

This couldn't be happening. How could everything be going wrong? I suppressed a sob. Then Andy was on top of me, kissing me fiercely and roughly grabbing my breasts. He seemed angry, not loving. He was somewhat hard and he tried to push himself inside me. I cried out so loudly in pain that he withdrew and jumped out of the bed.

"This isn't working. I don't know what's wrong." And then Andy said those words that still lived in my head,

"Maybe it's you. Maybe I'm just not attracted to you. Maybe you're not woman enough."

It was my fault. Maybe I wasn't woman enough to interest or excite any man. That was the reason Mark had chosen Danielle and Billy had broken up with me. I had to get out of there. I had to get away from Andy, away from the scene of my humiliation. I threw on my clothes and raced out of the house.

I didn't go to school the following Monday. Sure that my failure would be the subject on everyone's lips I'd concocted an excuse to stay home, pushing away Sunday night's dinner complaining of nausea and dizziness.

I actually did feel ill when I thought of having to confront the amusement in the eyes of my classmates. I wanted to stay home on Tuesday too, but my mother, not convinced my illness was genuine, refused to let me miss another day.

I walked briskly down the hall keeping my head low, listening for snickers, but detecting none as I passed other students getting ready for their first class. I sighed with relief as I opened my locker, then allowed myself a little laugh. Did I really think that Andy was going to tell anyone.

I grabbed my chemistry book and closed my locker just as Leslie and Megan came out of the girls' bathroom, their heads thrown back in laughter. My face went white. I couldn't remember if they had started laughing when they saw me or before. I felt weightless and my skin began to tingle. The books fell out of my arms and crashed to the floor, immediately followed by me, landing with a thud.

"Hunter, are you okay?" Megan asked, worry filling her face.

"I don't know. I guess so." My voice was so weak I barely heard myself speak.

"You should have stayed home. Let's get you to the nurse and have her call your mom," Leslie said, taking charge of the situation. "Get her books," she commanded Megan, who responded like a well-drilled soldier.

As Leslie lifted me up and guided me down the hall with Megan trailing behind, a tiny smile crept across my face. They knew nothing. By the time we reached the office of Mrs. Otto, the school nurse, I was completely recovered.

"Do you want to go home?" Mrs. Otto asked as she pulled the thermometer out from under my tongue. "You don't have a temperature, but fainting isn't a good sign. Have you eaten breakfast?"

Mrs. Otto frowned, all two hundred pounds of her, at the negative response. "You girls and your weight. Coffee, cigarettes, no food. It's not healthy. Go to the kitchen and ask Mrs. Kretchmar for an apple. And eat lunch today."

I went to my classes, assiduously avoiding Andy, and it hurt that he never sought me out. But then why would he want to waste any more time with me. As I came out of Mr. Johnson's Spanish class I saw him talking to Lee Sinclair, a very cute, bubbly junior with big tits and long legs who had all the boys in the school drooling. Why wouldn't he want to be with her. He'll want to be with a real woman. Thank God, graduation was only three weeks away.

I told all my friends that Andy and I had broken up for some vague reason. Our friendship wasn't restored until one summer day three years later. I was home from college and Andy showed up at the house, cajoling me out for a ride in his new Mazda. He parked the car in Atwater Park overlooking Lake Michigan and said gravely that he had some- thing to tell me. He's getting married. He has cancer and has six months to live.

"I'm gay."

"What?" It was a reflex response. I was pretty sure I'd heard him right.

"I said I'm gay. I've think I've known for years, since grade school, but I could never admit it, not until two months ago. I told my parents. My dad cried. My mom sat there, looking at me like I'd sprouted horns, just like you." He cocked his head, crossed his eyes and stuck out his tongue.

I laughed, then my face fell. "You mean you knew in high school? Prom night? You let me believe it was my fault all this time. You were my best friend."

"God, if you only knew how terrible I feel about that. I've spent hours talking to my therapist about it," he said putting a hand on my shoulder. I shrugged it off.

"Will you take me home now. I need to think about this."

"Hunter, please forgive me. I never meant to hurt you, but I was so messed up and scared." I saw sincerity in his eyes.

"I think everything'll be okay, but I really just need to be alone and think."

Once I was in the privacy of my room, I relived that painful night over and over again in my mind. Hearing with great clarity the cruelty in Andy's voice as he told me I wasn't woman enough. As I played the scene out for the twelfth time it dawned on me that if Andy was gay then the fiasco that night was his fault, not mine. Maybe I was attractive and sexy after all. I fell back on the bed, smiling. But a woman who was really sexy and beautiful could have turned on a gay man. There were lots of gay men who had been married and fathered children before coming out.

I ate only a few bites of casserole and helped myself to glass after glass of first the Pinot and when that was gone, the Syrah I'd brought. Andy and Danny watched me with troubled faces, saying nothing. My eyelids weighed a hundred pounds each. My head lolled to one side then jerked upright as I tried to rouse myself. In another minute, it was lolling to the other side. Andy guided me to the guest room, laying me down on the bed. He slipped off my sandals and tossed a thin blanket over me. He turned off the light as he left the room, closing the door behind him.

The red wine toyed with me, letting me drift off then teasing me awake. I awoke with a start at one AM, fully dressed and in a strange room with hideous, glowing sad clowns faces surrounding me. The diamonds in the crown of Andy's clown painting collection. I rolled over and went back to sleep. I awoke again at four, eyes wide in terror of being alone and unloved, the clowns frowning in sympathy. "We know how you're feeling," they seemed to say, "If it weren't for Andy we'd be forgotten in some attic or rotting under mountains of trash in a dump."

First my parents and now Michael was gone, too. But Michael wasn't dead and how could I even compare losing him to losing them. But how could he leave me when he knew better than anyone what I was going through. He'd lost his dad. He should know how much I needed him. But how could I ask that of anyone? What guy wanted a needy chick? Had I acted too needy? Is that what turned him off? I tried to remember instances of blatant neediness and could come up with one, the night I woke up from a dream about my parents, sobbing, my heart beating so fast I thought I was having a heart attack. Not exactly a constant hand tugging at his sleeve. So if it wasn't that, and if I believed Andy that I was woman enough, then why?

Maybe Michael was scared. Maybe he really liked me, but was afraid of getting hurt. Guys did that, didn't they? They sometimes backed off when they felt themselves getting in too deep. Fear of having their wings clipped was how Mom had put it. Of fuck, what did it matter. He was gone.

At five I gave up. I got dressed, bid the clowns farewell, scrawled Andy and Danny a short thank you note and stole out of the apartment.

The street lamps on Stansfield Street threw haloes of greenish light onto the sidewalks, only the occasional chirping of a sparrow broke the silence. In the car, I stared at the house, hand on the key still in the ignition. The house frightened me more at this hour than it did at midnight. In the gray dawn light it looked like it had been abandoned years ago, its windows cold and lifeless. I didn't want to go inside. There'd been an all-night diner near the university where we used to go for greasy eggs and coffee after the bars closed. Maybe it was still there.

The red neon OPEN sign in the window of Ma Fisher's flashed on and off as it had in the past. The same three waitresses, slower and heavier, waddled up and down the aisles in blue uniforms with white aprons and outdated beehives. They could have been triplets. Possibly the same grizzled old men were hunched on their stools at the counter, searching the pockets of their dingy, threadbare jackets for enough change for a cup of coffee. I slid into a booth and grabbed a laminated menu from its place between the salt and pepper shakers. It hadn't changed either. One of the triplets appeared, a pot of regular in one hand, decaf in the other. I turned over the white mug on the table and asked for regular.

"What'll you have?" a triplet asked when she returned, coffeeless, ticket book at the ready.

"Two eggs over easy, bacon, hash browns and cinnamon raisin toast. And more coffee, please." I'd already drained the cup. My stomach ached like it was being scraped with a metal rake.

My breakfast had just been dropped onto the table when the door of the diner swung open. A guy in his early thirties, his long, strong body clad in cycling shorts and shirt, a bike helmet tucked under his left arm, strode in. He greeted the triplet wiping down a table near the door.

"Good morning, Ms. Trudy. How are you this fine day?"

"Well, Mr. Philip, I'm overworked and under paid, thank you very much," Trudy replied gruffly then grinned revealing their exchange to be a well-worn routine.

"The usual?" she asked.

"You betcha. Gotta get those neurons firing."

"Coming right up. Hey, Stan," she yelled to the old man in the kitchen who was wiping a greasy hand on his apron, "the usual for Philip."

Oh shit. Just what I needed. Philip Cox. I shrank down in the booth, hoping he hadn't seen me. The clack that the clips of his bike shoes made on the floor grew louder and then he was there, leaning over the back of the booth, wearing an easy smile.

"There are only three reasons why anyone is in this place at six on a Saturday morning. You're seeking hangover relief after a hard night of partying, you're a trucker just getting into the city after driving the whole night, or you're down on your luck, like the gentlemen at the counter," Philip said. And not waiting for an invitation, he sat down, continuing, "You're obviously not two or three so that leaves number one, but the partiers usually aren't alone."

"I could be a trucker leaving on a long haul."

"No rig outside."

"What about you? You didn't mention a category for annoyingly perky cyclists," I said, taking a bite of egg and hoping I didn't dribble yolk down my chin.

"I live around the corner. Come here after my morning rides."

"You've already been on a ride. It's not even light."

"And it's not too hot, either."

"So wait, you're into fitness and you're a computer nerd. I thought the two were mutually exclusive."

He shook his head in mock dismay, "Guys in the computer industry are as maligned as you blondes. I'll have you know

Steve Jobs was a competitive swimmer and Larry Ellison mountain bikes and sails."

"Larry who?"

Trudy delivered Philip a bowl of granola, a small bowl of plain yogurt, a side of fresh fruit, wheat toast and a glass of orange juice. "I forgot the extra banana. I'll be right back."

I looked at the mess of yolk, potato, and bacon crumbles on my plate and felt guilty about my dietary choices.

"Danka showny macaroni," Philip called out as Trudy shuffled off.

Danka what-y? He sounded like a preschool teacher.

"Something my dad used to say to me."

"What, when you were like five?"

Philip shrugged, "The ladies here think it's funny." He dumped the fruit and yogurt onto the granola.

When Trudy returned with the sliced banana, which Philip added to the mix, he told her to add the beautiful woman's food to his bill. I raised a hand to object, but he cheerfully waved it aside, "I insist."

"And here I wanted to believe all men are shits," I sighed.

"Aha, love troubles. Reason number four, forgot that one. Care to talk about it? I've been told I'm a great listener."

I feared talking about Michael would expose our relationship as a joke, that it would be obvious to Philip that Michael wasn't really into me and I wanted to hold on a little longer to the possibility that Michael left me because he was falling in love.

"Not really. I think I'd better go home, I'm exhausted. Thanks for breakfast."

By the time I stood up I'd forgotten about Philip and was wondering what Michael was doing. Was he sleeping or had his night been as disturbed as mine?

"My pleasure. See you Tuesday."

"Huh? Oh yeah, see you Tuesday," I muttered and drifted out the door.

Thank God it was Saturday and I didn't have to work. At home, now alive with morning light, I took a bath, lying with my head half submerged, hearing only a rushing in my ears, till the water turned cold. Putting on the black sweat pants and a baggy tee shirt, I settled into the den couch and spent the weekend gorging on old movies and pints of ice cream.

II

Something about Natalya Haven brought to mind an odalisque in a Turkish harem. She had thick chestnut hair woven into a loose braid falling to the middle of her back, almond eyes accentuated by black liner, and delicate features. Thin wrists emerging from the sleeves of an Indian cotton print shirt jangled with silver bracelets. Around her neck was a coral and turquoise necklace of Nepali design. She stood only an inch above five feet and couldn't have weighed more than a hundred pounds. She also had a deer-in-the-headlights vulnerability that confirmed my suspicion that Janine was a sadist. Natalya had come into the bookstore on Saturday, was interviewed, hired and on the floor in less than an hour. I put her chances of survival at no more than a couple of weeks.

"You don't sound like you're from the Midwest," I commented to Natalya, who spoke with no accent to give away where she was raised.

"No, I just moved here couple of weeks ago."

"From where?"

"Nowhere you've ever heard of," Natalya responded, struggling to lift a book-filled box before acknowledging defeat, "I guess I'll have to make two trips."

But why Milwaukee. She couldn't have moved here for a job at bookstore. I had difficult time accepting that anyone would move to the city voluntarily.

"Bad relationship. Needed to put some distance between us," she said as she emptied half the box into another, "And I have a really good feeling about this city. I think my life's going to be a whole lot better here. It'll be just like *Happy Days*. I loved that show when I was a kid."

"Hunter, have you finished that Random House shipment? I want those books on the floor today. And Natalya, where're those books for biography," Janine called out from the top of the stairs.

Natalya rolled her eyes, "That woman really does have the ears of a bat."

❧

"Hey, wanna get some dinner after work, then go for a drink maybe?" Natalya asked me two days later. "Derek's having the guys over, poker night, and I so do not want to be there."

Natalya had gone home with Derek the night she arrived in Milwaukee and had never left. "He's so into me he's driving me nuts. If I was home tonight, he'd want me to sit on his lap while he plays cards. How crazy is that?" she asked just before taking an enormous bite of Veneta's spaghetti, sucking up a dangling noodle and giggling when it slapped her on the nose before disappearing into her mouth.

Leaving the restaurant, Natalya spied a trio of young, kinda cute guys walking south on Brady. "Come on, let's follow them. The one in the middle is totally fuckable. Oh,

I'm not going to fuck him, but it's fun to look" she added, reading disapproval of her in my frown when there wasn't any. I just didn't think the guy was anything to get excited about.

The trio led us to Wimpy's Hunt Club, Milwaukee's nod to Seattle, the hipster homeland. Lots of plaid shirts and Doc Martens. Nirvana on the stereo. Natalya grinned like a cat in a bird shop. "God, a girl could go crazy in this place. So many hotties to choose from. Wanna play a game? It's super fun." The Fucking Game (TFG) was rating guys we saw as TF (totally fuckable), FDR (fuckable in a dark room), or UF (completely unfuckable no matter what). Most guys were fuckable to Natalya. Did it mean she won because she had twenty TFs to my eight? When I got home, heading whirring from one too many beers, I realized I hadn't thought about Michael once.

❧

Natalya was really fun. She made herself instantly popular with the staff by coming up with an idea to keep Janine honest without her knowledge. Instead of shelving the Not for Sale review copies, she suggested, why not stash them somewhere for the employees to take home. It got a smile out of Stephanie who wished she'd thought of it.

She and I quickly became inseparable. We took lunch breaks together, salads from Salvador Deli eaten under the cool canopy of an ash tree in a nearby park. I'd tell the horror stories I'd heard about the Bat and Natalya'd describe the panoply of customers who streamed through the shop. Like Walter, a customer who was in every week buying a new book on health and fitness and was now ogling Natalya. His style of flirting was to lecture Natalya on her diet and how she should train with him at the gym around the corner, though he evidenced not a single bulging muscle. Natalya joked that he was more Chip 'n' Dale than Chippendale.

Because Derek didn't get home until after seven and Natalya didn't like being in the apartment alone—there were some real weirdos in the building she said—she and I'd go out for beers after work. She had fresh ears to hear about my parents. I had her undivided attention and a comforting arm around my shoulder. No interruptions from crying toddlers like Leslie, no mention of the dreaded therapist like Andy. And Saturday, after she finished her lunch shift at some restaurant she worked at she got me to take her to the zoo. She'd never been to one before.

"Hey, it's me. We're going to 'Disco Night' at The Factory tomorrow. You wanna come with? No better way to get over some asshole than immersing yourself in a sea of sweaty, gyrating gay men," Andy had said when he called.

"Can I bring a friend along, if she's free?"

"Ooh, I'm in love. I'm in love. I'm in love, I'm in love. I'm in love..." Lights whirled overhead in time to the synthesized beat bathing the dance floor in green, red, blue and white. Dancers, vintage nylon shirts open to their abdomens, gold medallions nestled in chest hair or laying flat against waxed skin, trousers hugging their asses, sequined dresses sparkling, spandex stretching, arms in the air, bodies swaying, spinning. The chemical odor of poppers spiked the air. Behind the polished aluminum bar, bartenders, both male and female, in tight purple satin mechanic's

jumpsuits worked swiftly and intently, like medics in a surgical unit, to get drinks out to the crush of thirsty patrons.

Men greeted Danny with effusive hugs. He seemed to know everyone there. We'd already breezed to the front of the line and the bouncers, both Danny's clients, waved us in.

"We're not here merely to have fun," Andy informed us, "This is work. Danny hands out a few business cards for the gym then writes off all the drinks."

A curvaceous, dark-skinned, big-haired redhead in a leopard print dress planted a kiss on Danny's cheek then Andy's, leaving fiery red smears.

"No way!" Natalya shrieked when Danny told her the woman was Steve, his hairdresser.

"The hands. Check out the hands," Andy said, "They're a dead giveaway."

"Oh my God! He's gorgeous, and you're a cutie pie," Natalya shrieked again, and grabbing Andy pulled him onto the dance floor. From the sidelines, Danny and I watched Natalya throw her arms around Andy's neck, grind into him with her hips then shimmy away, bending forward slightly so that the neck of her blouse gaped open giving Andy a clear view of her small bare breasts. Danny laughed at Andy, who didn't know what was happening or where to look. Minutes later, the tables were turned and it was Andy's turn to laugh at Danny's dancing discomfort.

Sipping vodka gimlets at one of the tall-top tables placed throughout the club—not even Danny's minor-celebrity status could snag us a red velvet couch in the ultra-popular lounge overlooking the dance floor—Andy amused us with the story of a man who wanted to sue the city because his wife refused to have sex with him after she fell on an icy sidewalk.

"He was short and fat, with a comb over. She probably thanked God she didn't have to get naked with him anymore."

Natalya, opening her mouth wide, let out a short, sharp volley of laughter, more than the story deserved, and gave him a big hug. "Oh, you are so adorable!"

Andy, encouraged by Natalya, regaled her with further tales of frivolous lawsuits he'd heard about until her face was wet with tears of laughter. During the telling, Natalya occasionally squeezed Andy's forearm, and when she tossed her head back it would come to rest on Danny's shoulder. "If you two weren't gay, I don't know which one of you I'd go home with," she declared as coy as Scarlett O'Hara.

Recognizing the opening beats of 'More Than a Woman,' Danny took Andy's hand, "C'mon baby, they're playing our song," and led him onto the floor.

"Look at me, I'm hitting on gay men. I gotta break up with Derek," Natalya said, "but I don't know where to go. I haven't got enough money to get my own place."

"You can move in with me." The words slipped out before I knew what I was saying.

"Are you serious? Oh my god, that would be so awesome." Her voice bubbled with barely contained excitement.

With Michael out of the picture the house was feeling big and empty again and I couldn't bear the thought of that.

And Natalya was a person in need. Letting her move in was another way I could help out others with my inheritance. It was a noble act. And maybe Natalya was what was missing in my life: a really great girl friend. Someone I liked all the time, someone fun and free (*Leslie was an amazing friend, but she was rarely free*) I could just hang out with, talk to about anything without worrying that I was acting too clingy, or that she was going to dump me. And of course there'd be no sex to really fuck everything up.

"Yeah, I'm sure."

"What about rent? I don't have a lot of money."

"Don't worry about it. Just put in some money for the utilities."

Was it far from downtown or the bookshop? Natalya relied on her bike and buses to get around so she didn't want to be too far. My assurances that there was a downtown bus stop five minutes from my house and that riding a bike could often get you to The Printed Page faster than driving sealed the deal.

"It'll be sooo much fun. We'll be just like Laverne and Shirley."

12

It didn't take Natalya long to move in. All she had were a suitcase and a shoebox. I marveled at the compactness of her life. Regardless of my vagabond lifestyle, I accumulated possessions requiring the purchase of another suitcase with every move.

I put Natalya in my old room and I moved completely into my parents.' I'd been sleeping there since Michael left so it made sense.

"Let's go to Doc Holliday's," Natalya suggested to celebrate our new roomie status, "Do you know it? It's this really awesome restaurant. I've just got a couple of lunch shifts there right now, but I'll get dinner ones soon. My boss loves me. And Trey's working tonight and he's totally into me. I wanna tell him I've moved out of Derek's."

Doc Holliday's ads claimed it had the best burgers in Milwaukee and people must have believed them because the place was packed. Its location near downtown made its bar, done up like a western saloon, a popular stop for an after-work drink. Women in suits, men in suits, women who came looking for men in suits. There were also plenty of sales assistants from area shops and university students. The staff were young and generically pretty in their jeans, white western shirts and bolo ties. The wait for a table was already twenty minutes, but we waited even longer so we could sit in Trey's section.

"I broke up with Derek," Natalya informed Trey as he was handing us our menus. "Living at Hunter's now. We're here to celebrate."

Trey wasn't at all the type of guy I thought Natalya would be into. I pictured her going for an older, more hippy, Eastern philosophy kind of guy. Trey was cute, but he was young and conservative, his hair neatly clipped around his ears. Who knew, maybe he was a wild man. And he was obviously besotted with Natalya so maybe that was the main attraction. He directed everything he said to her. I didn't exist. And Natalya played it up, calling him over to the table asking for more ketchup, some mayo, another beer, touching him often.

"We're going to keep the party going, aren't we, Hunter?" Natalya said when Trey delivered our bill. "You should meet us when you get off. We're going to Wimpy's. Do you know it. It's super cool."

Going out was news to me. I'd been planning on an early night. I relented when I saw the eagerness in Natalya's eyes. Being flexible and open was going to be part of the new me, good friend Hunter.

"I get off at nine, only an hour from now. Why don't you wait for me in the bar," Trey said.

The bar had quieted down. Most of the patrons had gone home to their wives or husbands. The remainder were putting the moves on their targeted prey or settling in for a long night of drinking.

"See what I mean. Isn't this like the most awesome place ever? I wish my mom could see it. She'd love it. She's really cool like that. Really fun. More like my best friend than my mom. Oh fuck, I'm such a bitch going about her like that when yours is... I'm sorry Hunter."

What was I going to do? Go through life refusing to let people talk about their parents. It was great that Natalya and her mother were so close. I knew darts of regret and envy were always going to prick when people talked about their parents, but maybe I could serve as a kind of advocate, telling people to cherish their parents while they were still around. I tried it out on Natalya, "Keep it that way cause you never know what's going to happen."

There was a flicker in Natalya's eyes, maybe sympathy for my loss, and then she was back to Trey. How hot he was. How into her he was. How glad she was to be out of Derek's place. "Derek's cute and all and the sex was pretty hot, but he was getting so clingy. Lesson learned, don't move in with a guy after fucking him just one time."

A few minutes after nine Trey, out of his uniform and in a Pearl Jam tee shirt and khakis joined us. He looked much cuter in his own clothes. He and Natalya talked and flirted, the space between them getting smaller and smaller and the world around them, including me, fading into nothingness. Neither one put up any resistance when I announced my intention of going home. I wasn't even sure they heard me.

❧

It was all Trey's fault that I didn't see Natalya again for two days. "He's a very bad boy. He won't let me leave," she said when she called, "Ow." Laughter. "I gotta go, he's biting my toes. I'll be home tomorrow, promise." More laughter. The line went dead.

A pang of jealousy. She was living in my house. Our friendship was just beginning. I wanted to hang out with her. I should be her priority. I wasn't ready to share her.

Good as her word, Natalya was back the following day with a stack of videos and bags of groceries intent on cooking me a great dinner as a way of apologizing. And she wasn't sure Trey was the right guy for her. He was cute and all, and totally into her, she said, but "He smells like sweaty gym clothes. How could I not have noticed that before?"

She made green chile stew, taking care to make it mild because not everyone could handle the gut-burner version she and her mom loved. On Sunday nights, she and her mom always made a huge pot and watched a black and white movie usually starring one of the Hepburns, Audrey or Katherine. Taking our steaming bowls into the den, we plopped down for a marathon of Audrey Hepburn movies that kept us up laughing and talking till one. It was more fun than I'd ever had with Michael.

The following night we were back at Wimpy's. Another round of TFG. Natalya found one guy so TF that she didn't come home for another two nights. Another pang of jealousy. I didn't want to be a supporting player in Natalya's life, a second banana who only had a couple of scenes. "You depend too much on one friend." "Get your own life," advised the voices—mainly my parents' and Andy's—in my head. But it was really hard to get my own life when everyone else was always busy. Who was I supposed to hang out with? I told Natalya she didn't have to always go to the guy's place. She could bring him here. I was cool with that. So Sam spent the night, and I watched them cuddle and coo on the couch, feeling more alone than if they weren't there.

Michael. I missed Michael. He was gorgeous. The sex had been amazing. He was an artist and that was so cool. Thinking a girl friend could replace him was crazy. A girl friend wasn't going to fulfill me both emotionally and physically. A girl friend wasn't going to make me forget Michael. There'd been no phone call, no change of heart, no pleading to take him back. No nothing. Maybe Michael needed to see me, be reminded of what he was missing, and then I'd make him work his ass off to win me back.

"Natalya, have you and Sam ever been to Hanrahan's?" I asked the next day at work.

"Oh, I ended it with Sam, but I'd love to go somewhere new."

"Wait, when did you do that? You were so lovey-dovey this morning."

"Just before he left, when you were in the shower. I pretty much knew last night I wasn't feeling it, but he'd brought me those roses and he was so into me that I had to let him down easy."

The bar was full for a Tuesday night. The Freeloaders were just taking the tiny stage. I couldn't have chosen a better night. Michael designed their posters, the lead singer was the bartender and poster girl. He was sure to be here.

I was already jealous and wary of her because I was pretty sure she'd slept with Michael. Then she started to sing and I hated her. She had a voice like Janis Joplin, every bit as intense but minus the hard liquor roughness. The men in the crowd whooped and called out to her. Natalya sized her up and said, "I don't see what the big deal is. Look at her thighs. She's got saddlebags."

Waiting for our whiskeys, Natalya's head was practically doing three-sixties. "There're some really cute guys here. I'm going to check the place out," she announced loudly and vanished into the smoky haze.

My eyes were trained on the door expecting Michael to walk in any minute. My stomach flipped every time it opened and I was both disappointed and a little relieved every time it wasn't him. If he did come and tried to talk to me, I'd respond with feigned nonchalance I decided. And if he ignored me, I'd ignore him too.

The bartender had just delivered a second whiskey when the door opened again and a pretty, petite redhead came in, pausing to smooth down her miniskirt. Following closely behind her was Michael. He slapped the redhead's ass and she scooted across the floor laughing. She turned around and playfully slapped his face. He grasped her hand and led her to the bar. It was worse than I imagined. I had to get out of there. I couldn't watch him with another woman. It wasn't that he hadn't wanted a relationship, he just didn't want to have one with me. Like a total masochist, I had to look back just once. Maybe I'd be rewarded with a whip smack to the face and he'd be kissing the redhead. He was looking right at me, with a sheepish smile and a pathetic wave. I kept on going out of the room.

Natalya was in the middle of a game of pool against a pair of burly guys with heavy mustaches and a biker club insignia tattooed on their upper arms. Her partner was a baby-faced blond in an oxford cloth shirt and plaid shorts. He wasn't much to look at, but Natalya was definitely interested. I watched them play the game: the way Natalya high-fived him when either one sunk a shot, her shirt rising to expose her flat stomach. The way she flipped her hair out of the way as she aimed at the cue ball. The way she laughed when she missed an easy shot. The way she hugged him, pressing her hips against him when he sank a particularly difficult one.

"Don't you say hello anymore?" Michael had stolen up behind me.

"You looked busy," I replied, my body stiffening. "Who is she, by the way?"

Michael laughed, "You mean Wendy. She's an old friend. She's not an ex or even a maybe." He breathed in my ear, "I've missed you."

His nearness was unsettling and I stepped away, my eyes still on the pool game. The bigger, burlier biker dropped the eight ball in a corner pocket. Game over. Natalya pouted then hurled herself at the biker, planting a kiss on his cheek. "Maybe we can be partners one night," I heard her say, and caught the glint of a gold tooth in the biker's smile. Her partner, put off by Natalya's defection, walked away. Natalya caught him and putting her hand on his crotch whispered in his ear. He smiled and led her to the bar.

Letting a bit of anger slither out, I said to Michael, "Is that so. You could have called me."

"I thought about it, but I wasn't sure you'd want to talk to me."

I finally turned to face him and God did he look good. "Not really," I lied.

"I've come here a bunch of times hoping you'd show up," he said taking a step toward me, trying to close the physical and emotional distance between us. I countered with a step back.

"C'mon, let's go back to your place and I'll show you how much I missed you." He again moved closer.

Do not give in. Do not give in. Not tonight. Do not be too damn easy. But another look into his sad puppy eyes and my resolve was in a puddle on the floor. I closed my eyes to think. Maybe he'd decided a relationship wasn't a trap waiting to ensnare him. Or maybe his feelings for me were so deep he no longer cared he'd been caught. Arms thrown around my neck. He was now so close I felt his breath on my cheeks, which burned in anticipation of his kiss. But instead of a kiss I heard Natalya's voice in my ear, "Marcus is going to spend the night at our place, okay?" I opened my eyes to find Natalya's face inches from my own and her arms about me, not Michael's. He, startled by the intrusion, had taken a few steps back, his head cast toward the floor, hands in the back pockets of his jeans.

"His ride ditched him, and he really wants me. And I grabbed him, you know, down there and he's huge," Natalya was so infatuated with Milwaukee's answer to John Holmes that she failed to notice she was interrupting

116

something. And then, as if a switch flipped, she saw my flushed cheeks and noticed Michael for the first time. Thinking she was both helping her cause and mine, Natalya turned to Michael, "Why don't you come, too. Keep Hunter company."

"That'd be cool, if it's all right with Hunter," Michael replied so hopeful that I let go of any lingering doubt.

Two hours later in my bedroom, exhausted from love-making, we were on the verge of sleep. Michael had kissed me so ardently that my lips ached and with each thrust he'd touched something deep inside me. I could never tell anyone because it was so corny, but I felt he'd been touching my soul. Suddenly, a female howl of rapture ripped through the silence. Maybe having Natalya bring guys home wasn't such a great idea after all.

13

Legs curled under me on the den couch, beer in hand, a stack of albums chronicling the lives of my family in front of me. Five months ago I couldn't touch them. In the past month, I'd flipped through them hundreds of times. There were three photos that consistently captivated me.

The first: my parents on the steps of the Hotel de Ville in Paris the day of their marriage, taken by a passing stranger waylaid for that purpose. Dad in a camel hair Chesterfield, mom in a plaid knee-length coat and black pill box hat, her left hand indiscreetly showing off a thin white gold band on the all-important finger. Their eyes locked on each other, smiles as big as the sky.

They'd met three months earlier, in September, only a few weeks after my mother arrived in Paris to study French. Dad had left for the continent immediately after graduation to make the Grand Tour before joining his father's investment company and was only supposed to be in Paris for a few days. At the Louvre, seeing my mother standing before the Venus de Milo, he was jolted by the electric shock of "she's the one" and knew instantly he was going to marry her.

For the next thirty-one years they had as close to a perfect marriage as a couple could have. They'd had their fights, certainly, but while they'd witnessed many of their friends' marriages implode, theirs seemed to become more in tune.

Which is why I loved the second photo: fifteen years later, Dad in a tuxedo, Mom movie star glamorous in a green silk evening gown, mink coat draped elegantly over her shoulders. The same love-filled looks. Theirs was a love that existed more in the imagination of writers and teenage girls than in reality, and my dreams of experiencing a love like that were swirling down the toilet. At thirty, eight years older than my parents when they'd met, I was attaching myself like a limpet to a guy who'd voted for Reagan and Bush. If I'd known that from day one I would never have gone home with him. Never assume all artists are liberals.

The third: a photo of me, age eleven, and Nana, my mother's mother. We were standing by the pool at her and Bopa's house in Florida. I was in slightly blurred mid-leap, lopsided grin, hair in lopsided pigtails, the crotch of my one-piece bathing suit, red with white stars, hanging almost to my knees. I'd made Nana buy it for me even though it was way too big because it was the only one left and I claimed I'd die if I didn't have it. Nana, as cool as the voile blouse and Bermuda shorts she wore, was holding my hand as if trying to keep me from floating away. I loved the photo because it was one of the few of me looking goofy, free and happy.

The unconfined joy with Nana summed up our relationship. I'd always felt closest to my true self with her. With everyone else, even my parents, I felt I was acting a part. And with me, Nana let loose her inner girl, playing dolls and Candyland, letting me make a chocolate-chip-cookie mess of her gleaming kitchen. It was relationship she'd never had with her own daughter.

If it hadn't been expected of Nana, I doubt she would have had any children. She wasn't cruel to my mom, or ignored her or anything like that. It was just that she wasn't really interested in raising a child. She was not a born nurturer. Cooking meals every day, helping with homework, listening to teenage girl problems bored her. She'd wanted more. She could have been an executive had her parents raised her to believe that was a possibility. Rushing to meetings in Manhattan in immaculate designer suits, smoke from the omnipresent Winston held in a gloved hand mingling with the scent of Shalimar around her stylish curls. Being a product of her generation, she settled for being secretary to Bopa who owned several hardware stores in Michigan. Frustrated ambition made Nana particularly hard on my mom. All those years showing her daughter that a life outside the confines of the home was possible—with a nanny and a cleaning woman, of course—only to have her daughter say no thanks. Married and a mother by twenty-three.

The back door opened and slammed shut. The refrigerator door opened and slammed shut. A beer bottle cap popped. Natalya dropped onto the couch next to me. She grabbed an album and absently opened it to the center pages. She let out a fusillade of laughter that was like fingernails on a chalkboard to my ears over a photo of me in college.

No school in the States had been far enough away from Milwaukee for me. I'd had to cross an ocean. At St. Alban's College in London I peeled off the last of the nice-girl skin I'd been wearing and slipped into a darker, badder one. I didn't feel or behave like a good girl so I shouldn't look like one either. In the photo, my hair was pink and spiked straight up with lots of teasing and copious applications of hair spray. Thick black lines drawn under my eyes extended out toward my temples. I wore a black shirt and a white gauze skirt with a prayer and cross stenciled on it. Around my neck were various silver chains and crucifixes. Nine earrings dangled from my left ear. My black lips were drawn into what was meant to be a threatening sneer but fell a bit short. More like I had menstrual cramps.

"You look ridiculous. What were you thinking?" Natalya demanded to know through her laughter.

I sat up straighter. I could laugh about my punk days with Andy and Leslie, but it bugged me that she was treating my rebellion as a joke.

"I bet your parents were horrified."

"Not really. They always encouraged me to express myself (*Actually, my mother cried when I came home for the summer. I think it was the only time she was ever glad I was only home for a few weeks.*) If they'd hated the look, why would they keep the photo?"

"Probably to embarrass you in front of your children."

"And your parents have no pictures of you that you'd like to tear up."

Natalya threw her head back with the feigned irritation girls use when something secretly pleases them. "My mom's always taking pictures of me and that gets kinda annoying, but it's 'cause she loves me so much. One whole shelf in her house is lined with photo albums. Thank god I'm photogenic."

Natalya was always telling me how much her mother loved her. I couldn't tell if it was part of her habitual gushing or she if she was intentionally poking my open wound. I'd heard countless times that they wore each other's clothes. That they told each other everything, there were no secrets between them. That they loved the music of Tom Waits and the novels of Jack Kerouac and Herman Hesse, the poems of Sylvia Plath and Anne Sexton. That her mother could have been a model she was so beautiful, but, alas, she was only five-two. That she was so kind and generous heavenly light shown out of her ass. Those weren't the exact words Natalya used, but when she'd follow up lines like that by telling me that she and her mother looked so much alike people mistook them for twins, what else was she doing but bragging about what a fabulous specimen of womanhood she herself was. Nauseating.

Don't ask some chick you've just met to be your roommate was one of life's lessons, along with don't fuck a guy on the first date, and pay off your credit card every month, that I was having trouble learning.

An examination of my friendship histories and the rare experiences of co-habitation would have demonstrated that the house-sharing offer I'd made to Natalya had been pretty idiotic. Most of them had been like relations between England and France: convenient, competitive, jealous, at times openly hostile and only occasionally harmonious. Leslie and Andy were anomalies of amicability and continuity. That I'd never lived with either of them might have had something to do with it.

In high school Hannah Nicholson, not Leslie, had been my best friend. We'd been joined like a wishbone with unseen hands tugging us apart. Our friendship had demanded constant vigilance. Most nights, especially Sunday nights, I'd call Hannah, fake-casual calls about the usual best friend stuff. Did you get the math homework? Did you read Chapter 10 in *The Grapes of Wrath*? Isn't Polly's haircut hideous? But I was really trying to predict her mood, like a meteorologist predicting the weather. Would it be a calm, warm day at school tomorrow or was a sudden cold front moving in. Hannah's moods shifted as fast as clouds blowing across the sky. I could arrive at school to discover that not only she, but none of my other friends would speak to me. I had unknowingly committed some hideous gaffe between the end of the school day and the next morning, like maybe I had looked at her funny or said something that could be taken two ways and she took it the wrong way. Hence the phone calls. But they could be as unreliable as a weather forecast. After several hours in the freezer, Leslie would grab my frostbitten hand and pull me into a girls' bathroom to spill the beans.

Hannah flirted with the boys I liked and claimed in conference afterwards that she was helping me. "I've arranged for us to meet at the game tomorrow night. Then you can talk to him." When she dated Billy Maxwell sophomore year she boasted he'd used me to get to her. Andy transferring to MA meant I had to contend with her jumping into his lap and acting like we were a triad with Andy in the middle.

I wasn't exactly Snow White. I'd parry her flirting with jabs at her vanity, like asking if the small red splotch on her cheek was a zit. Tit for tat. I'd be banished to Siberia for it, but at least then I knew why.

College did nothing to alter the friendship topography. I met Andrea in my Modern Popular Music class. Half her head was shaved, the remaining hair dyed black with red tips. She wore combat boots, a black leather jacket with the anarchy symbol stenciled on the back, a studded collar around her neck. A kindred spirit. She suggested we get a flat together and I jumped at the chance to quit my lonely dorm existence. Cheryl, another friend eager to live independently, joined us. A few months of splintering camaraderie finally perished when the two sat me down and through the hash haze that hung like a curtain in our flat enumerated everything that was wrong with me as a roommate and as a person.

I'd had such high hopes for my friendship with Natalya. I thought it would be different. I wasn't in school anymore. I was older. I'd imagined us as my mom and Gale, only Natalya was much cooler than Gale. Best friends forever. Sisters.

And Natalya was like a sister, the nightmare little sister whose sole purpose in life was to drive her older sister nuts. She was a good housemate. She was neat. She helped out with cooking and shopping. She liked housework. The house hadn't been that clean since I'd moved back in. But she had habits that ran from odd to annoying to kind of creepy.

Odd: She refused to eat grapes. Not because she didn't like them, but because she was afraid of them. Who's afraid of a grape? Also, either all her food had to be mixed together as a stew or none of it could touch. I told her I was going to get her one of those cafeteria plates, the kind that are divided into sections. She didn't think that was funny.

Annoying: the gushing. Everything—dogs, cats, clothes, people, cars, flowers—was cute, really cute, soooo cute. Her favorite topic to gush about was herself. Didn't I just love the new shirt she'd bought. It was so so so cute and looked so good on her. How everybody at the bookshop loved her, even Janine. Jeremy wanted to open her chakras. How Mr. Busalacchi, who owned a small grocery a few blocks away, gave her a piece of fruit every time she went there. He was sooooo adorable. The need to feel loved was extremely important to Natalya, followed closely by the need to share how much she was loved with anyone who would listen.

Creepy: I was losing track of the men she'd slept with. There'd been Trey, then Sam, then Marcus, then Gary, then Charles. Or was it Charles, then Gary? And was his name Gary or Jerry? It didn't matter as he, like the others, was out of the picture fast.

Natalya met them at Wimpy's or Hanrahan's She gushed about each one: how cute he was, how badly he wanted her, how maybe he was The One. By the third or fourth night he was all wrong and Natalya was onto her next conquest.

Who was I to judge, but I did any way. Natalya had slept with more men in the past month than I had in a whole year. Of course, I hoped that any guy I went home with would turn out to be my soul mate, but she was so desperate. She'd have sex anyone who came onto her.

It had gotten to the point that almost everything she did bugged me.

Her latest thing was making a big show over this homeless guy who hung out near work. "Today, she came back from lunch and told us how she took him to the deli for lunch. 'I wanted to teach all those snooty rich bitches a lesson.' Bullshit, she just wanted everyone to know how open-minded and generous she was," I'd griped to Andy, one of many gripes about Natalya he'd heard.

"Jesus, Hunter, stop bitching and tell her to move out. It's your house," he'd told me, like doing it was as easy as ordering a pizza.

But it was complicated. There still were times when I really loved hanging out with Natalya. Like the day when we went thrift store shopping and at each shop we took polaroids of each other modeling the most hideous outfits we could come up with. Then over beers at Wimpy's we asked the bartenders to choose the winner. Robby and Alan said it was a close call but my oil-well-themed polyester shirt and mustard yellow suit with brown stitching won. It was so ugly Robby said, it was almost cool.

And if I asked her to move out she might hate me.

Natalya continued absently paging through the album, until one photo startled her. I saw nothing special about the image of me and my parents in front of a snow-covered abode wall, mountains behind us, a cerulean blue sky over our heads. Mom and Dad smiling, I almost grimacing. "That's Chamisa, New Mexico. We went there for Christ-mases and summers for years. Look at my face. Shows how much I enjoyed those trips. But I didn't like anything much back then. My parents were going to retire there."

"Really, I—" Natalya began then abruptly stood up, "I'm gonna get another beer. You want one?"

She left the room without waiting for an answer and when she finally reappeared she'd changed into an Indian silk skirt and a halter top. Silver bracelets were stacked on her wrists and a heavy silver ring adorned the middle finger of her left hand. She'd applied both eyeshadow and blush, more makeup than was usual for her. She looked like she'd just escaped from a seraglio. I half expected her to begin belly dancing.

"Going out?" I asked.

"Yeah, I'm antsy. I need," Natalya shook her body, "something."

I was pretty sure what that something was.

There'd been a mini dry spell since she'd dumped Brian—the most recent guy du jour—because he stayed home to study for the GMATs rather than go out with her. I'd told her that seemed like a legitimate reason. "It was just a practice test," she'd replied. "He could've met me if he really wanted."

Natalya snatched her purse off the floor. Michael was on the steps when she opened the door.

"Wow! You look hot. Where are you off to?" he asked, "I just got here."

"Hanrahan's. Hunter doesn't want to share, so I have to find my own fun," she replied pinching his cheek.

"Oh shit! The Airmaster Blues Band is playing tonight," Michael said. "They're fucking great."

"I love the Blues," cooed Natalya.

"Hey Hunter, you wanna go?"

Not really, but I could see Michael was keen and I didn't want him going out alone with Natalya when she was on the prowl.

That was another thing about Natalya. She and Michael together made me nervous. The nights Michael came over he would tell her how hot she looked and playfully tug her braid. And Natalya would hug him, slap his ass, muss his hair. If we were going out and Natalya didn't have plans she'd want to tag along. Michael's unvarying response of "the more the merrier," irritated me. I sometimes wondered if Michael had come back to me because of Natalya. No, I'd remind myself, he came up to me before ever seeing Natalya (*or did he?*). So why did he always want her around.

I wanted to believe they'd never go behind my back and I hated those moments of jealousy, but I didn't completely trust them. In the month since we'd slept together again, Michael and I had never discussed the status of our relationship, whether we were a couple or just hanging out. I'd been trying to keep things light and easy, like he was Teflon and I was a can of Pam.

Natalya was on the tiny dance floor as soon as we arrived. She took one look at the bass player and pushed her way to the front of the stage. At first she ignored him, slowly spinning round, her torso and hips undulating like a ribbon, her arms moving rhythmically in front of her face, eyes closed. She appeared completely lost in the music. The bass player noticed her right away, watching her during the next few songs while she continued to ignore him. The fifth song was raucous and raw and Natalya's dance matched its mood, she ground her hips, tossed her hair and shimmied low. Her desire was so obvious only a blind man would have missed it. When the first set ended, the musician was asking her name and buying her a drink. By the end of the break, they were kissing. Goal achieved. Watching it unfold, I felt like an ornithologist observing the mating dance of an exotic bird. I had to hand it to her, she was good.

14

The stone hall was vast. On its walls hung tapestries of dense, twisting jungle vines and red, vulva-like flowers. A wrought iron chandelier dazzled with the light of dozens of flame-shaped bulbs. Clad only in brightly colored tulle tutus, or completely naked, faces hidden behind animal masks—bears, lions, hawks, pigs—women and men danced to a slow and rhythmic melody that gradually increased in intensity until it had whipped them into a carnal frenzy, kissing, fondling and groping one another. Balloons clung to the ceiling as if seeking refuge from the revelry below. A female body in a pink tutu, glittery daisy pasties on her breasts and a kitten head, flew through the air and landed on all fours at my feet.

"Meow," she said rearing up, both hands raised claw-like. I fell back in alarm.

Ripping off the mask, Natalya laughed, "I got you."

"Thank God it's you," I cried, "I don't know anyone here."

"Come on." She took my hand, "Let's go upstairs."

Like thieves, we stole up the grand, stone staircase as in an English castle. Natalya looking over her shoulder to ensure we weren't followed.

"All the men here want me, but they all have bad breath," she said, sticking out her tongue in disgust.

At the top, long hallways extended to the left and right. Natalya chose the hallway to the left. Doors lined both sides and portraits of my parents and grandparents decorated the pale yellow walls. Was this my house? Natalya tried the first door. It was locked. She tried the door across the hall. Locked. The next door opened. The room was small, taken up almost entirely by an ornate canopy bed. A man and woman were making love in the bed. It was Leslie and Danny.

"Shh," Leslie said, "Don't tell Tom, please. He'll leave me."

Natalya closed the door. "C'mon, let's go."

It wasn't curiosity driving us to try every door. We were desperate to be alone. We tried others. All locked. One door remained. The handle turned and we entered a room lit by candles, a fire blazing in the fireplace, as though we were expected. Ignoring the large bed covered in burgundy velvet, we lay down on a sheepskin rug in front of the fire. We kissed. Natalya rolled on top of me, pinning down my arms with her knees and ripping open my shirt. Her tongue caressed first my right then my left nipple.

"I am going to show you what making love is really about," she said.

I woke up, aroused and ashamed. It wasn't the first sex dream I'd had about a woman. It wasn't the first sex dream I'd had about Natalya. What did the dreams mean? I thought I was pretty clear with my sexuality. I'd never even kissed a woman in real life. Was I in full-blown denial and only in my subconscious did the truth reveal itself? Had I never found true love because I'd trying to find it with a man instead of a woman? But dreaming about a woman who drove me nuts? The thought that I wanted to get it on with Natalya made me sick. If I was lesbian, couldn't I be one with good taste?

❧

Michael, Natalya and the bass player, whose name was Justin, and I were sprawled out in the dimly lit den, too full to speak after gorging on Natalya's green chile stew and numerous bottles of wine.

Michael was on the floor, propped up against the couch, my head in his lap. On the couch, Natalya was wrapped around Justin's long, lean frame, twirling a strand of his hair with her fingers and running the tip of her tongue up and down his neck. Her foot was playing with Michael's ear. I shot Natalya a disapproving look and removed the offending extremity. I reminded Michael that he was with me by nibbling his ear, then kissing my way down his cheek to his mouth.

Natalya broke the silence asking, "Do you guys like porn? I've got a great video we can watch."

Justin and Michael nodded enthusiastically. I tried not to appear shocked and expose myself as a complete innocent. I'd never seen a porn film.

Natalya disentangled herself from Justin and left the room, returning with the tape and a fresh bottle of wine. She popped the tape in the VCR, turned off the light and wrapped her body around Justin's once again.

"I've got like some really choice blow, if you wanna do a few lines," Justin said, reaching into the pocket of his jeans and pulling out a small vial filled with white powder.

❧

My ass and left arm were numb. My head pounded with a wicked Merlot headache. I tasted aspirin when I swallowed. Getting up from the den floor, my foot found a red wine puddle on the carpet. The kitchen clock read nine-twenty-nine. Shit, I was supposed to be at work now. I stumbled upstairs, clutching the bannister. In the bathroom, my search of the medicine cabinet for the ibuprofen sent other vials pinging into the sink. I caught my reflection in the mirror. How had I ended up in Justin's REM tee shirt? My stomach did a barrel roll as I remembered. I tore it off, threw it on the floor and hopped in the shower. As sick as I felt, I was going to work. I couldn't be in the house when the others woke up. The hot water made me weak and I sat down on the tiles wishing I got the forget-everything kind of drunk instead of the remember-enough-to-make-me- squirm kind.

I surveyed the scene back in the den, Michael was passed out on the bedspread from Natalya's room (*When had that come downstairs?*). A fat clump of hair was plastered to his forehead, his mouth open, a thread of drool clinging to the corner. He looked really ugly and I wondered for the hundredth time what I was doing with him.

Natalya lay next to Michael, the afghan from the couch wrapped around her small, naked body. Her arm was draped over a spread-eagle Justin, naked too and snoring. He had the body of a boy, without muscular definition and hairless, except for a tuft of ginger pubic hair. How would I face any of them again? At least Justin would be out of the picture soon enough.

I didn't care if I was crazy leaving those three alone in my house. Natalya was too freaky for me. I wanted to be far away from all of them. If I hit no traffic and sped the whole way I'd be twenty minutes late for work. But I needed coffee. The only way to face the wrath of Janine was with the courage of caffeine. I pulled into a convenience store and bought a large cup of super bad French Roast, and a bag of barbecue potato chips and a large bag of M&Ms. I caught a break, Janine wasn't in yet.

"A breakfast meeting with a distributer," Stephanie informed me, "You look like shit. You better not be contagious. I'm going to Door County this weekend and if I get sick you're a dead woman."

"Only if hangovers are contagious, but, hey, I appreciate the sympathy," I replied and retreated into the cool, quiet basement.

I hoped throwing myself into work, cranking up the music as loud as I dared, would block out the night before, but cringe-inducing snatches kept intruding. Snorting a couple lines of coke. Natalya doing a drunken striptease, tossing her underwear onto Justin's head. Natalya kissing Justin, then Michael, asking them, finger on her lower lip, if she should kiss me. Michael and Justin, their faces hot with lust, egging her on. Natalya kissing me, shoving her tongue deep into my mouth, putting a hand on my breast. Justin telling me to get naked, seconded by Michael. Fearing that if I freaked out I would be left out. Closing my eyes and pulling off my shirt. Natalya tearing off my jeans and

135

pushing me onto my back. My dream was coming alarmingly to life. Thinking I had conjured it. Natalya's tongue on my breasts, then teasing my clit. My body responding but my mind telling me it felt all wrong. Relief that I wasn't secretly in love with Natalya. Thank God, I knew who I was, at least sexually. Then fear that because I kissed Natalya, had let her touch me, Michael would dump me saying maybe I'd rather get it on with women. Going crazy and fucking both him and Justin to prove I was into men. Afraid I was going to lose Michael because he couldn't handle my wanton sexuality. It didn't matter that he'd been totally into it, that he had fucked me, and Natalya and messed around with Justin. That wouldn't stop a man from playing the old double standard card. And just what game was Natalya playing? Maybe the whole night had been an elaborate set-up to seduce me.

Cocaine? Cocaine?! What the hell was I thinking? I'd only done it a few times and it had never ended well. In college, doing a few lines and writing the night before it was due the most brilliant essay ever. It was total crap. My Poli Sci professor gave it a C minus saying it lacked coherence. Saucer-eyed, hunched in a corner expecting the cops to raid the place any second. I pounded my head at my stupidity making it throb harder.

"I heard you weren't feeling well so I brought you some chicken noodle soup from the deli." It was Philip, at the bottom of the stairs.

Couldn't I just be nice and say thanks instead of sounding like he was nuts for offering me soup on a day when it was nearly ninety degrees.

"Doesn't matter, chicken soup settles the stomach and hot food will actually help cool you down on a hot day, ask anyone from India." He placed the cup on the table, "It's here if you feel up to eating it."

Pink linen shirt, mothering tendencies. Gay, definitely gay, no matter what Stephanie said.

15

"If Michael doesn't call tonight it's a good thing. An early night, alone, will do me good." I repeated the lines over and over trying to believe them. There were dark circles under my eyes. I was clammy with sweat and mortification. I sure as hell wasn't ready to talk to him about what had happened. I'd probably never be ready for that conversation. But when he didn't he call, my relationship DEFCON rose from yellow to orange.

The following evening he called only to tell me he was tied up, had a painting finish, laundry to do.

"I thought your roommate did your laundry," I joked uneasily.

"Roommate's night off," he said. "Maybe tomorrow."

DEFCON RED.

I'd joined in the foursome, not anything I ever thought I'd do, because I was drunk and Michael seemed into it and I wanted to show him I wasn't a prude, and that I wasn't possessive. He could get it on with another woman, even a guy. I didn't care. Now did he think I was some sex-crazed wild child? Or was he freaking out because I'd seen him kiss a guy?

On the third night, however, he suggested we meet at Veneta's. The place was quiet and Michael, usually talkative, hardly said a word as we ate a large pepperoni and onion pizza. No mention was made of the activities of three nights ago and I was hoping we'd pretend it never happened. As hard as I was trying to forget, every once in a while an image of Natalya kissing me popped into my head and I shivered with embarrassment.

"Wanna go bowling?" Michael asked pushing his plate away. "The Red Carpet Lanes are only a few blocks from here."

The guy at the cash register, snapping a wad of gum, his purple mullet clashing with his red uniform shirt, slapped two pairs of blue and red paneled bowling shoes on the counter telling us that lane 12 would be available in about a half an hour.

We sat down in the alternating red and blue plastic modular seats at 12, changed into our shoes and waited for a family—rare nocturnal humans only able to tolerate artificial light and subsisting on junk food—to finish their last game. The father, mother, a teenage son and daughter were all twenty pounds overweight with almost translucent white skin. The table was littered with the detritus of their meal: empty bags of cheese puffs and potato chips, thirty-six-ounce soft drink cups, a spilled box of Milk Duds and a wet hot dog bun. Not bothering to clean up their mess, they headed home—a house, I was sure, where all the windows were blacked out.

My first ball went straight into the left gutter. My second knocked down one pin. By the seventh frame, I'd scored a meager fifty-four points to Michael's one hundred-eighty.

After releasing a ball that wobbled into the right gutter, I turned in time to catch a grimace on Michael's face.

What did he expect. We North-siders weren't bowlers. We played tennis and golf. Factory workers and mechanics were bowlers, not stock brokers and bankers. On the verge of making a snide remark, I held my tongue and chastised my snobbery. I didn't want to marry a banker, send our kids to MA and play in a ladies tennis group.

"Why are you kicking your left leg out? It's totally messing up your follow through," he asked impatiently. He took his ball off the return and demonstrated the correct way to hold it and how to send it down the center of the alley, rather than having it go way off to the left or right.

Following his tips, my score had increased to one-hundred-twenty by the third game. Michael's irritability persisted, however, and his scores went down with each successive game. Something else was bugging him, but I wasn't going to ask, fearing all he was waiting for was the invitation to tell me that the other night had been too freaky for him and he wanted nothing more to do with me.

Leaving the bowling alley, Michael, looking at his watch, suggested we go out for one last drink. He wasn't eager to get rid of me, so that was a good thing. On the other hand, he wasn't rushing to be get me into bed either.

Floyd's Tap, wedged in between two much larger buildings, was long and narrow with a bar running along one side and tables set up against the other. Men went there, leaving wives at home, to down twenty-five cent beers and argue about sports. Would the Brewers ever get out of the cellar?

141

Who was a better quarterback, John Elway or Joe Montana?

I took a seat at a table while Michael got two PBRs from Floyd himself, seventy-five and still pulling the taps six nights a week. Michael set the beers down and dropped onto a chair. He lit a Marlboro, fixing his eyes on the closer of the two TVs suspended over the bar. The Brewers were playing the A's at Oakland and were down five to zero in the sixth inning. I hated baseball, but I watched the game. I didn't feel like smoking, but I lit one of his cigarettes. I had to do something. Michael's silence was unbearable. The smoke burned my throat on the way to my lungs. I tried again with a shorter drag. Still awful. I stubbed it out.

"Hey, don't waste 'em," Michael said, grabbing the cigarette out of the ashtray. He brushed away the ashes clinging to it, broke off the tip and put it back in the pack. His attention returned to the game.

Draining the last of his beer, Michael consulted his watch again. "Let's go to my place."

It was the last thing I expected him to say. Michael rarely mentioned where he lived, and he'd never invited me there. Had the other night not been the disaster I thought? Maybe the whole girl-on-girl action made me more exciting (*Oh fuck, I hope it didn't mean he'd want me to do it again*) and without coming out and saying it, he was finally acknowledging me as his girlfriend. Letting me into his life in a more intimate way. But he'd been so distant all night. He wasn't acting like a man who was about to take that kind of step. Or maybe he just didn't want to be around Natalya, that he was as wary of her now as I was?

I pulled up behind Michael's Corolla on a treeless block in Cudahy, the south-side neighborhood where he lived. A set of ancient plastic lawn chairs slept on the covered porch of the small two-story red brick house. The front door opened into a quiet living room lit only by a light in the stairway. An oak sofa and matching love seat upholstered in a highly flammable plaid material were arranged in front of an electric fireplace. Above it hung a water color of the lakefront. The latest issue of *Ladies' Home Journal* was on the coffee table. Adorning one wall were a photo of a man in a wide tie and wide-lapelled jacket, hair slicked down; a photo of a teenage Michael and his younger brother, and a crucifix. In the small dining room, the table was covered by an inexpensive lace runner, a plastic flower arrangement in the center. It didn't look like a place where two guys lived.

Upstairs, there was little space to move in Michael's tiny bedroom. Half of the walls were taken up by bookshelves. One held Michael's collection of comic books protected by plastic sleeves, and wrestling trophies. The other was filled with LPs and CDs by musicians that ran the gamut of genres: Muddy Waters, John Lee Hooker, Dusty Springfield, The Rolling Stones, Led Zeppelin, The Grateful Dead, The Cure, Dinah Washington, Sarah Vaughn, Queen, Bauhaus, Nirvana, among hundreds of others, all filed alphabetically, and the records, like the comic books, in plastic sleeves. Sketches, drawings and watercolors were tacked to the wall behind his bed. A half-finished watercolor, also of the lakefront, was on an easel in one corner. The table next to it was a mess of brushes, squeezed tubes of paint, a palette smudged with a rainbow of colors, paint-smeared rags, an ash tray, and an assortment of pencils, pastels and charcoal sticks.

We undressed and got into the bed. The sheets smelled fresh, so maybe he really had washed them. It was strange to be in the small house with his roommate in the next room. I could hear snoring through the thin wall. Michael began to kiss me and fondle my breasts. I froze.

"I don't think I can do this. I mean, your roommate might wake up and hear us."

"After the other night, I can't believe anything would phase you," he scoffed.

There it was. The first mention of that night.

"Well, you'd be wrong. I don't know who that was, but it wasn't me. You seemed pretty relaxed, though," I said, getting him back.

"Fuck, man, I was so drunk, I didn't know what I was doing. That was the first and last time for me. That Natalya is one crazy chick."

"Tell me about it. I'm not sure I can handle living with her."

"Hey, don't worry about the roommate. Deaf as a post," he assured me, sounding amiable rather than derisive.

"Can we put some music on? It might help."

Michael flipped on the bedside lamp and jumped out of bed. He chose a record off the shelf and popped it on the turntable. Nina Simone. He went over to the table and opened the center drawer. When he got back in bed he had a pipe and a bag of weed.

"This should help you relax," he said, tapping some pot into the bowl. He lit the pipe, took a hit and passed it to me. "Be careful, it's pretty strong," he warned.

A couple of hits and I'm high as a kite, a total light-weight. I really thought I was being careful, holding the smoke in my lungs for a few seconds no more, but oh shit, my head started spinning and my limbs turned to rubber. I collapsed on the bed, legs falling open, beckoning Michael to lie down with a lazy wave. His roommate could watch us for all I cared now.

Michael was on top of me in seconds. The noises he made while we were making love reminded me of the grunts of a pig. I giggled. His nose looked more like a penis than ever. I wondered if he was going to fuck me with his penis nose. I couldn't stop laughing.

"Shh!" Michael hissed.

Trying to stop only made me laugh harder.

"Shut up or you'll wake up my mom," Michael said, putting a hand over my mouth.

His roommate was his mother? He lived with his mother?

"God damn it. Would you shut up?" Michael barked.

"I thought you said she was deaf as a post," I replied, sides splitting now.

A door opened in the hallway and a groggy voice called out, "Michael is that you? Are you okay?"

"Everything's fine, Ma. Go back to bed." And to me he chided, "Now look what you've done." He rolled off me and went over to the stereo and put the needle back on its rest. "This was a bad idea."

"Oh Michael, I'm so sorry, really," I said, "I should never smoke pot. The tiniest bit too much turns me into an idiot."

He pulled the pack of cigarettes from his jacket pocket and lit one, pacing back and forth as he smoked.

"Why didn't you tell me you live with your mom?"

"For just this reason, hysterical laughing." He stubbed out the cigarette, lit another and resumed pacing. His nervous energy was infectious and my silly, amusing high took on an agitated edge.

"But you just can't drop a bomb like that on me, especially when I'm stoned, which was your idea, by the way," I said and immediately regretted my tone. The night was spinning out of control and that wasn't the way to get it back. Michael's biting response confirmed it.

"How'd I know you'd cackle like a hyena."

I had to get us back on the right track. I got out of bed and crossed over to him. I removed the cigarette from his mouth, took a drag and crushed it in the ash tray.

"What the hell are you doing?" he asked.

I was going to prove how sorry I was. I pushed him onto the bed, straddled him, and began to gently play with his cock.

"I'm not in the mood. I need to get some sleep," he said in half-hearted protest.

"Are you sure?" I asked, feeling his cock grew hard in my hand. I took him in my mouth.

Michael groaned and said softly, "Keep that up and maybe I'll forgive you."

In the morning, Michael woke me up with a cup of coffee and the news that his mother had left for work. My coffee sat on the floor untouched, getting cold, as we made love. Our relationship was definitely moving to a different level.

16

"His mother? And he never told you? What about when you called him, didn't she ever answer the phone?" Leslie asked when I called excited and confused by the significance of last night.

"He's got his own phone line."

"It seems like a big step," Leslie said.

"I mean, he's never called me his girlfriend, but he's never said I wasn't either."

"Well, if he's never taken you there before and you're spending so much time together, it could mean he's getting serious. Did you meet her?"

"No, but I'm sure she knew I was there. She was in the kitchen when Michael made coffee, and he made two cups."

"But he didn't introduce you." Leslie mulled over the possible meanings. "Hey, who knows, maybe he felt awkward, having shagged you only a few hours earlier. Why don't you come over for dinner tonight, and bring him, if you're not worried we'll embarrass you. Dinner won't be anything fancy, but I'll at least try to have the girls fed before."

I waited a few hours before calling Michael. I rehearsed what I'd say and how I'd say it with the right degree of casualness. I hoped his machine would pick up. It did.

"My friend Leslie, she was at Hanrahan's that first night (*"the night we met" implied too much importance*) invited me for dinner and she wanted to know if you could come too (*saying "invited us to dinner" implied coupledom*). So let me know what you wanna do. I'm probably going anyway (*implying independence*).

He called an hour later, the distant tone of the previous night was back. "I got your message. Actually, I was sitting right next to the phone." He paused. I heard him lighting a cigarette. I could almost smell the fumes through the receiver. "I've been thinking a lot, you know, after what happened the other night and all. And I don't think we're in the same place. We're into different things. And I think, you know, you want more. I told you before I don't wanna get tied down. I think it's better if we, you know, cool it."

How could I have misread the situation so completely? How could my sixth sense have been so off? I couldn't go to Leslie's now and explain that once more I'd been dumped. Screw Natalya for drawing me into her demented sexual web. It was all her fault. And screw Michael for being such a coward. He hadn't been sitting on the sidelines. Now he was blaming me. And screw him for using me. How could he spend all those nights with me and not think he was in a relationship? What an idiot I'd been. Again. And for what? A Republican. I'd call him and tell him he could go to fucking hell. But wait a minute, had Michael actually broken things off? He said, "cool it." He didn't say he didn't want to see me ever again. Maybe it was like the last time. Maybe he just needed time to relax, to miss me a bit. Maybe if I played it cool, didn't scream at him, he'd be back in a few days. Brightened by the idea that Michael was not gone for good, I set out for the Leslie and Tom's.

❧

"Solo tonight? Dinner with toddlers too much for Michael?" Tom asked when he answered the door of the half-Tudor home, his daughter Emily, three and a half, in his arms.

"He might've decided parenthood looks like so much fun he'd start pressuring me to have his baby," I joked, "Couldn't risk it."

"Well, we would have helped you out. Schuyler could have thrown up on him and Emily could have made him play Barbies."

"Who knows, he may love Barbie. Couldn't take that chance. Actually, he promised to help his mother."

"Cute, or so Leslie tells me, and conscientious. Sounds like a good guy," Tom pronounced.

A bit of a shit, really. I don't think I'll take him back after all.

"Les's in the kitchen. I gotta put this one to bed," Tom said tickling Emily's tummy. The little girl squealed with delight until he started up the stairs. Then the wailing began, "Don wanna go bed. Wanna play wit Hunner."

I made my way through the living room strewn with toys, past Tres, the three-legged pound puppy, to the kitchen where I found my friend sitting with Schuyler. The eighteen-month-old's face was smudged with bright orange cheddar cheese and her high chair tray was covered with macaroni, cracker crumbs and applesauce.

"I know I promised you wouldn't have to witness this disgusting display, but Schuyler refused to get in her chair an hour ago," Leslie apologized.

The girl, excited by the arrival of a new face, let out a high-pitched squawk and struck her little fists down on the tray knocking over her bottle of water and sending macaroni flying into the air and onto the floor.

I admired how calm Leslie remained. One toddler, let alone two, would have driven me to a nervous breakdown long ago. But Leslie and I were as temperamentally different as friends could be.

Leslie's world was small and she had no driving ambition to conquer a larger stage. She'd known from a young age what she wanted: marriage, children and a house in the suburbs, and she'd gotten precisely that. She and Tom met in college and they'd married soon after graduation. Tom had a good job selling insurance allowing Leslie to stay at home with the girls, and the pets—in addition to Tres, there were two more dogs who stayed outside, and a deaf cat.

Their home was littered with toys, the upholstery stained from spilled food and drink, the refrigerator and cupboards crammed with juice boxes and sugary cereals, and the laundry room piled high with dirty clothes. It was chaotic and cluttered, but it was also happy and filled with love. It wasn't a life I wanted for myself, but I did want a relationship like Leslie and Tom had, one founded on mutual respect, support and genuine fondness. Like my parents. I enjoyed watching Tom playfully tease Leslie about her questionable culinary skills, which he called "unique," and Leslie rib Tom about his increasing girth despite her bad cooking. They were relaxed and confident with each other, qualities that I rarely, if ever, had had in my relationships.

"So has Michael made last night any clearer?" Leslie asked, picking the pieces of pasta off the floor.

"Not really. And I've been thinking, do I even want to be his girlfriend. I'm not sure I'm really that into him. Thinking of, maybe, ending it."

"If you're not sure, cut him loose. Ho hum is not promising." God bless Leslie for not pointing out the sudden change in my attitude.

"And what about life with the sex maniac?"

I'd told Leslie about Natalya's lovers, but not about the foursome. "I may have to break up with her too. If I was afraid of being lonely, I should've gotten a cat."

A bell chimed in the front hall.

"Ah, that'll be dinner. I ordered Chinese. I know I'm not letting anyone down by not cooking," Leslie said and headed for the front door. "Can you watch Schuyler for a minute. Make sure she doesn't do a face plant into what's left of her dinner."

The orange-smudged face stared at me, sizing me up. I stabbed some macaroni with the Mickey Mouse fork. The child refused to open her mouth. Choo-chooing like a train, I chugged the fork toward her. She pursed her lips more firmly and shook her head defiantly. I felt ridiculous. I stuck my tongue out at her. She giggled. I made the face again. And again, the child laughed. I tried once more to get her to eat. This time Schuyler opened her mouth, took the food and spit it onto the tray, laughing and clapping, immensely proud of herself. I put down the fork in defeat.

"Don't get too frustrated," said Tom, who'd been watching me from the doorway, "She won't let me feed her either. Only Mama, isn't that right, boo boo?"

"Mama, Mama!" Schuyler shouted.

"Here I am," Leslie called out as she returned to the kitchen with two brown bags of food. "Tom, will you get us some plates and put the food into something other than styrofoam. I'll put this one to bed and be back in a minute. I hope."

When dinner was finished, fortune cookies were opened and we each read aloud our fortune. Tom went first, "Flattery will go far tonight." Then looking at his wife, he added, "Honey, that was the best meal you ever made."

"Haha. How appropriate for you, Tom darling," Leslie said, reading hers, "Don't mistake temptation for opportunity."

Now it was my turn. "Get a life.

"It doesn't say that," Leslie scoffed and snatched the slip of paper out of my hand. Her eyebrows rose. "Really! What kind of fortunes are these."

I don't know, it sounded pretty accurate to me.

17

The ivy-covered basement window of The Printed Page let in only thin shafts of daylight and all that was visible were the feet of infrequent passersby in the alley. A stack of books sat ignored on my desk. Natalya had disappeared. When exactly she'd disappeared I wasn't certain. She hadn't come home two nights ago, the night I went to Leslie's. It wasn't unusual and I was happy to be alone. Dreading a confrontation about 'the craziness,' the name I'd given that night in the rare instance I let myself think about it, I'd been avoiding Natalya. If enough time passed I hoped 'the craziness' would be such old news there'd be no reason to talk about it. And it had been easy to avoid her. For the first few days she had shifts at Doc Holliday's and I made sure I was in my bedroom with the door closed when she got home. Holed up, staying quiet, I imagined telling Natalya to move out and Natalya quitting The Printed Page, or getting fired. Then she would be out of my life completely. It was pretty pathetic not having the courage to tell her the housemate thing wasn't working out and she needed to find another place.

When Natalya failed to show up for a shift at The Printed Page I still wasn't worried. No one asked me where she was so I didn't give it much thought, but when she didn't come home that night or to work the following morning, I got anxious. If something had happened to her how would I ever find out. If she wasn't home by tonight, I'd file a missing person's report with the police.

Philip, with his familiar bouncing gait, descended the steps. Roused to attention, I assumed he was there to mess up my day with a new computer function. He rarely ventured down into the bowels of the shop for anything else. I opened my mouth to express my dismay, but he cut me off.

"Save your complaining for another time. Today's only a reboot," Philip said, "Five minutes max."

"I wasn't going to complain," I replied, rising from my stool to give him access to the computer, perturbed he'd so precisely anticipated my thoughts.

"Well, if you were going to ask me out tonight, I'm really sorry, but I have plans," he said with a wink.

"That was definitely not what I was going to say."

His fingers began rapidly tapping on the keyboard. The screen went black, followed by the hum of the computer restarting.

"Done! And it only took four minutes and twenty-three seconds," he announced, pumping a hand in the air like he'd won a bike race.

"Do you think Natalya will be well enough to work tomorrow?" Janine's voice snapped, though she herself was unseen. She often did this, starting her question or complaint or reprimand from the top step, completing it and heading back up before she reached the bottom. Seeing Philip, she came all the way down.

"I didn't know you were down here," she cooed and touched her hair. In a softer voice, she asked me again about Natalya.

She'd called in sick so she was alive. But then where the hell was she and why hadn't she called me? If I wanted to get her fired this was my chance. I could tell Janine the truth, that Natalya wasn't sick and I had no idea where she was. Janine would swear and say the little bitch shouldn't bother coming back. Instead I said, "I don't know, maybe." As much as Natalya annoyed me, I couldn't sacrifice her to the Bat.

"Well, I'll find someone to fill in just in case," Janine said. She remained on the bottom step, as if waiting for Philip.

"Sorry, I can't go out with you tonight. I hope you're not too disappointed," Philip said.

"Excuse me, you're not the only one with plans," I retorted with a smile.

I didn't take him seriously. He flirted with all the girls at the shop. A few wished his teasing meant more, like Janine, who now wore a jealous scowl, "Tell Natalya, she'd better get better soon or there won't be any shifts for her." And in a manner that forbid any response other than compliance, she said to Philip, "Come to my office. I have an idea I want to discuss with you."

Alone once again, I was seized by a terrible thought. What if Natalya was with Michael? That was why she hadn't called. I'd been convinced Michael would be back if I gave him time, but days had passed and I hadn't heard a word. He'd just pretended to think Natalya was crazy so I wouldn't suspect what was really going on. No, that was ridiculous. Natalya was many things, but she wasn't deceitful. Or was I telling myself that because the truth was too painful to contemplate. She wasn't as sweet as she wanted everyone to believe.

The hours ground slowly by and I spent them in distracted agitation, paying little attention to my work and making mistakes I had to go back and correct. At five o'clock I raced home. Natalya's bike was in the garage. She was back.

With my stomach in knots I entered, the coming scene with Natalya playing out in my head like a movie. She'd be waiting for me in the kitchen, smugly triumphant. Yes, she and Michael had been together and it wasn't the first time. Their affair had been going on for weeks and they laughed at what a fool I was, how easily they'd deceived me. The foursome had been a ruse, a way for them to make love right under my nose. No, Natalya wouldn't be that willfully callous. I reset the scene. Natalya would be lying on the couch, a look of love blended with exhaustion on her odalisque face. When asked where she'd been, Natalya would reply dreamily that she'd been with Michael, that their lovemaking had gone on for days without stopping. No wonder I was trying so hard to hold onto him, he was incredible. Again it seemed wrong. Take three. Natalya on the couch crying, wringing her guilty hands. When I entered, she'd throw herself at my feet begging forgiveness. She and Michael had tried to fight it, but they could hold out no longer. They loved each other passionately, madly. They had to be together. Could I find it in my heart to rise above my own misery and not stand in the way of true love. It was a bit melodramatic, but Natalya was over the top.

The kitchen was empty, as was the den. I went upstairs. The door to Natalya's room was open. She was on the bed, her cheeks wet, shoving some photographs into a shoebox. Two empty beer bottles were on the floor.

"What's the matter? Where have you been?" I blurted out.

Wiping her eyes and nose, Natalya replied, "Nothing, I'll be okay in a minute."

"But where have you been? The Bat's threatening to fire you if you're sick another day."

"Sorry, I never called. This guy I met at Holliday's tells me he's got tickets for both Phish shows in Chicago and the next thing I know we're on our way. Is Janine really pissed?"

"You know how she is. But you better show up tomorrow," I said, a smile creeping onto my face. I'd been crazy to think Natalya and Michael were together, but I had to be sure.

"Who's the guy?"

"Scott. Sweet, totally into me, but not really my type. Too small, if you know what I mean. Got to see Phish, though. Shit," Natalya said looking at the bottles on the floor, "Two beers. I better watch it."

I'd been so preoccupied with a Natalya-Michael hookup that it only just occurred to me that I was seeing her for the first time since 'the craziness.' It was like it had never happened.

"How's it going with Michael?" Natalya asked.

I looked at the floor.

"Is that asshole pulling that shit on you again?"

"He needed some space. He'll be back in a couple of days, I'm sure." I wasn't going to step into a minefield by telling her the real reason Michael'd left.

"I'd tell him to get lost if I were you," Natalya said coming over and giving me a hug. My arms remained hanging rigidly at my sides. Hugging was unnecessary touching and I wanted to be perfectly clear, without saying it, that there was never going to be a repeat of the other night.

"I'm going out with Danny and Andy tonight. I'm sure it'd be okay if you tagged along," she said.

Andy, my oldest and closest friend, had made plans with Natalya. And she was telling me I could tag along, lying back down on the bed like she was the Queen of fucking Sheba. She was either trying to goad me as payback for not hugging her back, for avoiding her, for whatever, or she really had no idea how obnoxious she sounded. Both options were equally hideous. Suddenly, my life was like a horror film I'd once seen. Earth was attacked by plants from outer space. They wrapped themselves around their victims choking them to death, except it was Natalya wrapping herself around me and slowly squeezing the breath out of me. I should have gotten her fired. I never should have asked her to move in.

"You invited Natalya to come out with us?" I snarled into the phone when Andy picked up.

"She called Danny crying. He didn't know how to tell her no," he replied, his voice steady.

"You should have heard her, 'tagged along,' like I'm the one who just met you," I fumed.

"Listen, it's just tonight. You're one of my best friends and nothing's going to change that, unless you do something grotesque like become a neo-Nazi or join the MA alumni board. So, are you still coming out or are you going to stay home and mope?"

"Go out, I guess."

"That's a good girl. Now get yourself gussied up and we'll see you in a bit," Andy drawled.

❧

Natalya kept bugging me about not being ready. She finally pushed me over the edge when she said that she and 'the boys' really wanted to get to the club early so they could get a couch in the lounge. I sized up her peasant blouse and jeans and asked if that was really what she was going to wear. We were going to Disco Night not Woodstock.

And when we arrived at The Factory the place was practically dead, only twenty dancers on the floor. Natalya fell back into one of the mostly vacant couches, pulling Danny down with her. He landed on top of her and she unleashed her shrieking staccato laugh. I cringed. God, that laugh, how I hated it.

"What'll it be?" asked the cocktail waitress, bending down to place napkins on the table, her skin-tight mechanic's jumpsuit stretching to contain her enormous breasts, which were inches from Danny's nose.

"Ooh, I want a very dirty double Martini, three olives," Natalya purred to Danny, snuggling against his arm and throwing a leg over his, making it clear to the waitress her prior claim on him. She was like a dog marking its territory, except Danny wasn't hers. Andy was reading the specialty cocktail menu, oblivious or unconcerned and only let out a low chuckle when he raised his head to order a Manhattan and saw Natalya draped over his boyfriend.

"God, her tits are ridiculous. I don't get why some guys are so into big tits," Natalya said, claws outs, when the waitress was not quite out of earshot. If she heard she didn't react.

"I'm not into tits at all, big or small," replied Andy.

Lifting her Martini glass high when it arrived, Natalya made a brief toast, "Thank God I don't drive so I can really have fun." And catching the waitress as she was leaving, ordered another double. "I'm in a wild mood tonight."

Midway through our first round of drinks, Natalya starting on her second, Danny traded looks with Andy, who nodded after checking his watch. "C'mon Natalya, let's dance," Danny said.

"Oh, baby, I thought you'd never ask," Natalya cried. The two went down the steps and merged with the undulating mass.

"It doesn't bother you, them dancing together? She's throwing herself at him. I'm surprised she doesn't lie on the floor and tell him to fuck her now." I said.

"Meow. Let's not be catty. Women hit on him all the time. They don't want to believe a guy that gorgeous isn't straight."

"What about men?"

"Them too, but I trust Danny. Maybe she tries a little too hard. I think she's a little lost, a bit like someone else I know."

Even that small comparison to Natalya made all my cattiness leap out of the bag. How I couldn't take living and working together much longer. How much I hated her laugh. How she bragged about how much every guy wanted her. How she took off, missed work, never bothered to call me.

"I'd have thought you'd have been rejoicing about that," Andy remarked, pointing out my inconsistency.

"What are you looking at?" I demanded, swiveling my head over my shoulder. The entire time Andy's eyes had been zeroed in on the steps behind me.

"I invited someone to meet us. Making sure I spot him when he gets here," Andy said, then giving a little cry, jumped up, waving eagerly.

"You know each other?" I gasped when Philip Cox joined us.

"You know each other?" exclaimed an equally surprised Andy, and to Philip he added, "You sly dog, you never said a word."

"We work together, so to speak," I said.

"So do we," said Andy. "I didn't know you were such a computer slut, Philip."

"Just don't call me a cheap slut," Philip laughed.

Homing in on the new customer, the cocktail waitress made sure Philip, who'd joined me on the couch, got an eyeful of her assets when she bent over way more than was necessary to give him the drinks list. Philip waved it away. "Don't need it. I'll have a Maker's Mark on the rocks. Who else wants a drink?"

"If you're buying," Andy said, "I'll have another Manhattan."

"Hunter?"

"I'm good, thanks."

Andy was commenting on how many of the same countries Philip and I had traveled to when we were aurally accosted by a baby pig.

"Oh my God! Philip!" Natalya squealed, "What are you doing here, cutie pie? You've just got to dance with me." She took a big swig of her drink, grabbed his hand and dragged him away. Danny gave a helpless shrug to the dirty look he got from Andy. "She was thirsty," he said.

"So, what do you think of him?" Andy asked me with a little too much interest.

"Of Philip? Honestly, I've never given him much thought. He's okay, I guess."

"He's way more than okay. He's hot, and ripped," Danny piped in.

I wasn't really into 'ripped'. I found 'ripped' kind of freaky. I preferred my men on the skinny side, like Michael.

"And smart," added Andy.

A klieg light went on above my head. Andy and Danny were playing matchmaker. Andy had known me most of my life and still had no idea what kind of man I was attracted to.

"He's not really my type."

Andy replied, spreading the sarcasm with a knife, "Not your type, like, you mean, he has his own business, doesn't live with his mother and not only knows where Bolivia is but has actually been there?"

"Anyway, he's gay, isn't he?"

"If only," sighed Danny.

"Well, it doesn't really matter, even if I was interested," I said, pointing to the spot on the dance floor where Natalya was giving Philip her now familiar mating dance.

"She may want it, but I she ain't going to get it. I saw how he looked at her and how he looked at you. He's not interested in Natalya," Andy declared like he was making an argument in court.

I watched Philip throughout the night. He treated Natalya no differently than the friendly way he treated the other girls at the shop. Natalya on the other hand, fueled by a steady consumption of martinis, was getting wilder and more blatant in her pursuit of him. On the dance floor, she shimmied and shook around him, slithered her body up and down his. Leaned on him and whispered in his ear. It was hard to know what Philip thought of her antics. He wore the same Mona Lisa smile through it all.

In the rare moments Philip and I found ourselves alone together, I didn't get the vibe that he was especially interested in me, either. If anything, he was probably exasperated by my asking him to repeat everything he said at least three times. At ten o'clock the music had been turned up so loud I could barely hear my own thoughts let alone anything anyone said.

Returning to the couch after some awkward dancing—Natalya, Philip and I were supposed to be dancing together though Natalya did her best to cut me out—Natalya flopped into Philip's lap like she had into Danny's earlier. I spied her hand creeping between his legs. Philip looked at his watch and announced he had to go, an early breakfast meeting. A strategic move or an escape plan?

"Can I catch a ride with you?" Natalya asked.

"Didn't you come with Hunter?"

"Yes, but she's a total partier, aren't you, Hunter? I can never stay out as late as you, can I?" A wink told me I was supposed to play along, confirm the lie, help her go home with Philip.

If Andy and Danny hadn't been off somewhere 'working' I might have had the courage to tell the truth, or Andy would have. But if Philip wanted to fuck Natalya, why should I stop him. Please God, let them go to his place. I didn't want to find him in my kitchen tomorrow morning, naked like Marcus whose unembarrassedly bare ass had shocked me, half awake, into complete alertness one morning. I'd never be able to work with Philip again.

I smiled lamely, "Never in bed before three, that's me."

18

Dressed for work, ears ringing from last night's music, I was in the kitchen pouring a mug of coffee when Natalya staggered in, her skin as pale as raw chicken. And I could see a lot of it because she was barely wearing a blue terry cloth robe. I looked at the floor, over her head, anywhere but right at her. She pulled it closed and tightened the sash.

"I didn't expect to see you this morning."

"Yeah, well, Philip's a total gentleman, but really not my type. Too old. Did you know he's thirty-one?" Natalya said, flopping down in a chair at the kitchen table, "Fuck, I really tied one on last night," She pointed to the coffee, "A cup of that would be a big help. Pour me a big one, would you?"

It was clear she was suffering from more than a hangover. Puffy eyes showed she'd been crying again. "Are you okay? You want something to eat? Some toast?" I asked in a ten-second burst of motherly concern.

"No thanks. I can't think about food right now. What time is it?"

"Eight-thirty."

"Oh good, I can get a shower in before work. Hey, can I ride with you?" Natalya asked, putting the mug of hot coffee to her lips.

"Sure, I guess," I replied wishing I were quicker at coming up with an excuse for why that wouldn't work, "But I thought you were off today."

"Working for Stephanie. I can't tell you why, but she really needed today off."

Acting like it was a big secret about Stephanie, one that she was in on and I wasn't. Except I was. Stephanie was meeting with the editor of an underground literary magazine in Chicago who wanted to publish some of her stories.

In the car, we'd driven less than a mile when Natalya blurted out what she thought was a brilliant idea. She'd ask Janine for only morning shifts then we could ride together.

No. No. No. No. No. The rides to work were precious to me. I didn't have to talk to anyone. I could just think. They were also brief moments of freedom from her and I wasn't going to give them up. Taking time to gather my nerve, I fiddled with the radio tuner until it landed on 'Sympathy for the Devil.' When I spoke, I lied. "Yeah, I don't know. We'll have to see. Not sure if I'm going to keep working there."

"You're thinking of quitting?" Natalya seemed shocked.

"It's just retail and who really wants to work for the Bat?"

"What would you do instead?"

"I don't really have to work," I said, then, detecting a hint of disdain in Natalya's eyes, quickly added, "But I may go back to teaching English. Maybe get a job in Africa, or somewhere like that."

"God, that would be so cool. I'd be an amazing teacher. Kids love me," Natalya said in the syrupy tone she used when gushing about herself.

"I teach adults." If she'd be so amazing at so many things, what the hell was she doing working in a book store?

"That would be fun, too." Natalya took hold of the Africa theme and ran with it all the way to work. I drove in irritated silence, trying to tune her out. I arrived at work jittery and with a dull headache. I regretted the second cup of coffee I'd had while Natalya showered.

Janine, hopping from leg to leg like she had to pee, was signing for five boxes from UPS. It was the shipment she'd been pestering me about for days, coming down every few hours to ask if it had arrived, knowing full well the morning and afternoon delivery times. She fretted that *A Poison Kiss*, the latest romance from the ridiculously successful Milwaukee author Noelle Martin, wouldn't be there in time for the scheduled reading and book signing at the shop the following week. Get them on the floor ASAP was her parting directive as she sped upstairs to get a table ready to display them.

I was opening box number four when Philip appeared.

"I've made a minor adjustment," he said with his usual good humor. Claiming only a minor adjustment to the inventory program was his way of introducing every major change to the system and it usually meant that all the information I'd just entered would disappear and I'd have to start over.

"Please don't tell me I'm going to have re-enter everything," I sighed thinking about the seventy-five books I'd already received.

"You won't and you don't even have to move," he said coming up behind me, preventing me from getting off the stool. His arms encircled me. His face was so close that his cheek brushed mine. He smelled fresh and sunny, like clothes hung on the line to dry. It made me dizzy.

"You look pretty good for someone who went to bed at three."

"You know that was Natalya's little joke, right?"

"I figured, but then Andy confirmed it. He also told me you played doctor together when you were ten."

"Never. I'll admit to playing dolls and Hot Wheels with him, but never Doctor. Are you really down here to work or just to bug me?"

"Seriously, with this new function quantities will be filled in automatically based on our orders. You'll only have edit the numbers when you're short-shipped."

"Hey, slow down on the innovations or I'll be out of a job soon."

"You? Never."

"You keep up the sweet talk and I may start to like you."

As he typed the few last lines of code, he asked, "So, you doing anything tomorrow night?"

"No idea, probably staying home," I replied, not even thinking his question might signify more than casual interest.

"Want to have dinner with me?"

"If I say yes are you going to tell me too bad, you already have plans?" I asked.

"If you say yes then I'll have plans."

He was seriously asking me out.

"Is that funny?"

"Oh no. You just surprised me, that's all. I thought you and Natalya..."

Philip laughed. Not a I-wouldn't-be-caught-dead-with-her laugh, which was good. I was glad he wasn't a mean guy. It was a self-conscious laugh, like even the implication he'd had sex made him uncomfortable. "She's a sweet girl. Too young."

I'm not sure why I said yes. An ego boost. Of all the girls at the shop who'd kill to go out with him, he'd chosen me. New found respect because he'd turned down Natalya. The temptation of being the one in control after the bruising my heart had taken with Michael. Curiosity.

"I'll tell you all the things Andy told me about you."

"Sure, why not. Where do you want to meet?"

"I'll pick you up. Where do you live?"

On hearing my address, Philip said one of his favorite restaurants wasn't too far away. He'd take me there.

"Really," Natalya said, her gaze remaining out the car window, when I told her about my date on the drive home. It gave me perverse pleasure telling her a guy she pursued wanted me instead. "You don't have a problem with that, do you?"

"Me? Why would I?" she said with not quite the easy delivery she was aiming for.

Not that I would have backed out if she'd said yes. (*Okay, so I'd be breaking the girl friends cardinal rule, but were we really friends?*)

"Well, I know you said he wasn't your type, but I just want to make sure we're cool."

"Yeah, we're cool. And since he's most likely gay, I doubt it's even a date. Got any smokes? Don't know why, but I could really use one. Fucking hangovers."

There was a pack in the glove box. She took a couple deep drags and blew the smoke out the window. "What about Michael?"

Just last night she'd been encouraging me to forget Michael.

"No, but I mean you're the one who's so into him. Would you sleep with him?"

"With who? Philip? Not planning on it. I'm not sure he's my type, either."

"Poor Philip," she said in a low voice, twirling the cigarette between her fingers and staring into the sun.

My brilliant plan for the evening was to use Philip to make Michael jealous. I'd convince Philip to go to Hanrahan's for a night cap, use the possibility of live music to sweeten the deal. TomKat Killers were playing, one of Michael's favorite bands. He was sure to be there and when he saw I wasn't waiting around for him he'd realize what an idiot he'd been and come back to me. I chose the sexiest dress I owned, the green floral one I'd bought to wear for the aborted anniversary celebration with Michael. I didn't want Philip, but he sure had to want me. And Michael had to regret ever letting me go.

Natalya was meeting up with Kevin—"He looks a little like Philip, but way cuter"—a guy she'd met the previous night. She was in such a good mood she even offered to help me get ready and I, wanting to look my absolute best, let her. She gathered my hair in a low, messy bun leaving two long tendrils framing my face. She applied a little eye shadow and liner. "Your eyes'll look bluer, and bigger, 'cause they're kinda deep set."

She stepped back to admire her work, "You're going out looking like that and you're not going to sleep with him. Poor Philip." That was exactly the point.

Philip arrived on time. I had to admit he looked pretty damn good in his tailored khaki linen suit and multi-hued striped shirt. He looked like a man, handsome and sophisticated, not a man-child like Michael. He presented me with a single daisy. Michael hadn't given me so much as a dandelion and Philip had chosen my favorite flower. Who'd told him it was my favorite?

"I thought if you were a flower what kind would you be."

He escorted me to his spotlessly clean VW Golf and opened the passenger door, something Michael'd never done. Inside it didn't look like a rat's den, there was no dust on the dashboard, no candy wrappers or empty coffee cups on the floor, no crumbs on the seats, no brown stains on the carpet and seats where coffee had spilled.

Pastarovya was an Italian-Russian eatery with lots of atmosphere and customers. Each table was decorated with a red and white checked cloth and an old vodka bottle thick with the wax of countless candles. On the walls vintage Italian travel posters and Soviet propaganda posters were interspersed with wicker baskets holding bouquets of plastic flowers and shelves lined the *matryoshka* dolls.

Philip greeted the maître d', asking after his wife and sick father-in-law. The man threw up his arms in frustration. "I swear he only pretends to be ill so Julianna will take care of him. She would even if he was healthy, so I don't get it," he said leading us to a quiet table near the back.

Minutes later, a waiter brought us a bottle of Valpolicella and Vladimir Respighi, the Italian-Russian owner and chef, popped out of the kitchen to say hello.

"Do you come here every night?" I asked.

"Not quite that often. I've done computer work for Vlad."

"Ah, so you get free dinners. Now I understand."

"It's because I come here so often that I got the job. Vlad's so generous. He never wants to charge me. I have to force him to take my money."

I perused the menu, asking Philip what he recommended. His favorites were the *braciola* and the *pelmeni* with sour cream sauce.

"What's pelmeni?" I asked.

"Russian ravioli stuffed with pork and sauerkraut. As a Milwaukee girl you gotta love sauerkraut."

I ordered the braciola when the waiter returned.

"Then I'll have the pelmeni. And to start, can we have the calamari and the *fondi di carciofi*, please."

Philip, originally from Cleveland, told me about moving to Milwaukee five years ago with his now ex-wife, who was a local girl.

He'd met Kathryn in Bangkok, staying at the same ramshackle hostel I'd stayed at. They got married six months later on Bali. When it came time to decide where they would live, Kathryn wanted to be close to her family. The marriage lasted two years.

Philip shrugged when I asked him what happened. "Kathryn's great, but we got married too fast. We were caught up in the romance of travel and when we came back to earth, so to speak, we found we wanted different things. She wanted kids right away and I wasn't ready. Still not. She got pregnant with the first guy she dated after we split up."

It turned out Kathryn's desire for motherhood was greater than her desire for couplehood. The guy was out of the picture before the baby was born.

Philip's computer programming business was heating up as his marriage was flaming out, so he stayed on despite having no other ties to Milwaukee. But when the whim took him, he said, he'd leave in a heartbeat. The beauty of his job was that he could do it almost anywhere. He wanted to travel more. He hadn't made it to Africa yet.

I told him that just the other day I was talking about going off to teach in Africa. "I don't know where the idea came from, but now that I've said it it's starting to sound more like a real possibility. Since my parents died I've been in a kind of stasis, not knowing where to go or what to do, but I know I'm not going to be at the bookshop forever."

We spoke of art, movies and literature and though we hadn't read many of the same books, my great love was nineteenth century English novels while Philip preferred mid-20th century American writers, he read books that had more words in them than pictures.

Philip was everything Michael wasn't. He was smart and funny. He was curious about the world. I liked him far more than I expected. Sometime between the entree and dessert I revised my vision for the end of the evening from a thank-you and a handshake to an invitation upstairs. And when I suggested we go to Hanrahan's for a nightcap it was no longer to make Michael jealous. Now it was to show that loser I'd found someone else, someone worthier. I envisioned Michael's penis nose bending out of joint at the sight of the woman he'd spurned enjoying the attentions of a real man.

Entering the bar, I saw it with different eyes. It was smoky. The floor was sticky from spilled beers. The speakers were blasting Deep Purple. I'd gotten the date wrong. Tom Kat Killers were the next night. A few patrons looked the worse for drink although it was only a little past nine. It was a dump. I shot Philip a quick glance to gauge his reaction, fearing it would indicate a diminished opinion of me. He was smiling.

"I can't believe I've never heard of this place. It's great," he exclaimed.

We found two empty stools. The bartenders, who were wiping down glasses, greeted me. Chris, my favorite, came over to take our orders and give my companion the once over. He gave me a discreet thumbs-up.

"I did some work for the owner, that's why they all know me, not because I come here a lot. I try to get my drinks for free, but they always make me pay," I joked.

"Ha, ha. Very clever. For that, you can buy these drinks too," he said and took a sip from one of the whiskeys Chris placed before us.

For fifteen minutes I kept track of every patron who drifted in on that unusually slow Friday, but as I was drawn in, along with the underworked staff, to Philip's tale of a summer he spent as a cowhand on a ranch in Arizona my vigilance waned. He was a gifted storyteller giving all the character he'd met their own voices, even the cows had different moos. He described, with slurps and squelches, what the mud sounded like after a heavy rainstorm, and what the wind was saying when it blew so hard at night that the walls of the bunkhouse were ready to surrender. When we got up to leave an hour later I'd forgotten completely about Michael.

Full of fantasies of the how it would be with Philip, I got so far ahead of myself that by the time we arrived at my house and Philip was walking me to the front door, I had us walking down the aisle. Philip said he'd had a wonderful time. He gave me a hug, neither a quick I'm-not-gay hug guys give each other nor a long I-want-you-to-ask- me-in kind. It was a vague, medium length hug followed by a peck on the cheek. Then he left. He just left.

19

Natalya usually worked at the bookstore Saturday mornings, and for someone who worked with books I'd never actually seen her reading one, so I was doubly surprised, when I came downstairs at ten to find her seated in the breakfast nook, chin hovering just above a bowl of cereal, nose in a book. I was also annoyed because I'd anticipated having the kitchen to myself. I was about to retreat when she caught me. "I hope you don't mind. I borrowed this from the den," she said holding up the book, "I remember Philip saying it was one of his favorites."

"What is it?" I asked coming all the way into the kitchen and helping myself to a banana.

"*East of Eden.* I think it's yours. There's an inscription in it."

"May I see?"

Natalya handed me the paperback. Its cover was tattered and its spine split and many of the pages dog-eared. My father had given it to me for my eighteenth birthday. I opened the cover and saw Dad's precise script on the end paper.

November 12, 1980. Susu, I read this book when I was eighteen and it has been a favorite ever since. I hope it's as meaningful to you as it is to me. Love, Dad.

So like him to rescue it from my room when Mom packed up all my things. Though he had liked to keep it hidden, my father had been sentimental. Once, as a girl, searching his desk for paper, I'd discovered at the bottom of a drawer, tied up with string, every birthday card I'd ever made him. I was embarrassed I'd learned his secret, like the cards were Playboys or a box of condoms.

"I know I'm only on page ten, but it's kinda boring," Natalya said, "I prefer Hesse and Kerouac."

"Well, if don't like it, I'll put it in my room." If Natalya didn't love the book from the first page as I had, I didn't want her to read it, especially that copy, which was too precious to be in the hands of an indifferent reader.

Natalya undid her knot of hair and shook out the long tresses, running her fingers through to untangle them. "So how did it go last night?"

"He's not what I expected at all. I had so much fun," And that was true up until he'd left me on the doorstep, but I wasn't going to let Natalya know about that.

"Well, you're here, he's not and you're not acting like a woman who got laid, so I'm guessing nothing happened."

The cruelty lay in the words Natalya chose, not in her voice, which maintained its normal tone. She was usually sweet, super sweet like a Jolly Rancher, yet when she wanted she'd viciously pull a cat's tail.

"Not every date has to end in bed, you know," I replied. "Speaking of ending up in bed, where's Kevin?"

"The girls at work say he likes you, but personally, I don't see it," Natalya said. Nasty, and ignoring the question. Her date must have tanked. She had a ninety-nine percent conquest rate—Philip the single exception—and if she didn't like the guy she always explained why, often in more detail than I wanted, like Mike whose cock smelled like, well never mind. Had she bombed out again?

The phone rang. Natalya, seated closest to it, answered. "Hello?.....Oh, hi there. You sound sexy this morning..... Me? Just got out of the shower. You should see me." She laughed, then after a pause, said, "You are a bad boy..... Mmm, I'll get her." She handed the phone to me, "It's for you."

I took the handset and walked into the den.

"Hey, it's Philip. My meeting this morning got cancelled so I was wondering if you'd like to go for a ride on the bike? We can go along the lakeshore. Stop at a beach for a swim."

Already asking me on a second date. I couldn't contain my happiness.

"I heard it might rain today," Natalya said.

I didn't pay any attention to Natalya's weather forecast. I was wrestling with a bigger problem: I didn't own a bike. I couldn't tell Philip I lacked the central element for our date. He might've changed his mind if I confessed the deficiency. I wasn't going to ask Natalya if I could borrow hers, too small anyway, so I hoped Philip would somehow intuit I had no bike and bring one for me.

The Golf arrived at the house with its bike rack empty. "Change of plans. The bike wouldn't start, so we're going for a drive instead," Philip said.

"I don't get it. How does a bike not start?"

"Who knows. The Triumph's a temperamental machine."

"Oh, you mean a motorcycle," I laughed at my own cluelessness.

"You thought I meant bicycle? I wasn't sure you knew how to ride one."

"As long as it's got training wheels, I'm good."

❧

The only Lake Michigan beach I knew had been blocks from our house, an urban beach where people who didn't belong to a country club, or have a summer home on one of the interior lakes went to cool off. Located at the base of a steep bluff, access was either by a zig-zagging path or cable car. The beach extended only a few hundred yards, its reach stunted at both ends by private property. The toilets and the concession stand were in a white concrete building that upon entering dropped a cold and clammy shroud onto sun-tingled skin. The floor seemed to be made of layers of slimy, slippery sand that slithered up between bare toes. To even tempt me into the frigid waters of the lake, the air temperature had to be kissing ninety degrees and the humidity almost visible. Why would I go there when I could swim in the cool, refreshing water of the club's pool, followed by a hamburger, fries and fresh lemonade on the shaded, sand-free patio (*God, what a snob I'd been in my youth. Now I hated pool water. All that chlorine*).

Only an hour north of Milwaukee, the beach Philip took me to was of another world. Crossing dunes of green and gold, we came upon a golden beach that stretched as far as the eye could see. The water was calm, gently lapping against the shore and just a shade bluer than the sky. Only experience told me it would not be Caribbean-warm. Gulls

182

swooped and swirled in the warm air, darted up and down the shore, and pecked at microscopic prey buried in the sand.

Under beach umbrellas and shade tents, sprawled out on towels and blankets, picnic baskets and coolers filled with sustenance for the long, hot day ahead, families, couples and a few clusters of teens were scattered about.

No sooner had we claimed a small patch of sand with a black and red checked blanket than Philip was tearing off his tee shirt *(I liked him so much that I could forgive him his almost six-pack abs)*, running into the surf and diving under the waves. He called to me to join him, "C'mon in, it's energizing."

I knew I was never going to go deeper than my knees, yet I presented the illusion I was a daredevil and full immersion a possibility by stripping down to the bikini I wore under my clothes and shucking off my sandals. I strode to the water, hoping I wouldn't degenerate into some ultra-girly girl, a Natalya, who shrieked when a cute boy asked her out, when she saw a spider, when cold water hit her feet. I stopped at mid-calf with a single, barely audible gasp, and watched Philip frolicking like a dolphin, a species he must be related to in order to tolerate the icy temperature. When I was no longer sure my feet were still attached to my ankles, I hobbled back to the blanket and wrapped myself up in a towel. I popped open a beer and waited for Philip to come ashore.

"What?" he exclaimed a few minutes later, slightly blue-lipped, drying off, when I confessed my ignorance that a beach like that existed.

As a family, we had never explored Wisconsin. We'd always gone to Florida, New Mexico, California or Europe for vacations. I came to believe my home state was not interesting, not beautiful, that there was nothing to do or see there. There'd once been a bumpersticker to promote tourism: *Escape to Wisconsin*. I covered the '*to*' so it read *Escape Wisconsin* like the state was a prison. Truth was, as a kid, I could've been living on a white sand beach by an aqua blue sea, the sun shining three-hundred and sixty-five days a year, the temperature never dipping below seventy nor rising above eighty-five and I would have found reasons to hate it. It's always warm. It never snows. Sand gets into everything.

"I might as well tell you that I've never been to Door County, Madison, Taliesin or a Bucks Game."

"I'll forgive you the Bucks Game. Not a big basketball fan myself, but the others, girl, you and I have some trips to make."

"Ah, but you'd never been to Hanrahan's," I said, thinking I was getting one back on him.

"One bar in a city with thousands of bars. I could go out for a drink every night for years and never go to the same place twice. But I'll give you an 'A' for effort," he said with a laugh, "Hey, I'm famished. Let's eat." From his small daypack as from a magician's top hat, he began pulling out Brie and crackers, roast chicken, green salad, potato salad, apples and a bar of dark chocolate.

Drowsy from food, beer, sun and talk—we'd talked about everything and nothing, of things important and trivial— we lay back on the blanket side by side and let ourselves drift off. A shadow falling across my body awakened me. I pulled off the hat that covered my face, having no idea how long I'd been out.

The owner of the shadow was a woman in her mid-seventies, wild grey hair, stained men's shirt and overalls, a nearly full fifty-five-gallon garbage bag at her feet, and radiating goodness and compassion like a beloved, kooky godmother. Not exactly thief material, but she was holding Philip's tee shirt in her hand. "Oh, I didn't mean to wake you. I just wanted to cover your husband up. He's getting awful pink."

My husband! How nice did that sound. I wasn't going to correct her. "That's very kind of you. I'll do it."

"Being so late in the season, people forget that the sun can still get 'cha."

I nodded in agreement and thanked her again. Since I had the situation in hand, she remarked what a handsome couple we made and tottered off down the beach to perform more good deeds.

I gently put the tee shirt over Philip noting, that indeed his skin was turning the color of a newborn mouse. I lay facing him, watching his chest rise and fall; noticing a tiny mole just below his ear, a few whiskers on his jaw line that the razor had missed; his thick, nearly-black eyelashes twitching. I wondered what he was dreaming. His head rolled toward me and his eyes opened. His mouth crept into a smile. "Did you cover me up?"

"I only finished what the old lady started."

"What old lady?" he asked, full of excited curiosity.

"I don't know. I opened my eyes and there she was. Said she was worried you were getting burned."

"I can't believe you saw Grannie Weigell. I've been here a dozen times and never seen her. She's either just left, or shows up after I'm gone, or hasn't been seen in a few weeks. And you see her your first time."

"Who's she?"

"A kind of guardian angel for this beach. She picks up garbage, cares for injured birds, looks out for burning bathers. You know what this means, don't you? You're a lucky charm. I'm going to have to bring you with me every time."

I'm free tomorrow and the next day and the day after that said the voice inside my head while outwardly I asked which charm? Yellow moon, orange star, pink heart or green clover.

Back in the city, Philip took me for frozen custard at Karl's.

"I don't believe it," he exclaimed when I admitted it was my first time there too.

"How is that possible? It's been around since the early seventies. It's got the best frozen custard in the whole state."

I shrugged. A deprived childhood?

❧

A raincheck. Philip wanted to take a raincheck on my offer of a drink. His cycling club met Sunday mornings and tomorrow's ride was a long one. If I was free in the evening, maybe we could catch *The Fugitive*. Another vague hug. Another blink-and-you'll-miss-it kiss on the cheek. And he was gone. Again.

Okay, Hunter, relax. He'd asked me out, again. It would be our third date in three days. He talked about us in the future tense, of taking trips together. Door County couldn't be done in a day. He wanted to spend time with me. He paid for everything. He had to like me. Tomorrow would be the day. I could feel it in my bones. I could almost feel his lips touching mine. Third time's the charm. Definitely pink hearts.

20

Gordon's gin, a half-empty bottle, full the day before, was on the kitchen counter. Next to it a glass holding three ice cubes. Natalya twisted off the bottle cap and poured three fingers of gin over the ice, got a jar of olives from the fridge and dropped three into the glass. She dubbed the cocktail Three Cubed. I could tell from her leftward list that it wasn't her first drink. Natalya's new routine since the night of her disaster date with Kevin was staying in, stumbling up to her room after one too many, coming down each morning looking thinner and frailer. When I first spied her ferrying bottles up and down the stairs I thought she didn't trust me, then I realized she was trying to disguise how much she was drinking. Natalya was falling apart and I had no idea how to help her and, honestly, I resented being expected to.

She had two drinks in her, but still she spotted my hastily banished frown at the steady red light of the answering machine. Enunciating carefully, she said, "No messages when I got home and the phone hasn't rung." She took a swig of her drink, scooping out an olive with her tongue. She continued, "In my experience, when a guy's into you, he wants to be with you all the time. If Philip hasn't tried to fuck you, he's probably not going to. And he hasn't called in days. I'm not being cruel, but you just may have to face facts that he's just not into you."

"Is that your wisdom or the gin's? Have another. See if it makes you any wiser."

Not sure which one of us started it, but cruel was how we were with each other most of the time.

Philip and I had gone to the movie Sunday. He'd bought popcorn, Junior Mints and a large Coke to share. He'd put his arm around me in the dark theater, the prelude to a long-awaited kiss. I hadn't made out at a movie since Andy and I saw *The Blue Lagoon* in high school. We'd sat in the back row, Leslie and her then boyfriend, Peter, four seats over. Andy faked a great yawn, stretching out his arms so he could put one around me. I laughed at the corniness of it and told him if he wanted to make out to just say so. He replied that he'd always wanted to test out that move.

Once in a while, Philip's hand brushed against my bare skin giving me goose bumps. Thinking I was cold in the air-conditioned theater, he offered me his sweater. I put it on, thrilled to be wearing something of his, something that had touched his skin and it made up for the kissing that never came.

Only self-control kept me from running to the car when the movie ended. An aura of anticipation had been in the air the entire evening. I'd wanted the movie to end as soon as it began. I'd wanted to push the clock forward to the moment Philip pulled his car into my driveway, I invited him in and he finally accepted, not with words but with a kiss. A real kiss, not another peck on the cheek. Our passion would steam up the car's windows. Then I would lead him into the house and up to my bedroom. I'd kept his sweater on even though it was sticking to me in the sultry night air because I wanted Philip to take it off and heard him saying, as he lifted it over my head, "Let's get rid of this damn thing."

Philip pulled his car into the driveway. I asked if he would like to come in.

"I'd love to..." The words were almost tangible, floating in the air feather-like. Blood rushed from my head, my heart thumped in my chest. My instincts were right, it was going to happen. "...But I have to drive to Madison tomorrow morning, deliver some hardware."

'Days' the way Natalya had said it sounded like it was weeks ago the last time Philip called rather than three days. And it seemed like three weeks to me, but probably only three hours to Philip. Three days only seems like an eternity to men when sex is involved.

Philip liked me, I was pretty sure about that. Why else would he want to spend so much time with me. What I couldn't understand was his reluctance to make a move. Was he a man who followed the old rules of dating, the type who didn't try to bed women on the first date, or the second, or the third. They must still exist in nature, somewhere. Or maybe Natalya was right. Maybe it was never going to happen. Maybe Philip was gay. Maybe that was the real reason his marriage had fallen apart. He was friends with Andy after all. And here I was stupidly falling in love with him, like I had Andy, and he was only interested in friendship. But if he was gay, why didn't he just tell me? Maybe he hadn't admitted it to anyone, not even to himself. Still dating women, feigning interest. I'd been so certain Andy and Danny were trying to set us up, but maybe I'd misread their intentions. He'd turned down Natalya, but that might have been a display of good taste. There was that girl from the bookshop he'd had a fling with. Maybe that story wasn't even true. Maybe the girl made it up knowing Philip would never contradict her. Or maybe, the worst of all possible reasons, he saw me as one of the guys, a buddy, and not as a woman to be desired. I beat down the voice in my head, Andy's voice, that said I wasn't woman enough.

అ

Thursday was Philip's first day back at The Printed Page. His schedule was down to two or three days a week as his project for the shop neared completion. Stephanie had cornered him in Fiction with a joke. Stephanie collected jokes like some kids collected stamps and she had a new one nearly every day. "And Jesus said, 'God damn it, Mom. Sometimes you make me so mad!' The walls of the shop resounded with Philip's laughter. I, entering unseen, hastened to my basement lair. My confidence in Philip's feelings had slipped with every day that passed without a phone call and I dreaded seeing him, imagining his abrupt, awkward hello, eyes averted, or God forbid, a friendly greeting as though I were Stephanie or Alice or any of the other girls at the shop and the time we spent together had never happened.

An hour later, I recognized his footfalls on the stairs. I grabbed some invoices and with mock purpose, leafed through them.

"Hey there," he cried. I raised my head briefly with a terse hello. It was enough time to wish I could return to the days before I'd noticed his mouth or had my head filled with his scent. If he was here to put me out of my misery, please let it be swift.

"Sorry I haven't called. I feel terrible. I ended up having to stay in Madison to fix a crashed system. Got home yesterday and slept for fourteen hours."

I dropped the pretense of the invoices and looked directly at Philip. There was something different about him, something eager in his stance, like he'd missed me.

"I wish I could see you tonight, but I've got to meet a client I was supposed to meet yesterday. Are you free tomorrow? We can go out for sushi."

"The place better be good. I lived in Tokyo, so I know sushi," I teased.

❧

I was a Zen master Friday night, a real switch from my usual freak-out before a date with a guy I really liked. I would be happy whatever happened that night. If nothing happened then it would be the next time or the time after that, but it was going to happen. I knew that from the way Philip had looked at me yesterday. I chose a blouse I'd bought in Mexico, white with flowers embroidered in celadon thread. The blouse didn't show lots of skin, but in place of buttons it had tie closures that I decided was sexier and less obvious. I calmly rubbed *4711* onto my arms, neck and sprinkled it in my hair and applied little makeup.

We were welcomed into the crowded Sushi Hattori with a merry "*Irasshai mase*" from the owners, Yoichi and Mariko, a couple who'd moved to Milwaukee decades ago from Kagoshima. Yoichi, the sushi chef, wore the traditional white coat and apron, but in place of the white hat he had on a Brewers baseball cap. Mariko, who acted as hostess, offered us a table. We declined, preferring to sit at the sushi bar.

Though I'd lived in Tokyo, I really knew almost nothing about sushi—I'd survived on cheaper fare like *yakisoba* and *gyoza*—so when Philip encouraged me to order whatever I wanted, I stuck to California rolls and spicy tuna.

"So, Janine asked me to be manager of the catalog today," Philip said as he filled two small ceramic cups with *sake*.

"What'd you tell her?"

"That I'm not a nine-to-five kind of person. She looked at me like I'd refused to marry her. I'd heard she liked me, but I guess I didn't believe it till then."

"You mean you never noticed her batting her eyelids and touching her hair every time she talks to you? She's gotta be desperate to find a way to keep you around."

"Yeah, well, in three weeks I'm outie kapoutie."

"Another one of your father's sayings?"

"No, that's one of my own. Just made it up, in fact." Then Philip raised his cup saying, "*Kampai.*"

I wondered how he knew the Japanese toast.

"You think you're the only one who's been to The Land of the Rising Sun?"

"No, of course not," I replied, embarrassed that I'd been called out for being condescending, "It's just you never mentioned it."

"Got to let my history out slowly, keep you interested."

We engaged in a bit of friendly traveler's one-upmanship. I went first with a story of a disastrous rafting trip in Nepal when the guide tried to kick me off the boat for being a bitch and we discovered the bloated and sun-burned body of a man floating face down in the river. He'd been stabbed in the back. Philip countered with a story of being so broke in the Swiss Alps in the middle of winter that he was forced to camp out on peoples' porches, wrapped in whatever he could find to stay warm.

Just as I began relating a Bolivian bus ride from hell, the door of the restaurant opened. "It was one o'clock in the morning and the town turned off the elec..."

"Irasshai mase!" Yoichi and Mariko sang out to Michael and Wendy, the redhead.

Wendy saw me immediately and tugged Michael's sleeve. From her arching eyebrows and twitching feet I guessed she wanted to leave. I tried to beam my thoughts into Michael's brain: "Yes, leave. Wendy doesn't want to be here. I don't want you here. Go. Get out of here." Michael gave his head a violent shake as though ridding it of an intruder, and scowling, dragged Wendy, her upper lip quivering, by the hand to the only available table. Right behind us.

Not an ex or even a maybe, that liar. That shit. That asshole. Our relationship wasn't even cold and Michael was already sleeping with someone else. And when had he started up with Wendy. Weeks ago no doubt and waited until it was a sure thing before dumping me. And there I was sitting with a guy who I couldn't even get to kiss me, who was probably gay. It was humiliating. Well, that was going to change. I was going to emerge victorious that night or else. The only visible sign that I was preparing for battle, however, was a grip on my chopsticks so tight it dug furrows in my index and middle fingers.

During Philip's next story, my voice got louder, my laugh grew more enthusiastic and I touched his shoulder too often. And like I'd spontaneously developed a tic, my head kept snapping backwards to see what Michael was doing, what his reactions were. Then remembering the *sake*, I downed the cup in one gulp. I needed something stronger. I ordered a whiskey and shot it down as soon as Yoichi served it. My voice got even louder and my laugh more hysterical. Philip, noting how much the guy with the redhead was staring at me and how he was getting more and more peeved, wondered what was going on. I drained a second whiskey. When I asked for a third, Philip suggested he take me home instead.

"Yes, you should take me home." And getting right up close to his face, I added breathily, "I'd like very much for you to take me home." As I rose, I staggered back and realized I was a little bit beyond tipsy. Philip immediately provided a supportive arm and escorted me out.

I leaned heavily on Philip, more than I needed to as he walked me to the front door. I wanted him to feel my body pressing against his, breathe in the citrus scent of bergamot in my hair. I wanted him to be unable to resist me.

"Do you wanna come in?" I asked.

"I'm not sure that's a good idea," Philip said.

"Is there anything I can do to change your mind?" I put my arms around his neck and kissed him, trying to slip my tongue into his unyielding mouth. Undeterred, I slithered my right arm down between his legs and caressed him with my hand. Philip gently removed it and pulled away from me.

"Don't you like me?" I pouted.

"Yes."

"Then come inside."

"I don't feel comfortable about this. First, you've had a bit too much to drink. And second, I think there's something's going on that I don't want to get in the middle of. Something to do with that guy in the restaurant."

"He's nobody. Don't let him stop you." I reached out to put a hand on Philip's shoulder and missed.

"I'm definitely not interested in some kind of love triangle."

My body slumped in defeat. "That was Michael, and whatever there was between us, it's over. He broke it off."

"Well, it didn't seem over to me."

"Yeah, well, believe me it is. He's just the last person I expected to run into there, and with Wendy. It threw me."

Philip was silent for a moment then said softly, "Well, we've all had bad run-ins with exes. But maybe it means you need some time, you know, it's too soon."

He was letting me go. This was the last I would see of him. His work at The Printed Page would be over soon and then he'd be gone, out of my life. I couldn't let that happen.

"No, believe me, I am so over him. I really had a great time tonight."

"Yeah, me too, for most of it," he said in a voice tinged with defeat. "I'll call you."

He turned and walked into the darkness.

21

God, I was such an idiot! I'd probably just fucked up any chance I had with Philip. Why did I have to get drunk? What a loser. No wonder Philip wasn't interested. And why the hell did Michael have to show up? He didn't even know what sushi was. And what was he doing right now? Was he fucking Wendy? Or were they making love? I pictured them in bed together, Michael kissing and touching Wendy the way he had me, but more passionately because it wasn't me. Michael and I had only fucked. That's the word he used, never 'made love.'

I flew into the house and straight to the powder room. I gripped the towel bar to steady myself, my head spinning like a top. I retched the *sake*, whiskey and self-contempt into the toilet. In the kitchen for a glass of water, I heard the TV in the den.

"Hello?"

No response.

I found Natalya passed out on the couch, an empty bottle of gin on the floor next to her. She looked how I felt, bad. She'd been crying again.

"Hey, wake up," I said loudly and without a trace of sympathy.

When Natalya didn't move, I poked her. "Hey, Natalya, wake up."

She stirred. Her eyes fluttered open. "What time is it?" she asked groggily.

"No idea. Go to bed."

"How was your date?"

"Great, until I fucked it all up. I don't want to talk about it. I just want this fucking night to be over. And I don't want to find you on this couch in the morning."

Just as the bed spins were ebbing the doorbell rang. Letting out some choice expletives, I rolled out of bed and went to the window. Michael's car was in front of the house. The doorbell rang again. I ran downstairs forgetting I was in a tank top and underwear. Or maybe I hadn't forgotten. Maybe I wanted to tease him.

"What the hell are you doing here?" I hissed.

"Is he here?" Michael yelled up the stairs as if to draw the culprit out.

"None of your business."

"Well, is he?" His voice was shrill.

"What do you think? Do you see a car in the driveway?" I responded with irritation. "By the way, where's Wendy? I hope you haven't left her in the car."

Michael continued, ignoring my comment, "So, who is he?"

"As I said before, it's none of your business. You dumped me."

Michael changed tack, his voice softened, "It's just when I saw you with him I got so jealous."

My expression questioned his sincerity.

He moved closer to me, "You don't believe me, but it's true. You looked so hot. You look even hotter now. I want you so badly. See." He took my hand and guided it to his crotch. He was hard. Not thirty minutes ago I'd stood on that same porch kissing Philip, yet I did not remove my hand.

Philip hadn't explicitly said he wasn't interested, but he'd implied it. If he liked me why would he walk away? Why wouldn't he fight for what he wanted? Michael had deserted Wendy and rushed to be with me, risking the chance I'd tell him to get lost. Maybe I was supposed to be with him. Really, what were the odds that tonight of all nights he decided he wanted to try sushi and showed up at same restaurant I was at. It couldn't be coincidence. It had to be fate. And the universe had sent Philip into my life to bring Michael back. But why didn't the universe want me to be with Philip? I liked him so much more.

Michael's hand was in my underwear, between my legs, a finger entering me, gently moving up and down. He whispered in my ear, "Oh my god, you are so wet." I unzipped his jeans. He groaned as I took hold of his cock and stroked it. His excitement increasing, he pushed me against the wall. "I want to fuck you here, now."

Not wanting to be seen by a night owl neighbor, I suggested we go upstairs.

Once in my room, Michael threw me down on the bed, ripped off my underwear and entered me. If I'd felt empowered by my hold on him, it was gone as soon as Michael came with a grunt and rolled off, like I was a whore there to please him. There had been no tenderness, no consideration for my enjoyment or satisfaction.

Without saying a word, we got under the sheets. Michael immediately fell asleep. I lay awake staring at the ceiling wondering how I'd deluded myself that his desire meant anything more than seeing a woman he'd dumped enjoying herself with another man. Michael didn't want me, but he didn't want me to want anyone else. Ugh, it sounded like me before my first date with Philip. I deserved whatever I got.

I fell asleep around five and when I awoke two hours later, Michael was gone. A note on the pillow read, "I'll call you." I ripped it up and threw it in the trash. God, how I hated those three words.

❧

I'd been to Jordy's only once and swore I'd never go back. The California-beach themed bar, surf boards on the walls, surf music on the stereo, was a popular hangout and hookup site for Wisconsin State students. But after a day and a half of telephone silence and the dismal prospect of spending another night staring at the phone, I called Stephanie and begged to go with her. There was little chance I'd run into either Philip or Michael at Jordy's.

Why Stephanie, who I considered a smart girl, wanted to hang out shoulder to shoulder with the frat boy crowd, listening to sixties surf music, shoes crunching on the peanut shells that littered the floor while sipping Long Island Iced Teas, I didn't get.

Tonight the surf music blared but the action was all outside. It was the wet tee shirt finals and the crowd was gathered around a plywood stage set up in the sand-pit volleyball court. Five hundred dollars in prize money, a tiara, a sparkly sash and her boobs cast in Plaster of Paris and mounted on the wall so that one day she could bring her children to see them.

"Ok everyone!" shouted Jordy, grizzly bear voice, upper arms the size of my thighs, and a chest bench-pressed to cartoonish proportions, over the din. "It's the moment you've been waiting for. All summer we've been introducing you to the most beddable babes in Beer Town and now it's all come down to tonight when we crown Miss Wet Tits, I mean Tee Shirt, 1993."

The eight weekly winners were lined up on the stage, high heels, short shorts, bikini bottoms, their names—Staci, Kelli, Cyndi, Amber, Tonya—emblazoned on thin white tee shirts, purchased from the girls department at the nearest K-Mart that were straining to cover breasts not one pair smaller than a D-cup. They giggled. They flipped their hair. They blew pink, water proof, glossy-lipped kisses at the appreciative frat boys and slimy men who only showed up on contest nights.

"And away we go!" Jordy cried, "First up is Tiffani Hoffmann. Bang! Zoom!"

A live band ripped into Aerosmith's 'Walk This Way' as Tiffani, dance-strutted to the front of the stage, her back arched to thrust out even farther her double-Ds.

"Tiffani's twenty-two. She's from Bayview and works in the billing department at Wisconsin Gas. She likes puppies,

Pac-Man and popsicles and couldn't give a damn about world peace."

Two guys dressed as firemen opened their hoses on Tiffani. She threw her arms up in the air, then ran her hands over her breasts. Brown aureolas and erect nipples were now visible through her drenched tee shirt. The frat boys and slimy dudes whooped and hollered. Tiffani pulled up the tee and wrung out the water. She spun round, bent over and wiggled her ample, bikini-clad ass. The men went nuts.

The next contestant, Tonya, looking like she had no idea how she'd gotten there, had dance moves that were as sexy as The Lawrence Welk Show. Having to top Tiffani's performance would have made all but the most seasoned stripper nervous. An ill-timed jerk of the head and Tonya was hit in the face with a blast of water. She sputtered and stumbled and was hit with another blast.

"Poor thing," Stephanie said, "She needs some more liquid courage."

Tonya had consumed a lot of liquid courage last Sunday night and entered the contest on a drunken dare.

The crowd showed little compassion.

"Show us your tits," someone yelled.

"Yeah, take off your shirt."

"Some of us missed 'em last week."

"Get off the stage."

"It's alright, Tonya. They've all got tiny penises," Stephanie shouted out to the shell-shocked contestant.

"And I bet you've got three tits, Spock," yelled some frat boy dickhead with a ha-ha-I-got-you look on his smug face (*I guess I wasn't the only one to see the likeness*).

Stephanie seemed to grow taller, her eyes narrowed to slits, her lips formed a sinister smile. In a flowing top, her hair in a high, tight ponytail, a thin braid hanging down over each temple, she looked more alien than ever (*Was it my imagination or were her ears slightly pointed*). She extended a pale arm and pointed a slender finger at the frat boy, "*Kavtan veggan seelplat, flegrot.*"

The strange words flew like photon torpedoes. The guy didn't know if he should laugh or run for cover. And then, just as abruptly, she was Stephanie again, "Jordy should really even things out by having a tighty-whitey contest. Then the winners could date, procreate and unleash some truly hideous hybrid into the world."

"Wait a minute. What just happened? What did you say to that guy?"

Total gibberish. The guy got up in her face every time she came to Jordy's, always with some lame alien insult. She'd been working on the routine for a week hoping he'd give her a reason to use it.

"Why do you come here?" I asked, "Please don't tell me you like this place."

"Hell no, I'm doing research for a story I'm working on. A jock-strap asshole is murdered after leaving a bar like this. It's a comedy."

Only contestant number six, Staci—twenty-one, a server at Wendy's from Wauwatosa who liked cheap wine, cheap beer and football players—surpassed the raunchy heights achieved by Tiffani. Smaller boobs, but even less shame: she stuck her hands up her shirt and grabbed her own ass in her bid to win the title.

The thrill of seeing Staci crowned Miss Wet Tee shirt couldn't entice me to stay after a freckled teenager in definite possession of a fake i.d., eyes three-quarters closed and swaying like a stalk of wheat in the wind, threw up inches from my feet, spattering my shoes with droplets of vomit.

☙

A silver Ford Festiva was parked in the driveway, but no lights shone in any of the windows. Behind Natalya's closed door I could hear the muffled voices of Natalya and some guy. God, why had I ever suggested she bring guys home? It was bad enough having to share the kitchen with her in the morning, but I would've confessed to crimes I didn't commit to not have to watch her and the guy grope each other, listen to her giggling and whispering in his ear. I'd really have to talk to her about it in the morning.

I was slipping on my pajamas when I heard the guy shout with the exasperation of someone who'd said it a hundred times, "I'm telling you that's not going to happen!" Maybe my morning was saved. Another fling sounded like it was off to a bad start. The bedroom door opened and there was an anguished cry from Natalya, "Please, don't go! I love you."

"Yeah, well, I don't love you anymore."

Love? Who could the guy could be. Natalya hadn't gone out in days. When had she met him? I stole over to my door, cracked it open and peeped into the hallway. Too late.

He was already down the stairs and out the front door, slamming it behind him. Natalya was in her doorway, naked and weeping. I debated whether I should go to her. Before I could make up my mind, she withdrew into her room.

When I gathered my things for work Natalya still hadn't appeared. It wasn't my problem if she missed her shift. She, too, had to suffer the consequences of bad choices. I stopped at the car. God damn it! Back inside I went and lightly tapped on her door.

"Natalya, are you up? Are you okay?"

I heard sheets rustling and a nose blown, but no response followed. I asked again if she was okay, if she needed anything.

"Just leave me alone, please," Natalya said at last.

"Do you want me to tell Janine you're sick?"

A sniffle, then, "I don't give a shit if she fires me."

I'd thought about calling in sick myself, but Philip didn't work at the shop on Mondays so I was safe. I'd save the sick day for Thursday in case I wasn't up to seeing him.

The garage door was up when I returned home. Natalya never remembered to close it when she went out. I'd have to talk to her about it when she got back. For about the fifth time. But her bike was in its usual spot against the wall and the door to the house was unlocked. She was home.

Natalya never came out of her room that night. And the following morning when, again, she didn't appear and I could discern no movement in her room, I got worried. I knocked and called out her name. No answer.

"Natalya! Are you okay?" I called out more loudly. Again no response nor movement. I turned the handle and cautiously pushed open the door.

Natalya was on her stomach, naked, her head turned away from me, her left leg bent at the knee. The sheet had been kicked to the end of the bed. Her thick, wavy hair cascaded down her back. She was still and pale, like she'd been turned to marble. I foolishly asked if she was awake. Something was seriously wrong, but I wasn't ready to acknowledge it. I approached the bed slowly. Natalya, wake up, please. I nudged her. My hand recoiled in fear and revulsion. Her body was cold. No. This couldn't be happening. I wanted to run away, but I forced myself to walk around to the other side of the bed. There, on the floor, were an empty bottle of gin and an empty amber prescription vial. On a leaf of lilac paper, in Natalya's loose, loopy script was written:

> *when the waves reach my feet*
> *i will return to the sea*
> *letting it carry me out*
> *till i feel nothing*
> *not pain...not desire*
> *not want...not love*
> *not you*

22

When I was in the viewing room of Hillier & Sons, my parents' bodies before me, mind and body cleaved. My body felt weightless, like it was hovering inches above the floor and a thousand needles were pricking my skin. My mind, on the other hand, stayed grounded and clear, studying with detachment the thinly disguised damage to my parents' faces. As much as I wanted to be dreaming, I knew they were dead. My mind noted the physical changes I was experiencing with an eerie calm that it maintained even when I was about to throw up. How utterly different was my response to finding Natalya. A scream so deep, as though it were born in my feet, surged through my body and came out with such ferocity I thought the windows would shatter. My arms shook. My legs buckled. I crashed to the floor. I broke down body and soul, wailing for a woman I hardly knew and didn't like. No, I couldn't let myself fall apart. I had to do something. Maybe she wasn't dead. Maybe she could be saved. But her eyes were fixed and glassy and I could feel no pulse. Help. I needed help. I couldn't go through this alone. Maybe Andy was still home. So weak I couldn't stand, I crawled to my room and blindly reached for the phone and punched in his number.

Surprised and confused when Michael answered I couldn't speak, but I didn't hang up.

"Hello?" Michael said again, "Is anyone there?"

"Oh Michael, I'm sorry, I thought I was calling Andy, but can you please come over. I need help."

"Hunter is that you? "

"It's Natalya, I think she's dead."

"What do you mean you think she's dead?"

"She's not moving. I touched her and she's cold. There's an empty bottle of pills. I don't know what to do."

"What do you want me to do? What can I do if she's dead?" Panic was taking hold of him. The pitch of his voice was getting higher. "Call the police. Call an ambulance. I can't do anything."

"Can't you come over here? I'm so scared."

"I don't wanna be in a house with a dead body. Too many memories of my dad. I can't handle that."

His dad had died twelve years ago. My parents hadn't been gone a year yet my suffering never occurred to him. Even when I begged, he refused to come. He told me to call the police and hung up.

Fucking bastard! Asshole! Coward! Loser! I banged the handset back in its cradle. But he was right about one thing, I had to call the police. I fought down my anger and dialed 911. I'd just put down the phone when it rang again.

"Hello?"

"Hey, it's Philip—"

I didn't give him the chance to continue, words spilled out of my mouth, "Something terrible has happened and I really need some help. Natalya's dead. The police are on their way, but I can't do this alone. Could you come over, please?"

"I'll be right there."

❧

Squad cars, a boring official-looking brown sedan, and an ambulance were already at the house when Philip arrived. Curious neighbors congregated on the sidewalk. I was on the front porch talking to a detective.

"Now, you arrived home an' heard Ms. Haven arguing with a man in her room," asked Detective Schmidt, a heavy-set man of fifty, with a puffy, ruddy face and bushy mustache that curled around his upper lip. Put him in *lederhosen* and he could have been the accordion player in a polka band.

"I couldn't hear what they were saying, only the last things he said, 'That's never going to happen' and 'I don't love you anymore.'"

"An' ya never saw him? Did ya recognize his voice?"

"No."

"So you have no idea who he was?"

"No, and I remember being surprised about the love part. Natalya'd never mentioned meeting a guy she really liked. She said she moved here because of a bad break up. Maybe it was him."

"Where'd she move here from?"

"I don't know. She never told me. She talked about her mother a lot, but I have no idea where she is or how to contact her. I don't even know her name."

211

"So ya didn't see Ms. Haven in person after the man fled the house Monday night?"

I shook my head. "The next morning, I knocked on her door and spoke with her, but didn't see her."

"An' when ya came home from work that evening?"

I shivered in the late summer heat, "She'd been out. I could tell because the garage door was open. But I never saw her. She never came out of her room. I thought she was sleeping. I didn't want to disturb her."

"What about her mental state in recent days? She seem upset? Did she appear despondent? Ever talk about killing herself?" Schmidt asked.

"No, never. She'd been crying a lot and drinking more, but I thought it was just, you know, a bad patch. I didn't think it was serious." I shifted uncomfortably. How would I have known if it was serious since I'd made it pretty clear in the last few weeks that I wasn't receptive to any type of soul-bearing. Hiding out in my bedroom, ignoring her, making cruel remarks, wanting her out of my life.

"Hmm," said Schmidt.

(*What did the 'hmm' mean? Crying a lot and drinking? Ms. Grayson, those are the greatest indicators of potential suicides. You should have known that, called a suicide helpline days ago. You failed Natalya.*) I felt compelled to justify myself, "I've had plenty of bad patches and I've never wanted to kill myself. I'm so sorry I didn't go in. Oh god, I'm so sorry."

Philip touched my shoulder, telling me soothingly that it wasn't my fault.

"Your boyfriend here's right. Don't blame yourself, Ms. Grayson. It's hard to know what's going on in someone's head. Just trying to establish a motive for suicide, or determine if we're looking at something else," Schmidt said and turned his attention to Philip, "Mr. Cox, you also knew Ms. Haven?"

"Yes, but not well. I mean, she wouldn't share her problems with me. The three of us work together at The Printed Page. I'm only there a couple days a week."

Schmidt's partner, Detective Jablonowski, appeared and handed him two small plastic evidence bags. One contained the amber vial. The other the suicide note.

"Who's Margaret Grayson?" he asked, looking at the vial.

"My mother," I replied through my tears.

"The prescription's made out to Margaret Grayson. It was refilled yesterday." He handed the bag back to Jablonowski.

"That can't be. My mother died last January. That vial was in the medicine cabinet in my parents' bathroom."

"May I use your phone?" Jablonowski asked.

"There's one in the kitchen."

Schmidt turned his attention to the note. His brows furrowed in puzzlement. "I guess this could be a suicide note."

"It's a poem by Grace Newhall. She drowned herself in the Thames. Natalya loved her poetry, tried to get me into it. Too grim. It goes to places I don't need to go."

"We'll compare the handwriting to a verifiable sample."

"Coming through!" called out an EMT as he and his partner maneuvered the gurney holding Natalya's body out the front door. I watched them load it, small and insignificant under the white sheet, into the ambulance. It was hard to comprehend Natalya was dead and I would never see her again. I'd wanted her out of my life, but I never wanted it to happen that way.

Jablonowski returned saying the pharmacist recalled a young woman picking up the prescription. She'd show him a photo of Ms. Haven. See if he could i.d. her.

Putting his notebook back in the pocket of his jacket, Schmidt said right now it was looking like a suicide. "There's yer booze and pills. No signs of a struggle. Signs of depression. If the note's authentic and she filled the prescription, that's a slam dunk to me. Course, it's not up to me. The ME makes the final call. There'll have to be an autopsy and a tox report."

The police departed soon after the ambulance, Detective Schmidt telling me that he or Jablonowski would be in touch and to call them if I had any concerns or questions.

"You can't stay here, that's for sure," Philip said as the last squad car drove off and the neighbors returned to their homes with plenty to talk about the rest of the day. "Get what you need. You can stay at my place."

"I wouldn't be in your way?"

"Nah. We're friends, right?"

I thought about my parents dying while living in the house and Natalya dying there. I really hated the place now. It was time to move on, time to sell. But who would buy it? Who would want a death house?

23

The stairwell to Philip's duplex housed a road bike, a couple pairs of skis, and a tennis racquet. His apartment was furnished minimally and decorated haphazardly. The living room contained only a round table with mismatched chairs, a black leather couch and a coffee table covered with cycling magazines. Photographs of his travels competed with cycling posters for prominence on the walls. It definitely lacked a woman's touch.

Reading my mind, Philip explained, "The ex took most of the furniture. I haven't gotten around to buying new stuff. Just more crap to eventually put in storage."

The adrenalin that had been keeping me going since the morning evaporated. I was weak and unstable. My body swayed. Philip was instantly by my side.

"The bathroom's got a big clawfoot tub. How 'bout I run you a bath."

"Really?" I replied, touched by his attentiveness, "That sounds perfect."

Philip turned on the taps and poured in some Dead Sea salts. "Brought them back from Israel. Very relaxing, use them after long rides."

He handed me a towel and a fluffy robe, "If you need anything else, just whistle. And you know how to whistle, don't ya, Steve?" (*I loved that he quoted one of my favorite movies ever.*)

I put my lips together and blew. A dying chickadee. I'd never been able to whistle.

"Ok then, just scream."

After the bath, I could barely keep my eyes open. I'd just lay down for a bit on the futon in the office-guest room. The sun was low in the sky when I finally awoke. I checked myself out in a mirror. Definitely not hideous. The bath and nap had helped. I ran a brush through my hair a few times then wandered to the living room. Philip was doing exercises, shirtless, his toned back glistening.

I watched him do sit-ups on an incline bench that must have been hiding in a closet. His movements were confident and unhurried. He noticed me when he moved to the floor to do a set of push-ups.

"Hey, you're awake. Feeling better?"

"Much."

"Hungry?"

"Starved."

"Great. I made dinner, nothing fancy, just chicken stir fry." He easily knocked out fifty push-ups. "I'm going to jump in the shower, then we can eat."

We ate on the apartment's balcony to enjoy the last of the twilight. The air was calm and pleasantly humid, though the sky was clouding over. In the back yard of the house to the right, a couple was barbecuing. They gave Philip a hello wave. And to the left, some boys were playing basketball. A flash of lightning was quickly followed by a rumble of thunder. A light rain began to fall and we moved inside to the couch.

I stopped Philip when he tried to turn on a floor lamp, "Don't, I prefer the dark."

We sat in silence for several minutes. I spoke first, "You know, she kind of drove me nuts. I hadn't told her, but I was going to ask her to move out."

"She was a bit of an odd duck," Philip concurred.

"Do you think I'm a terrible person? I knew something was up and I never asked her about it."

"Of course not. Like Detective Schmidt said, we can't hold ourselves responsible for another person's state of mind."

"Even when you know something's wrong, but the person bugs you so much you don't want to know?"

"Well, did Natalya try to confide in you and you ignored her?"

"No, but I might have."

"I don't believe that, but we'll never know." Philip put his arms around me and pulled me to his chest. "Don't be too hard on yourself."

"But her mom. Natalya was so close to her mom and I don't know where to find her, to tell her what's happened. Or Mystery Man."

"The police'll handle all that from now on. They'll find him and her mother." He stroked my hair and kissed the top of my head. He put a hand under my chin, tilted my head up and kissed me softly on the lips. Was it just a friendly kiss or was it the beginning of something more? No second kiss followed the first, but his hand traced the length of my back.

"Hmm, no bra. Very naughty," he teased. He slid his hand under the tee shirt and moved it up and around my side to cup my right breast.

There was no mistaking this. With a sigh of delight, I rolled over onto my back. Philip leaned over and kissed me again, this time slipping his tongue into my mouth. The heat grew between my thighs. Taking my hand, he led me to his bedroom.

God, I wanted him, and in ways I'd never wanted a guy before. Sure, I wanted him lying naked on top of me, but I wanted him emotionally, intellectually, spiritually and every other good way there was to want another person. I liked him so much that even the hideous green Goodwill Naugahyde chair where he put my clothes after he removed them was adorable because he'd chosen it.

"I've wanted to see you like this since the first time I saw you. You are so beautiful," he said.

Those new feelings I was experiencing were kind of exciting, but mostly they were terrifying. I didn't know what to do with them, so I became a sexual dervish. I was kissing Philip, grabbing at his belt, the buttons of his shirt. I wanted to rip him out of his clothes. I was so wild that I bonked him in the mouth with my head.

"Hey, slow down," Philip said, rubbing his lip, "There'll be plenty of time for that."

"Really? You're not just saying that to let me down easy?"

He said he'd wanted to make love to me for weeks, but it changed everything. Not giving in had been hard. His relationship with his ex had gone at warp speed. They were getting married before they really knew anything about each other. He wanted us to know each other so when we made love it meant more than two people satisfying a carnal urge.

When he enveloped me in his strong arms, it was the first time I'd really let a man hold me. I'd never been a hugger. I was from a family of non-huggers. I'd never been comfortable with that kind of intimacy, but with Philip, I felt safe and calm. Despite all that had happened I felt happy.

"I'm so glad you called this morning. I never could've handled the cops and everything on my own. So thank you," I said. "By the way, why did you call?"

"I was going to give some lame reason about a final run through I was gonna do before the catalog launch tomorrow, but I was really just giving you the head's up that I was going to be in the shop, in case you wanted to wear some steel-toed boots to kick my ass for leaving you Friday night. I knew you were a little confused. I should have explained why I'd been holding back a lot earlier."

I was a fucking idiot. I'd slept with a complete asshole because I was drunk and stupid and feeling rejected, which I wasn't, which I would have realized if I possessed an ounce of intelligence, explanation or not. What would Philip think of me if he knew what I'd done. God, I was crap. Crap daughter. Crap friend. I'd failed my parents. I'd failed Natalya. And then, of course there was all the other crap: the aimlessness, the zero life achievements. I didn't deserve Philip. I didn't deserve to be happy.

I had to get out of there right away. I was out of the bed and into my clothes in seconds. You gotta take me home I said, rousing Philip out of a semi-slumber. It was after midnight he countered. He was right. Stay in bed, I told him, I'd call a cab.

"No, I'll take you if you really want to go, but I don't get it," he said, shaking himself awake when he realized I was serious.

"I don't deserve you."

"What are you talking about?"

"Just take me home. Believe me, you're better off without me."

He drove saying nothing. I stared out the window saying nothing. When he turned the Golf into the driveway, the dark, dead house glooming grey in the blackish night, I nearly cried out I don't want to go in there. I don't want to go into that tomb full of my dead parents' things, where Natalya's cold, naked body was just a few hours ago. I want to be back in your warm bed feeling your warm, sweet breath blowing on my ear. I want to be happy with you.

Philip said, "I can't pretend I understand what's going on with you. Maybe a little PTSD. You should talk to someone. First your parents, now Natalya. That's really rough. Just remember, I'm here for you whenever you need me."

God, why was he being so nice? Why wasn't he angry having to drive some wacko around in the middle of the night? I struggled to open the door, tears singeing my cheeks. Philip reached over and pulled up the lock. I spilled onto the pavement, not bothering to reclaim the flip-flop that fell off my foot, and ran into the house. Too scared to go upstairs, I slept on the den couch, like a monk's pallet. No soft cozy bed for me. I woke with a stiff neck and an aching heart. I found my shoe by the front door.

❧

All the evidence was pointing to suicide Detective Schmidt told me when he called. The pharmacist had i.d'd the photo of Natalya. The handwriting of the note matched a sample taken from her bedroom. Only her finger prints were on the gin bottle, and hers and the pharmacist's on the vial. No one at the book shop or Doc Holliday's had any ideas who Mystery Man was. The manager at Holliday's said Natalya was a good waitress, if a little flighty, but she wasn't real close with the other waitresses. "Too popular with the male staff and customers, if you catch my drift. A lot of jealousy. Same at the book shop. Seems she didn't confide in anyone."

Finding the next of kin was going to take a little time and could be tricky. Natalya'd told no one her mother's name. They hadn't found an address book anywhere in her room. In her purse there were no credit cards or a debit card, not even a checkbook. Only four-hundred dollars in cash and a Colorado State I.D.

The first three digits of her social security indicated she was born, or at least spent some of her childhood, in New Hampshire. The family, or Natalya herself, could have moved frequently.

The license gave her name as Natalya Lawless. The discrepancy in last names didn't mean much. Lots of divorced women went back to using their maiden names. Natalya'd just never gotten around to changing her i.d. Or possibly, Haven was her husband's name and she was still using it. Either way, a divorce fit with what I'd told him about a bad break up.

Schmidt said they'd try tracing her through her past employment and public records. Perhaps they'd luck out and Natalya'd ended her marriage in Colorado. They'd also check missing persons and wanted lists. (*I tried to imagine tiny Natalya with her schoolgirl voice as a badass bank robber waving a gun and shouting at people to get on the floor.*)

And what if they never found her family?

"Well, the morgue's had one body in the freezer for more than ten years."

No bank account. Two last names. A possible ex-husband. A nameless mother. Who was Natalya really? She was far more intriguing in death than I ever thought she was in life. The sad part of all the mystery she'd surrounded herself in was that she'd condemned her body to lay year after year on a metal tray with all the other unclaimed bodies, the Jane Does; the John Does; the vagrants; the children, parents, aunts and uncles whose families didn't know or didn't care they were dead. There'd be no family or friends to say a few loving words over her grave. I wouldn't have done that to my worst enemy. If the police didn't find her mom in the next few months, I'd pay to have Natalya buried, whether it was what she wanted or not.

24

Schmidt's and Philip's assurances that Natalya's suicide wasn't my fault didn't cease the hammer pounding in my conscience, every stroke telling me I should have done more. I needed to do something to get Natalya out of my head.

I toyed with going to work even though I'd been given another day off until I realized what that would mean: all the questions I'd be asked and couldn't answer; all the theories being tossed around that I'd have to listen to; seeing Philip.

Tackling the pile of mail on the dining room table was a task that required just the right amount of concentration. Daily I'd scoop the bills, the magazines whose subscriptions I never cancelled and that I never read and the catalogs from companies whose products I'd never buy off the floor where the mail slot dropped them and dump them on the table. There they'd sit until the day, once a month, that I sat down and went through everything.

My eyes immediately fell on a shoe box tied up with string and a manilla envelope that hadn't been there two days ago. The envelope was addressed to me in Natalya's hand.

I tore it open and found inside another envelope and a single sheet of paper.

Dear Hunter,

Thank you for letting me share your house and for being such a good friend to me when I needed one. I'm sorry for all the shit I am going to put you through. There's no reason to continue this joke of a life. I'm all alone. I have no one.

Would you please deliver the letters and the box for me. I don't want them to learn of my death from the police or receive a note from me in the mail. I know it's a lot to ask you to go across the country, but you already know how to get there.

Maybe it was fate that brought us together. Even though we've only known each other a short time, and we didn't always get along, I probably wasn't the easiest person to live with, I trust you and know you have a good heart.

xxNatalya

Relief. There were people out there to claim her and I knew where to find them.

I examined the first envelope. Luna and Sierra. The logical assumption was that one of them was her mother. But Natalya'd always talked about my mom this and my mom that so why had she suddenly given her mother a name? And was Luna her mother, or was Sierra? Either one could be a woman's name. And who was the other person? Natalya'd never mentioned her father so I'd assumed he'd disappeared from her life a long time ago. Her stepfather? Her mother's girlfriend?

The second letter was tucked under the string tied round the box. It was addressed to Giles. Was he her father? An ex-husband? An ex-boyfriend? A brother? Or yet another person she'd never told me about? Was he Mystery Man?

Chamisa, New Mexico was where I was being asked to go, a town that had been a part of my life for years. Natalya'd seen the photo of me and my parents there and had said nothing.

Reading the letters and opening the box would solve the mystery of Natalya, but that was a violation of privacy I could never commit. The idea of someone snooping through my belongings, reading letters I'd written and never sent nor thrown away, was akin to being stripped naked in front of a hundred strangers. And what if I damaged the envelopes trying to steam them open. Or the steam made the ink run. Or clumsy attempts to reseal the envelopes made it obvious they'd been opened. I imagined the offended looks on the recipients' faces when I handed them over.

I didn't need any time to decide if I would honor Natalya's request. She was giving me a chance to be the friend she believed me to be. Maybe by doing so, I'd learn the truth and silence the hammer. And as sad an errand as it was, it was also perfectly timed. I needed to get out of town. Milwaukee and I were a bad combination.

There was a dose of morbid nosiness to my decision as well. I saw nothing romantic in what Natalya'd done—I always thought Romeo and Juliet were silly— but I did want to find her Romeo, discover what kind of spell he'd cast that made Natalya so desperate that death was preferable to life without him. Would I come under his spell, too?

I called Schmidt, "I forgot to ask about Natalya's stuff. What do I do with it?"

He said the crime scene team had gotten everything they needed so he didn't see a problem with packing up her belongings.

"And I'm supposed to go out of town day after tomorrow. The trip's been planned for weeks. Can I still go?"

"I don't see a problem with that either. Just leave a number where you can be reached."

It was incredibly easy to lie to him. It might have been harder if I thought I was doing something wrong, but if he knew about the letters he might make me hand them over. Incurring the anger of a cop was worth the price of not failing Natalya again. I'd tell him once I'd delivered them.

"She really killed herself, huh? I never saw that coming," Stephanie said.

"Makes two of us."

I couldn't go in Natalya's room alone. Andy was working. Leslie had the girls. Phillip was no longer an option. So I called Stephanie. She was efficient and not easily freaked out. I didn't mention the letters because I was pretty sure that reading them would have presented her with no ethical dilemma, and she probably knew how to open and reseal them leaving no one the wiser.

"Why do you think she did it?" Stephanie asked.

"I don't know. She had a really bad fight with a guy the night before."

"Yeah, that's what that cop said. I didn't believe him. Our little Natalya with a man? Never," Stephanie said, a Vulcan eyebrow arched in mock disbelief.

"They think he might've been an ex-husband. She ever tell you why she left wherever it was she came from?"

"Seriously? I'm about the last person Natalya would've discussed her love life with. We weren't exactly close. Too much of a Hallmark card for me."

Neither Stephanie nor I wanted to linger in the room so we got down to the task at hand. There wasn't much to pack up, just some clothes, the coral and turquoise necklace Natalya'd always worn, the silver Indian bangles, and a few books. Examining the books—*The Dharma Bums*, *On the Road*, *Siddhartha*, *Steppenwolf*, *The Book of Folly*—the bindings stiff, the pages smooth, Stephanie exclaimed, "These books are new. I knew she hadn't read them the hundreds of times she claimed."

"Maybe she wore out other copies," I suggested.

"Then why when I quoted, 'What a horror it would have been if the world was real, because if the world was real, it would be immortal,' did she have no idea what I was talking about?"

"I have no idea what you're talking about."

"You would've, if you'd read *The Dharma Bums* that many times."

"Have you read *The Dharma Bums* that many times?"

"Yuck, no. I hate Kerouac, but I had to read him for a class last semester and liked that line."

25

Backpack loaded in the car, a brief, impersonal I-quit message left for Janine, and I was on my way the following day. It was a relief to watch the city diminish in my rearview mirror and with it all the scenes of misery of the last eight months. Philip was the one bright spot, and I wasn't going to think about him.

I got as far as Kansas City the first night. I'd wanted to make it to Topeka, the half way point, but I couldn't keep my eyes open. I was back on the road early the next morning, fortified by a cup of crappy coffee and a packet of Hostess powdered donuts.

The long, unvarying stretches of Kansas highways rippled under the intensity of the mid-September sun. Fields of wheat ready for harvesting swayed in the hot wind. Country music dominated the airwaves, barging in on other stations like party crashers. I turned the radio off.

Any second thoughts about my mission, a desire to throw the letters out the window and be done forever with Natalya, letting her keep her secrets, were overruled by the desire to spare her family the agony of uncertainty, of hoping she would one day walk through the door, and when she never did, not knowing if she were dead or alive, not knowing what had really happened to her.

Natalya's family and I were bound by loss. A child who'd lost her parents. Parents who'd lost their child. We were halves making a whole. Forgetting I knew nothing about the people I was driving over a thousand miles to meet, I fantasized we'd become an ad hoc family. And really that had to be why Natalya'd come into my life. Seriously, what were the chances that she'd be from the very town that my family had vacationed in.

With her parents, my slate as a daughter was clean. I could start anew, be the daughter I'd never been to my parents. It was the relationship Gale had wanted with me, but I felt no connection with her, not emotional, not intellectual. It would be one thing to have real parents you had nothing in common with, but why choose a mother you didn't like.

I envisioned Luna as a cooler, hipper version of my mother, possessing her kindness, generosity and sense of fun. Luna would love more than just Kerouac and Hesse, but opera and Jane Austen and Thomas Hardy, too. And she wouldn't be as annoying as Natalya, who was just bragging that she and her mother were so much alike.

And if Sierra were Natalya's father, he'd have Dad's dry humor and love of travel. I would listen to stories of his adventures as I had listened to Dad's pre-mom adventures. We'd drink whiskey and play backgammon together.

A second flight of fancy had me and Giles, who I hoped would turn out to be Natalya's brother, falling in love and getting married, making her family my true family.

❧

I drove north from Santa Fe to Chamisa because we'd always come that way, like it was a pilgrimage route. The view that greeted me took my breath away. The sky was the same rich blue it had always been with heavy clouds in the distance tinged pink and orange. Looking to the west, I saw the land in muted tones of green, grey and brown, severed by the ragged, gaping chasm of the Rio Grande gorge. To the east were the Sangre de Cristo Mountains, so named by the Conquistadors because the rising sun painted them blood red. I stopped the car by the side of the road and stepped out into air redolent of camphor-scented sagebrush and the dirty-sock-smelling, ocher-bloomed chamisa that gave the town its name. It was warm and dry with hints of the chill the setting of the sun would bring.

I was twelve the first time I came to Chamisa. Wanting to give me an Old West experience, my parents booked us on the Southwest Chief that left Chicago in the late afternoon. Sleepers were more expensive than airline tickets, so we were going to spend the day's journey in coach seats. After a dinner of dry chicken, canned green beans and rehydrated mashed potatoes, not staring at the unaccountable Amish family, I fidgeted in my seat trying to find that elusive position most conducive to sleep. Every time I managed to drift off, the train pulled into a station and the conductors walked the aisles intoning the name of that dot on the map.

The sun, when it finally rose, illumined flat, dull country. The only excitement was our arrival in Trinidad, Colorado, rumored to be the Sex Change Capital of the World. We examined disembarking passengers for likely candidates.

In the afternoon, we were deposited in Lamy, New Mexico, a forlorn depot out of a spaghetti western. We spent a couple days in Santa Fe and then, in a rented car, traveled north to Chamisa, known for its quaint charm, its ski resort, its artist colony, and its Indian pueblo.

I hated it immediately. The landscape was brown. Everything was made of dirt, dirt buildings, dirt streets, even the residents looked dirty. And it was cold. I didn't care that the sun was shining or that the sky was an unblemished blue. I'd wanted to escape winter for Christmas break, go to the beach, like Andy, whose parents were taking him to Acapulco.

We went back that summer. The sky was the same shade of blue. It was hot, and the brown of the land was brushed with green. And I still hated it. My parents, however, fell even more in love. They bought a casita for after Dad's retirement. A good investment Dad said. Holiday rentals brought in a small but steady income.

Until I graduated from college, I spent every Christmas in Chamisa and was hauled out there every summer. The small town bored me. There was nothing to do. I didn't know anyone my age. I didn't enjoy skiing. I didn't like hiking in the mountains. The lone movie theater showed films I'd already seen and its floor was sticky with the residue of hundreds of spilled soft drinks.

The summer I was seventeen I was ripe for rebellion. Hannah invited a bunch of us for a long weekend at her family's cabin on a lake in northern Wisconsin. I'd miss it if I went to New Mexico. There would be swimming, water skiing, cookouts and drinking games, but, of course, no mention was made of alcohol when I demanded I be

232

allowed to stay home. I was too old to be forced to do something I hated and old enough to take care of myself.

The weekend at the lake was a blast, but the rest of the time alone in the house was horrible. I was lonesome. The house was spooky at night. I missed my parents, especially at meal times. I'd never earned a Girl Scout merit badge in cooking and MA was too pretentious to have anything like Home Ec. I survived on cereal and frozen pizzas. Because I'd been vehement about my maturity and ability to go it alone, I was too proud to tell my parents how miserable I'd been. Now at thirty, I wished, even more than having told them the truth, that I'd gone with them to New Mexico. What was two weeks out of my summer if it had made my parents happy.

It had been more than four years since my last visit and as I drove into town, I noted the changes taking place. The main road, which had once been flanked by open fields, was developing fast with motels, two big chain super-markets, a Walmart, and a multiplex cinema. In town, formerly narrow, twisting streets had been straightened and paved.

The small plaza remained as it had been with its mix of art galleries and cheap souvenir shops. The rusticity, organic lines, flat roofs, exposed *vigas* and turquoise blue window and door frames of the pueblo-influenced architecture now reminded me of the towns and villages I'd loved in South America. For the first time I saw the beauty of Chamisa that my parents had seen.

I pushed the cart up and down the crowded aisles of Safeway dumping in eggs, coffee, butter, bacon and a few other essentials. My fellow shoppers were a motley bunch: short, old hispanic women, their hair tightly permed. Their younger selves with bangs teased and shellacked upright looking like the *latilla* fences so common to the area, a shock of blue shadow over each eye, lips traced with maroon liner. Young anglo couples, the guys dressed in dingy tee shirts and jeans so holey they defied definition as clothing, the girls in long, full Indian print skirts, both with matted, dreadlocked hair. Middle-aged Texans in pressed denim, cowboy hats and Lone Star State belt buckles, accompanied by immaculately coiffured wives, diamonds twinkling on their ears, wrists and fingers. Broad-bodied and broad-faced Indians from the nearby pueblo, their skin coffee with cream.

Ahead of me in the checkout lane, a guy, in a once-white tank top and jean shorts was counting the coins from his pocket, seeing if he had enough for a pack of Camels. His body pitched back and forth and he steadied himself on the counter. His stash of quarters, nickels and dimes came out a dollar short.

"Can I pay with a credit card?" he asked the young, blonde and imperturbable clerk.

"Sure," she replied with a smile she applied along with her lipgloss.

When the guy tottered off after leaning in for a rebuffed kiss, the girl's smile slipped. "If I have to wait on one more drunk guy. He's the fourth and I've only been here an hour," she sighed.

A mile north of the plaza, I turned onto a road canopied by enormous cottonwood trees, their golden orange leaves glimmering in the last rays of sunlight. I turned again onto a driveway that immediately crossed a small river via a narrow wooden bridge. The small adobe house was surrounded by a low wall with a turquoise blue gate in the center. I cursed when I saw the courtyard. Weeds had taken over the garden and the crab apple tree was dying. The gardener I was paying monthly to maintain the place was a thief.

The house was hot and musty. A fine layer of gritty dust covered all the surfaces. As I dragged my feet about what to do with the houses I'd inherited, the casita had sat vacant of renters. I opened windows in the living room, kitchen and master bedroom letting in the cool evening breeze. I'd call the rental agency tomorrow to get someone over to clean the place. I didn't bother to put away the food, just shoved the bag into the fridge, or to unpack my bag. I fell into bed fully clothed.

❧

I stared at the objects of my mission as I ate bacon and fried eggs. The journey to New Mexico had been so filled with thoughts of new family that the contents of the letters and shoe box, out of sight, were never contemplated. Now I tried to imagine their mood. Natalya had never discussed her family, and despite all her gushing about her mother, her mother had never called or written. Her father was a big question mark. He'd never even been mentioned. Was she asking for her parents' forgiveness or telling them it was all their fault? It was then that I was hit full force by the burden of my task. I'd have to meet them face to face,

235

possibly stay as the letters were read, watching their faces crumble with grief, or worse, relief, joy, or indifference. I didn't see how I could just slip the letters under the doors and run away. Natalya'd wanted them delivered by hand to the recipients. When I went out later, the letters were left behind.

With no idea where to go or what to do, I headed to Mo' Joe, a tiny coffee shop on the corner of the plaza I'd noticed yesterday. Overwhelmed by the choices and sizes on the wall-mounted menu board, I let several more decisive patrons go ahead before I made up my mind.

I examined the posters taped to the windows as I waited for my *Americano*. An art exhibition opening on Friday. A play that's run had ended the day before. The Bohemians at Old Martinez Hall. And at the Kiva Bar! The Giles Lawless Band! Tonight! 8:00!

26

What was a guy as charismatic, as confident and as beautiful as Giles Lawless doing in a northern New Mexico backwater? He should've been playing to sell-out crowds in arenas. Teenage girls should've been plastering his picture on their bedroom walls and dreaming he'd spot them in a concert crowd and send a burly roadie to bring them backstage, like I had about David Bowie when I was sixteen. Actually like I was doing at that moment. And from the size of the mostly female crowd, I wasn't the only one.

Giles's complexion was fair and smooth, his lips full and red, his eyes a piercing blue, all made more dramatic by the intense blackness of his hair, which had to have come from a dye bottle. The rolled-up sleeves of his blue cotton shirt exposed lean forearms, the thinnest skin stretched over tensile muscle, nearly hairless, that ended in hands with every bone and vein discernible. I memorized him in ten minutes.

The Kiva Bar was located in the lobby of The Chamisa Inn, once the home of a local legend, a patroness of the arts who'd lured many East Coast artists to the town with promises of money and easy access to her bed. While the band played guests checked in, diners made their way to the quieter restaurant and the wait staff weaved through the tables to deliver Margaritas, a house specialty, and towering plates of nachos. A waitress flitted by once, twice, three times always smiling coyly at Giles, before I caught her attention. I shouted my order into her ear then waited a lifetime for her to return with my beer.

It was ridiculous, the fantasizing, or was it? Thinking Bowie was going to single me out in an audience of thousands was ridiculous. But Giles wasn't an out-of-reach rock god. He and I had a tangible and intimate connection. Anything could happen when we met. Maybe that was what Natalya wanted. Maybe that was why she asked me to deliver the letters. His age had eliminated the possibility that he was Natalya's father so I crossed my fingers that he was Natalya's brother, not her ex-husband. Since Natalya's death, I'd been laying off the heavy criticism, but the idea of sleeping with a guy she'd slept with was still a little gross.

I had to stop staring. I looked like a love-struck owl. I contemplated going home, except that seemed extreme so I gave up my seat to a grateful twenty-year-old girl with gapped teeth and moved to the highly polished oak bar located opposite the stage where I was less conspicuous.

I ordered a second drink, this time moving on to something harder. Sipping the Maker's Mark, I wondered again why I was staying. I wasn't going to give Giles the letter. It was on the kitchen table. Besides a bar wasn't the appropriate setting for its delivery. I threw back what was left in the glass and put on my sweater, unaware the music had stopped. A voice said, "Leaving already. Hope it's not 'cause of the band."

Oh crap. Giles Lawless, a glass of water in his hand, his face glistening with perspiration, was standing next to me. "I've never seen you at one of our shows before."

Okay, Hunter, you're thirty years old, keep it together. Don't say anything dumb. "You know every one of your fans?"

"No, but I notice the pretty ones."

(*He thinks I'm pretty!*) "Ah, aren't you a smooth talker. Does it work for you?"

"I'd say I'm batting around three-fifty."

Confident on and off the stage. And just as beautiful up close.

Giles cast a critical eye at my hair. "Is that some grey I see?"

(*What?*) "I think your average just dropped a few points."

"Hey, take it easy. Just means you're older than you look."

"It must be the light in here."

"No, no, it's cool. I dig older women. And I really dig grey hair."

"Just out of curiosity, how much older do you like us?"

What was I doing? I couldn't flirt with Giles. Coming here was a mistake. Now he'd seen me, spoken to me, and I was going to show up at his house having to explain myself. It was absurd to say I hadn't known who he was. But then, it wasn't odd to want to see, in advance, someone to whom I had such grievous news to impart. No, distance had to be maintained until the letter and box were delivered. "I gotta go," I said, making for the door, leaving behind a bewildered Giles.

My room but not my room. Smaller. The colors were wrong. Curtains were missing. Nightgown (*Nightgown? I hadn't worn one of those since I was thirteen*). Philip caressing my cheek. Kissing. Intense happiness. Then he was pushing me away, morphing into Giles, eyes full of venom. Hissing that I'd no right to happiness. You let Natalya die. She's dead because of you. I didn't know. I didn't know. She wanted to be left alone. And your parents? Did they want to be alone?

I awoke with a start, gasping, confused by my surroundings. It was still dark and the absolute quiet was disconcerting. No glare of streetlights streaming in the windows. No low rumble of traffic. My eyes adjusted. I recognized the bedroom of the casita.

I tried to gather the threads of the dream. The harder I tried, the more elusive they became until all that remained was a whisper of self-loathing. I eventually fell back into dreamless sleep and awakened again when the sun was cresting the mountains.

People. I needed to be around people. I threw on some clothes and drove to Mo' Joe. It was busy, as I hoped it would be. The woman ahead of me ordered a Borgia. What was that? I scanned the menu board. Espresso, hot chocolate, whipped cream, orange. Sounded good. I ordered the same.

"Morning Giles," the barista called out, "You guys nailed it last night."

'That we did, that we did." Giles replied.

Cocky first thing in the morning, and wrecking my plans. I attempted to retrieve my coffee and exit the cafe unseen.

Giles blocked my path, "Hey, it's the dasher. Where're you dashing off to this morning?"

"Got to be somewhere at nine. Bye."

As I was going out the door, I heard him ask the barista if she knew me.

"Never seen her before."

I almost ran into Giles again the next day at the supermarket. He was coming up the ice cream aisle I was about to turn down. I hastily retreated to the safety of the feminine hygiene section. The town was too small. I couldn't keep trying to avoid him. I had to deliver the letter.

Back at the house, I consulted a map of the town in the phone book. Torres Road was located off the main road that headed east from the plaza. I grabbed the letter and the shoebox and jumped in the car.

An old Toyota Land Cruiser and a beat-up VW bus missing a front wheel were parked in front of a small adobe house with a sagging roof. I knocked. Peering through the diamond-shaped window in the door, I saw Giles emerge from a room at the back of the house, softly shutting its door. His expression was one of pleasant surprise when he found me on his doorstep. "I knew you wouldn't be able to resist me for long, but how'd you know where I live?"

I tried to set a serious tone, "I actually came to Chamisa to see you."

"Fuck, you're not some crazed fan, are you?"

"You're not quite Mick Jagger yet. It's about your ex-wife."

"You got the wrong guy. I've never been married."

"Then who's Natalya?"

Now he was wary, "She's my sister. What about her?"

"Can I come in?"

He shot a quick look over his shoulder at the room he'd just left, "It's not a good time. Can I meet you somewhere in an hour or so?"

Did he have a girl in there? I gave him the address and phone number of the casita. It was the only place I could think of that was private enough.

I paced the room, my eyes frequently coming to rest on the letters and the shoebox. I picked up the letter addressed to Luna and Sierra and hid it away in the bedroom. How should I give Giles the letter. Just hand it to him and let the letter explain everything? Or tell him Natalya was dead first? I hadn't made a decision when he knocked on the door.

"Who the hell are you?" Giles demanded once inside the house. He wasn't angry but confused and a bit frightened. The preceding hour had given his mind time to create many possible scenarios for my being in Chamisa.

I picked up the envelope and the shoebox and handed them to him saying only I was asked to give him these.

Giles instantly recognized the handwriting, "Is Natalya okay?"

"I think you better read it."

He sat down on the couch and opened the envelope slowly, dreading the news it bore. I watched as he read, seeing his face slide from trepidation to anguish. And when he read the last line, he let out a howl of pain that tore into my heart. And then Giles was gone. I heard gravel spray as his Land Cruiser tore out of the drive.

27

I was curled up on the couch watching *From Russia With Love*, my Dad's and my favorite James Bond film, on video. Dad thought everybody loved James Bond. The casita had the complete set of the Sean Connery films for guests to watch, minus *Never Say Never Again*, because among the Connery purists like the Graysons, a remake of *Thunderball* didn't count.

The phone rang. A wrong number for sure. I picked up anyway.

"It's Giles. Can I come over? I really don't want to be alone tonight."

The first night I was back in Milwaukee the house was so still and I'd felt so alone in it, my only relief from the flood of memories a little blue pill, the same blue pills Natalya would use to end her life. No one should be alone on the first night.

I turned off the movie, brushed away the slimy film the almost entire pint of mint chocolate chip ice cream had deposited on my teeth and tongue, and dug through my clothes for something to wear. Nothing was right. Shit, I wasn't getting ready for a date. I stayed in my tee shirt and sweat pants.

The knock was so faint that at first I didn't hear it.

"Sleep, I just want to sleep. Is that ok?" he asked when I opened the door.

I drank in the silhouette of his thin, taut arms, of his strong legs encased in the denim of his well-worn jeans. Even with red-rimmed eyes he looked like he'd stepped out of a Calvin Klein ad. It wasn't exactly going to be penance sharing a bed with Giles Lawless.

I stood at the edge of the bed. Clothes on or off? On, definitely on. I climbed under the covers. I heard him removing his jeans then felt the softness of his shirt as he found my body under the covers.

"Will you hold me?" he asked, his voice shaky.

I awkwardly put my arms around him. His body began to shudder. He was crying. Giles's suffering unleashed my own desolation. I told him I knew what he was going through. My parents' deaths were lacerations on my soul that would never heal. I cried for them like I hadn't cried in months. Then, not knowing how, Giles and I were kissing and pulling at each other's clothes. It seemed natural that two people in torment should want to feel something else.

Giles tore off my shirt and bit my nipples so hard I flinched. But I didn't push him away, I wanted to be handled roughly. Punishment for my sins. I yanked his head back up by the hair and thrust my tongue into his mouth. I bit his tongue just hard enough for him, too, to flinch.

He gave me a queer smile, "Are you a bad girl?"

"The worst," I replied.

"Bad girls have to be fucked hard."

He tore off my sweatpants and told me to get on my hands and knees. He pinched and slapped my ass before driving his cock deep inside me, sending a jagged spasm of pain through my knees. That I could be in real trouble flashed through my mind. Being Natalya's brother didn't make him safe, but when Giles realized what he'd done, he backed off.

"How?" he asked softly when I returned from cleaning up.

"Valium and gin."

"Do Luna and Sierra know?"

"You haven't told them?"

He shook his head.

"Well, I have a letter for them, too." I put my arms around him (*It was easier now that he'd been inside me*).

If they were brother and sister, I asked, why was Natalya using the name Haven. Giles sighed, "Some other time. I'm tired. I just want to go to bed"

❧

Giles dragged me to Chamisa Diner, a place popular for breakfast with everyone in town.

"Are you sure you want to be in such a crowd?" I asked.

"I always meet my buds here on Fridays."

The three friends gave looks of surprise and concern as we joined them in the booth.

"Nathan told us about Natalya. A real bummer," said a guy with a wispy beard wearing a Rasta tam bulging with trapped dreadlocks.

"Yeah, I'm real sorry. That sucks, man," added a guy whom I recognized as the bass player in the band.

"Have you told Kaela?" asked the third, a young woman with large breasts, thick red hair and a perma-pout mouth.

The other two looked at Giles, who shook his head, "No, gotta figure out how."

"Who's she?" the redhead, who'd been eyeing me warily, asked Giles.

"Natalya lived with her in Milwaukee. She found her. Hey, can we talk about something else?"

"Creepy, man," mumbled the bass player whose name was Jason.

"What's she doing here?" It was the redhead again.

"Jeez, ease up, Magpie. It's none of your fucking business," said Nova, the guy in the tam.

"Don't call me that. My name's Maggie."

Nova informed me that she was called Magpie because she could be a total fucking pest.

Giles turned angrily to Maggie, "Natalya asked her to bring me something, okay? Are you done with your questions?"

"Creepy, man," said Jason.

"You know what," Giles said to me, "maybe this was a bad idea. Let's go."

"Oh, dude. Don't go. Magpie'll shut up. Stay," said Nova.

"We gonna cancel the gig in Santa Fe tomorrow?" asked Jason.

Giles shook his head emphatically, "No, we're playing."

"You sure?"

"Yeah, I'm fucking sure."

Everyone shut up after that. Hardly a word was spoken during the rest of the meal. Later, at the car, I advised Giles to go easy on his friends. It was hard to know what to say. When my parents died, I stopped talking to people. I couldn't bear to watch them squirm and fidget.

"Hey," he said, making me think he hadn't been listening, "You wanna take that letter to Luna and Sierra now? Might be easier for you if I'm there."

❧

The portal of Sierra and Luna Lawless' house was strung with Tibetan prayer flags. A wooden post with the word LOVE carved into it, the letters painted red, was stuck in the lawn. A frayed, faded rainbow flag with a peace sign in the middle hung limply from a flagpole.

Giles's firm rap on the door set a dog barking and scratching on the other side. A gruff female voice admonished it to settle down. The dog paid no heed. A hand thwacked the dog's nose, a whimper followed.

"How many times do I have to tell you not to hit the dog," Giles scolded the woman she when opened the door.

"What do you want?" she snapped, as if Giles were a Jehovah's Witness or a Mormon missionary or some other unwanted caller.

"You'll have to excuse Luna," Giles said to me, "To her, politeness is just bourgeois hypocrisy."

The squat woman, a red and white striped *huipil* covering her pendulous, braless breasts, black hair streaked heavily

249

with grey falling to her elbows was Luna? She was the great beauty Natalya had raved about? The woman so like Natalya in looks and sentiments they could have been twins? Natalya and Luna looked as much alike as I looked like Audrey Hepburn, which was not at all.

"Hey Che. How's my boy? The big meanie didn't hurt you, did she?" Giles affectionately mussed the ears of the small, muddy brown dog of indeterminate breed. "Is Sierra here, too? You both need to be here."

"Yeah, he's here. Who's this?" she asked with blatant suspicion. I was scoring poorly with the women of Chamisa.

"You'll find out soon enough." He brushed by his mother and into the house, dragging me along with him.

The living room was furnished with heavy, distressed Mexican furniture. The walls were adorned with Bolivian mantas, Mexican carnival masks, Tibetan mandalas and a Che Guevara poster, the iconic image of him in the beret with a scraggly beard. Fantastical birds, carved from wood and painted bright colors, were arranged in small clusters on tables and bookcases. A large metal ashtray on an end table was full of butts. Cardboard file boxes labeled PETITIONS, CHARTER SCHOOL, HEART HOUSE were stacked on a blue-washed pine dining table and on the floor around it. Also on the table were an old Corona typewriter, a coffee mug and another, nearly full ash tray. The stink of cigarettes permeated the walls, the carpets, the cushions.

"Health care reform," said Luna, moving a file box off the couch so she could sit down. She'd need it if all those butts were hers.

"Politics has always come first for my parents, even before their children," Giles said with thinly disguised scorn.

"Giles, my son, the ends you serve that are selfish will take you no further than yourself, but the ends you serve that are for all, in common, will take you into eternity," said a man with a deep baritone and the vocal style of a well-practiced orator, who entered the room, a steaming mug of tea in his hand.

Sierra immediately dropped Giles down to the second most gorgeous man I'd ever seen. He was tall and lean like his son, with the same penetrating blue eyes and full mouth. His dark hair, was worn short around the ears and back, a bit longer on top. Running my fingers through it, as I immediately fantasized doing, would be like running them through threads of thick silk, cool and smooth. The lines evident at the corners of his eyes and mouth gave him an aura of wisdom and experience, as though applied by an artist for that affect. After my eyes first beheld that god-like being, I turned away for fear of staring, mouth agape. The love-struck owl again.

Sierra spied me hiding behind his son. His eyes lit up. "I wish I could claim those words as my own, but Marcus Garvey said them," he said, flashing a high wattage, movie star smile and eyeing me with little more finesse than a wolf eyeing a juicy spring lamb. "And they epitomize the difference between Luna's and my approach to life and our son's." A little unnerved by such obvious attention, I was also flattered that he found me attractive, alluring. Luna's eyes narrowed to a death ray stare.

 Giles, ignoring his father, cut straight to the chase, "She's got something for you from Natalya."

251

Sierra's and Luna's countenances changed at the mention of their daughter. Sierra became curious while Luna was harder to read. Fear, possibly?

"Natalya asked me to deliver this to you," I said holding out the envelope, unsure of which to give it to, but looking right at Sierra.

Luna impatiently seized it from my hands, "What does she want? Money?"

"I don't know what it says," I replied, shocked by her hostility.

"When did she ever ask you for anything?" Giles snapped and walked over to a picture window, Che trailing him. He ran a hand through his hair as he looked out onto a large garden of browning bean, tomato and pea plants.

"Open it," Sierra encouraged Luna. She slit the envelope with her finger and removed the two sheets of paper it contained. She glanced at both and handed one page to Sierra saying, "This one's for you."

Sierra read only a few lines before groping for a chair, his tanned face paling. Luna read standing, motionless, emotionless. Then she strode out of the room. A door closed.

I turned to the window. Giles and the dog were gone.

Sierra, voice cracking, "When did this happen?"

"A little more than a week ago. I'm really sorry."

"How tragic, but then she was so like her mother."

I was definitely missing something. Natalya'd been all blue-birds and rainbows. The woman I'd just met was about as cuddly as a wart hog, and kind of looked like one, too.

"For parents to lose..." I began a sentence I didn't know how to finish so I left the words hanging.

Sierra balled his hand into a fist, crumpling the letter it held. Realizing what he'd done, he gasped and smoothed the paper out on his knee, "She was an angel, too fragile and lovely for this world. Where is she?"

"In Milwaukee, waiting for someone to claim her. Here's who to contact," I handed him Detective Schmidt's business card.

He fingered the card absently then dropped it on a table and said, "C'mon, I'll take you back to your hotel."

"But Giles brought me..."

"He's gone. Took off a few minutes ago. Always running when the going gets tough."

I was skeptical until I opened the front door and saw the Land Cruiser was gone. Under other circumstances I'd have been furious, but how could I blame Giles for giving precedence to his emotions. I hated burdening Sierra, who was also suffering, with having to take a stranger home.

"Please, I can walk. It's not too far."

"Don't be ridiculous," Sierra said, "You came all the way to New Mexico, the least I can do is give you a lift. Where're you staying?"

"My parents have a house here," I said as we got into his truck.

"Who're your parents? Maybe I know them."

"I doubt it. They only used to come at Christmas and for a month in the summer."

"Used to? Not anymore?"

"They died in January. So you see, we have something in common. And I have a history with Chamisa. I think it's why Natalya gave me the letters. This is it," I said indicating he should turn right into the drive.

"Well, blow me over, this is Walker Reedy's old place. Man, we had some wild parties here back in the day."

Sierra got out of the truck and opened the door for me. Placing his hands on my shoulders and squeezing them gently, he looked me right in the eyes, "Thank you so much for bringing us the letters. You must have cared a lot for our girl."

Unable to bear the nearness of his face, too handsome and too full of gratitude I didn't deserve, I looked at the ground, "I hardly knew her."

"That's makes what you've done even more special. You have a beautiful soul," He lifted my chin. I thought he was going to kiss me on the mouth, but his lips moved up to my forehead at the last minute. "You've lost your parents. I've lost a child. We're like halves of a broken heart. Maybe we can help make each other whole again."

Zoom! My imagination was off and running. Sierra'd articulated my thoughts almost to the word, and with sincerity. That couldn't be a coincidence. It had to mean something big. Maybe Sierra wasn't meant to be my surrogate father. Maybe he was meant to be my husband. He was what, maybe fifty-two or -three. A twenty-two-year difference wasn't outrageous. There were plenty of couples with bigger age gaps than that who had very happy marriages. And Sierra didn't look that old. His already being married wasn't a big stumbling block. Men left their wives all the time. He couldn't really be happy with a woman like Luna. Giles was more of a problem than Luna. I shouldn't have slept with him. But maybe in the future Sierra and I'd make it part of our story: Tragedy brought us together, then I got a little confused about which Lawless was meant for me. Sierra had to set me straight on that one.

28

The road followed the twisting course of the muddy, shallow Rio Grande River as it slithered south towards Mexico. The leaves of the giant cottonwoods flanking the shore shimmered like golden sapphires. An old wooden bridge sagged so low it almost touched the water. Only sheer determination kept it from dropping completely into the river. The sloping walls of the canyon were strewn with rocks that looked ready at any moment to cascade onto unsuspecting cars. Giles told me that once a three-hundred-ton boulder moving at seventy miles an hour put a deep crater in the road before landing in the river.

We were on the way to his band's gig in Santa Fe. Giles had turned up at the casita that morning full of apologies. There were too many memories of Natalya in the house. He had to get out.

He asked me to come with him. I understood what he was going through and he wasn't sure he could survive the night without me. His bandmates had urged him to cancel, but he knew they needed the money. Besides, when he was playing he only thought about the music.

It was okay to go with him I told myself, as a friend. No more sleeping together. We'd only done it once and it was kind of like drunk sex. It wouldn't have happened if we'd been emotionally sober. I could tell Giles it had been a mistake and he'd agree. No harm done. And Sierra was adult enough to accept that stuff like that happens.

Giles entertained me with a flow of stories of his and Natalya's crazy upbringing as the children of political activist parents who dragged them all over the country to rallies, marches, music festivals, anywhere they could carry around placards or hand out flyers. For his tenth birthday, when what he'd wanted was a G.I. Joe and a birthday party, he was melting in the heat at a No Nukes rally in D.C. He didn't even get to go to the Air and Space Museum to see the Apollo Lunar Module.

He confessed his real name wasn't Giles. It was Cloud. "Who the fuck names their kid Cloud? The dogs were named after political heroes. There was Jack then Bobby, named after the Kennedys. Now Che Guevara. I was named after the weather. Natalya's was worse. Sunflower Dewdrop. Luna and Sierra got to choose their names, they're really Arlene and Larry. So when we were in our teens we chose new names. Wouldn't answer to anything else."

He couldn't remember why he'd chosen Giles. He just liked the name. Later he found out about Giles Corey who was accused of being a warlock in Salem and refused to plead guilty. He was pressed to death. That was pretty rad Giles thought. Natalya's name came from the Van Morrison song 'Natalia'. "You know it?" He sang a few bars. "Luna has all his records."

"Sorry, my parents were squares. I grew up hearing show tunes and symphonies. I can sing you something from

Oklahoma, if you want. Went from there straight into David Bowie, The Ramones, X. Kinda missed the whole Van Morrison thing."

"'Natalia' was the one song Luna hated. Used to skip it when she played *Wavelength*. I think that's why Natalya picked it. Spelled it with a 'y' though. Thought it looked more foreign."

Giles was in a relaxed and sharing mood. Maybe I could ask him my questions now. With cautious steps, I entered the territory of Natalya's bad relationship. Giles fixed his eyes straight ahead. Yeah, he knew the guy, he said. A real asshole who didn't deserve her, but for some reason she was crazy about him.

Could he have been the one with her the night before she died?

"Who knows. Maybe. He was always jerking her along. It was pretty fucked up. Does it matter now?"

"No, I guess not, but I kind of think he should know."

"I'll tell him."

He didn't say a word for a long time then announced he was thinking of changing the name of his band to Queen Victoria's Secret. "It seems so cheesy to have it named after me."

The rest of the band were already at the venue setting up when we arrived. Giles introduced me to Vanessa, the percussionist, and Nathan, the drummer. Jason, the bass player, I'd met already.

El Chiquitito lived up to its name. It was tiny, with a tiny stage at one end, a tiny bar along another wall and a dozen tiny tables. Even the owner was tiny, but he packed in the people and probably violated a few fire codes. Maggie was among the crowd and not pleased to see me. She was the only person I knew in the audience, but the message came in loud and clear that I wouldn't be welcome to hang with her. At one point, finding ourselves next to each other at the bar, Maggie sneered, "A little obvious don't you think. Coming all the way to Santa Fe to see his band. I know Giles and I don't think you're his type."

"Strange that he asked me to come with him then," I mused aloud.

Maggie permitted only a flicker of despair to cross her face before turning on her heels, whipping her hair, and marching away.

"There's a saying in Chamisa. No one ever breaks up, you just lose your place in line," Vanessa, a no-nonsense, straight shooter, informed me during a break. "Magpie dated Giles for like ten minutes and she's been waiting ever since for him to come back to her, but it's never going to happen. I've known Giles forever and he doesn't do reruns. And just a heads up, he isn't in for the long term, either."

No, no, I was just interested in being his friend I assured her.

"Wise move."

The band played until midnight. I was ready to leave at ten. Giles's plea that he needed me there didn't extend to actually wanting to talk to me. During the breaks, he preferred to stand alone at the end of the bar knocking back shots of tequila. We did talk once—an overstatement, I commented on the music, the crowd. He grunted monosyllabic replies. Maybe he was thinking about Natalya. Maybe he'd realized he didn't want me around after all. Maybe he was drunk. He'd just downed his fourth shot. Don't worry, he said. He could handle his booze and besides he sweated it all out playing.

Giles finally announced the band's last song. It was about love gone wrong written by his sister. She had real talent and could have had a brilliant career if fate hadn't had a different plan. "She died a few days ago. *Vaya con Dios*, Natalya. This one's for you."

It was a haunting ballad made more poignant by Natalya's death and the undisguised misery in Giles's voice. Vanessa was crying by the end and unable to sing harmony on the final chorus. The entire audience was brought down.

"Shit!" Giles shouted. "We can't let you go home sad." And after a moment's consultation with his bandmates, the Giles Lawless Band ended the night with a rousing merengue-inspired tune that got everyone dancing again and stomping the floor for more.

"Sorry folks," said the owner of the club, "It's already past twelve. Hasta la bye bye."

❧

Two more shots of tequila from a bottle stashed in the back of the Land Cruiser while he helped load the van and Giles was really in no shape to drive back to Chamisa. He protested he was fine. "I've driven worse than this," he

261

said. He'd already dropped an amp and fallen down the steps leading from El Chiquitito to its tiny parking lot.

Visions of my parents' accident, of the smashed car holding their dead bodies, of Giles driving too fast, like my dad, up that curving road, of us plunging into the river made me sick. I begged Giles to give me the keys. Nathan told him not to be such a dick and give me the keys. Jason told him he was way too drunk to drive.

"Jesus Christ, back off. I said I'm fine."

"Please Giles, give me the keys," I said, holding out my had to receive them. "I understand why you're drinking, but..."

"Like hell you do," he cried knocking away my hand so forcefully that I lost my balance and fell to the pavement. "Oh fuck, I'm sorry." He tripped over his own feet trying to help me up.

Vanessa wanted to know why we didn't crash at Daniel's place like the rest of them. Daniel, I assumed, was the big dude—shaved head, goatee, the tail of a tattoo rattle snake peeking out from the cuff of his shirt—who was leaning against the van watching Giles's drunken antics with a satisfied smile.

"Got stuff to do. Gotta pick up..." Giles's mouth hung open. He'd forgotten what he was going to say.

"When? At three in the morning? Drive up early tomorrow. Tell him it's okay, Daniel," Vanessa said in a stern mother voice, one she must have used often in a band of boys.

"I wouldn't stay with that asshole if you paid me," Giles declared, pointing an accusing finger in Daniel's general direction.

"Yeah, well I'd have to fumigate the place if you did."

"You are a fucking dickhead," Giles shouted and charged at Daniel, which was stupid as Daniel had fifty pounds of muscle on him, was stone cold sober and looked like he might beat people up for fun.

"Oh man, you so have this coming," Daniel said. His fist connected with Giles's face, knocking him to his knees. Giles stood up slowly, his eyes unfocused, blood dripping from a small jagged cut on his cheek thanks to Daniel's skull ring. He took a shaky step towards Daniel.

"You come any closer and you're going down again," Daniel warned, ready to throw another punch.

"My god, can you two grow up already. For Natalya's sake can't you two let it go for one night?" Vanessa snapped, and to Nathan and Jason, who stood watching mouths agape, she commanded, "Don't just stand there, do something."

Jason, who looked like killing a fly would be a traumatic experience, pleaded, "C'mon dudes, Vanessa's right, think of Natalya."

Nathan, however, sprang into action, coming up behind Giles, grabbing his right arm and pulling it behind his back. "Sorry bro, but I gotta do this." Giles writhed around trying to free himself, but Nathan's grip was too strong. Nathan grabbed the keys out of Giles's back pocket and tossed them to me. To Daniel he said, "And you, bro, I thought you already settled that score."

Vanessa went over to Daniel and gave him a kiss on the cheek, "I know Natalya's death's hit you pretty hard. It has all of us, so why don't we just cool down and forget this ever happened."

"I think it's better if we go to a motel," I said.

"Probably," agreed Vanessa.

"The Turquoise Trail on Cerrillos is cheap." The recommendation came from Daniel.

❧

The neon 'The' in the motel's sign was burned out. A faded, peeling mural of a Western scene—Indians observing a wagon train from a rocky ridge—decorated the detached lobby. A handwritten notice taped to the window told me to ring the bell after eleven. An enormous woman stuffed into a pale green robe and a hairnet shuffled out from a room behind the desk and unlocked the door. Filling out the registration card, I could hear a jumped-up televangelist promising the eternal fires of hell to those who turned away from Jesus. The lobby was plastered with signs. Zero Drug Tolerance. No Excessive Noise, Drinking, Talking. No Loud Music. Only Registered Guests in Rooms. Smoking in Smoking Rooms Only! No Pets!

"What's the car's license number? Gotta have that. It's the only way I can tell cars apart. I don't get the number and bam! every car that drives up is the same."

It was after one in the morning. No other cars were parked along the U-shaped building. Highly unlikely there'd be a sudden rush, but I got her the desired information.

"Number four. Checkout's at ten, either on or before."

"Come on, Giles. You gotta get up," I said softly, removing the bottle of Jose Cuervo from his hand, almost gone. After finally accepting defeat, he'd crawled onto the back seat and was so quiet I thought he'd passed out, instead he'd continued drinking. "I can't carry you."

He didn't resist when I tugged him out of the car. He stood, gangly-legged like a new born foal. Walking arm around my neck to the room, he began, slurry and teary, singing Natalya's song off key.

"Izabowuss," his words came out stuck together, "Thesthong, izabowuss." I had no idea what he was he was trying to say.

I dropped him on the bed. Thirty dollars in Santa Fe got you a double bed, a chair, a table, hideous shit-brown carpeting and cheesy prints of Pueblo women making tortillas. The place wasn't even bottom drawer.

When I returned from the bathroom with a dampened washcloth, Giles was out cold. I dabbed the dried blood off his cheek.

❧

My vow not to sleep with Giles again lasted less than twenty-four hours. He woke me up early, a thin band of grey light streamed through the gap in the blinds making the room appear even more dingy. He looked like a dejected, hungover cherub, and was apologizing non-stop for getting so drunk that I had to do something. And seriously, Sierra was old enough to be my father. When I was forty he'd be sixty-two. He was married.

"The grey is definitely hot," Giles said after, dropping the lock of my hair he'd been holding and rolling back on his pillow.

"So are you going to tell me what's up between you and Daniel? Is he the asshole boyfriend?" I asked.

Giles shot straight up, "Oh, shit, what time is it?"

"Five after eight."

"Fuck!" He was immediately on his feet, "We gotta go. I gotta pick Kaela up in two hours."

"Kaela?" I asked rubbing my eyes against the assault of sunlight when Giles tore open the blinds. Who was Kaela? She better not be a girlfriend he forgot to mention.

"She's my daughter. I can't be late."

"You've got a kid? You never said you had a kid." The possibility of him having a kid had never occurred to me.

"Does it make a difference?"

Not once in my life had I ever experienced a single pang of maternal longing. Procreative apathy ran in the family. My parents were only children. My four grandparents had two siblings between them. I liked kids the way I liked monkeys at the zoo: cute and fun to watch, but I didn't want to have one. Both times Leslie'd told me she was pregnant I did the excited girl thing—Oh my God, that is such fantastic news!—and thanked God it wasn't me throwing up, getting fat, giving up my life for some bawling brat. Her girls were the only children I'd ever been around and every encounter left me feeling like a sponge squeezed dry. Not all women are cut out for motherhood. I'd never even been involved with a man with kids.

Giles hustled me into the car. When I wanted a coffee for the road, he wrung his hands and grumbled about how long it took to make a "fucking latte."

The drive back to Chamisa was at breakneck speed. I twice spilled my Americano down my shirt when Giles swerved to pass another car. Slow down, I implored. He'd comply for a minute then was flooring it again. Once in Chamisa, he told me I'd have to come with him. No time to drop me off.

He turned right at the plaza intersection onto the road going east out of town. A further two miles down, he turned right onto a potholed dirt road that passed several houses and dead-ended at a double wide trailer. There'd been feeble attempts at landscaping, a tree here and there, a flower bed marked out with rocks spray-painted white. A forgotten doll flopped on a lonely canopied swing bench on an uneven paving stone patio.

Giles asked me to stay in the car. "Melissa can be kinda moody. And she hates it when I have other women around Kaela."

He climbed up the steps to the trailer's door. It opened while his hand was raised to knock.

"Daddy!" cried a small girl, smiling from ear to ear, as she jumped into Giles's arms. Behind her was her mother, hands on her hips.

"What happened to your face?"

"I don't want to talk about it."

"What else is new. Can I borrow some money? I have to pay the pre-school."

"What about the money I gave you last week?"

"It went for rent."

"I thought I was supporting Kaela, not you."

"Sorry. Rosario quit her job and couldn't come up with her half. I'd ask my parents, but my mom went back in the hospital yesterday."

"Again? That sucks."

"Yeah, well, cancer sucks."

Putting his daughter down, Giles reached in his back pocket for his wallet, drew out fifty dollars and handed it to Melissa. Then turning to Kaela, asked her to wait in the car. He needed to talk to Mommy. Kaela, gripping her pink Hello Kitty backpack, jumped down the steps. Half way to the car she stopped and pointing a chubby finger at me asked, "Who's that?"

"That's a friend of *Tía* Naty's from out of town, so be nice to her okay, sweetie."

"Okey dokey, artichokey," she replied and skipped the rest of the way.

I got out of the car and opened the backdoor for the girl.

"I'm Kaela. I'm four. Daddy said to be nice to you. You know my Tía Naty? I love Tía Naty. She always gives me presents. Do you have a present for me? I hope it's Ariel. She's so pretty. I wish I had red hair, but not a tail, then I couldn't walk," the girl spoke without stopping for air, "My car seat's not here. I need my seat. Daddy sometimes hides it, 'specially from girls he likes. Look in the back."

Installing a car seat must have been a skill that was automatically acquired with parenthood, along with bottle-feeding and interpreting baby talk. I got no farther than figuring out which end was up. "Let's wait for your daddy."

"Okey dokey. I miss Tía Naty. Do you know where she is? I haven't seen her in a long time. Daddy said she moved, but she didn't say goodbye."

Melissa walked to the car with Giles. She knelt down before her daughter and took her little hands in her own, "I want you to be a super, super sweet girl to Daddy. Do everything he tells you and give him lots of love, okey dokey?"

"Okey dokey artichokey."

To Giles, Melissa said, "I can try to get off work tomorrow if you can't handle it."

"We'll be fine, but thanks. This is Hunter, Natalya's friend."

Melissa reached out to shake my hand, "Wow, it's a really cool thing you've done. I know Giles really appreciates it and I'm sure Luna and Sierra do too."

I wished they'd all chill on the gratitude. It was a response I'd neither anticipated nor sought. Would they still feel so grateful if they knew how I really felt about Natalya?

Kaela talked non-stop on the way to the casita. She talked about her mom; her sick granny; her aunt, Rosario, who also lived in the trailer with her sons, Victor and Oscar, who weren't very nice to her sometimes, hiding her dolls and not letting her watch her cartoons; her favorite food, pizza, and the food she hated most, spinach. "Daddy doesn't like it either, he says it looks and tastes like pond scum," she snorted.

When father and daughter dropped me off, Giles said he'd be busy for the next two days. He'd call when Kaela went back to her mom's. "You'll still be here, right?"

Kaela was only with Giles two days a week. How hard could that be? He and I would still have five days alone together. And perhaps it was time to discover if I was really devoid of mothering skills. At the least I'd learn how to put in the car seat. And Vanessa's warning? Just because Giles had never committed to his old girlfriends didn't mean he never would. Maybe he just hadn't met the right woman.

਒

I spent the first day Giles was with his daughter playing tourist, falling for the charms of Chamisa I'd so ardently resisted as a kid.

My first stop was the Rio Grande Gorge Bridge. At twelve, I'd rolled my eyes at the suggestion that I walk a thousand feet to stand on a dumb bridge. I stayed in the car. This time I joined the other tourists, cameras slung round their necks, and trekked to the midway point, girders rumbling under our feet from the weight of crossing cars. Standing on one of the small overlooks that jutted out over the chasm, I looked down at the river six-hundred feet below. The walls of the gorge appeared to vibrate, my head spun and despite the high guardrails, I felt I could topple over the edge. It was safer to gaze out at the endless views in all directions. To the north and south, no evidence of human habitation was discernible giving the sensation that I and the few others on the bridge were far from civilization.

A visit to the pueblo was foiled by a sign posted on the gate informing me that due to an unexpected death, it was closed to the public. I'd visited the pueblo before. My parents wouldn't let me stay in the car there. I found the maze of multi-story adobe structures, inhabited for a thousand years and still without running water or electricity, fascinating. I wanted to explore, to climb the ladders to the upper levels, to see how the people lived, but held back, refusing to give my parents the satisfaction that they'd been right when they'd told me I'd love it.

We rented horses at a stable run by Ona, born and raised on the pueblo, and his huge Anglo wife, Jessie. As Jessie was helping my mother get on Cesario, a rust and grey appaloosa, she grabbed her side and moaned. Mom asked if she was all right, and she replied that her labor had started an hour ago, but she'd rather be at the stable than in the clinic.

They sent us off, guideless, with instructions to head for the water tower when we'd had enough. As we rode along, with no idea where we were going, just killing the hour we'd paid for, we began to notice some odd things: a frying pan, shirts hanging on bushes and other signs of human activity, but no humans. Mom kept looking over her shoulder as if she expected an arrow in her back. It was kind of spooky and exciting, like we were starring in our own Western. Back at the stables, Dad reported the things we'd seen and Ona surmised that they must have been left there by boys from a kiva who were undergoing initiation and weren't allowed to be seen by anyone. Jessie asked how I'd enjoyed the ride. I kicked the ground with my shoe and said it was just okay.

On the plaza, businesses had come and gone, but the clash of lowbrow and highbrow persevered. Shops selling authentic Indian jewelry sat next door to those selling cheap knockoffs. Art galleries offered works ranging from original members of the early twentieth century Chamisa Artists' League to hokey pastels of hollyhocks against adobe walls. The movie theater had closed, but Chamisa General Store with its soda fountain and array of New Mexico-themed tee shirts, hats, shot glasses, and food continued to draw in customers. Even the old man who repaired watches was still in his tiny office at the back.

I chose a jar of salsa for Andy and a package of blue corn pancake mix for Leslie. At the sales counter I was surprised to find Vanessa filling glass jars with penny candy. Jason was watching her with the rapt attention of a man in love.

"It's the family business. My mom inherited it from her dad and someday it'll all be mine. Woohoo."

"That's why I'm with her. Free candy," Jason said, helping himself to a handful of nonpareils.

Vanessa slapped his hand away, "Someone's paying for it, *pendejo*."

"You seen Giles since the weekend? I bet he's got one hell of a shiner." Jason asked.

Alright, the Saturday night fight between Giles and Daniel was out in the open. "So, what was that all about? Giles didn't want to talk about it."

That wasn't surprising Vanessa said, and poured a bag of Bit-O-Honeys into a jar. Giles and Daniel had been playing 'My dick's bigger than yours' ever since grade school. They were always trying to outdo one another. "I love' em both, but they can be real *cabrónes* sometimes."

The rivalry came to a head over Lisa. Chamisa guys were like bloodhounds, sniffing out fresh women almost as soon as they pulled into town. Daniel was the first to scratch at Lisa's door and she let him in for a few nights, but when he returned from a trip to Phoenix, he found Giles had taken his place. It'd been one of Giles's more boneheaded moves.

"C'mon V, the thing with Lisa was different. Giles really loved her," Jason said.

"Well, Daniel didn't see it that way. Went right for the jugular. Started banging Natalya."

I recounted what had happened the night before Natalya died, what Giles had said about Natalya being involved with a real jerk and wondering if Daniel could be that guy.

"Whoa, trippy," Jason said.

Vanessa stated firmly that, no, Daniel was not the ex-boyfriend. And whoever the guy was, what was I going to do? Talk to him about Natalya's suicide? Make him feel more guilty than he probably already did?

"I'm not looking to cause trouble."

"Then don't." In Vanessa's opinion, it was best to leave it alone. It wasn't really my business nor anyone else's what happened that night.

There'd be no more information from her, or Jason who was too meek to defy his girlfriend whether he agreed with her or not. "I'm starving. Where's the best New Mexican food in town?" I asked trying to restore a friendlier atmosphere.

Vanessa suggested Jaime's.

"Oh yeah, for sure," concurred Jason, "and get the chicken enchiladas. They're awesome."

Jaime's Chow Cart was no longer a cart. It was now housed in the former Taco Bell location when the fast-food restaurant acknowledged that nobody wanted its mediocre versions of the local cuisine and left town. The current tenants didn't inspire confidence that their food was going to be any better. The place had as much atmosphere as a morgue. I hoped Vanessa and Jason hadn't sent me there as a joke and were back at the store holding their sides with laughter thinking of me biting into food that was a notch or two above dog food. Most of the tables, however, were occupied and not by diners exhibiting the telltale tourist trappings. They appeared to be locals. The owners were apparently just decoratively deficient. "Red, green or Christmas (*a combo of red and green*)?" asked the pimply kid who took my order, referring to my chile choices. Whichever was less spicy. He marked the ticket with a big capital R. Pimply kid told me they'd call the number on the bottom of the ticket when my food was ready.

I sat down at one of the only available tables, grabbing a wad of napkins from the dispenser to wipe up the mysterious brown splotches that were dribbled across the tabletop. Waiting for my food, I got angry recalling what Vanessa had said. Who was she to tell me it was none of my business? Natalya'd killed herself in my house. I'd found the body. I had to deal with the police. I'd driven a thousand miles to deliver the letters. I was entitled to know what had happened. And bullshit that it wasn't Daniel. Vanessa'd been so fast denying it that she'd given him away. But how to find him since the only sources I had weren't cooperating.

"Number 57!" a voice called out. That was me.

Just the tips of the blue corn tortillas were visible under the deep red coating of chile and the gooey layer of melted jack cheese that smothered the enchiladas. Accompanying them were a mound of rice and a blob of refried beans, which did resemble Alpo. I was so hungry my stomach was practically leaping out of my throat to get at the food, which had a roasted, woody aroma. I took the first bite ready to be dazzled.

Holy crap! Had pimply kid misunderstood me? Had I messed up? If the red chile was milder, the green would have killed me. All I tasted was heat. Scraping it off the enchiladas didn't help. The heat had penetrated everything. I now had a pretty good idea what a fire-breathing dragon's insides felt like. How did the locals do it?

I ditched the box in the garbage and went somewhere safer, McDonalds, refueling with a decidedly spiceless quarter-pounder with cheese and a chocolate shake.

"Don't they have answering machines where you are? Been trying to call you for days. I was beginning to think you'd given me the bum steer. Where's that 505 area code anyway?" It was Detective Schmidt and he didn't sound like he was about to read me the riot act.

"New Mexico."

"But how come I didn't have to dial a country code?"

"Because New Mexico's in the United States."

Americans made that mistake all the time. Letters addressed to New Mexico were returned to sender stamped by the post office 'Returned for Additional Postage.' Potential visitors to the state asked if they needed visas and immunizations, and was the water safe to drink.

"Well, whadda ya know. Never been west of the Mississippi myself." He was way too friendly. Was he making small talk, trying to keep me on the phone until the Chamisa police showed up with a warrant for my arrest. "So were you ever going to tell me about the letters?"

I meant to call the day I'd delivered them, but then I figured Luna or Sierra would show up in Milwaukee and Schmidt would be so relieved that the search was over he'd never ask how the Lawlesses learned of their daughter's death.

"Are you going to have me arrested?"

"Well, that all depends on you being straight up with me. Did you remove them from her room before the officers arrived?"

"No, I swear I didn't. I found them on the dining room table the next day."

"That's good. Cause if you'd taken them from the crime scene, you'd be finding yourself in a big ol' pot a trouble."

I explained why I'd kept them a secret. Give the police some credit, he said. They weren't ogres. They had feelings and compassion. He would have respected Natalya's wishes.

And it was a good thing Natalya had written those letters because it turned out her I.D. was a fake and the social security number she was using was issued to one Dolores Mercer who'd died back in 1978. "If you find out what her story was would you let me know. I don't like loose ends."

29

Natalya's suitcase. I'd forgotten all about it until I accidentally pushed the trunk release instead of the gas flap. I wasn't risking rejection by taking it to Giles. He hadn't called after his days with Kaela ended nor had he responded to my two messages about the bag. That left me with one not so pleasant option: taking it to the Lawlesses.' Maybe I'd luck out and Sierra would be home, alone.

Che's barking was the only response to my knocks. I was writing a quick note when the door opened. Luna, pulling off a pair of leather gardening gloves asked, "What are you still doing in town?" She spied the suitcase on her doorstep. "If Sierra told you you could stay here, he was dead wrong."

I wondered if that was that her version of a pleasant conversation opener. "I have a house, I mean my parents have, or had, well, they still have, a house here. The suitcase is Natalya's. It's her clothes and stuff. I thought you and Sierra'd want them." I was fumbling my explanation like a kid in the principal's office.

"Neither of us are really sentimental people. The clothes can go to the women's shelter. Maybe Giles'll want the rest."

Unable to part with even the smallest object of my parents, keeping the house as almost a shrine to their memory, I marveled at Luna's detachment.

"Bring it inside, will you? I love the garden, but my back hates it. It's killing me." She waved to a spot near the door where I should deposit the bag and walked off.

That done, I stood dumbly in the foyer. Now what? Was I supposed to follow her? Let myself out?

"Who are your parents?" Luna asked from somewhere nearby, sounding almost friendly now.

"Jack and Margaret Grayson."

"I can't hear you. Come in here."

I found her in the living room hopping around, lifting up pillows, digging between couch cushions, lifting boxes.

"My parents are Jack and Margaret Grayson."

"Never heard of 'em," Luna said, looking under the couch, "Aha! There you are, you little bugger."

The little bugger was a Bic lighter in a silver case adorned with a large turquoise. "Always losing this damn thing," she complained as she tapped a cigarette out of a pack of American Spirits and lit it. She inhaled deeply and let the smoke out slowly. "Fucking awful habit, but God, I love it. From the first drag I ever took I knew I'd found my best friend." She took another and let loose a phlegmy cough. Then she surprised me with an invitation to go down to the Rio Grande.

"Sierra's in Milwaukee and I'm trying to keep my mind off D.C. The health care hearings started this week and I wanted to be there, but that's not going to happen now," she said, seeming more angry to miss the trip than sad about the reason why. "And you should really see it while you're here."

I told her I'd driven along it and looked down on it from the bridge.

"The bridge is impressive to be sure but I like being right next to it, though this time of year it's pretty low."

Meeting Luna was like biting into what I thought was cantaloupe and getting papaya instead. It could have been the most delicious papaya in the world, but it was still going taste awful because I was expecting cantaloupe. I'd been expecting Edie-Sedgwick-meets-Maria-von-Trapp in beads and bell bottoms and I'd gotten a surly, dumpy, warthog. Now Luna was offering an olive branch. Maybe I'd been too quick to judge her on the day she discovered her daughter was dead. Maybe the woman Natalya had raved about was waiting to pop out like a jack-in-the-box.

"I'd love to," I said, determined to like the woman.

Luna tossed a file box into the back seat of her Jeep Cherokee so I could sit down. Air freshener that was supposed turn the car into a pine forest, a synthetic version of a pine forest failed to cover up the reek from years of cigarettes smoked with the windows up. I rolled down the window despite the coolness of the day.

Ten miles north out of town, Luna turned left at a gas station with two lonely pumps onto a road that meandered through an eclectic collection of adobe houses, mobile homes and trailers that fell short of its goal of being a village. Rusting hulks of abandoned cars littered some yards, in others there were collapsing swing sets, piles of logs, chicken coops or vicious dogs on short chains.

"That's New Millennium, the commune Sierra and I used to live on," she said, pointing to a large circular adobe structure, its windows and walls obscured by a wild jumble of browning rose bushes and hollyhocks.

"Not much to look at now. Shit, it wasn't much to look at back then either," Luna snorted. "We didn't know a thing about building. It's a miracle it's still standing. Course, back then, there were tepees, old school buses and VW campers, too. And a lot more land. Most of it's been sold."

Scrub pine and oak took over the landscape as we left the houses behind and headed toward the jagged shadow of the gorge. The pavement ceased and the Jeep bounced down the rutted gravel road churning up clouds of tan dust. After a mile we began to descend into a narrow gorge carved by the Rio Hondo, a tributary of the Rio Grande that sprang from the mountains to the east.

At the confluence of the two rivers, a metal bridge crossed the Rio Grande and on the other side the road switch-backed up the high, steep western face.

Luna parked and we walked across a rocky beach, exposed by the receding waters of the big river.

"We used to bring Giles and Natalya here to swim in the summers," she said, "Giles was brave, jumping off the bridge, just like his father and me. Natalya would barely stick a toe in. It's too cold, she'd whine. But she was always afraid of things, the water, the dark, spiders. Can't be afraid of those things and live in New Mexico." She kicked a stone and it skittered over other stones and plopped into the water. "Any idea why she did it? She's dead now so don't feel you have to keep any of her secrets."

"Not sure. Well, maybe because of a guy."

"So, she didn't tell you some sob story about how horrible I was? How she was unloved and unwanted?"

I shook my head, "Just the opposite."

My answer surprised her, but she didn't pursue it, "She ever talk about Sierra?"

"No, just you."

If Luna was seeking an answer to why Natalya had killed herself, I had none to give, though I wanted to say something to ease her conscience. "I've been restless, unhappy, searching for something most of my life, never contemplated suicide, but those feelings did kind of drive me away from my parents, even though it had nothing to do with them."

"You close to your parents now?"

"They were killed last January. Car accident."

"That's tough."

"What I'm trying to say is that killing herself may have had nothing to do with you."

"I know that," Luna stated in a manner that told me I was stupid for even suggesting it.

I felt responsible for my parents' accident though I was a continent away when it happened. Luna had no self-doubts about her and her daughter's relationship, no 'if onlys' or 'I should haves,' just certainty that she was in no way to blame.

Luna, up to that moment straight as a pole, dropped down on a large rock and drew out her American Spirits. "You know how we got her, right?"

I was pretty sure I knew where babies came from. My mother had taught me about the birds and the bees when I was in the fourth grade.

"Any fool or junkie can bring a baby into this world, but that doesn't make her a mother. I was the only mother that girl ever had."

"Wait, you're not Natalya's biological mother?"

Again I got the Is-Earth-your-home-planet look. "Do we look like mother and daughter? Her mother left Natalya with us when she went off to rehab. Never saw her again."

Adopted. That explained a lot. Why all Natalya's talk of mother-daughter harmony, their mutual loves of music, books and movies had felt phony. It was phony. She was nuttier than I thought, making up all that stuff. Like that girl I met at summer camp who claimed to have the same birthday as me. I believed her until she asked me what time I was born, then announced with great glee that she'd been born at exactly the same hour. It didn't, however, explain the fake I.D. and social security number. My gut told me Luna wouldn't appreciate me prying so I left those questions unasked.

Luna continued she wasn't a bad mother, just not one of those smothering types whose life was her kids. The work she and Sierra were doing to create a better world for them, for everyone, was much more important than lots of cooing and silly toys. Over the years they had protested the Vietnam War, Apartheid, Reagan's tax cuts, the invasions of Grenada and Panama, Iran-Contra, cuts in the NEA. They had campaigned for nuclear disarmament, racial equality, universal healthcare, better education and the charter school law that had passed the previous year in New Mexico. They'd started a food pantry in Chamisa. Luna was a co-founder of the women's shelter. They both had served on the boards of directors for numerous local non-profits.

"Natalya was lucky to have you in her life," I said.

"Hell, let's be frank here. We didn't like each other much. She was a strange girl, so sensitive and cloying. Like her mother but magnified ten times. I guess that stuff's genetic, too. But every child needs to be brought up in a stable home, not bounced from foster home to foster home, which is where she would have ended up if it hadn't been for me."

Most people were weak, especially women, Luna continued. They said they had convictions, but when asked to live by them, they let petty feelings, jealousy or envy, get in the way. She wasn't one of those people (*Okay, that was a new one. When speaking of adoption, people generally praise the unselfishness of adoptive parents, not call out their pettiness*). And she wasn't being arrogant only honest when she said she treated both children the same. She never showed Giles any favoritism.

I was trying to like her. Really I was. She did more than sit in a cushy chair and jab her cigarette at the world's problems. She was out there fighting for what she believed in. Trying to be the change, or whatever it was that Gandhi had said. But she sounded so superior, looking down on the rest of us from her mountain top. If she'd had just a tiny bit of Gandhi's warmth and compassion I might have taken to her, but peeling away the warthog exterior I'd only found bones of steel and organs of ice.

"Was she drinking a lot, or doing drugs? Samantha, that's her mother, was an addict so it wouldn't be surprising." There again was that contempt for weakness.

"I don't think so. I mean, she got drunk once in a while, but it only took a couple of beers. She was so light."

"What about men? Did she fuck around like her mother?"

"Not that I ever saw," That was a lie, but Luna's derision triggered me to come to Natalya's defense. Natalya was dead and she still couldn't say one nice thing about her.

"What about you? Did the two of you have something going on? She was obviously pretty special for you to come all the way out here."

"Oh my God, no. Never." My denial was contradicted by a blush at the memory of 'the craziness' that Luna picked up on instantly.

"What do I care if you were lovers."

"I'm not into women. I don't sleep with women. I like men. I mean, I'm straight," I stammered, "And Natalya was in love with Daniel."

"Daniel Martinez? That ape? It figures. What about Sierra?"

"I'm sorry, I don't understand. Are you asking me if Natalya was in love with Sierra?"

"No, I'm asking if you're attracted to my husband."

"He's married."

"Very married, but that doesn't stop women from trying. And it doesn't stop him from flirting, either. So if you're sticking around hoping you and he have a love connection, think again." She flicked the cigarette into the river and marched back to the car.

The trip to the river hadn't been an offer of friendship. It had been a ruse to grill me about Natalya and warn me off Sierra. I'd given it the old college try, but there was no way, not in a million years, that I could ever look at that woman as a mother figure, as a friend. I didn't even want to run into her in the street. The only good thing to come out of the trip was Luna'd given me Daniel's last name.

Instead of going home I headed toward the mountains. An old Chamisa guide book, found on a shelf in the casita, reminded me about hiking trails on the road up to the ski valley and now was a perfect time to check one out. I could walk Luna out of my system.

On the side of the road, heading north like me, stood a guy, thumb out, earnest smile telegraphing the message 'I'm safe' to passing cars. I hit the brakes. It was Jason.

"Yo, dude, thanks" he said as he hopped in the car, followed by, "Whoa," when he realized who'd picked him up. His destination was a little town on my way, but I'd have taken him to Denver if it meant he'd tell me where to find Daniel Martinez.

He was going to the studio he shared with a few other potters. He made *raku* ware, a Japanese technique. He loved the process of hand-shaping the pieces, but he was slow and a little lazy and was way behind for an upcoming show. "V's riding my ass so I gotta get some work done today. Oh yeah, I hope she didn't upset you the other day. She's pretty direct and she can go all mama bear about her friends."

I sensed Jason was as soft and malleable as the clay he worked with, and a little afraid of women. Stating my case in just the right way so he felt he was doing the right thing, which he would be, was key. Too much pressure and I'd have a big mess.

"I get it. She's being a good friend. I respect that. And like I told her, I'm not trying to stir up trouble. But try to see it from my side. Natalya died in my house. That was pretty traumatic. I'd just like to understand what happened."

Jason didn't say anything yet his face betrayed his inner conflict. His mouth twitched from side to side. He looked to the car roof then to the floor. He squinted one eye then the other. To tell or not to tell. Finally, with a sigh, he said, "He works at Gabe's, or Abe's, Auto Body on St. Michael's. But you didn't hear it from me. If V ever finds out I told you, I'll be dead meat."

I promised his secret was safe with me.

30

It was Gilbert's Collision Center and fortunately it was the only auto body shop on St. Michael's. A chainlink fence enclosed a yard full of automobiles of every make and condition. In the small office, there was a plywood counter painted dark blue, candy and soda machines and a TV tuned to CNN with the sound off. A pair of old truck benches were placed on either side of a small table covered with ancient copies of *People* and *North American Whitetail*. The guy behind the counter, the name Gilbert embroidered in red thread on his stained coveralls, asked what could he do for me.

"I'd like to talk to Daniel, if he's available."

"If you've got a job for us, I can help you with that."

"It's personal."

Take a seat he said, giving me the once-over before opening the door to the garage and shouting, "*Oye, primo, ven aqui.*"

"In a minute."

"*Ahorito. Te metes en líos. Hay chica que quiere hablar contigo.*"

Daniel, even bigger than I remembered him, entered the office wiping grease off his hands then shoving the rag in a pocket. That Giles had limped away from the fight with only a cut on his face showed Daniel had exercised restraint. He wasn't surprised to see me because he didn't remember me.

"Do I know you?"

It was probably a good thing he'd forgotten he'd seen me with Giles.

"Wait, you're the chick who was with Dickhead at El Chiquitito. What do you want?"

I'd rehearsed what I was going to say the whole way down to Santa Fe and almost every word was a lie. I told him that Natalya and I had become very close in the short time we'd known each other. I'd come to see her as the sister I'd never had. She had been a very private person and hadn't told me much about her past, but she'd mentioned him, how she'd cared for him very much. And since I didn't know a delicate way to ask, I was going to come right out with it. Was he the man who'd been with her the night before she died? The man she loved?

Daniel was snuffling, as unexpected from a guy with a skull ring as the truth was from a politician, "It wasn't me. Honest. I'd never have left her. Never."

He'd always had a thing for Natalya, maybe partly because, being Giles's sister, she was forbidden fruit, but it was more than that. She was like a china doll. He wanted to protect her. He'd kept those feelings to himself and she'd been so loyal to Giles, "that when we hooked up everyone thought I was getting revenge for Lisa. And maybe I was a little, but I swear, Natalya was the one who came on to me. She was all over me when I ran into her at The Dingo in Albuquerque. It was kinda like a fantasy come true, really."

They were only together four times, but he'd have done anything for Natalya, anything. Then one day she was gone, disappeared, no one knew where. First Lisa dumped him, then Natalya. That's when he decided to accept his cousin's offer and move to Santa Fe.

As for the identity of Mystery Man, he couldn't shed any light on who he was. Before the night at the bar, he hadn't seen her in a year, but with a chick as hot as Natalya, there had to have been a few exes.

❦

Sierra's red truck was in the drive when I pulled up to the casita. The owner was slouched on the bench by the casita's front door. His cowboy hat pushed forward to block the late afternoon sun from his eyes, a leg propped on the knee of the other. A hand resting on the raised knee held a cigarette, a long ash clinging to the tip. He didn't move or speak until I was right next to him.

"I brought her home," he said, placing his leg on the ground and leaning forward to rest his elbows on his knees. The ash dropped and then Sierra dropped the cigarette and crushed it with the heel of his cowboy boot on the flagstone. He picked up the butt, slipping it into the front pocket of his jeans. "Better remember it's there. If it goes through the wash, Luna'll have a fit."

He removed his hat and ran his hands through his hair, just the way Giles did. "I hope I never have to go through something like that again. No matter how prepared you think you are, there's nothing like seeing someone you love on a slab."

"When my parents died, I asked to see their bodies. It was a huge mistake," I shuddered at the memory.

"By the way, Detective Schmidt isn't real happy with you. Seems he knew nothing about the letters."

"Yeah, he called me the other day."

"He says she OD'd on pills and booze."

"My mother's pills. I wish I'd thrown the bottle away ages ago. I'm so sorry."

"If it wasn't the pills, she'd have found another way."

The lines of sadness and exhaustion that carved his face made it seem as if the slightest pressure would crack him wide open. It fueled my desire even more. I imagined his hands, hands that had known hard work, hands that were veined and rough, caressing my body, learning its every contour, finding new ways of giving pleasure. I bet he knew how to make love to a woman. I remembered the way he'd looked at me when we'd met, like the rest of the world had fallen away leaving just the two of us and he couldn't wait to get me naked. Luna had seen it, too, and she was scared. Scared he might leave her for me. Scared enough to warn me off. I might have felt bad about that if she weren't such a bitch. What was twenty-two years? And Giles? We'd slept together twice. I hadn't heard from him in days. He was a guy. He would never think he and I were in a relationship. Michael'd slept with me for months without ever once considering me his girlfriend. Okay, maybe it was a little creepy leaving a guy for his father, but it wasn't Woody-Allen-Soon-Yi-Previn level creepy. He wasn't my mother's boyfriend. Invite him in. Invite him in.

"Would you like to come in? I can make you some tea or coffee."

"It can't be today, but one day very soon I want to talk with you about how you've dealt with your loss. How you cope with it. What you've learned from it," Sierra said, taking my hand and caressing it, "Luna doesn't feel things as deeply as I do, as I can tell you do. I feel a connection to you, like I can tell you anything, be myself with you. I felt it the moment I met you." Both of us knew if he came in we wouldn't do all that much talking. That we would make love was not in doubt, it was just waiting for the perfect moment when time could stand still. "Just one thing before I go 'cause I don't understand it. What the heck was Natalya doing in Milwaukee?"

"Because of *Happy Days*."

"Happy days?"

"You know, the TV show. She envied the Cunninghams."

Sierra gave a low, wistful laugh, "I don't blame her. I'd love to know that kind of easy happiness."

If Sierra felt he could tell me anything he would never think me nosey for asking questions about Natalya.

Poor kid, he said, life had treated her pretty rough. They were sure she'd been born in the US, but since Samantha didn't leave a birth certificate they couldn't prove it because they didn't know where or if her birth'd ever been registered. And as he and Luna had had a few run-ins with the law, they never pursued it. The state might have taken Natalya away from them. The social security number came from a buddy's dead mother so Natalya could at least get a job. She must have bought herself the license.

In the last few years, Sierra admitted, he hadn't been the father to Natalya he should have been and he'd regret that till his dying day. When she moved to Albuquerque, she didn't come up to Chamisa much. "Once Natalya knew the truth she didn't want to burden Luna anymore." He looked at his watch, "Shit, I really gotta get home. Luna's expecting me."

Wait, what truth? "Wait, what…"

Sierra was already halfway to his truck. "No time now. And, just a suggestion, get rid of the grey. You'll look prettier."

31

Day number three.

Day number three of asking myself what was I still doing in Chamisa. I'd done what I came there to do. I'd honored Natalya's request and delivered the letters. There was no (*good, smart, rational*) reason to stay. Playing detective had been a bust. I was no closer to finding Mystery Man than when I arrived. He could have been from anywhere. My would-be surrogate mother had turned out to be more Mommie Dearest than Carol Brady. I wanted to jump in the sack with my would-be father, whose son I'd already slept with, who was the reason it was also day number three of my coffee shop stakeout. I'd get to Mo Joe's early, make one Borgia last as long as possible in hopes that Giles would turn up. I know I'd decided he and I weren't happening, but I hated the fact that he'd decided it too and completely blown me off. Or maybe he was grieving, which was what any normal person would be doing after the death of a loved one and if I weren't so insecure I'd have realized that was why he hadn't called.

Just as the Borgia was losing its last trace of warmth and I finished the final article in The Chamisa News—a part-time embroiderer named William Holden shot his best man on the wedding night for dirty dancing with the bride—hope fading for another day, Vanessa slid into the seat opposite me.

"Uh oh, you're still here," she said.

First Luna, now Vanessa. Wasn't I allowed to hang out for a few days? Did everyone want me gone?

"Sorry, didn't mean to offend. Just wondering if the Land of Entrapment had trapped you, too. Happens all the time. Nathan's family came here in '79, just for a few days, supposedly. His mom announced she and the kids were staying. His dad could too, if he wanted. Been here ever since. Jason was on his way to LA. His car broke down just outside town. That was three years ago and he still hasn't gotten the damn thing fixed. It's because of the mountain."

What mountain?

Chamisa Mountain, a sacred mountain on the Indian reservation, the big one you saw when you looked to the east. Lots of people believed it was a source of great power. If it wanted you to stay in Chamisa, you stayed. It was why certain businesses succeeded while others failed. It was why some people thrived here and others didn't. The mountain decided if you stayed and when it said it was time to go, you went.

I had a vague memory of my dad telling me the legend. But I didn't think my being in Chamisa had anything to do with the mountain. There was definitely no good reason for me to still be there, except I didn't want to go back to Milwaukee. I had reasons for staying away.

"Well, I get that. As long as Giles Lawless's got nothing to do with it."

"Oh no, not at all," I lied, maybe too emphatically because Vanessa gave me a yeah-right smile.

"Ok, do whatever you want, just don't say I didn't warn you. Giles's my friend and I'm not going to dis him, but trust me, you really don't want to go there. Well, gotta go sell cheap crap to the tourists. And if I don't see you again, have a great life."

Ok. That settled it. Leaving Chamisa didn't mean I had to go back to Milwaukee. I could go farther west. Check out San Francisco. Spend a few days at my friend Megan Brenner's place, then head up the coast to Portland, maybe even go as far as Seattle. I went home to pack.

The phone rang.

"Hey stranger, long time no talk." It was Giles.

"And whose fault is that?" I wanted it to be light, but it came out peevish.

"Yeah, sorry. I haven't wanted to be around anyone, talk to anyone. From wanting to surround myself with people to spending the last few days alone in the dark."

"And I'm sorry. I should know better. How're you feeling today?"

"Wiped out and in need of some rejuvenation. Heading down to Paloma Springs. Mineral waters, a mud bath. Wanna come with?"

My ego heaved a sigh of relief. Giles's disappearance had nothing to do with me. And when he emerged from his cave, I was the one he was called. But if he thought the trip to the springs was a date, I'd let him down easy. He was a great guy and I'd liked hanging out with him, but I had to get to San Fran. If he brought it up. I didn't want to sound presumptuous.

Did I mind driving, he asked. The Land Cruiser's fan belt was loose and every time he changed gears it screeched like a banshee. Was that why he'd called, because he needed a ride? I shook it off. He must've had friends with cars. Or maybe they were all busy. Oh god Hunter, just shut up.

It was a good thing I drove. I had to stare at the road and not at Giles. For all my vows of keeping things platonic, I just wasn't the type who could look and not think about touching, kissing, fucking. And I'd already proven my resolve not to sleep with Giles to be as solid as jello. So why couldn't he give me break and have a huge zit on his chin or fart or something. But if I did pull the car onto the shoulder and jump him, what did it matter. I was leaving the next day.

Giles sprawled out in the passenger seat, put a foot on the dashboard, hung an arm out the open window. He looked peaceful and I hesitated whether it was fair to bring up Natalya. But I had driven over a thousand miles to bring those letters, so was it too much to ask that he clarify a few things for me.

"Sierra said something about when Natalya learned the truth. What did he mean?"

"When did you see him?" Giles sat up in the seat, his foot dropped to the floor. There was mistrust in his eyes. Oh god, maybe he was the jealous type. I'd only hooked up with that type once so I'd almost forgotten they existed. Did he think our sleeping together twice made me his property? Is that why Vanessa had warned me off. Was Giles going to smother me with his doubts and suspicions?

"He stopped by for about five minutes when he got back from Milwaukee. He wanted to know why Natalya'd moved there." My breezy response seemed to satisfy him.

"He meant when Natalya found out he was her real dad."

"Her real father? From what? A previous marriage?"

"No."

"So how? I don't understand."

The only thing Giles inherited from Luna was the look, the dismissive look, the 'you idiot' look, the look he gave me right then. "Christ, how slow are you? He cheated."

In an ill-conceived attempt to exonerate Sierra I stated that there was usually a reason a man strayed (*and married to a woman like Luna there'd have been a lot of reasons*).

"I could maybe excuse once, but basically, Sierra's never met a woman he didn't want to fuck. I could have dozens of half brothers and sisters out there. The guy can't keep his dick in his pants."

No. Not possible. Sierra couldn't be as bad as Giles made out. A man that gorgeous probably had women throwing themselves at him all the time. Maybe Giles just assumed Sierra'd slept with them all because he'd slipped with Natalya's mother. "You're exaggerating. Sierra's a sensitive…" I began earnestly before Giles cut me off.

"Christ, don't tell me you're falling for his crap. He just knows all the right things to say to sound like he cares. He wants everyone to think he's God's fucking, and I mean that literally, gift to the universe," Giles said.

It was obvious from the one time I'd seen them together that there was some serious father-son tension, most likely a power struggle, like chimps fighting over a banana, or Giles rejecting everything that was important to Sierra. Every man talks about wanting a son, an heir, all that patriarchal crap, but they usually have much less complicated relationships with their daughters. Defending Sierra, however, was only going to get me in trouble. "What woman would put up with that?"

"Luna. And Natalya's mother was her best friend."

That explained all the stuff Luna'd said about rising above jealousy and it would take me a while to come up with a defense for the kind of betrayal she suffered.

"Luna's not super warm and she sure as hell isn't going to win any prizes for motherhood, but I admire how she stands by what she believes in and doesn't let emotions control her decisions," Giles said.

For Luna, not being the maternal type, to take in Sierra's child from a prior relationship would have been a big enough deal, but that she took in his child from an affair with her best friend made what she'd done even more admirable. And if Sierra was so unfaithful why did she stay with him, or couldn't she afford to leave?

Giles shook his head, "No, the money's hers. If you wanna know why you'll have to ask Luna. I gave up trying figure those two out a long time ago. Hey, your hair. Why'd you dye it? The grey looked hot."

L'Oreal #8 Medium Blonde. Purchased immediately after Sierra'd left the other day. And he'd been right. I did look prettier. I should have done it months ago. Maybe Michael would have stuck around. Then Natalya would never have moved in. Then I never would have come to New Mexico and been lying to Giles about why I dyed my hair.

I shrugged saying I could handle thirty or forty, but not more than half my head.

❧

Set amidst a landscape of gray sandcastle-like basalt rock formations, Paloma had been operating as a health spa since the 1860s, making it one of the oldest in the country. Centuries before that it had been the center of a thriving Pueblo culture. In 1993, it was in need of some serious TLC. The entrance to the pools was through a shabby trailer heavy with the smoke of a sage smudge stick. The pavement around the pools was cracked and the woven plastic lounge chairs were faded with straps torn or missing. The women's changing room smelled of sweat and disinfectant. The floor was dotted with so many puddles I stood on the bench to change into my suit.

I waited for Giles in our arsenic pool meeting point for what felt like an eternity. I was the only one in it whose hair didn't smell like a grease trap and who wasn't wearing a tank top and cutoffs as a bathing suit. Then I saw him, a towel wrapped tightly around his waist, slinking out of the old bathhouse. He whispered in my ear that we should check out another pool, there were too many 'mesa rats' in this one.

We darted into a low stone building that housed the soda pool and I learned the true reason Giles desired privacy. Under the towel he wore a pair of girls' baby blue Champion athletic shorts that hit him just inches below his crotch. He'd forgotten his suit and the shorts were only thing in the Lost and Found box that fit.

"This goes no further. What happens in Paloma stays in Paloma. Got it?"

I nodded, my face contorting to hold in my laughter.

The stone walls oozed moisture. Water dripped from the blue, green and red glass roof. The air smelled like the lazy tropical humidity of Florida. Floating on my back, eyes closed, I was transported to my grandparents' house, surrounded by hibiscus and gardenias and overlooking the Intracoastal Waterway north of Palm Beach.

I was ten. Dad, Bopa, and I were fishing off the concrete sea wall. A fish, my first ever, had just taken the bait on my line and I was shouting excitedly, the reel spinning wildly, as the fish swam off with its dubious prize. Competing advice on how to land it came from Dad and Bopa, so I ignored both and did it my own way.

Bopa was sure I'd hooked a sheepshead, but the fish I reeled in was ribbon-like, its silver body tapering to a pointed tail, with sharp teeth and a mean disposition. It cracked like a whip as my dad struggled to remove the hook and toss it back. I'd caught my ichthyological equivalent.

Dad and Bopa made a big fuss about my skill, but I saw the disappointment behind their show. It wasn't a good fish. I was the problem kid, the one who threw temper tantrums, caught fish we couldn't eat and almost lost the fishing rod in the process (*my way had involved dropping the rod in the water where, luckily because it was Bopa's favorite, it got hooked on a mooring and Dad retrieved it and handed it back to me so I could land my twin*).

To end the day, Giles and I sat in the one-hundred-five degree hot tub followed by a plunge into the cold swimming pool. Rather than brutal, the transition was invigorating, any tension that hadn't melted in the hot water was washed away by the cold. I swam a few laps until Giles stopped me and gave me a kiss. Letting him kiss me was permitted. Just a kiss from a friend, meaningless in any sexual way.

"Thanks for coming. Just being you around relaxes me. I feel that if I was racing towards a cliff you'd stop me," he said.

After my parents' death that's how Andy made me feel, most of the time, when he wasn't harping on me to bare my soul to a therapist. I couldn't tell Giles then I was leaving the next day and wasn't going to see him again. I'd do that later, maybe on the phone.

Giles gave me another kiss when I dropped him off. This one with tongue, long and deep. I felt it all the way to my toes. A goodbye kiss, though he didn't yet know it.

"You doing anything tonight?" he asked, "I could bring over a pizza and a movie."

There was no harm in having him come over. It was my last night in Chamisa. Most likely, probably. Maybe I should keep my options open.

My heart beat double time, my usually dry palms moistened. I shot a quick look into the rearview mirror. Not gorgeous, but not hideous. The kiss from Giles completely forgotten.

Sierra was in his spot on the bench. Today was the day. It had to be. He'd sensed I was leaving and knew he had to make his move or lose me forever. I saw how the meeting would play out: I'd invite him in. He'd wordlessly lead me to the bed and we'd make love, the most transcendent love making I'd ever experienced. Afterwards, I'd ask him about all the other women. He'd admit that he'd strayed a few times, though nowhere near as many times as Giles charged, when he and Luna were going through particularly rough patches. She'd lock him out of the bedroom for months at a time and a man had urges. But unlike me, none of those women had meant anything to him. I was something completely different. I was true love and he was leaving Luna. We'd travel for a while, then find some new and wonderful place to settle, marrying as soon as his divorce was final.

"You here for your cup of tea?" Hoping I sounded sexy rather than nervous.

He jumped up, "Can't dillydally today. Just wanted to give you this." In his hands was a wooden bird, like the ones that roosted on the tables and shelves in his house. It had long, wide tail feathers and a short, fat beak, thin metal legs and painted in merry reds, greens and blues. "My way of saying thank you for all you've done. I know it isn't much, but I made it and Natalya loved my birds."

What the hell? He could sit on the bench for hours waiting for me to come home, but he couldn't come in. Was he ever going to venture inside? Was he holding back, knowing what would happen were we to make love, but the need to see me was so intense he couldn't stay away, devising the thinnest of pretexts for stopping by. I sought a sign of internal struggle. His eyes were calm pools, not churning seas of frustrated desire. Had I misinterpreted everything? Was I flying solo? It wouldn't be the first time I'd thought a guy and I were soaring together only to discover he'd never left the ground.

"I also wanted to let you know there's gonna be a memorial service for Natalya at our house day after tomorrow. I hope you'll be there."

Oh God, not a memorial service. "I don't know. I was thinking of taking off tomorrow. Gotta get home."

"Can't you stick around a couple more days? It would mean a lot to Luna."

"Luna wants me there?"

There was the tiniest pause before he said, "Yes, she thinks you two got off on the wrong foot. She wants to start over. And it would mean a lot to me, too."

"Well, I'll think about it," I kept my head down as if admiring the bird, knowing I couldn't look him in the face. Even if his eyes were free of the lust I'd hoped to find, I'd never be able to refuse him.

❧

I didn't want to go to the memorial. I would rather do almost anything than go to a service full of people I didn't know. I didn't want to get on the right foot with Luna. I didn't want Giles to come over. He might try to convince me to stay and I didn't want to be backed into a corner. I called him. No answer, and a voice told me the answering machine tape was full. When he showed up, I'd tell him I was really sorry but he couldn't stay. I was leaving in the morning and had a lot to do to get ready. Until he arrived, I moved restlessly around the house. I packed. I turned on the TV and flipped through the channels. A rerun of *Happy Days* was on one. I turned the TV off. I tried to read, but couldn't concentrate. Sierra's gift stared at me from atop the TV. I shoved it in my backpack. I didn't want more accusations of falling for Sierra's 'crap.' Those birds. He gives them to women so he can get in their pants.

Giles arrived, a pizza in one hand, a copy of *Batman Returns* resting precariously on top, and two six-packs— one missing three beers—in the other. His nose was pinkish. His hair looked like he'd tried to rip out hanks of it. His breath was beery. There was no way I could tell him to go home. I grabbed the pizza and video and pushed him in the direction of the bedroom. I got extra pillows and piled them behind him. Then I pulled the TV and VCR into the room, and climbed into bed.

The pizza and beers were finished, the Penguin was ruining Christmas in Gotham City, and Giles laid his head in my lap. I stroked his hair. We were like mother and son until I felt his hand opening the zipper of my jeans. It happened every time we were together so why should I fight it. And if I was really leaving tomorrow why not give him a parting gift.

Usually when eyes meet while making love it's pretty awkward, especially when you're just a few steps up from being total strangers. Your faces are so close. Yet, when it happened to Giles and me, we didn't flinch. We held each other's gaze as a wave of pure energy, of love even, flowed between us. The sex was crazy hot, but I sensed instantly that it meant more to us than the gratification of a physical urge. Our connection was so real that I quit denying it. Natalya's lack of enthusiasm about Philip was suddenly clear. She'd arranged a wonderful gift for me, and I'd been a total bitch to her. And I wasn't completely loco. I didn't think Natalya'd made the ultimate sacrifice just to get Giles and me together. Were she still alive, she'd have devised another less extreme match-making ploy, but her intuition had been spot on. I let go of the ludicrous idea that I was meant to be with Sierra—Luna would probably make the divorce super nasty—and surrendered my heart to Giles. He didn't leave till three the following afternoon with the promise to be back later.

"There's a memorial service for Natalya tomorrow," he said after a lingering kiss goodbye and an embrace so tight the buttons of his shirt left marks on my cheek, "I won't survive it without you."

"I'll be there. And with you for as long as you want me." I didn't actually say that last part, but I thought it.

32

A locked closet in the casita kept clothing and shoes my parents only wore in New Mexico, along with dishes, linens, and other household items they didn't want holiday renters to use.

In Milwaukee, my mother had dressed in wool crepe skirts and dresses, silk blouses, pearls, and high heels. On the trips to New Mexico, she'd leave the conservative style at home and wear broomstick skirts, cowboy boots, velvet Navajo shirts and concha belts. It was the only time she ever wore denim. Embarrassed by what I saw as affectation, I'd accused her of going native.

The morning of the memorial service I opened the closet for the first time since my arrival. If I had to go to Natalya's service then I was going to honor my parents in some way. I pulled out an array of skirts and blouses and laid them on the bed. Mom had been a size larger than me, but a skirt could be held up with a pin. I tried on several, finally choosing one in dark blue cotton patterned with tiny red, pink and yellow flowers. I could devise no flattering remedy for her blouses so I threw on a white one of my own and fastened her concha belt around my waist.

Putting on a pair of Mom's cowboy boots made me feel like I was playing dress-up. I couldn't clomp around in boots two sizes too big. Back in the closet they went and I pulled on my own brown leather boots.

From the wooden box holding Mom's jewelry I chose a traditional Navajo turquoise and silver squash blossom necklace that she'd bought on one of our early trips to Chamisa. The silver *naja,* the crescent-shaped pendant that adorned the necklace, was an ancient protection symbol that had come to the Navajo from the Moors by way of the Spanish. I figured I could use some protection that day and clasped it around my neck. It was heavy and combined with the belt added a few pounds to my weight.

There was nothing of Dad's I could wear. He never wore jewelry and had only kept a pair of hiking shoes and a few tee shirts in Chamisa. He did, however, have a bottle of twelve-year-old Glenmorangie stashed in the closet.

I raised the bottle to my departed father, "Here's mud in your eye." It was Dad's and my favorite toast to each other. I threw back a long draft, gasping as it burned my throat on the way down. God Dad, are you trying to get me drunk? I took a second swig.

❧

The outfit was a mistake. Even though it was in memory of my parents, I didn't have the confidence to carry it off among the Peace, Love and Granola crowd, the shrinking band of 60s holdouts, and their 1990s incarnations. Wispy clouds of pot smoke drifted by, courtesy of a tight circle passing around a pipe. I saw one other elaborate silver necklace, around the neck of a Pueblo woman who wore it like it was coded in her DNA. I'd wanted to blend in, go unnoticed, yet I'd achieved the opposite. I was a poseur, just as I accused my mother of being when she'd worn the clothes, saying it in the French to heighten the affect. My mother's rebuttal was to correct my pronunciation.

I headed straight to the wine table and filled a glass to the rim with Chardonnay. Maybe if I kept the buzz from the whiskey going I'd cease to care if everyone was staring at me and whispering. "Who's that?" "Never seen her before." "She's the one who found Natalya." "Oh, the one who never checked on her, never asked what was wrong." "What the hell is she wearing?"

If I'd arrived with Giles, I'd have felt more secure, the reason for my being there evident to everyone. "Where are you going?" I'd asked when he slid out of my bed at seven that morning.

"Gotta help Luna and Sierra set up." Could he pick me up later? Too much to do, but I was a big girl, I could handle it he'd said. Right, the day was about his family's mourning not my comfort.

I took a seat in the last row of chairs that faced a large photo of Natalya in a gilt frame, flanked by vases of dahlias, her favorite flower. Natalya was about seventeen, her big brown eyes looking upward, the setting sun transforming her hair into a shimmering halo as diamonds of light danced around her shoulders. She looked like an angel.

Avoiding obvious gestures, I tried to will Giles to my side through the sheer power of my presence. He was standing with Nova and Maggie holding Kaela's hand, along with some others I'd never seen before. He gave a quick wave of hello, but remained with his friends. Ok, he had to be host, not babysit me. But I was a guest, too.

Sierra, in a dark gray shirt and jeans, strode to the memorial table and in a loud voice asked everyone to please sit down. Giles again stayed away. He sat in the front next to Luna. That was to be expected, he should be with his family. But why was I relegated to the seating equivalent of Siberia? Where was the loving, tender Giles of the morning?

When all were seated and the chatting had dropped to a murmur, Sierra thanked everyone for coming. "Luna, Giles and I know you all loved Natalya in your different ways and we thought there'd be some of you who'd like to share a few of your memories of her with us, so rather than having a set program, we'll let whoever wants to come up and say a few words. And as long as I'm already up here, I'll go first."

He spoke of the day Natalya had first come to them, how he wasn't sure he wanted another child, but she was so darn cute that he was soon hooked. He spoke of a father-daughter ritual—he'd sensed their blood connection before it was confirmed—of making dandelion crowns every summer. What happened was so unfair, so sudden and so senseless. And while they would never know for sure the reasons that led to that terrible tragedy, he encouraged us not to linger in that gray place of why but instead remember the kind and generous, loving and fun-loving girl she was, to see her face in every flower, hear her voice in every bird's song.

Next, a woman, late-forties, in a black polyester pant suit, feet stuffed into sensible black shoes, walked to the front, giving Sierra a hug as they passed. Anita Hernandez had been Natalya's government teacher and remembered a young woman with a bright smile and a curious mind who had been a joy to have in class.

Anita was followed by another teacher, a former boss, the director of the animal shelter, all saying what a kind, sweet, person Natalya had been and sharing a cherished memory of her. To Vanessa, Natalya was her sister of the heart and she would forever remember the time she'd had mono and was in bed for weeks. Natalya would come over almost every day after school to bring her homework, dish the latest gossip and sneak in foods her mother had forbidden like Milky Ways and Cokes. Maggie credited Natalya for making her a non-smoker. When they were twelve, Natalya stole a pack of smokes from Luna and behind old Ramon Tafoya's ginormous woodpile, they smoked the entire thing in about an hour, turning white as ghosts and throwing up. Maggie never touched another cigarette after that.

By the time Sgt. David Ferguson marched to the front in his olive dress uniform, hat tucked under his arm, like he was reporting for duty, I'd polished off the first glass of Chardonnay and was making my way through a third. I was feeling a little drowsy.

David led off with the typical eulogy lines, how Natalya had always been a positive person, how she wouldn't want us to be sad today, how if she were here she would tell him to cheer up, smile and think of all the great memories they shared. Those memories had me hoisting up my eyelids. As seniors in high school, they'd skipped school, apologies to Mrs. Hernandez, and went to Santa Fe.

They spent the day doing dumb teenage stuff like going to the mall, hanging out in the plaza and trying to get served beers at a local bar. The bartender had told Natalya she could stay, but David had to go, and for a minute he thought she would stay, the bartender was pretty good-looking. Another time, they went camping in Utah, pitching their tent where there was nothing higher than a rock for miles. During the night a storm rolled in hurtling down lightning bolts all around them. Fleeing to the safety of the car, they laughed at how terrified they'd been, then spent the rest of the night scaring themselves even more telling ghost stories.

He definitely sounded like an ex-boyfriend. Had I finally found the ex? I scribbled a slightly sloppy mental note to speak to him after the service.

David ended by saying it was inexpressibly sad that he'd never again see Natalya's beautiful smile and returned to his seat with a less confident stride. When no one else stood up, Sierra rose again and addressed the gathered. "There is one here who I'm sure you'd like to hear say a few words. I know I'm putting her on the spot, but Hunter would you please join me?"

All heads turned towards me. Stunned, I cursed Sierra, Giles, Natalya, the universe, but mainly myself. Why hadn't I just delivered the letters and gotten the hell out of town. Then I wouldn't be at this fucking service, having had too much to drink and about to make a complete ass of myself. Because I'd slept with Giles, that's why.

Holding my hand, Sierra said, "Natalya lived with Hunter in Milwaukee and Hunter unselfishly honored Natalya's last wish and drove all the way to New Mexico to tell us of Natalya's death."

"I don't think that's anything I should be especially commended for. Anybody in my situation would have done the same thing," I began, fighting the wine that was encouraging me to tell the truth. That Natalya drove me crazy, I wanted to tell them. That I was going to kick her out. She was weird. Everyone thought so. I bet you all thought so too, you just won't admit it. She slept around, a lot. She was into men and women and all sorts of kinky shit. But that wasn't exactly in line with memorial service protocol.

I observed Giles, his emotions under uneasy control; Luna, as inscrutable as a cipher; the expectant faces of the mourners. I sensed the tension in Sierra's hand. I realized I hadn't said anything for several moments. I continued that I didn't know Natalya very well or for very long, but in that brief time I'd learned she was a caring and generous person. She gave a homeless man food or money every day. I'd really admired her for that. Everybody at the bookstore where we worked liked her. And like some of you, I could see she was depressed, but couldn't get her to open up about it. She didn't want to burden anybody with her problems.

My voice dropped low for a final thought, "We all wish we could help someone, save them, but sometimes we can't, either because they want to figure it out for themselves or they don't want our help. Or we're thousands of miles away wrapped up in our own stupid lives. That's really all I have to say."

With my head down, I returned to my seat. I couldn't bear seeing anyone's face. It was all Sierra's fault if I'd fucked it up.

Sierra called upon his good friend from the pueblo, Frank Bernal, to say a prayer for Natalya to bring the service to a close. Dressed in a sky blue shirt under a vest made from an old wool blanket, his long hair worn in long braids, the old man, his body bent almost in half with age and hard work, slowly made his way to the front with the help of a roughly hewn cane. He asked the crowd to rise and in a strong, clear voice that belied his years, he chanted verses in his native *Tiwa*.

A profound quiet fell over the attendees as Frank's prayer ended, then everyone rushed to the well-supplied food table set up under the back portal and helped themselves. Another funeral, another feast.

I remained in my chair needing Giles's support now more than ever, but he was nowhere to be seen. I noted David Ferguson standing alone, taking sips from a hip flask. After my fiasco, I didn't have the nerve to talk to him.

Maggie approached with Kaela behind her, a plate in her small hands.

"Nice speech. As long as you're not doing anything, watch Kaela for me. I gotta pee." Even when asking a favor she was bitchy.

"Isn't Melissa here?"

"No, her mom's sick. Can-cer," she said exaggerating the syllables like she was talking to a moron, which was the word I'd have used to describe myself at that moment.

"Oh, right," I replied weakly to no one, Maggie had already walked away. I held Kaela's plate as the little girl hopped onto a chair. The plate held three pieces of cake, a slice of pie and a tamale.

"That looks healthy," I said, and thinking of Leslie's daughter Emily, continued, "I know a little girl who won't eat anything green. Are you like that too?"

"No. I like green M&Ms," the girl replied and took a bite of chocolate cake.

Kaela finished the slice, licked all the icing off the other two, spit out a bite of pie and didn't touch the tamale.

Where the hell was Maggie? How long did it take to pee? I scanned the crowd for her only to find Giles at the corner of the house in the company of Vanessa and Jason, but his eyes were watching me. I waved. He ignored me. He'd insisted I attend and now he was avoiding me. Instead David was making his way over.

"Do you mind?" he asked, pointing to one of the chairs before spinning it round to face me, "You look as out of place here as I do, except I grew up here and you didn't."

"I look out of place most of the time."

But at least you weren't viewed as the enemy, David said. To the Sierra and Luna types, he'd chosen the wrong side to fight on. The day he told Natalya he was enlisting after they'd been going out for about six months, she made Sierra try to talk him out of it. She didn't really give a shit about the politics, she just didn't want him to go and thought Sierra could convince him not to. David didn't understand half of what Sierra was talking about and the other half didn't make any difference. All David cared

317

about was not going to jail. He was on a collision course with the law, drinking a lot, jacking cars. His uncle, who was a cop, told his dad what he'd been up to. They gave David an ultimatum, join the army and get his shit straight or face the consequences because there'd be no get-out-of-jail-free card. The day he left for boot camp Natalya refused to see him off. He wrote her a few times, but she never wrote back. He got the message. He'd only just returned from a year's stint in Korea the previous week.

"Hunter, I wanna swing," Kaela announced. "Will you push me?" She jumped off her chair and not waiting for an answer, trotted off in the direction of a stand of trees.

"Sorry, I better go after her," I said.

"No sweat, I gotta check out anyway. Left Jeong, that's my wife, back home with my dad, and he's probably trying to get her to clean the house." He put on his hat, "You know, if I'd thought Natalya really loved me, I might've stayed."

&

The swing was a plastic disc threaded with a length of nylon rope tied to a thick branch of a half-dead cotton-wood. Its arc took it out over the edge of a gully.

"Are you sure you can do this?" I asked, fearing Kaela would slip off and break a leg.

"Luna always lets me. Gimme a push."

I did as instructed, but tentatively, not wanting her to swing too high. Unsatisfied, Kaela demanded to be pushed harder.

"I want to go really high. As high as Tía Naty in heaven."

"Kaela, that's enough. No more swinging."

"But Daddy, I want to go higher."

"I said that was enough." Giles, his voice firm but not angry, brought the swing to a stop.

"Why's Kaela still with you?" With me, he was angry, "Where's Maggie?"

Could this day get any worse? First the speech and now this. I went on the defensive, "Don't be mad at me. She left Kaela and never came back."

"I'm right here," said Maggie who, like Giles, appeared out of nowhere and snidely added, "Lovers' quarrel? Come on Kaela, let your daddy and his friend work it out." She took the girl's hand and walked her back to the house.

"What the hell is your problem," I whined, "You avoid me the whole day and then you yell at me. The only reason I came is because you said you needed me here."

"Right, I wanted you here for me. To be here if I needed you. Not running around playing with my daughter or throwing yourself at Dave fucking Ferguson."

"What did you expect me to do? Let Kaela run off by herself. If you want to yell at someone, yell at Magpie. And David came over to me."

"Not making insulting speeches."

"Insulting?"

"Yeah, we were too busy with our 'stupid lives' to help Natalya."

"I didn't mean...I was talking about me, being in Peru rather than near my parents. Do you think I wanted to get up there in front of a bunch of people I don't know, but what was I supposed to do, refuse?"

Ignoring me, he continued, "I wanted you to be beautiful too, but what are you wearing. You look like a Texas matron."

"Fuck you, these are my mother's clothes. I wore them in her memory. She's dead too, you know."

I ran off toward my car, checking once or twice if Giles was following me. He remained at the swing. Looking one last time, I almost collided with Sierra coming around the house.

"Hey, where're you dashing off to?"

"I've got to go," I said, tears tracking down my cheeks.

"What's wrong? Shit, are you upset about the service?"

"No, that's not it, but, I mean, that was a disaster."

He wouldn't let me drive in my state and led me down a short wood chip path to a west-facing bench for watching the sunsets. "I'm so sorry for putting you on the spot like that. It was a terrible thing to do. I shouldn't have listened to Luna."

"Luna?" I sniffled and wiped my cheeks on my sleeve.

"Yeah, it was her idea. She said you wouldn't mind. I knew as soon as I called you up it was a mistake."

That bitch.

33

I needed to be in the outdoors to clear my head, sweat out the whiskey and wine, and come up with a strategy for defeating Luna. I went home, changed into jeans and a sweater, and headed to the mountains for a vigorous hike.

The woman really disliked me. If I'd given her cause, like shagging Sierra, I could understand, but I hadn't. Ok, I'd slept with him dozens of times in my daydreams, but how could she know that. And I hadn't since I'd committed myself to Giles thirty-seven hours and forty-seven minutes ago. Did she know about me and Giles? Was she as jealous of her son as she was of her husband, some kind of Oedipal thing? The woman was so heinous she may even have told Giles lies about me. He'd confessed to her that we were in love when they were setting up that morning and Luna had scoffed, "She was getting it on with Natalya. She tried to deny it, but it was obvious. Driving a thousand miles for someone she hardly knew. Right. I'm only trying to protect you." Giles wasn't angry, he was hurt, hurt that I hadn't been honest with him.

The trail I'd chosen crisscrossed a stream that in late September was a mere trickle, and eventually it brought me to a grove of aspens in full autumnal splendor. Breathing hard, as much from anger as from exertion, I rested on a fallen tree and gazed up at the canopy of gold set against the intense blue of the sky. My anger abated. What significance did Luna's schemes have in a setting such as this. I began to wonder if she was even that conniving. Maybe she was just clueless and it had nothing to do with my being with her son. Thinking she'd say anything about me now sounded crazy. And if she were trying to sabotage our relationship, Giles, if he were any kind of a man, wouldn't allow it. If he had questions, he should ask me, not be mean.

Just what kind of man was Giles. On the hike down, I replayed the nasty comments he'd made earlier. He had a cruel streak not revealed before. With every cross of the stream my mind changed about him. Either I made allowances—he was at a memorial service. His emotions were running high. Not everyone responded to grief in the same way, give him a break—or no excuse was acceptable for the way he'd treated me. It was uncalled for. The latter emerged victorious and I returned home furious.

ॐ

There was the crunch of gravel on the drive as I got out of the shower. Sure it was Giles, I threw on a robe and went to the door ready to give him an earful only to find Sierra there.

"Just wanted to see if you were okay," he said.

Damn. I'd committed to the wrong man. Sierra consistently showed he cared about me, was concerned for my feelings. Giles had been an ass. He hadn't come over to apologize. He hadn't even called. Sierra was a true gentleman. No wonder Giles disparaged him. He'd never be even half the man his father was.

"But if you always answer the door like this, I'll stop by more often," Sierra added, gazing appreciatively at my wet hair and loosely tied robe. "If I remember correctly, I have a rain check on a cup of tea."

If Giles caught us in bed together, he deserved every agony that tormented him.

Sierra followed me into the kitchen as I filled the kettle and set it on the stove to boil. Opening a cupboard and rummaging around, I declared, "I don't think there's a lot to choose from. I know there's some Earl Grey. Wait, here's some green, too."

"Earl Grey's fine."

He half-sat on the counter and ran a hand through his thick silken hair. His grey shirt, the same one he'd worn at the service, was unbuttoned to mid-sternum offering me glimpses of his sun-browned skin. Men bared their chests all the time, but those brazen displays were never as sexy as sneak peeks into an open shirt. It made me want to rip the shirt off, press my cheek against his chest and feel the beating of his heart. He'd arch my back, raising my breasts to his mouth. He'd suck one while massaging the other with a calloused hand. His tongue would wander the distance to my pussy and—

"Got any sugar?"

Blushing, I smacked down a mug, teabag in it, next to him. I darted back to the cupboard, took out a small glazed bowl, set it next to the mug, then jumped over to the stove.

"Relax, you're hopping around like a rabbit. Come over here. I'm not dangerous."

I stayed at my post. Sierra was finally in my kitchen. I was one yank of a sash away from naked. A fantasy was crossing the threshold into reality and I was as nervous as a virgin on her wedding night. What if he thought I was a terrible lover? What if he thought all my moves were teenage-girlish. What if he lost interest mid-way? What if he only wanted a cup of tea?

"Any milk?"

I retrieved the carton from the refrigerator and as I placed it next to the sugar, Sierra took hold of my wrist and drew me into an embrace. "Now I've got you," he purred, "You know how beautiful you are, don't you. I'm sure men tell you all the time." He dropped his head so that it was almost touching my hair, "I had a bet with myself that you'd smell like lavender. I was wrong, but you sure smell good. More like a wheat field after the rain."

"It must be my conditioner," I said sounding like a bad TV commercial.

"And I bet you taste like heaven," he murmured in my ear.

An electric charge ran through my body. It felt all wrong. I couldn't add sex with a father and son to my list of shameless acts. I had to put a stop to it right away. But in depressingly typical fashion, I did nothing. Sierra, emboldened by my lack of resistance, pinned me between himself and the counter. He drew his finger down the V of exposed skin from the base of my neck to the cleft between my breasts, then used it to begin tugging on the sash. It gave way and the robe fell open exposing my naked body.

He cupped my breasts in his hands and pressed his hard cock into my abdomen.

"Giles is a boy, not worth any woman's tears. Do you think he could ever make love to you like I will?"

The whistling of the kettle brought me to my senses. "You'd try to get me in bed knowing I'm sleeping with your son?" I knew in an instant that he'd tried this with some, maybe all, of Giles's girlfriends. I was not going to let my name be added to his list of conquests. I pushed him off, closed my robe, and darted to the stove, turning off the burner and grabbing the kettle at the same time. I was infuriated to see Sierra was laughing at me.

"And if I hadn't said anything, you'd have fucked me right here even though you're fucking my son."

I assumed an expression of indignation.

"Come off it, I know when a woman wants it. You could've gotten dressed, but you stayed in that robe."

"I think you better go," I stammered.

Ignoring my request, Sierra returned to his position against the counter, "Don't I get my cup of tea?"

"What the hell's going on here?" The question came from Giles, who was walking into the kitchen.

"Just stopped by to check on Hunter. She was pretty upset earlier today. Seems you weren't very nice to her." Sierra said with disturbing serenity.

I tried to match his calm, knowing that if there had been no comment about Giles, I might well have been caught in flagrante with the father by the son.

"Yeah, I know. I was a total asshole. But you can go now, I'll handle it from here," Giles said, dismissing his father with a wave of the hand.

Sierra admonished his son to treat me better and departed.

Giles turned to me and eyed my robe suspiciously, "Is that really why he was here? I mean, he didn't come over for something else?"

"I'd just gotten out of the shower. I heard a car. I thought it was you."

"Why didn't you get dressed?"

"I don't know. After what you told me about him, I thought he might follow me into the bedroom."

"So nothing happened?"

I avoided his eyes by putting away the milk. "No. He may have been hoping, but he was going to be disappointed."

Giles relaxed and dropped onto the couch. He kicked off his shoes and asked if I had anything to drink.

"There's hot water. I can make you a cup of tea."

"Hell no, after today I need hard liquor. Tequila, if you've got it."

I poured him a glass of the Glenmorangie. "This is all I've got."

"It'll have to do, though Tequila'd be better."

"Does Luna have a problem with me?"

"If she thought you were fucking Sierra, she'd have a huge problem with you. I would, too."

"Would she have a problem with us?"

"She's got zero interest in my girlfriends (*He called me his girlfriend*). Pretty much zero interest in my life. If she knew she wouldn't care. Sierra's all that matters to her. Why?"

"It was her idea to call me up to speak. I thought maybe she wanted to embarrass me..."

"How do you know that?"

"Sierra told me."

"Oh man, that's fucking Sierra all over. He gets some crazy idea in his head and when it all goes to hell, he can't stand anyone thinking it's his fault so he passes the buck, usually to Luna, cuz most people don't like her. And all that bullshit about Natalya, the dandelion crown. They made one once when she was like four. He didn't give a rat's ass about her even after he found out he was her father. He may have cared even less, cuz he couldn't fuck her."

Now that was Woody-Allen-Soon-Yi-Previn level creepy. Giles was right, Sierra was a sleazebag. And Luna was a bitch. Raised by people like that it wasn't surprising Natalya was so desperate for love. Giles was the only normal one in the family. He did show up to apologize and maybe he'd stopped by earlier when I was in the mountains cursing him. My love meter hit nine.

"Now get that robe off and get on top of me," Giles said.

34

Giles's behavior at the memorial service marked a change in him, or he dropped the normal guy act and was his true self. He was erratic and moody. At times he was on a high talking about us in the future tense, mapping out our life together in minute detail: two children, a boy named Galen and a girl, Natalya, in memory of his sister. He'd chosen the house we would live in, one that he, and Natalya, had always loved. On its three acres we would have a big vegetable garden and raise goats and chickens. We'd spend our nights around the wood-burning stove eating what we'd grown. In those moments, I was carried away by his fire, driving by the house noting all the changes I'd make, how I'd decorate its rooms, where I'd put flower beds. With my inheritance we could really do the place up right, and Giles could quit his landscaping job and concentrate on his music. Get a demo made, then a record deal, then out on tour with thousands of screaming groupies throwing themselves at him. Was I crazy? Probably better if Giles was a farmer who played music as a hobby. I could even kind of, sort of, a tiny bit, see myself being a stepmother to Kaela.

A lot of the time Giles, however, was class-bully mean, making snide comments about my clothes. I had no taste and I should let him pick out what I wore. Or my cooking.

Northern New Mexico cuisine with lots of green chile was all he liked. When I wore my hair up he preferred it down and when I wore it loose, he wanted it in a braid.

He was raring for fights and picked them over the tiniest of reasons. I was five minutes late to pick him up. I bought Tecate instead of Corona. He didn't want to do the dishes. I failed to respond to his every suggestion with Stepford wife-like obedience—Yes, dear. Whatever you want, dear. What a great idea, darling.

And as after the service, each nasty episode was followed by remorse, begging for forgiveness and passionate make-up sex that left me exhausted and chafed.

And it was not just me that Giles sunk his venomous teeth into. Vanessa was a stupid bitch for moving his kapo right before a gig. She threatened to quit the band if he didn't apologize. He wouldn't so out she walked.

Another night he threw a punch at a Kiva Bar bartender who refused to serve him. Inhibited by alcohol, the punch was stopped mid-swing by its target, who suggested with a firm grip on Giles's collar that he take his party home.

The worst was when he told Maggie she was a fucking cunt and to get a life. He was never coming back to her. For once Maggie's icy facade cracked and a single tear tracked down her cheek. She slapped him and turning to me said, "You can have the asshole."

At first, I bore the mood swings out of empathy for Giles's suffering. He was grieving. And I was pretty skilled at justifying the actions of any man who treated me like gum stuck to his shoe—he lost his job; his last girlfriend really hurt him; his mother died when he was young; his soccer team lost a big game. Not a team he actually played on, but like Chelsea or Real Madrid. I soon came to see Giles as the agent for my well-deserved punishment. Payback for all my bad behavior. I ceased arguing with him, ceased defending myself against his insults and scorn. His wanting to be with me in spite of my failings, and his descriptions of a shared future were signs that he was my destiny. We wouldn't be happy together, but I didn't deserve happiness.

"Your destiny? Are you nuts?" Vanessa said giving me an incredulous look, "He treats you like crap."

"He's treating everyone badly. He's grieving. It'll pass.

"Maybe with his friends, but he wasn't grieving when he was going out with Melissa or with Denise, or with Tara and he treated them like crap. He's either nasty or completely shut down. Lose-lose scenarios," Vanessa said.

We were leaving Fleur de Lis, Chamisa's priciest restaurant, where Giles had invited Vanessa, and Jason, to atone for his rude behavior. Vanessa accepted with a caveat: no matter how messed up he was, for whatever reason, Giles was never to speak to her like that again or he could kiss their friendship goodbye.

In full Ghost-of-Christmas-Present mode, Giles encouraged us to order starters, entrees, bottles of wine, and desserts. When the bill arrived it totaled way more cash than he had on him. "Give me some money," he said to me.

"How much do you need?"

"Don't be fucking stingy. Gimme everything you got," he said loud enough for the others to hear that I was Scrooge in his minor financial drama.

That interchange had inspired Vanessa to pull me aside to offer the unsolicited advice.

"Listen, I love Giles, but I warned you not to get involved with him. And don't tell me 'But he's so gorgeous.' If I hear that one more time I'm going to puke. As a boyfriend, he sucks."

"He's always sorry."

"Whoopee. You can do way better than a guy who's always apologizing for fucking up. You should be with a guy who treats you like a queen. And listen, please don't hate me for saying this, but you're rebound. Lisa dumped him in August and he was totally gaga for her. And with Natalya's death, he's totally bad news right now. You've been together what, four weeks? Get out now before you're in so deep you start to believe all that shit he's dumping on you."

I had just enough wine in me to think Vanessa was right. I did deserve better than what I was getting. My indignation was at a roiling boil by the time we got to the casita.

He'd invited the three of us out and I shouldn't be expected to foot the bill for his act of contrition, I said jabbing a finger inches from his face.

"Fleur de Lis was your idea," he charged.

"All I said was that you had to take them somewhere nicer than Jaime's Chow Cart."

"I said I'd pay you back."

"Yeah, you always say that, but you never do. And when you want me to do you a favor you shouldn't talk to me like I'm some idiot you're forced to put up with."

"Yeah well, sometimes you can be pretty fucking stupid. It was fucking obvious that I was embarrassed." His eyes flashed, and he rolled onto the balls of his feet, the signs that he was ready to go another round, but I was in no mood to hear it, or for the apologies and the sex that would follow. I told him to leave. The first time I'd ever done that. Confused and disappointed, Giles made no move to go, confirming my theory that he saw these interactions as parts of a sadistic game that I now didn't want to play.

"Go, now, I mean it," I said crossing my arms on my chest. Obeying my command like a dog who'd peed on the carpet, he left with a solemn, "I'll call you tomorrow."

❧

Kaela was at the front door the next day holding a bouquet of red roses almost as big as she was. "These are from Daddy. He says he's really sorry for being such a…" She began to giggle and snort so that I could barely make out what she said next, "such a big stinky poop last night." She turned around to the SUV where her father sat. "I said big stinky poop, Daddy, just like you told me. But I forgot the other part."

"Walmart," Giles cued her.

"Oh yeah." The girl faced me again, "We're going to Walmart to buy me some shoes. I wanted to get blue sneakers but Victor says blue's a boys' color and everyone'll think I'm a boy if I wear them, so I'm going to get pink ones instead. Blue is my favorite color but I don't want anyone to think I'm a boy. And then we're going for ice cream. Wanna come?"

I'd immediately regretted kicking Giles out last night. The possibility that he might never return made me feel ill. It'd been all Vanessa's fault, getting me so fired up. Of course she'd think Giles was a crap boyfriend. She was so demanding and bossy. Giles would never have let her push him around like she did Jason. She treated the poor guy like a servant, constantly ordering him to do this or get that for her. For Giles, our fights were tests, tests of my commitment to him, how deeply I loved him and I had to find the right balance of tolerance and firmness to show I was all-in but not a total pushover. I grabbed my purse and hopped in the front seat.

❧

There were no pink sneakers only red or white, but when it came to shoes, Kaela wasn't fussy. The moment she slipped on a pair of red Keds and after Giles assured her that red was not a boy's color, she deemed them perfect. Entrusting them to my care, she declared she had something very important to show Giles and me and dragged us to the sad, soulless aisles of the toy department. The shelves were packed with luridly colored plastic toys encased in layers of plastic packaging, obviously done to discourage theft, but having the unintended consequence of discouraging play. Kaela, having never been to a real toy store, didn't know what she was missing and pointed her chubby finger at Sea Fashion Ariel, a cascade of synthetic orange hair and a green-sequined fish tail.

"We're only looking, not buying," Giles told her, but the girl was determined to use her wiles to leave the store with Ariel. When her father again told her no, Kaela looked like a koala plucked from its favorite eucalyptus tree. Tears poured from her eyes, and a few shrieks were thrown in for maximum effect, "But Daddy, I want Ariel."

Everything Giles wasn't as a boyfriend he was as a father. Patient. Loving. Kind. Never were Kaela's hundreds of questions brushed off with a harsh word. The tedium of reading *Goodnight Moon* three times in a row was performed with good humor. Cups of Kaela's imaginary pickle juice tea were sipped in a tiny chair, a plastic tiara on his head. He was strict but calm when she misbehaved, never a voice raised (*Even during our fights he never shouted, which made the fights even worse*). Except today. It was the first time I ever saw him get angry with his daughter. He lifted the writhing, wailing child under his arm and carried her out of the toy department shouting, "I can tell you right now, that's not going to happen."

Those words. I knew those words. I'd heard them shouted in anger before. I knew that voice. It was the voice shouting at Natalya the night before she died. The sneakers slipped from my grip. It was Giles's voice.

The thud spun Giles round. He glared at the shoes on the floor, then at my stunned face. "What's the matter with you?" he snapped.

"It was you. You are Mystery Man."

Shocked and sickened by the knowledge, I rushed past him, the acid burn of bile rising in my throat. In the parking lot, bent over, hands on my thighs, I breathed in the crisp high desert air.

What did it mean that Giles had been in the house. Had he raped his sister? Why else would Natalya have been naked. No, that wasn't possible. I'd made some bad choices in men, but I couldn't have slept with a man who raped his own sister. Natalya was telling the man she loved him so it couldn't have been rape. If it wasn't rape, then it was consensual. Giles and Natalya as lovers was just as repulsive. Maybe Natalya had been so off-the-chart wild that she'd tried to fuck her own brother. That's why Giles told her she was crazy. That it was never going to happen. He found the idea as disgusting as I did. That had to be what happened.

But I had to know the truth. On a cracked, weed-plagued and occasionally nonexistent sidewalk, I walked the three miles to Giles's place, arriving hot and tired, a blister forming on my left heel.

He was seated at a circular dining table, holding a bottle of tequila, the contents of Natalya's shoe box spread out before him: photographs, cards, letters, a small toy kitten with a pink bow.

"You know, when I opened her suitcase and saw the books and the Indian clothes, I didn't understand. They weren't Natalya's style, but reading that," Giles said, pointing to a sheet of lilac stationery, "it all makes sense."

"Where's Kaela?"

"I took her back to Melissa's."

"Why was Natalya naked that night? Was she trying to seduce you?"

"Yes, I mean no, she didn't have to try." His implicit confession hung in the air for several moments. When I was finally able to speak, I spat out the words like hot coals, "But she was your sister."

"Half-sister, not that it makes any difference. It's still against the law and every moral code. When it started we didn't know, honest." He was crying, "I loved her. She loved me. God, it's such a relief to tell somebody that. Holding it in for so many years has been killing me. It's part of what killed her, too."

35

Luna and Sierra were true radicals, SDS, the New Left, ardent civil rights activists, Vietnam War protesters. Anything establishment they hated. The assassinations of Martin Luther King and Robert Kennedy shocked them into a different form of action. If they wanted a world more equal, just, community-focused, and respectful of the land, they had to create it from scratch. They bid goodbye to San Francisco and headed for New Millennium, a recently formed commune in Chamisa committed to pacifism, the sacredness of the earth, and sustainability. It would also be a better environment in which to raise Cloud, their newborn son.

The little family became part of the extended communal family for a year until a disagreement over the direction the commune should take resulted in them buying their house.

"I'm sure my parents thought their ideas were the best ones and everyone there were morons."

On a spring day a year later, Samantha Haven, Luna's childhood friend whom she hadn't seen since her husband was killed in Vietnam, showed up with a drug problem and a two-year-old daughter, Sunflower. Father unknown or his name forgotten. She wanted Luna's help to get clean and off she went to rehab on Luna's dime, leaving Sunflower behind, supposedly for a couple of months. They never saw her again. So Luna and Sierra raised Sunflower. There was no one else to look after her.

"I think Luna secretly loved being praised for being so unselfish, you know, raising another woman's child."

And Luna never failed to remind Sunflower how lucky she was to live with them. Her own grandparents didn't want her and she would have ended up in foster care, a ward of the state, if it weren't for them.

Sierra never reminded Sunflower what lucky girl she was because he rarely talked to her, or to his son. His time and undivided attention went to his political causes. He was advocating for this, or protesting that, or at the food pantry he and Luna had set up. It was intended for the local poor, but most often served the hippies who floated in and out of Chamisa in the seventies. And at night, all the town's radicals hung out there arguing politics, planning for the revolution that never came.

Luna wasn't maternal. She didn't enjoy motherhood, but when Cloud and Sunflower were small she was forced to spend time at home. The two were told to play quietly in their rooms while Luna—never Mom or Mother, or, God forbid, Mommy—was working, which was most of the time.

The family never ate together, Cloud and Sunflower ate first and after Luna and Sierra had eaten, Sierra lectured them about the state of the world. The children were embryonic activists and Sierra was awaiting the day when they would emerge from the political womb, pamphlets in hand, ready to march. Eventually, the pamphlets they were given to hand out at school went straight into the garbage can.

It was natural that with such austere parents, Cloud and Sunflower turned to each other for support. They were each other's protector, defender, counselor, and best friend. In their eyes, they were brother and sister, and, depending on their moods, they were also Batman and Robin, Butch Cassidy and the Sundance Kid, or Lucy and Ethel.

When they started school full-time, Luna started going to the pantry and to more meetings. In the summers, the children were dragged to music festivals all over the country. Luna and Sierra manned booths to raise awareness for their latest cause often leaving Cloud and Sunflower alone to entertain themselves in the tented communities that popped up at festivals, or in cheap motels while they attended political rallies or conferences.

At fourteen and thirteen, they began staying home alone when Luna and Sierra travelled. They did the shopping, cooked for themselves, kept the house clean and got themselves to school. They pretended they were truly on their own. He wasn't sure when they began seeing themselves as a husband and wife rather than as brother and sister.

One night, when they were a year older and Luna and Sierra were gone for a week to Washington, D.C., Cloud, who now called himself Giles, and Sunflower, who called herself Natalya, were washing dishes. Natalya threw a handful of soapy water at Giles, who emptied a glass down the back of her shirt. Soon water and soap suds were flying through the air, drenching the teens and the kitchen.

Natalya ran screaming joyfully towards her bedroom with Giles in hot pursuit, in his hands a sopping sponge. He pinned Natalya to her door before she had a chance to open it, and wrung the sponge out over her head. Laughing, she turned to face him. She was so beautiful, hair wet, eyes dancing. He kissed her. He was afraid she would recoil, but she didn't. That night he slept in her bed and they kissed until both fell asleep.

The next day, they wanted to skip school and be alone to kiss the whole day, but feared their absences would get them in trouble. Maybe Luna and Sierra would hire someone to look after them. They would do nothing to jeopardize being left alone.

The school bus couldn't get them home fast enough. Each had spent the day dreaming of the other and once inside the house, they were in Natalya's bed kissing and holding one another.

Over the following months, any chance they got they spent in each other's arms. Kissing led to touching and fondling, which led to shyly removing their clothes, which led to more ardent touching and fondling. And when Giles was seventeen and Natalya sixteen, they fully consummated their love.

Making love was not a sin they assured themselves. They weren't doing anything wrong. They weren't really brother and sister. They weren't related. Luna and Sierra had never adopted Natalya. Luna, particularly, whenever the subject of adoption came up, always said it meant getting the government involved and without a birth certificate, they might take Natalya away.

Natalya and Giles were careful to keep their relationship secret. They sensed that Luna and Sierra wouldn't like it and they became expert at deception. And Luna and Sierra were such distant parents that it wasn't hard. Giles had a few girlfriends in high school and Natalya a few boyfriends, but no one came between them. Girls at Chamisa High gossiped that Giles was probably gay, he had no interest in sex with them. Natalya got a reputation for being frigid.

Giles graduated and went to University of New Mexico in Albuquerque, coming up to Chamisa some weekends, or Natalya visited him, telling Luna and Sierra that she slept on the floor of his dorm room when in truth the two went further south to Los Lunas and checked into a motel.

On Natalya's eighteenth birthday in March, Giles came up to celebrate with her. Now that they were both of age nobody could stop them and they were going to tell Luna and Sierra the truth. They were in love. Before the chance arose, Luna announced she had a birthday surprise for Natalya and would she, Giles and Sierra please sit down on the couch.

Luna sat in a chair in front of them, hands clasped. Only those who knew her well would recognize a smile from her slightly upturned mouth. She had a wonderful present for Natalya, something she'd promised Samantha not to tell till Natalya was eighteen. Sierra was her biological father. She was Giles's half-sister.

No one said a word, but inside, Giles's world was imploding. Natalya looked like she'd been pierced through the heart. Sierra stood up slowly and gave Luna a glare that would freeze water. "You've known this all along?"

The words came out calmly, but only with practiced self-control.

"Samantha swore me to secrecy. She may betray her friends, but I don't."

"I don't understand," Natalya said, looking first to Sierra then Luna.

Luna answered in a voice as smooth as polished granite, "Do I have to spell it out for you? Your mother slept with my husband. They betrayed me, then she left you for me to raise. But I knew my friend was in trouble, and that you needed a stable home so I took you in."

That was when it hit Giles, all Luna had been through over the last sixteen years. "I'd always hated how she'd treated Natalya, you know, always reminding her how she wasn't family. Now I knew why and suddenly I saw her as someone who'd done the best she could for a child who everyday reminded her what an asshole she'd married. And, I mean, what kind of person was Samantha Haven. She fucks her best friend's husband then asks her for money. I already knew Sierra was a sleazebag. Natalya and I'd seen him banging some mesa rat chick at the food bank. But I didn't hate him till that day."

Natalya tried to keep it together, saying it was the shock of the announcement that threw her. She was happy. It was what she had always wished for. But Giles knew she was shattered. They both were. He felt sick with shame, but they hadn't known they were brother and sister when they fell in love.

Giles went back to Albuquerque and didn't come home again that semester or even that summer. He got a job in the university library. Natalya never visited him, she started seeing David and tried to fall in love.

As his daughter, Sierra said he'd pay for any university Natalya wanted to go to. "I had to pay my own way. That's what men do, he told me. Sierra's really a sexist for all his progressive sermonizing." Natalya felt so guilty about the circumstances, she refused to take the money. Her and Giles's plan had been for her to join him at UNM. She'd already qualified for financial aid and been awarded a scholarship, and it was too late to apply anywhere else. They were sure too, that the months they'd spent apart had cooled their love. But some passions are hard to put out and the tiniest spark set theirs burning hotter than ever.

Natalya and Giles got an apartment together. There was nothing odd about them sharing a place. They talked about leaving New Mexico, about leaving everybody and everything behind, making a new life for themselves in a new city, a new state, where no one knew them and they could be whoever they wanted to be. Then Melissa, a girl from Chamisa Giles dated off and on, got pregnant. He half-heartedly suggested an abortion, which she refused outright. Melissa dropped out of school and moved back in with her parents.

As soon as Kaela was born and Giles held her, he changed. He vowed he was going be the opposite kind of parent that Luna or Sierra had been. His daughter was going to feel loved, have lots of toys, and never go to a fucking rally, ever. She was going to have as normal a girlhood as he could give her.

Giles finished school and returned to Chamisa. He and Melissa moved in together and tried to make it work for the baby's sake, but when you're twenty-two, have a kid, hardly know each other, and one of you is in love with someone else, the odds aren't great. Initial domestic unity deteriorated into constant bickering and fighting. They couldn't even agree on what milk to buy. After one particularly nasty fight—"I think I called her a fucking cunt"—Melissa kicked him out. The breakup didn't mean Giles wasn't going to be a great dad. A custody agreement was worked out giving him two days a week with Kaela.

Natalya stayed in Albuquerque, waitressing, wearing a veneer of happiness and normalcy, but always holding onto the dream that she and Giles would have the fairytale happy ending. And Giles fed that dream, continuing their relationship all the time he was with Melissa, and after they broke up making more frequent trips to Albuquerque. Natalya tried to persuade him to run away with her, but there was no way he'd leave Kaela. He would come home ashamed, swearing it would never happen again, but it always did.

This year, in early February, a letter arrived for Natalya in the Lawlesses' post office box. Natalya rarely got mail, not even junk mail, so Giles knew she'd be doubly, triply excited by an actual letter. Natalya held the lilac envelope with no return address, written in an unfamiliar hand, like it was a flawless, twenty-carat diamond. It's from her, isn't it, she asked, meaning Samantha.

Ugly thoughts about her mother—She chose drugs over me; she didn't want me, and later, she's deceitful—competed with Natalya's desire to be compassionate. She needed time to sit with her feelings now that the only thing separating her from Samantha's excuses and pleas for

346

forgiveness was opening an envelope. As curious as she was about the letter's contents, she didn't read it that day, nor the next. She taped it to the bathroom mirror.

The letter was still in its spot a month later when Giles told Natalya he was in love with Lisa, a woman he'd met around the same time the letter came—She reminded him of Natalya, fun and sweet. They even looked a bit alike— and he was committed to making that relationship work. He and Natalya had to learn to love each other in a different way. They had to move forward with their lives, find a new happiness. He told her they would never be lovers again. He tried to convince her that the letter and Lisa were part of God's, or the universe's, plan. They were finally being paid back for what they'd lost. But he'd ended it with her so many times only to fall in bed again that Natalya didn't believe him. He was adamant this time was different.

And to show he was serious, Giles stopped going to Albuquerque. Weeks passed and Natalya's calls became more and more pleading. He finally stopped returning them, a form of tough love that had him drinking more than was healthy and unplugging his phone at night.

He heard from a friend that Natalya was going a little wild, lots of guys, hard partying. He worried about her, worried he'd been too tough. A second letter from Samantha gave him an excuse to see her.

Daniel Martinez was there when he arrived and Natalya made a big show of saying she'd forgotten Giles was coming and how embarrassing it was to be caught in bed with a guy by her older brother. If she'd wanted to make him jealous she'd picked the right guy. And if he hadn't known that Daniel could kick his ass—"I'm only dumb enough to take him on when I'm drunk"—he would have punched Daniel in his smug face.

Several days later, Natalya left him a message. Samantha was the beautiful angel she'd always hoped, deep down, she'd be. She'd deciphered the letters' postmark and was off to Milwaukee to be close by when her mother was ready to meet. A little while later he got a message with a post office box where he could forward any future letters.

Then nothing, not a word till she called begging him to come to see her. She was drunk and despondent. Visits to rehab centers had turned up nothing. Privacy policies prevented them from even confirming that Samantha had never been a patient. There'd been no more letters. She was losing hope.

"I don't know what she was thinking. That she'd just waltz into town and find her mom. She wasn't very practical a lot of the time. But I hadn't tried to talk her out of it. I thought putting some distance between us would be a good thing."

And Giles wanted to see her, too. Lisa'd just dumped him, running off to California with some other guy. Giles was too clingy, Lisa said, the first time he'd ever been accused of that. "I was feeling sorry for myself and wanted to see someone who loved me. I missed Natalya."

The day before his flight, Luna called. Samantha was dead. She'd gotten a letter from the director of someplace called Golden Days Living Center in Racine, Wisconsin. Sounded like a nursing home, she'd sneered. A not very compassionate comment coming from such a great defender of the oppressed and downtrodden as she liked to think herself. She asked him to tell Natalya, if and when he heard from her. He'd never told his parents Natalya was in Milwaukee and had kept his impending trip a secret. Giles asked if he could have the letter. Luna said she'd tossed it, but he was welcome to look.

'Tossed it' meant the letter was in one of the file boxes dumped around the house. It would have been easier to find in the garbage can, but Giles eventually recovered it. Samantha had died during the night several days before. She'd been clean for eight months so her death was not directly drug-related, but the years of abuse had weakened her heart. Claire Hellmann, the director, further wrote that during the time Samantha spent with them, she had often spoken of her daughter and her desire to see her again. She was a kind and gentle woman who had been well-liked by the other residents and the staff. The few possessions Samantha brought with her had been boxed up and were waiting to be sent as soon as they received confirmation that the address was correct.

When Giles and Natalya saw one another again, they couldn't help themselves. Natalya used it as proof they were meant to be together. It was why none of their other relationships worked. She tried to persuade him to stay with her. She was crying and saying she'd give him children to make up for Kaela, and they'd be better because they were born out of their love. That's when Giles shouted she was crazy, that that was never going to happen, and ran from the house.

He didn't even tell her about Samantha. He just left the letter behind. If he'd stayed while she read it, watching yet another dream die, he'd never have left. He'd have forsaken Kaela, the one other person he loved as much as Natalya. Never see his daughter again. But he couldn't do to her what Samantha'd done to Natalya. "But I should have known how desperate Natalya was. I knew her better than anyone and I left her. The last thing I said to her was I didn't love her. It's my fault she's dead." Looking like a boxer who'd just completed fifteen grueling rounds, Giles was slumped on the couch, head hung low, eyes swollen. If psychic bruises could take visible form, he'd have been covered.

I'd gotten what I wanted. The blanks about Natalya were filled in. So why did I feel like total crap. Because, I realized, I'd been lying to myself. It wasn't answers I'd been seeking, but absolution. I'd wanted Natalya's lover to tell me that her suicide was all his fault and that she would've done it even if I'd been a better friend. Looking at the whimpering mess that was Giles I wondered how I ever thought I could possibly feel better by getting someone else to take the blame. Vanessa had sussed out my real motive right away and had wisely warned me against it. I should have listened.

Giles held down a sob with a long drink of tequila and groped for my hand. When he found it, he pulled me towards him.

36

I woke up alone in Giles's bed. I found him passed out on the couch swaddled in Kaela's Little Mermaid blanket. He looked like a little boy. I smoothed his hair and kissed him tenderly on the forehead. He yawned and rolled away exhaling a vapor trail of alcohol. Coffee was a definite must. Giles could barely function without caffeine on the best of mornings and that morning, I predicted, was going to be bad.

Mo' Joe's was quiet. The jitterbugs, as Giles called the group who every morning, rain or shine, hot or cold, sat out front smoking and drinking double espressos, were gone. Only one table was occupied. An older couple, a pot of tea between them, chatted about the adorable little moccasins the woman wanted to buy for their grandson. By now the baristas greeted me by name and prepared a Borgia and a double Americano, without my having to order.

A breeze followed me into the house, fluttering the papers on the table. I picked up a photo that drifted to the floor. It was of a happy Giles and Natalya, arms around each other's waist, heads touching, big smiles. I casually looked at the other mementos. The fur of the toy kitten was rubbed away completely in a few spots and its pink bow was frayed and stained. There was a birthday card with a puppy holding a bouquet of flowers in its mouth, signed "Cloud" in childish block letters; a pressed red rose; a photo of Natalya and Giles when they were small in Halloween costumes, a fairy and a pirate; the letter from New Day. And two sheets of lilac stationery.

February 23

My darling Sunflower,

I write knowing you might throw this letter away, hating me for leaving you so many years ago. I'd like to say I regret what I did but I can't. I would have taken you down with me and as bad as I am, I couldn't do that to my baby girl. And it pains me to say I couldn't clean myself up, not even for you. I've never been a strong person. I knew that Arlene and Laurence would give you a life you were never going to have with me. After years of struggling, I'm now at a point where I think I might be ready to walk a new path and I'm getting the help I need.

I pray that you are happy in a way I've never been. That you can forgive me. I want you to know that not a day has gone by that I haven't thought about you and loved you. I will write again soon.

With a heart full of love,
Samantha

May 27

My darling Sunflower,

I want very much to see you, to know about your life. I wonder if you look like me, are like me. Do the poems of Grace Newhall and Sylvia Plath touch you? Have you read and loved On the Road and Siddhartha? Have you seen Sabrina and The Philadelphia Story hundreds of times? Do you have every album Tom Waits ever recorded?

When I write next it will be to make arrangements to meet,
that is, if you want to meet me. I hope you do.
Loving you with all my heart,
Samantha
P.S. I have carried this photo with me always.

I found the photo in an envelope. On the back was scribbled Me and Sunflower, 16 months. In black and white, Samantha, in an Indian cotton blouse, a necklace similar to the one Natalya wore around her neck, held Natalya wearing a tiny version of her mother's outfit. Samantha looked directly at the camera, her expression a blend of pride and pure joy. It was hard to believe her life was already spinning out of control and less than a year later she was handing her daughter over to Luna and disappearing. And Natalya had grown up to look so much like Samantha. They had the same nose, the same wavy hair woven in a braid, the same smile. Something, however, stopped them from being identical, something I couldn't put my finger on.

It made tragic sense to me, too, why Natalya had tried to make herself into Samantha's spiritual as well as physical twin by dressing like her and claiming to love the same books, music and films. If I been raised by a lech like Sierra and a cold, unfeeling woman like Luna who'd constantly reminded me I wasn't family, denied the man I loved, feeling like I belonged nowhere and to no one, I probably would have done the same thing.

Unnoticed before, the wind had blown another piece of paper to the floor. It was a drawing of two hearts intertwined, an arrow piercing them both, a drop of blood on the arrow's tip and written below in Giles's hand dated Valentine's Day of the previous year:

I love thee to the depth and breadth and height/ My soul can reach, when feeling out of sight.

❧

The man held the stick aloft making the motion of throwing it into the river, once, twice, three times. His black lab jumped and howled in excited anticipation. The fourth time, the stick arced into the churning, mud-colored water of the Rio Grande. The dog splashed in after it, swimming easily with the current. It clamped its jaws around the stick and lumbered to shore, laying the stick at the man's feet. I was watching from the rocky beach on the opposite shore as man and dog repeated the routine again and again and again. How many times before one of them got bored and opted out.

How many more dead-end relationships would I endure before I cried, "Enough." Too much time with the wrong guy was like too many nights on a bad mattress. Eventually I'd morph into one of those gargoyles on Notre Dame, stony, hunched and grotesque. With Giles my back was already beginning to stoop. The Valentine was proof enough of how much he loved Natalya. It would take him years to get over her, if he ever did. Did I always want to be living in her dark shadow? Or was I going to suppress my needs to play nursemaid to his broken heart. And if by some chance he did come to love me, was he really the man I wanted to grow old with? The bucolic life he described was alluring, and my opinion of Chamisa had changed so much that I could actually see myself living there, one day, maybe, but certainly not yet. There was so much of the world I had yet to see, so many things I had yet to do once I dragged myself out of the sludgy sty of torpor I'd been wallowing in for months. Giles was tied down by fatherhood and wanted to tighten the ropes with more children. Kaela was a sweet kid, most of the time, but honestly, I wasn't ready to be her stepmother, and children of my own were a distant possibility, if one at all. And most importantly, being with Giles meant Luna and Sierra would be in my life. Reason alone to get the hell out of Dodge.

Giles was cut from the same cloth as other men I'd pursued. Beautiful. Artistic. Cool. Great sex, but that wasn't even true anymore. Coming in the wake of a fight, it was a product of anger, not love.

He and Michael and Paul, a writer I'd dated in Tokyo, and Oswaldo, the beautiful exotic, and Daniel, a photographer I was obsessed with in London, were like designer clothes I wore with the labels on the outside. Everybody could see how cool I was. Having a boyfriend who was an artist or an Inca was way more important than having a boyfriend who was good to me, who loved me and treated me well.

But like clothing, the guys were only cover for a darker and more complex drama. Asif was a super-sweet guy from Pakistan I went out with in England. I liked Asif. He made me laugh, and even though he was Muslim, our worlds weren't that different. Asif bought me flowers, never blew me off, never played games. Then he told me he loved me. I bolted. That's not completely true. I didn't bolt, I slept with Bobby Tan, a Chinese-Egyptian guy who was working his way through the female students at St. Alban's, and broke Asif's heart. Asif was too good and sooner or later he was going to discover I was not the woman he believed me to be. I was saving us both the pain of that discovery. I'd pulled that stunt a few more times over the years. I ran from men who declared their love, choosing instead to go for men who remained aloof, who withheld love, and whom I didn't really like.

I lay back on the stones, closed my eyes, and let the sun warm my face. The thought was born a mere speck deep inside that began to take shape, to grow, and then to swim in my blood like a fish, like that fish from my childhood, thin body snapping, silver skin shining. Constantly increasing in size and strength, the thought became so powerful that when it finally crashed into my brain, it exploded in a firework of intense bright white light. I knew why I chose the men I did. I knew that in moving from city to city, country to country, living in monastic austerity, I was not on a romantic quest for home but rather wandering the globe in self-imposed exile.

I leapt into the car, a pool of clarity and a fiery ball of urgency at the same time, and was immediately stuck behind my antithesis. A rusty brown pickup truck veered from the shoulder to over the centerline, doing thirty-five in a fifty-five miles-per-hour zone. The driver was in no rush to get anywhere. I banged the steering wheel, cursing for the eight miles before I could pass.

Gale Dickerson sounded happy when she picked up the phone. If she was bitter over my tacit rejection of her friendship she didn't let it show.

"I need to ask you something. How did my parents feel about me?"

"I know they were proud of you, that you were so adventurous and independent."

"No, did they like me?"

"Like you? What do you mean? They loved you."

I wasn't talking about that automatic, unthinking way all parents loved their kids. I wanted to know if they liked me as a person. If I'd been someone else's child, would they have let their daughter play with me, or would I have been that kid whose friendship was subtly discouraged. Tantrums, screaming, taking so much and giving so little. I'd treated their love so casually, so carelessly. I couldn't blame them if they'd disliked me.

Gale sucked in her breath. Oh yeah, it was going to be bad.

"Remember when I kept calling you back in February. This is what I wanted to talk to you about. I always believed you had a right to know and I'd finally convinced Margaret to tell you."

I was braced to hear what I feared I already knew.

"Your parents had a great marriage, you saw that. You've heard the story hundreds of times, how they met at the Louvre, fell in love almost at first sight, married three months later. All true. It's what happened next that's a bit, ah, different. Firstly, your grandparents weren't over the moon. Alice (*my Nana*) even wanted them to get an annulment. They're too young. How was Jack going to support Margaret and go to medical school. Jack should join Penner & Grayson. What if Margaret got pregnant. But your parents had an answer for every question. Children were several years in the future. Margaret wanted to have a career first. She was going to teach. Family business be damned, Jack wasn't interested in finance. Medicine was his calling. Your grandparents mumbled something about best laid plans.

"They moved into that tiny apartment on Wilson St. Margaret did it up so beautifully. She really had exquisite taste, your mother. They were so happy. Then three months later your mother found out she was pregnant. To say your father didn't take the news well is an understatement. It's all your fault. How could you be so stupid. You did it on purpose. You lied about a career. You're ruining my life. How can I go to medical school now. And I knew your mother. She didn't have a devious bone in her body. And then, oh lord, the mood swings kicked in to make everything worse. One minute, Margaret was locked in the bathroom crying, the next she was cleaning the entire apartment, twice. She was telling Jack how much she loved him, then planning to kill him for setting the table wrong. 'For the hundredth time, the knife goes next to the spoon.' It was awful. Remember that, honey, even when you think you're being careful, things can go wrong, and pregnancy's no picnic."

She was carpet bombing a story I thought I knew and acting like she was teaching a sex ed class. Meeting at the Louvre, the marriage at the Hotel de Ville were still there, but that was it. My grandparents weren't dancing for joy. Dad didn't happily don a grey suit and read stock reports. I was an accident that made him act like a total jerk. Mom was a hormonal nightmare. With breathe trapped in my throat, I waited for Gale to continue.

"And then when she was six months along, Jack walked out."

My stomach lurched. My dad had been one of those guys. The guys who skip out on their responsibilities as easily as skipping school. The "It's not my fault. It's not my problem" guys. I hated those guys.

"Well, obviously, he came back, but yes, for a time your dad was a turd. Went off to med school in Ohio alone. I moved to Milwaukee to be with your mom, to help out, take her to doctor's appointments, give her a shoulder to cry on. We told everyone that she was joining Jack once you were born, but in truth Alice took you both down to their place in Del Rey Beach. A rare maternal act on her part."

Gale's distaste shivered through the line. She'd committed to memory every one of Nana's failings as Margaret's mother, every thoughtless comment, every forgotten piano recital, every heartache suffered without true comfort. Or was it that Gale resented being relieved of her duties as my mother's caretaker.

"Despite vowing you'd feel loved and wanted in ways she never had, she'd stare at you in your crib trying to figure out where you'd come from. You were an alien who'd invaded her life, driven Jack away, taken away her teaching career. She'd hate you, then hate herself for it and smother you with affection. The cycle repeated for months. She also despaired what Jack's desertion would do to you. How does one tell a child her father fled at the thought of fatherhood. Alice's reminders that she should've waited to marry didn't help. 'I knew Jack wasn't ready,' Alice gloated. 'How are you going to support yourself and the baby. Not many men are willing to take on another man's child.'

"Then one day, Jack was on the doorstep, hat in hand, begging to be taken back. He missed Margaret, he missed the daughter he'd never met. He wanted to be a husband and father. Nothing had gone right since he left. The expectation that he'd work at Penner & Grayson had driven him into medicine. After two semesters, he'd diagnosed himself as completely unfit for the profession. He dropped out, returned to Milwaukee, took the job with his father and found he actually loved finance. All that mattered to your mom was he was back."

"How have I gone through my entire life not knowing this? Why didn't they tell me?"

"Guilt. They read some child development book that convinced them your unhappiness was their fault. Fear that you'd blame them or hate them, or both, if you knew. And maybe what happened did affect you. Does it really matter? How does blaming someone help? Being a victim is a very passive role to play." Those last words were delivered with uncharacteristic vehemence. Gale always presented a sunny face to the world.

"Oh sorry, my anger's mostly directed inward. How many years did I blame Jerry and Jonas. Sitting on my butt eating bonbons, getting fat, shutting myself off so I wouldn't get hurt like that again. And the stupidest part is I knew Jerry wasn't like other men when I married him, I just wouldn't admit it. If any good has come from losing Margaret it's that I'm finally taking my life back. I've been taking this course about learning to love myself, as hippy-dippy as that sounds. And I joined the Peace Corps, something I always wanted to do. I'm off to Romania in the spring."

Gale Dickerson leaving MA? For twenty-five years she'd sat primly behind a dark oak desk granting and denying access to the headmaster of Milwaukee Academy. She could recite the school's history by heart, she remembered every student, attended every football game and graduation ceremony, chaperoned all the dances. I could no more imagine the school without Gale Dickerson than I could a Brewers game without beer.

"Six months and twenty pounds to go."

"They knew I loved them, didn't they? I can't even remember if I told them."

"I'm sure they did. The only thing they wanted was for you to be happy and it broke their hearts that they may have caused your unhappiness. The worst thing you could do is spend your life being miserable. Ok, so you're weren't the easiest kid, but you never did anything so awful that you don't deserve happiness. Be happy, be fulfilled. And can I say one more thing? I think I know why you're holding onto that house, but honey, your parents' spirits don't live there or in the objects in it. Their spirits will live in your heart and will be with you wherever you go. Sell it."

37

For the first time in my life I truly knew what I had to do and I had to start that day while the fires of determination burned inside me. I wasn't going to be the third casualty of the accident that killed my parents. If Gail could reinvent her life then so could I.

The real estate agent whose calls months earlier I'd ignored was the first person on my list. I told her I was ready to put the house on the market.

Giles was next. I had to tell him I was leaving before I lost my nerve and took the cowardly way out and skipped town.

His car was in the drive but my knock went unanswered. Through the diamond-shaped window I could see he was exactly where I'd left him hours before, the Americano untouched on the table. Fear that he'd done something crazy prickled my spine. I shouldn't have left him alone. His right arm twitched. Thank God. I pounded on the door. He pulled the Little Mermaid blanket over his head. I pounded again.

"Please, I need to talk to you."

"It better be fucking important," he growled. His face, annoyed, appeared in the window. On seeing me, it shifted to embarrassed. "Sorry, I thought you were Luna. I'm not going to have to move to another state, am I?"

"No, but I am," I said as he let me in, "I mean I'm going home, back to Milwaukee. I gotta get my life together. We both know this, us, is never going to work."

"But it'll be different now. I'll be different. I promise. You know the truth. I don't have to lie to you," he implored.

I saw in the deep blue of his eyes that he truly believed what he was saying. Suddenly, the roulette ball that had been spinning around in my brain since I'd looked at the photo of Samantha and baby Natalya dropped into a slot. The eyes. That was the difference I hadn't been able to put my finger on. "The photo. I have to see the photo again." I grabbed it off the table. The grey of Samantha's eyes was so pale, they couldn't have been brown like Natalya's. They had to be blue. Sierra's eyes were blue, too, meaning he was not Natalya's father.

Someone had lied, the question was who, Samantha or Luna. My instincts told me Luna was the liar, but I needed rock-solid proof. The woman was too smart not to rip holes in a flimsy accusation. My watch read three o'clock. Four o'clock in Wisconsin. I found the letter I needed in the shoebox and dialed Giles's phone.

"Good afternoon, Golden Days Living Center. How may I direct your call?" the receptionist asked.

"This is Sunflower Haven. I need to speak with Claire Hellmann. It's urgent."

"She's just speaking with one of the nurses. Would you like to hold?"

Seconds passed like minutes, minutes like hours as I paced the floor, a soulless Kenny G-esque smooth jazz track filling the empty space between me and Racine, while Giles's stared at me, uncomprehending.

"Hello Miss Haven, this is Claire Hellmann. I'm so glad to hear from you. I was beginning to fear we had an old address," she said with the kind of lilting sympathy in her Midwestern nasal twang that came from spending lot of time talking to either old people or children, "But before I go any further, let me convey my deepest condolences for your loss."

"Thank you. I'm not sure yet, how I feel. I never knew my mother," I replied trying to account for any detectable lack of feeling.

"Well, your mother was a gem, just an absolute a gem."

"That's very kind of you to say…"

"No, no, really, she was very popular with the staff. We are all so sad about her passing."

Feeling guilty about deceiving the kind woman, I didn't want to keep the impersonation going for too long. I steered the conversation to Samantha's belongings.

"She didn't have much poor thing, only a few pieces of clothing, a couple of books."

"What about documents, birth certificates, anything like that."

"Hmm, let me look, I have the box right here. One of the nurses packed everything up." There was the sound of papers rustling, "Oh my goodness, here's a letter to you dated just days before she died. Never finished. Now that is just so sad."

"Would it be too much to ask you to read it? It would really help me to feel closer to her. I don't want to wait till the box arrives."

"I understand completely. Let me get my reading glasses." Papers being moved around again, Claire grumbling about never remembering where she put her dang specs, then a pleased "aha!"

Darling Sunflower,

I am sure you have so many questions and I plan to answer every one. Many can wait until we meet, but there is one thing I want to tell you now because no matter how committed I am to complete honesty, I'm not sure I could do it in person, seeing the despair in your eyes. I have done things I am ashamed of, betrayed friends, lied and sometimes stolen to get what I needed, and it is time to leave that version of Samantha behind, though I will never deny that she once existed.

Know that I loved you from the moment I knew you were growing inside me—

"This seems very personal," Claire interjected, "Are you sure you want me to continue?"

"Yes, this is what I need to know."

"—but I cannot tell you that you were conceived during an act of love. I slept with a man, not for the first or the last time, because it was the price of a bed for the night. I don't think Peter Evans was a bad man, just young and selfish. I never saw him again. I never told him I was pregnant.

Maybe Arlene already told you his name. That much I did tell her, but not the rest of the story. She already despised me and I couldn't bear to have her absolute contempt.

"The letter ends there," Claire sighed, "Not the kind of story a daughter wants to hear."

"Actually, for me, it redeems her."

Luna had wrecked two peoples' lives, one her own son's, and to what end. She was either your garden-variety wicked witch out to make trouble for the pure joy of it, or a woman so miserable that she needed to destroy the happiness of others. I was leaning toward the latter. But the life of her own son? How could any mother do that, even a crap one like Luna? And Giles thinking she was so noble for rising above her husband and friend's betrayal to raise their love child. He had to know the truth.

"Luna lied to you," I said to Giles and told him what Samantha had written.

When I finished, he let out an anguished howl and rushed out the door. It didn't take a genius to deduce where he was going.

❧

I found them in the living room. Giles, hands around Luna's throat, was shaking her like a filthy rag, wailing, "It's your fault. It's all your fault, you bitch." Hoarse gasps seeped from Luna's lips, her fingers pulled frantically at Giles's hands trying to free herself. He squeezed harder. Her hands flew to his face. Jagged nails dug deep into his cheeks, drawing blood. With adrenaline surging, Giles didn't even feel it.

367

He was going to kill her and I was standing there like one of those pathetic starlets in the movies, frozen in place, screaming, while the hero and the villain fought to the death. I had to do something.

I grabbed the heavy book on African art off the coffee table and swung it as hard as I could. It thudded into Giles's head sending him sideways onto the floor, his hands releasing their grip on Luna as he went down. She, face sunburn red, doubled over, alternately coughing and sucking in air, saliva dangling from her upper lip onto her tan cardigan. "What's all my fault?" she rasped.

Giles made no reply.

"What are you talking about?" Luna asked again, this time with her usual tinge of disdain. Still Giles said nothing. He was a tight ball of misery rocking back and forth.

I spoke the words Giles couldn't, "You lied about Sierra being Natalya's father."

Flaring nostrils, angry grunts, Luna prepared to hurl a how-dare-you at me.

"There's a letter from Samantha. She tells Natalya everything. You knew all along her father was a guy named Peter Evans."

The flames of her outrage quickly died. She collapsed onto her hefty ass and leaned against the couch. "Oh the hell with it, they're both dead, so what does it matter now." She pulled a fresh pack of blue American Spirits from the pocket of the cardigan, extracted a cigarette, and lighted it with her silver encased lighter. "It wasn't a lie exactly, more a useful possibility. Sierra could've been Natalya's father. I'd never seen a birth certificate. Samantha told me she'd been knocked up by some guy in Oregon, that the kid was born in March of '69, but she could've been lying. She was a junkie. She wanted my help, actually just my money. She might have said anything."

I sat down in a straight-backed arm chair, probably the same chair Luna'd sat in when she told that devastating lie, my feet planted firmly on the floor. I wasn't leaving until I heard the whole story.

❧

"I'm ugly," Luna began, "There's no getting around that fact, and when I was young, as I saw it, there were two options to deal with the cruelty of the other kids. I could be obsequious, try bribing them into friendship with candy or help with their homework, whatever it took, but that really was a non-option. I could never toady up to anyone who voted me the ugliest 'boy' in school. The second was to be hard as nails, never let them see my pain, so that's what I became.

"Samantha Miller, on the other hand, looked like she floated down to Earth from a cloud. Big eyes, full lips, all that hair, so beautiful. The boys were always panting after her, so naturally the other girls hated her. She was the only one I let in because, for different reasons, we were in the same boat. And I grew to adore her, and she was kinder to me than even my own parents sometimes. Beauty and the Beast everyone called us.

"Needless to say, I never had a boyfriend. Then the summer after I graduated high school I met Sgt. Jimmy Haven at a carnival. He was the first boy to ask me out. After we'd been dating a month I felt secure enough to

369

introduce him to Samantha. Five months later they were engaged and moving to Fort Bliss, Texas where Jimmy'd been posted. I found out he'd used me to get to Samantha. He'd seen her somewhere and doing a bit of detective work, learned the best way to get close to her was to befriend the gatekeeper who protected her from the creeps who came after her, wanting only one thing. Samantha was too trusting and had no discretion, she'd talk to anyone. When the wedding took place I was in Oakland at Mills College. Far enough away so their betrayal didn't burn so much.

"Sophomore year, I went to a Civil Rights rally at Berkeley. Sierra was one of the speakers. He was Laurence then, and you may not believe it, but the first thing I noticed about him was his charisma. By the end of his speech, if he'd told me to vote for Barry Goldwater I would've. He had the potential to be an incredible speaker, but he needed help. He was disorganized, he couldn't find his notes at first, his speech rambled. Afterwards, I told him I wanted to help, anything he needed. I was a better writer, and I was efficient and organized. If there's one good thing about being ugly is you get so used to rejection you've got nothing to lose. He said we should talk about it over dinner. He tried to get me in bed that first night. I think I intrigued him because I didn't go all moony over him. I held him off for a year. Not because I was some goody-two-shoes but because I knew once we made love I'd never love another man. The will power that took." She shook her head in disbelief as if she were talking about someone other than herself, "I wanted to become indispensable to him first. I wrote him brilliant speeches and with his powerful delivery, he was soon speaking all over the state. And I cleaned up his personal life too, cleaned his apartment, cooked his meals, washed his clothes.

"He called marriage a bourgeois institution, but I got him to marry me—a supremely satisfying 'fuck you' to all the bitches in my hometown. I had a husband more handsome than all theirs put together—though I had to agree that we were free to be with anyone we wanted. 'Humans aren't inherently monogamous.' 'Monogamy is a political and economic compromise imposed on us by the church and the state,' Luna said in an impersonation of Sierra's oratorical style, dropping to a basso voice, giving an extra punch to key words. "But I could never be with another man. Mostly he picked up hippy chicks into free love and no commitments, none of them very threatening. The nights he didn't come home I told myself he'd married me. It helped a little.

"Then Samantha showed up, uninvited. Jimmy'd been killed in Nam and damn if that young widow vibe didn't make her even more beautiful. A wounded bird, that's how Sierra described her, and we had to heal her. I knew what kind of healing he had in mind and I didn't want him anywhere near her. He knew about Jimmy. Some women should just be off limits, you know?"

She lit another cigarette, forgetting there was one burning in the ashtray. She exhaled, pushing the smoke toward the ceiling with her lower lip.

"Caught them in bed together. While I was at the doctor's, seven months pregnant, Sierra was fucking my friend in our bed. He confessed he was in love with us both. Together we made his ideal woman and with me loving Samantha like a sister, why couldn't we three live happily together. If it'd been any other woman. I have no idea what I screamed at them. I thought I'd gone too far and Sierra would leave me, but he didn't. That's when I knew he really needed me. I'm not stupid. I know everyone says he stays for the money, I inherited money from my grandfather, but there are plenty of pretty women with money."

"But if you had the money and he hurt you so much, why didn't you leave him?" I asked.

"Because the idea of living without him was more unbearable. And the truth is Samantha'd hurt me more than Sierra had. She'd been the first friend I ever had, the first person I let in. I'd loved her and now she'd betrayed me twice. Never had another close friend after that.

"I had us packed up and moving to New Millennium in a matter of days. I wanted Sierra out of the city, too many temptations, no more going on the road alone. If he wanted to keep living off my money, we were going to live where I wanted. And if he didn't end up enjoying life on the commune more than I did. Like an idiot, I'd put the rooster in a hen house. After a while the other husbands got together and threw us out. That's when we bought this place."

Why did she agree to raise Natalya?

"Somehow Samantha found us. Showed up in Chamisa claiming she wanted to get clean, somewhere along the line she'd become an addict, and was hoping I'd help her out. I sure as hell didn't want her around so I told her I'd pay for rehab and look after Natalya. She promised she'd be back in a few months, tops. Never saw her again. I think she really just wanted to dump the kid."

And Samantha's family, why didn't they take the child?

"Her parents had always been pretty strict Catholics, but after Henry, that's Samantha's brother, was killed in Nam, they really freaked on it, went super zealous. Wanted nothing to do with the bastard child of their fallen daughter. With one dead kid, you'd think they'd be falling over themselves to save the other one, but what do I know," she shrugged, "I'd trapped myself into keeping it with all my advocating for child welfare. Samantha knew me well enough to know I'd never surrender a child to the state. I'd've looked like a hypocrite if I had.

"And as the saying goes, no good deed goes unpunished. Natalya grew up to be just like Samantha, well, except for the brown eyes. The same come-fuck-me looks, that same 'save me shit' that make some men think they're fucking Superman. I saw what was happening. When she was a child, Sierra'd never paid her much attention, but after she turned sixteen, he was always coming up with some reason to be around her, touching her. I saw him looking at her the way he'd looked at Samantha. Even though he raised Natalya, he never thought of himself as her father. He doesn't think of himself as a father of his own son. And she'd prance around the house in skimpy tee shirts, braless, or in her bikini in the summer, always giggling and throwing her arms around him. This time I was going to stop it before it went too far. I wasn't going to share him, or lose him to her."

Luna's mouth curled into a nasty smile as she recalled the night of Natalya's eighteenth birthday. Telling them was her twist of the knife, her payback. The way they looked at each other, the complete distress on their faces was such sweet revenge.

"You fucking bitch," Giles snarled, on his feet and standing over his mother, coiled menace waiting to spring again, "You saw nothing real, just your fears. And to think I felt sorry for you, married to that worthless shit."

"You watch how you speak of Sierra. He's still your father," Luna said showing no fear of her son.

"He slept with your best friend. He's fucked half the women in Chamisa. Natalya would never have slept with him. He disgusted her. She loved me. She wanted to be with me. You destroyed our lives and now she's dead."

Luna's eyes widened, her mouth went slack. Her bafflement was genuine. The skin of steel she'd forged in childhood as protection against the taunts of classmates, and that had later kept Sierra's infidelities from breaking her, had restricted Luna's movements, forced her eyes straight ahead, blinding her to what was happening on the periphery. And the armor had caged her emotions as well. After so many years of captivity, when she finally set one free, it went wild, though Luna believed she was in control. She was so focused on killing an imagined love the possibility that Natalya's heart belonged to someone else never occurred to her. For the first time in her life, Luna's confidence in the rightness of her actions failed her and when she spoke, her words came out like a lament, "What have I done? Oh my god Giles, really, I had no idea. Why didn't you tell me?"

"Hey Luna, you'll never guess who…" Sierra called out, his delighted tone clashing with the somber scene he came upon, "What's going on?"

"Ask your wife. She's no longer my mother," Giles said as he pushed past the man and out of the house.

The last emotion I ever thought I'd feel for Luna was compassion. Hannah telling me I was just a stone Billy Maxwell'd trod on to get to her wasn't in the same league as what Luna had experienced, but I knew the twisting pain of being used. And the taunts of Luna's classmates reminded me of Lauren Feldman who'd been picked on so mercilessly at MA. Polly Vandercamp had pasted pictures on Lauren's locker that compared her to a member of the bovine family. Even though I knew it was wrong, I'd worn a complicit smile because I'd been too timid to stand up to Polly and because part of me still wanted to be her friend. Polly'd said Lauren deserved it because she was a bitch as well as being ugly, as if Lauren was obligated to be nice to compensate the rest of us for her lack of physical beauty. Maybe Lauren, like Luna, had been bitchy as a form of protection. Why did we punish people for something that was beyond their control? I wanted to both fall on my knees begging Luna's forgiveness and give her an empathetic hug, but mostly I wanted to get the hell out of there. Unfortunately, Sierra stood between me and the door. Then Luna came at me shrieking like an angry cat, "Get out of my house!"

I blew out of there like the wind and kept on going all the way to Milwaukee.

38

Winter had come early to Milwaukee. Temperatures were dipping down into the twenties and the sky was a sheet of grey slate, a welcome change after the relentless blue of the desert southwest. The cold, however, did not diminish my enthusiasm. A "For Sale" sign was planted in the lawn of the house on Stansfield Street.

As snow wrapped the house in a fine white cloak, I, in my father's brown cashmere turtleneck, was in the master bedroom folding and boxing up my parents' clothing. Leslie was in the dining room carefully wrapping the china in newspaper. I struggled whether or not to sell the Royal Doulton place settings that had been wedding gifts to my parents. In the end, realizing that it could be years, or never, before I would be ready to use them, I decided to let them go.

Andy and Danny had been tasked that day with packing up the library. They were free to take any of the books they wanted, except the old editions of Jane Austen and Thomas Hardy. I would never part with them.

Those books, family antiques, Mom's best jewelry, the few valuable paintings Dad had collected, the family albums were moving with me to an apartment with hardwood floors and lots of natural light in a three-story building down the street from Andy and Danny. Of the rest of the furniture, a few pieces were staying in the house until it sold. Elaine Marchison, the real estate agent, advised me that some buyers weren't very imaginative. "The place needs to be staged so buyers get a good hit when they walk in and know if their couch'll fit in the living room." The rest I sold, including the dreaded den couch.

With help from Andy, I'd wrangled my eclectic work experiences into a résumé and I got a job teaching English to Russians four nights and two days a week.

And I'd called Sonya, the therapist Andy'd been bugging me about. Long, wild hair, caftans and incense. A little kooky for staid Milwaukee, but she was serious about her work. Together, we were slashing through my guilt-choked past and I was learning to forgive myself and accept happiness as the greatest gift I could give my parents, and myself. It was possible I'd never be as happy as those who'd see their parents live into old age or who were blessed with more buoyant natures than mine, but I'd no longer believe that by being happy I was stealing something that didn't belong to me. I could be a happier version of Hunter.

Eventually the time came to seek out Philip. With all the wheels in forward motion, there could be no retreating into the Stansfield St. house and locking the door if he rejected me. I felt so empowered and free that I was sure that scenario was unlikely—I meant retreating, not Philip rejecting me, which was entirely possible—but I didn't want to be guilty of over-confidence.

The lights were on in the duplex and I could see Philip moving purposefully about the living room. I rang the bell. Footsteps on the stairs, a key turning in the lock, the door opening and he was before me, handsome, a smile illuminating his face. Except it wasn't Philip.

"Please tell me you're the Welcome Wagon, a month late, but I don't care," the stranger said eagerly, looking me up and down, hoping I had a plate of brownies stashed on me.

"Where's Philip Cox?" I prayed he would say he was a new roommate and Philip'd just stepped out for a six pack.

"You mean the guy who used to live here? Don't know. You could give the landlady a call. I've got her number somewhere in the mess upstairs."

"Don't bother," I mumbled. I slunk back to the car and burst into tears.

I'd prepared for Philip not wanting to see me, for him having a girlfriend, for him throwing his arms around me exclaiming, "You're back!" (*most desired*). The one possibility I hadn't prepared for was him being gone.

Gone. I couldn't get my head around it. All those wasted weeks in Chamisa with Giles. Why had I waited so long? I was such a fool. I should have gone straight over when I got back to town. All the progress I'd made was like a new shirt I absolutely loved, been wearing for days, then decided it looked terrible on me and threw it in a corner.

Sitting in her cozy office, Persian carpets on the floor, a fire blazing in the grate, Sonya, notebook on a *kilim* pillow in her lap, twisted in her easy chair and pulled her legs up under her, a tell that she was about to say something I really needed to hear. Everyone in therapy had setbacks, it was part of the process. It was how I ultimately responded to the setback that was important. I hadn't sought out Philip because I needed time to heal, she said, then asked if I'd tried calling him. Maybe he had the same number. Or what about Andy, weren't he and Philip friends. Maybe he knew where Philip was.

Call Philip. It was so simple and I was so stupid for not thinking of it. But I couldn't find his number. The Printed Page employee list hadn't made the move from Stansfield St. I looked in the phone book. No listing for Philip Cox. How were potential clients supposed to find him if he had an unlisted number? Maybe it was under his business. Try as I might, I couldn't remember what he called it. I began to think I'd never known.

It came down to Andy. I'd never told him I'd been sort of seeing Philip before I took off to New Mexico and had never mentioned it since my return. Too embarrassing. And Andy'd never brought him up, either because Philip had never told him anything, or, much worse, had told him everything. But I wanted to find Philip so I had to buck up and ask.

"See, I told you she'd ask sooner or later," Danny said pointing a victorious finger at Andy.

"This is one bet I'm happy to lose. The old Hunter would've let a catch like that swim right past her and into some other woman's net," Andy replied, accepting the glass of Champagne Danny offered.

"So you knew about me and Philip?" I asked.

"Not till after you took off out West like the Pony Express. He wanted to know why you weren't returning his phone calls. He was worried about you. I told him take a number. You weren't returning mine either."

I'd thrown the answering machine tape straight in the trash when I returned, preferring ignorance over hearing Philip tell me to take a fucking hike, or discovering that he'd never called at all. But he had called, and he wasn't angry, and neither Andy nor Danny had actually answered my question. Where was Philip?

"I'm sure he's still in town, but he finished the job at our firm a while ago, so I haven't spoken with him recently."

"Ok, but do you have his number?"

"Somewhere in here," he said, rummaging through his briefcase till he found the business card. Computer Solutions. I was right, I'd never known.

"Let's call him right now," Andy said, grabbing the phone and dialing before I could raise an objection. The three discordant notes that preceded the Not-in-Service message were audible from where I deflated three feet from the phone.

I turned up at my next appointment with Sonya looking like road kill. "Did you call the landlady?" I shook my head. "Don't give up hope till you've exhausted all your options. Call her."

What if she doesn't know where he is. Then you'll deal with it. What if he's left the country? Then you'll deal with that, too. But you won't know anything until you call. She wasn't going to let me 'what if' my way out of this.

"But I let him go and now I may never see him again."

She coiled her grey-streaked tresses into bun on the top of her head and secured it with a dragon-fly-tipped hair pin, "So what does this experience teach you?"

That maybe Philip wasn't the one (*but I so wanted him to be*). And when I meet another man who, like Philip, accepts me for who I am, faults and all, I won't run away.

Ș

It was a nutty idea to sit in my car and wait till I saw the tenant's lights go on, but I was up at six and it was better than pacing around the apartment watching the clock. I didn't know his schedule, he might have to be at work early and then I'd have to wait until evening.

My plan sounded more and more nutty the closer I got to my destination. What sane person would show up at someone's home just after dawn asking for a phone number. And if the tenant knew I'd been waiting outside for him to wake up, he'd probably call the cops. The nuttiness hit its apex just as I was driving past Ma Fisher's, its neon OPEN sign glowing in the cold February dawn light. I recalled that morning many months ago when Philip was just about the last person I wanted to run into. Now I'd give everything to hear 'Danka schowny macaroni' again. Maybe. I veered the car into an open parking space.

I sat in the same booth. Trudy, not a hairdo, apron or shuffle different, offered me regular or decaf and scribbled down the same order, two eggs over easy, bacon and cinnamon raisin toast.

My head was bent over my plate, egg yolk dripping from my fork as I guided a bite to my mouth when the door of the cafe swung open. A voice too energetic for such a cold morning, called out, "Good morning, Ms. Trudy. How are you this fine day?"

"Well, Mr. Philip, I'm overworked and under paid, thank you very much," Trudy replied, "The usual?"

"You betcha. Gotta get those neurons firing."

I froze. Had he seen me? If he had, what would he do? Sit with me? Ignore me? Leave?

The squeak of thick soles on linoleum grew louder and then he was there, leaning over the back of the booth, wearing a black leather jacket, plaid scarf, black watch cap (*the cap really suited him*) and that same easy smile, maybe a bit bigger than normal, or was I dreaming it. "Even you couldn't have been on a bike ride. It's fifteen degrees out there," I said.

"Just finished a swim at the Uni pool," Philip said as he slid into the booth. "You know, this is so crazy. I just tried to call you the other day. Wanted to leave my new number, in case you ever felt like giving me a call, let me know you were still alive, but it was disconnected. And now here you are, like you were summoned by destiny."

My heart did a little leap, though I remained cool on the outside. It could just indicate friendly concern. I told him I'd put my parents' house on the market and was living in an apartment on the Eastside now. I acted like it was news to me that he had a new number.

"Yea, a buddy of mine and his wife took off for a year and are letting me live in their place for real cheap. Too good a deal to pass up, and they have much nicer furniture."

Trudy dropped Philip's breakfast onto the table. Gone were the bowl of granola, the yogurt, the side of fresh fruit and the wheat toast. In their place was a heaping plate of scrambled eggs, four sausage links, a stack of pancakes. Only the glass of O.J. remained. "Be right back with the syrup."

Philip opened a pat of butter and smeared it on the pancakes, then drenched the stack with the syrup when it arrived. "This is my winter usual. Need the extra calories to stay warm," he said in reply to my stunned look.

My look, however, had nothing to do with his meal. It came from the realization that I'd truly made progress. It wasn't a mirage that vanished on closer inspection. I was stronger, more confident. I was an emotional risk-taker. One who would gamble everything not to lose that man, that incredible man, that man who had a smudge of butter on his nose, the sweetest thing I'd ever seen. I could come right out and tell that man how I felt. Kind of.

"Hey, I've got another type to add to your list of partiers, truckers, down-on-their-lucks, and chirpy cyclists who hang out in this place. Women who run away from wonderful men and then hope those men'll take them back because they're finally learning it's okay to be happy."

Philip looked around warily, like he'd accidentally wandered into a den of thieves, "Are there a lot of those types in here now?"

C'mon Hunter, just go for it. "Well, actually, I think there's only one today. Me. And if it's not too late…"

"It's about time."

Now my heart was doing leaps, handstands, somersaults. I was climbing over the table and straight into Philip's lap, knocking over coffee cups, dragging the fringe of my scarf through syrup, sending silverware clattering to the floor. We kissed. I heard trumpets blaring and saw stars and rainbows and unicorns. And it felt perfect.

Philip said, "Now let's go to your place and I'll can give you a proper welcome back."

39

The universe works in strange ways. I often ask why I had to lose my parents to find myself. I wish they were here to see their daughter now, settled, happy and in love. A year and a half later and Philip and I are still together, the longest relationship I've ever had. Even been living together for the last six months, my first time ever.

We've been to Door County, the Dells, Taliesin, the Circus World Museum and all the other important and silly Wisconsin sites I'd never been too. We even went to a Bucks game just so we could both say we'd been to one.

We've also been to Chamisa. The mountain accepted Philip right away, and after eighteen years, it finally accepted me, or I accepted it, if it works that way. We're holding onto the casita. We've decided we'll live there one day. Until then, holiday rentals bring in a small but steady income. I never would have guessed I'd honor my parents that way.

First comes Africa. We leave next month. A few months of travel, Morocco, Egypt, Tanzania, then we begin teaching jobs in Kenya. It's the first time I feel that I'm actually going somewhere rather than running away. When Philip suggested the idea, I worried we'd get caught up in the romance of travel and flame out somewhere in the Serengeti.

We didn't meet traveling, he reminded me. We met working for the Bat. We talked about going to The Printed Page to thank Janine for bringing us together, but decided if she really was a bat, she'd have heard us already.

acknowledgments

A great big thank you to Lauren Bjorkman and Lara Santoro, both writers, for their willingness to read and give comments on multiple drafts of the book. I am lucky indeed to have friends like them.

Thank you to Lesley Cox for working with me to create the beautiful cover design.

To my parents, Mary and Jim Burns, I am eternally grateful for their love, patience, and unwavering support of all my myriad career choices.

Cheers to my brother, Ross, my sister-in-law, Natividad, their children, Angelina, Victor, Oscar and Ophélie, and to my stepchildren, Dylan and Ryan. They make my life richer just by being in it.

And finally there is Andrew whose encouragement and love have been invaluable not only in the writing of this book but in every aspect of my life. He is so much more than I ever dared to dream of in a partner. Thank you for giving me the fairy-tale ending.

elizabeth burns

lives on a small farm near Taos, New Mexico with forty chickens, three goats, two horses, two dogs, one cat, one duck, two step-children, and one husband. *No Direction Home* is her first novel.